Entropy

Jennifer Hartmann and E.R. Whyte

Dedicated with deepest love and appreciation to Chelley St. Clair. For your keen eye, clever wit, and invaluable insight... yours is the emperor's thumb.

Contents

Foreword

Our sincerest thank you to Jake Hartmann for the beautiful design work on the cover of Entropy.

Photography credits to Jennifer Hartmann. Model credits to Rhylan Streloff and Nicole Vaughn.

Chapter One

Indie

WHEN MY HEEL CATCHES on a piece of upturned carpet, and the triple shot latte dapples my work blouse in shades of cinnamon dolce, I can't help but laugh…

I'm certain this will be the most eventful part of my day.

Tameka greets me with a sympathetic smile, her teeth the dazzling sort of white I've only ever seen in toothpaste commercials. Her eyes case my espresso-adorned belly. "Rough morning?"

"Oh, you know. Trying to find excitement where I can," I breeze, punching in my code as I clock in beside her. "Mondays aren't as thrilling as our Saturday night margarita-marathons."

"Girl, I'm still recovering."

Lord. Me, too.

As a recently divorced twenty-eight-year-old, my pastimes include being a single mother and not getting pregnant again… well, not for a very long time, anyway.

I finally have a routine—a system I've carefully established over the last eighteen months of debilitating chaos as I adjust to doing everything on my own. I'm a bank teller by day, mother to a precocious preschooler all day, every day, and by night… I can be found cozied up on the couch with my chamomile tea and a good book.

Needless to say, my tequila adventures with Tameka are still doing a number on me.

Tinkering with her boho headband, my best friend and co-worker shoots me a wink as she straightens her skirt. "Well, you wear your hangover as well as you wear your coffee stains."

"Homeless and inept?"

She snorts. "Sweetie, I've yet to see a homeless person rock a balayage like you."

My fingers lace through my lightly-curled hair on instinct, a timid smile tipping my lips. The compliment warms me, considering it wasn't long ago that I had fallen into a black hole of hopelessness, completely letting myself go.

The divorce was hard.

Endings are hard.

Losing my grip on something I'd tried so desperately to hold onto nearly crippled me.

If it weren't for my daughter, Daisy, and my small but mighty support system, I wonder if I ever would have found the strength to pull myself out of that dark place.

"I'm unlocking!"

Damien's chipper voice registers from the front lobby, signaling to us that it's time to get to work. Sucking in a breath of motivation, I take a few more sips of coffee and tuck my blouse inside the hem of my skirt to hide the stain.

Tameka nudges me with her elbow before sweeping past me. "Another day, another dollar."

"That's right," I smile, turning to follow.

The truth is, my job is predictable. Maybe even a little boring... but that's exactly what I love about it. I crave the monotony and order. I punch in every morning knowing what I have to do, and knowing that I'll do it well. It's a sense of security amidst my unraveling life.

Before I settle into my desk, I make a pitstop at the teller stations, noticing the lines in the lobby are already several people deep with customers waiting to make deposits or get something notarized.

A typical Monday morning.

"Oh, no, he did not." Tameka's voice is honey and vinegar in my ear as she moves behind me to her station on the counter.

"Hmm?" I nod a smile to a customer, taking in the gangly construction worker who stops in every morning to flirt with Samantha, the Asian convenience store owner from down the block, and the elderly Mrs. Captain, come to do her weekly coin deposit. I never have figured out how the hell she comes up with so much change every week. They're in the line to the left of the large modern-styled courtesy desk, and normally I'd give each of them a smile and a breezy good morning. It's part of what I love about my job as manager of this Seattle branch of Edgewater Bank: establishing an actual relationship with every client.

Only, my smile wanes when my gaze cuts to the man barreling in through the glass doors.

It's my ex, breezing devil-may-care into the bank with Daisy. Even from across the lobby, I see things. Jeremy's unshaven face and mismatched shoes, one navy, one black. His untucked shirt. Daisy's unkempt curls and the blob of jelly next to her mouth.

"Oh, yes, he did. You've got to be kidding me."

My muttered response barely has time to cross my lips, prompting another snort from Tameka, when he's setting Daisy down before me and pushing her backpack across the teller desk. "Hey," he says. "I have a meeting I can't be late for, so I figured I'd just bring Dee here. Right, Dee? Boop." He leans down and boops Daisy's nose. She's only four, but I swear she rolls her eyes—a unique shade of blue like mine. She despises being called Dee.

"Come here, baby girl." I bend and pick Daisy up, and she falls into a sort of boneless sprawl against my chest that she's almost too big for. I'll never reject it, though. It's the most precious weight I've ever borne. Jeremy turns to leave but I stop him with a hiss. "You figured?"

His hand reaches up to scratch his stubble, his eyes skating around the lobby as he looks for witnesses to our squabble. "Well, yeah. I mean, my work is just around the corner—"

"And you were late because you're obviously still drunk, so you figured why not just drop her with the adult who's already on the clock, already working her job like a responsible—"

"Okay, now just hold on a second—"

"No, this has to stop, Jeremy," I bite out, trying to rein in my outrage. I've always been the avoidant type, resistant to conflict and confrontation, and it's probably the reason I coasted along those choppy, marital waters for far too many years.

But Jeremy is the one person who can light my fuse like no one else, and I truly resent him for that.

"I'm heading to work, too... just like you, Indie."

My teeth clench in response. "You're nothing like me. I'm not an alcoholic."

Painful memories poke through my angry haze, tingeing my cheeks red. Images of my ex-husband incapacitated from an alcohol binge on our wedding anniversary only heightens my resentment. I still recall with sickening clarity the moment Daisy skipped into the kitchen in her princess dress as Jeremy stumbled through the back door. He was supposed to be working, but he'd left early and had spent three hours at the local dive bar instead.

He was utterly shit-faced that night. Slurring, falling over, speaking gibberish. Jeremy tried pulling the casserole out of the oven with his bare hands, causing second degree burns. His howl of pain had terrified our daughter as the ceramic dish crashed to the kitchen floor, breaking into tiny, fractured pieces.

Just like our marriage.

That had been the last straw for me. That was when I'd finally said I'm done. It was a decision I hadn't taken lightly then, and I still don't, to this day. The disintegration of my marriage is a stain I'll carry with me all my life. I don't like failure. I don't like calling it quits because I'll always question if I could have done more.

But as I gaze into the hollow eyes of the man I once loved, I know it was the right decision.

Jeremy sniffs, looking everywhere but me. "Aw, now, when a man can't drink a beer in the solitude of his own apartment—"

I try to ignore him, as his attempt to defend himself is absurd, but I can't help myself. "Let's just skip right to the part where you put my livelihood in jeopardy because you're foolish and irresponsible. I'm tired of this, Jeremy. I divorced you to get away from it. It's exhausting, being the one to have to deal with the fallout every time you can't bring yourself to think of anyone but yourself. I'm just..." I have to stop to take a breath, and I hate the hitch that it gives my breath when I continue. "I can't do this."

"You tell him, girl." Tameka murmurs behind me, segueing seamlessly into greeting her next customer. "And how are you doing today, sir?"

I shake my head a little to discourage her, but inwardly, I'm smiling. A single mother like me, only of a preteen boy, Tameka and I have been besties since I started working here. No one has my back like she does, because no one else has the same special brand of jackass ex that we do. We share a knowing glance as she sifts through change.

Realizing my voice rose progressively through my tirade, I glance around, hoping the customers aren't paying attention. For the most part, they're ignoring the domestic dispute playing out in front of them, occupied with their financial business.

All except for one.

A strikingly attractive man with tattooed arms and a piercing gaze, waiting patiently in Tameka's teller line. He's well-muscled and distinct, with dark waves of hair capped in gold. His eyes are on us, one eyebrow quirked.

Shit. That's just what I need... a customer reporting my utter unprofessionalism to my boss. Tugging on the dregs of my control, I run a hand down Daisy's back and pull my mouth into the semblance of a smile before I turn back to Jeremy.

I talk through my teeth. "You need to take her to preschool. Now, because it's after nine and she was supposed to be there at seven-forty. I can't leave, especially not now when the morning rush is beginning."

I've only been working here for ten months, the past two of which I've been proving my mettle as assistant manager. Jeremy has pulled this same stunt a grand total of sixteen times. My math brain kicks into gear, and I calculate rapidly. That's once every two-point-eight weeks, or in other words, enough times to be ridiculous.

Jeremy shakes his head. "I can't, babe."

"I am not your babe." An unladylike curse is on the tip of my tongue, but I hold it back, conscious of Daisy's curious ears. I would probably have an entire vacation's worth of quarters in a jar at home, reserved only for the secret obscenities I sling at Jeremy that I'll never say out loud.

"It's an important meeting. I'll be fired. And you know what that means..." He clicks his tongue, his hands slipping into ratty denim pockets as he demonstrates his poor attempt at swagger. "No alimony. No child support."

"Oh, please. As if you are that much of a provider, anyway."

"Ms. Chase, this gentlemen needs to speak with you." Tameka cuts in, thankfully saving me before this argument escalates into something ugly.

I cut my gaze over to see the tattooed stranger standing beside Tameka, his eyes patient. Now that he's closer, I can see that one eye is a soft, lambent brown, the other a greenish-blue. It ought to be weird, but it's not. It's hypnotic, pulling my attention from one to the other, then back again. The brown is pure comfort, the other electric blue sex.

Oh, okay.

That thought process escalated.

I feel myself flush as I fidget with a button on my blouse. Stupid pale skin. Even with my blooming summer tan, I still blush far too obviously. "I... yes, of course. I'll be right with you."

Jeremy huffs out a breath and shifts his weight, tugging my focus back to him. "Anyway, like I was saying," he continues. "I've got to split. We can argue about it later, but right now, you'll have to figure out something with Dee." He makes a show of looking at his watch, backing a few steps toward the glass doors as he does. "Because I'm officially off the clock for two weeks."

My skin prickles with indignation, my fingers balling into fists alongside my pencil skirt. I spear my ex-husband with a sharp stare and gritted teeth, doing everything I can to hold back a rage-infused meltdown.

"Tag, baby," Jeremy grins, a cheeky thing I long to smack. "You're it."

"Oh, for the love—this isn't a game, Jeremy. You—"

I break off, my attention snagged by the group of men who are entering the lobby behind Jeremy. He remains oblivious, continuing to back away toward them, his hands lifted in false contrition. They're dressed in dark coveralls, like painters wear, adorning inky black ski masks. Long-barreled guns are clutched in gloved hands, and these men are terrible, awful clichés, and yet... the possibility of something like this happening has been an apparition dogging every step since the day I started working here.

I stumble back from the desk, catching the tattooed stranger's shift in attention, the widening of his mis-matched eyes when he sees what I see.

The men in black. Their masks. The guns.

This isn't happening.

My blood runs cold, my arms squeezing Daisy in a fearful grip.

Daisy. Oh, my God... my daughter is here.

The frantic thought is barely given life in my brain when the man in front lifts his gun, and like a scene straight from Hollywood, points it at Marcus, our security guard standing a few feet away. He shoots without preamble. Marcus is still fumbling with the catch on his holster when he crumples to the floor, shot in the arm, his mouth opening and closing in a caricature of surprise. The sound of the automatic weapon, loud and vulgar in the bank's hush, prompts several screams and instant chaos. Jeremy whirls and ducks, hands still raised.

"Now that I have your attention," the man says, his voice low and unrecognizable. "Let's get things started."

Chapter Two

Dax

"DAX, YOU DEVIL. I had no idea you were in love with me."

Blake scrolls through his phone as he tries to match my long strides through the busy Seattle streets of Belltown. It's Monday morning, the weekday rush and our own hurried agenda a drive of motion pulsing along the byways of street and sidewalk. Blake's eyes narrow in on the latest gossip article while he sips bubble tea from a biodegradable straw.

I can't help my amused snort as the absurdity of his claim registers. "Surprise."

"Don't tease me. My heart is fragile and easily manipulated." His elbow jabs me in the ribs as we move swiftly side by side. "Besides, if TMZ says it, then it must be true."

I glance over Blake's shoulder, eyeing the ridiculous headline as I rub away the sting of his rogue elbow: Retired Hockey Hunk Dax Reed Gets Cozy With Longtime Manager. Swiping the phone out of my friend's hand, a scowl unfurls between my eyes. "Let me see."

"Hey," he barks, attempting to grab it back. "You can take away my phone, but you can't take away my hopes and dreams."

My gaze skims over the article, then settles on a corresponding photo of Blake and me hugging at a recent promotional event. "I can't hug my best friend without implication of us being lovers? Jesus."

"Keep scrolling," Blake encourages, twirling his finger in a circular motion. "The look in your eyes in the second picture shows distinct desire. And the eyes don't lie, Dax. Just admit that you want me, and maybe, possibly, if you say please, I'll reciprocate your undying love."

I toss the phone at him, and he catches it awkwardly, one-handed, almost dropping his bubble tea.

"Rude," he snaps. "And don't act so surprised. Our sexual tension is staggering. Combine that with your enviable good looks and love for pairing snappy dress shirts with a streamlined profile—and shazam. It fits."

A huff hits the humid air. "Your analysis of me is concerning," I deadpan. "And please don't say shazam."

Blake slips his cell phone into his slacks with a casual shoulder shrug. "Well, then there was that tweet about the Maltipoos."

"Pfft. Everyone loves Maltipoos."

"Denial doesn't suit you, Dax," Blake sing-songs as he smooths out his salmon polo and points toward the line of ruddy brick buildings. "Ooh. We're almost there."

A bubble tea slurp echoes over the bustling city noise, and I cross my arms over my "snappy dress shirt," as I glance up at the approaching bank, my mind wandering.

Retired.

The term boils my blood.

More like, I was checked into the boards so hard by that prick, Allanson, I separated my shoulder and was forced out of the game. Removed from my career. Ousted from my passion.

Maybe I was nearing retirement age anyway at almost thirty-two, but I wasn't fucking ready yet. I had a few good years left.

Instead, I lost it all in one dirty play. I lost the thing that set my soul on fire.

And I lost her.

Refusing to succumb to the toxic black hole I had festered in for far too many months, I blow out a hard breath and focus on the weeks ahead.

A fresh start. New possibilities.

Twenty days alone in a Hawaiian penthouse with coastal views, salty sea breezes, and the quieting lull of ocean waves to accompany my endless supply of Kona coffee. It's exactly what I need to dig deep and reevaluate my future.

"Dax Reed! Oh, my God! I can't even! Can I get your autograph?"

We're just shy of the cobblestone walkway that leads to the bank entrance when a young woman thrusts her cleavage and a pen in my face. Blake stands to the side, watching the crowd with deceptively relaxed posture. He's always on guard for the occasional crazy.

I hardly blink, signing the swell of her breast on autopilot and flashing her my teeth.

My smile fades as she skips out of sight, beaming, and my weary sigh travels over to Blake. There used to be a time when I liked signing breasts. When I enjoyed the spotlight. Craved it, even. The lights, the women, the blind adoration.

It gave me her.

It gave me Sabrina.

Then it ripped her away.

Notoriety is a lot of things, but mostly, it's exceptionally lonely.

Glancing at Blake, the words slip out with a solemn sort of yearning. "Will it ever let up?"

"It's called celebrity status, Dax. It's this shocking new development."

Blake doesn't appear to detect the earnestness in my tone. He's glued to his phone again as we make our way towards the glass double doors. I pause, offering, "Feel free to wait outside. I'm just going to make a withdrawal, then we can grab breakfast at Biscuit Bitch."

"I'm in this, big man. I've got your back." He slaps me on the shoulder blade with a wink. "Also, Damien works the lobby on Mondays. He's a snack."

A chuckle slips out as we make our way inside.

I've got your back.

Blake may be half-a-foot shorter than me, about one-hundred-and-seventy-pounds soaking wet, and has never, and will never, beat me at a game of arm wrestling—but despite his gangly stature and lack of muscle definition, his heart isn't lacking one bit when it comes to me. He's my most trusted friend, and there's no one else I'd want in my corner.

I've done a lot of stupid shit over the years, but Blake Johnson has cleaned up my messes, no questions asked, no conditions. We've been friends since junior high, and the fact that he's my manager—well, former manager—is only an added perk. He's had my back for two decades, and I've had his.

The sweet tang of lavender and lime permeates the air as we stroll through the crowded lobby and situate ourselves in one of the three teller lines. My fingers drag through my mop of dark hair, warmed at the tips from the summer sun and in need of a cut. Scanning my fellow patrons, I notice a woman standing beside the teller stations, smiling at customers as they filter through the ever-growing lines. She stands out because she's beautiful, but also because she's trying in vain to hide a giant coffee stain on her blush blouse... and I find that all too relatable.

Long, softly curled tresses, all butterscotch and honey, fall over two slender shoulders as she grins far too brightly for a Monday morning, and I find myself momentarily zoned out until Blake pokes me with his index finger. "Ow."

"Where did you find this place, anyway?"

I plant my hands along my hips and spare a glance at the phone screen Blake is waving in my face. The penthouse condo I rented in Maui glows back at me. "You found it. You even texted me, "I found the best place ever for your soul-searching retreat" with a thousand exclamation points."

"Yeah, well, shame on me for not researching the amenities more efficiently. I don't see a bar."

"Pretty sure I'll pull through."

Blake continues to thumb through his apps, pausing on a photo of himself with another man, their arms draped around each other. He glares at the picture with disdain. "Really, Casey? You had to tag me in this photo?"

"I thought you guys had a thing."

He balks at me. "It was a very brief tryst, Dax. It was not a thing." Blake sighs, attempting to un-tag himself from the photo. "Casey is too butch. He looks like his mother."

My laughter is interrupted by an argument, and I clear my throat, peering over at the golden-haired woman who is no longer smiling. A scruffy-looking guy has joined her near her desk, while a young girl with pig-tails lies draped across the woman's chest.

"I can't do this." There's a hitch in her voice, as turquoise eyes float around the lobby, inspecting the witnesses. When her gaze lands on me and my concerned stare, she wilts slightly, forcing a smile into place and reining in her anger.

Her tone softens, making the rest of the conversation hard to hear, but my instincts still prickle with unease. The bearded man looks hungover, maybe drunk, and he's towering over her with insolence and venom.

Not thinking it through, I wave over a dark-skinned woman with ruby lips and copper eyes. "Hey, can you get her attention for me?" My head nods in the direction of the ensuing scuffle. "I have a question."

She peers over her shoulder. "Ms. Chase?"

"Yeah, please. It's kind of urgent."

"Certainly."

Ms. Chase. Not married, then? Idly, I wonder who the dude is, how the kid figures in. I have no idea why, but something about the situation... about her... intrigues me. I watch with interest, my lips pursed, my arms folded, tuning out Blake's tirade about celebrity drama on Instagram. I'm transfixed, patiently waiting for those teal-tinged eyes to find me once again, eyes that are the complete opposite of Sabrina's in every way.

Sabrina had black eyes, onyx and coal.

She had black hair, too.

And a black heart.

The woman finally faces me, her arms full, gaze curious. She's all brightness and daybreak, and I squint my eyes, almost as if they need to adjust to the light.

Her irises flash with something heated, and she swallows, stuttering a reply in my direction. "I... yes, of course. I'll be right with you."

She probably recognizes me.

The woman severs the connection just as Blake steals my attention back. I glance at him, then do a double-take when I notice his familiar arched eyebrow. "What?"

"She's pretty."

I scoff. "You're pretty. Doesn't mean I'm interested."

"TMZ would disagree with that."

A smile spreads.

Then... it disintegrates into dust before I can take my next breath.

My focus shifts, firmly fixing to the bank's entrance as four masked men plow through the glass doors with murderous gait and weapons held high.

Before I know it, before I can think, yell, reach for my phone, they blast a round of bullets into the ceiling, prompting the lobby patrons to break into an uproar of terrified cries.

Holy shit.

Holy fucking shit.

"Now that I have your attention, let's get things started."

The booming voice of the ringleader, a beast of a man, echoes all around us, inciting my stomach to lurch with dread.

Blake latches onto my upper arm, his fingers bruising my bicep. "Sweet baby Jesus in a motherfucking manager," he whispers harshly. "Tell them you're famous. Give them your savings account and your firstborn."

"Shh."

Another round pops off like fireworks, plaster and paint particles raining down on us. A sinister hailstorm.

I move fast, pulling Blake with me. "Get down!" Tugging him by the arm, we lunge towards the nearest desk. It's where the blonde woman is now standing frozen, clutching the little girl to her chest, her panicked sobs piercing through the gunshots. Snatching her wrist, I drag us all underneath the desk for cover. The space is tight, my back plastered to Blake's chest, and the blonde clerk pulled into my lap on instinct.

"Oh, my God. Oh, my God." The woman is frantic, her fingernails digging into the child's scalp and back. "Is this real?"

"Shit, Indie, move over."

Indie. My brain registers her name despite the cloud of chaos.

The unkempt male who was arguing with her only moments ago, pushes his way into the cubicle, sweat marring furry brows. Only half of him fits in the remaining space, and I find myself recoiling as alcohol-laced breath wafts over to us. The man fumbles for his cell phone, his movements jerky.

"Phones! Wallets! Purses!" One of the masked men barks out orders, circling the lobby and stopping at each frightened patron. "Toss them in the bag and don't make a fucking sound. Any complaints, you die. Any hero antics, you die. Any phone calls, you die."

Indie presses her trembling body into me, an attempt to hide, to disappear. I wish I could make that happen, but all I can do is snake my arms around her and the little girl cocooned in her own lap. As if on auto, she pushes the child behind her, trying to wrap her arm around her in reverse. My arm goes around the little girl, shielding her without a second thought. She's tiny, fitting between the curve of my arm and behind her mother perfectly.

"Who are they, Mommy? Why are they yelling?"

"Shh, Daisy, baby, it's okay." Indie's petrified tone turns strong and valiant, as if she flipped a switch. As if she had no other choice. "You're going to be okay."

Butterscotch hair tickles my chin, and it's the only thing I notice beyond the footsteps approaching our pathetically obvious hiding place. The whispered pleas beside me fade out with my thumping heartbeats until all I hear are her breaths.

All I feel is her hair.

I turn this stranger into my anchor because I need a safeguard through the mind-numbing uncertainty.

I need a pillar to keep me from crumbling.

Indie will do.

My eyes close through a tight swallow as I focus on the warm bodies huddled atop my thighs. Each time a lock of honeysuckle-scented hair tickles my chin, I'm reminded that I'm still alive.

Clomp, clomp.

Heavy footfalls grow closer. Death is coming.

Tickle, tickle.

We're not dead yet.

"Purses! Phones!" An overbearing man with grey eyes ascends on us, roaring through his mask. "Now!"

"M-My purse… it's on the desk," Indie murmurs, one arm wrapped around her daughter behind her, while her other hand punctures my thigh with fearful claws. "My phone is in the purse."

The man slings the hobo bag into his satchel as I reach into my pockets for my own belongings. Blake tosses his phone and wallet into the bag, as does the nameless man beside Indie. The gunman moves on, and we all let out a collective breath.

My grip is still firm around Indie's waist, and she tips her chin up to glance at me over her shoulder. Her eyes glimmer with blue-green terror.

I inhale a shaky breath. "I'm Dax."

It takes a moment for the greeting to process as her tongue pokes out to slick along her bottom lip. She blinks up at me with a small nod. "Indigo Chase. Indie."

"Blake Johnson." Blake waves his hand from behind me. "It's nice to meet my fellow companions in peril."

"And I'm Jeremy-fucking-Wheeler. Now that we're all formally introduced, can we figure out a plan to get the fuck out of here?" Two brown eyes dip to my protective arm around Indie, his eyebrows following with a scowl. "C'mere, babe. You don't need this guy's paws all over you. I'll protect you."

"Not the time, Jeremy," she grits out, a grating whisper.

"Come here." He punctuates both words, his tone stern. "I've got an idea."

My hold on her loosens, but she makes no effort to move. I glance at Jeremy as he swats a greasy piece of hair out of his eyes. "What's the plan?" I wonder aloud. He reminds me of that douche in that old Bruce Willis Christmas movie, the one that thinks he's going to be a hero and save Nakatomi Plaza but is really just an idiot with a death wish. Foreboding skips along my spine at the thought.

Jeremy's focus shifts from Indie to me, then he reaches behind to his rear pocket, plucking out a second phone.

Shit.

"My work phone."

A flare of hope shoots through me, causing my heart to gallop.

But the sensation is fleeting, because the moment a grin teases Jeremy's lips, the barrel of a gun is pressed to his temple.

I go deadly still, my veins flushing with ice. It feels like time freezes, right along with the air in my lungs. The man's cold gaze appears unhinged, laced with something wild.

Something lethal.

Indie scoots further into me, pushing the little girl further back, a squeak of protest passing through her lips. "No, please."

"Did you not hear me?" the man questions, his voice chillingly even.

"Fuck, here, take it." Jeremy tosses the phone a few feet from the desk, then holds his hands up, palms forward. "I hear you, man. Loud and clear."

"Do you?" The man jabs the gun against Jeremy's temple, provoking a hiss. "Any complaints, you die. Any hero antics, you die."

"I got it, okay? I got it!"

"Any phone calls—"

Indie tenses, her fear palpable. "No!"

"You die."

I squeeze my eyes shut, bracing for the inevitable gunshot, my hold tightening around both girls. A harrowing moment passes, then another.

And another.

Nothing.

When my eyelids ping open, I'm greeted with maniacal laughter. The gunman doubles over, hands on his knees, his biceps flexing, causing the ink of his skeleton tattoo to distort, almost as if the image is laughing right along with him. My teeth clench as I watch with cautious interest, my fingers curling tauter around Indie's waist.

"Your fuckin' face, man," the armed stranger howls, trying to catch his breath. "Shit, that was priceless. Did you piss yourself? You pissed yourself, didn't you?"

Jeremy looks ruffled, shifting his weight further into the cubicle. Sweat dapples his hairline, his complexion ashy. Scratching at his unruly mop of hair, he mumbles under his breath, "Clown."

The laughter ebbs, dissolving into silence. It's an eerie sort of silence, the kind that causes my skin to itch and my throat to draw tight.

"What the fuck did you just call me?"

Blake plasters himself to my back in the same way Daisy curls against me. Three human beings are using me as a shield, a protectant, but I'm not even sure how to save myself.

Jeremy noticeably swallows, refusing to make eye contact with the towering gunman. "I didn't say nothin'."

"You motherfucking liar." In a flash, Jeremy is yanked from his place beneath the desk by his shirt collar with a pistol pointed at his forehead. His back is to us, maybe two feet distant at the most. "I'll ask you one more time: what did you just call me?"

Indie whimpers from her place on the floor, quiet pleas tumbling from her lips. "No, please, no."

I squeeze her tighter. It's all I can do.

Jeremy's back is to me now, but I hear his words. I hear his stupid, stupid words. He spits them out with defiance, struggling in the man's grasp. "I said you're a clown. You're nothing but a whipping boy."

Jesus Christ.

What an idiot.

"Jeremy, stop," Indie begs. "This is serious."

The gunman lets him go, and Jeremy twists around to face Indie, throwing his arms up. "What? He's not going to shoot me, babe. If he wanted me dead, he would've—"

A loud crack shocks the air, blasting my eardrums, shredding my senses, until all I hear is a high-pitched ringing sound.

All I smell is gun smoke.

All I see is flickering stars.

The moment filters by in a slow-motion wave, and for a startling instant, I'm lying on that Maui beach, sand between my toes, seawater in my hair, and my skin drenched in sunshine. That's where my mind takes me. That's where I go, because the alternative is too abhorrent, too vile to comprehend.

To believe.

But I'm not gone long. I'm not gone nearly long enough, because her scream rips me away, forcing me back to reality and tethering me to this nightmare.

The ringing fades out, morphing into pure hysteria.

All I hear is Indie shrieking in my arms, crazed, impaired by disbelief.

All I smell is death.

All I see is carnage as Jeremy falls over, his eyes wide and lifeless, his skull obliterated, while blood spatter paints our clothes and skin.

All I know is fear.

Chapter Three

Indie

MY EARS RING. BENEATH the incessant buzz, there are other sounds. Screaming, I think. A booming echo. Male voices, hard and brutal.

My daughter's terrified panting.

A smoky haze hangs in the air, obscuring a horror I can't unsee. It lingers all around me, a fitting companion to the viscous fluid spattering my face and clothing, the tang of copper and the burn of sulfur infiltrating my nostrils.

I can't—

Daisy is partially behind me, tucked half behind my body and held by a stranger's arm. His other arm, strong and hard and somehow safe, is wrapped around my waist, pulling me as far away from Jeremy and into his bulk as he's able.

"Shh. Shh. I got you... please stop screaming—"

Slowly I come back to myself, realizing the screaming I hear is me. I clamp my lips and eyes shut. I'm sorry. I'm sorry, I'm so sorry. Jeremy, oh my God—

I don't realize I'm speaking the words aloud until I feel a stranger's kiss on the crown of my head and feel him rocking me and Daisy back and forth.

Oh, God. Daisy. "Mommy," she whimpers. She just saw her father... my brain refuses to give definition to the horror, instead filling in the blank with gruesome imagery I can't escape.

My fingers scrabble behind me, searching for her little hand, and she slides it into mine. I squeeze. "It's all right, baby, Mommy's here —"

"You fucking idiot!" Yelling penetrates my daze. "I knew I shouldn't have given you a fucking gun!"

"He had a phone—"

"So? Fuck! Shit!"

The blood that coats me is making me ill. I scrub my hands against my thighs, aware of its futility. My pants, like my hands and my face and my shirt, are also covered in...

Jeremy.

A shudder rises in me, and I clamp it down. Ignore it. Find something else to think about.

Another one of the men paces the lobby in front of us, saying something to the gunman that makes him puff his chest up with defensive arrogance. His face is covered, but his posture is pissed, his fist rising and falling as he punctuates his words. Another man, the one at the door, makes a slicing motion and both of the others go silent.

I can't bring myself to focus on them. My bandwidth is full of Daisy. Full of Jeremy.

We were happy once. Visions of lazy Sunday mornings, Friday night movie dates, and lovemaking marathons fuse with carnage and bloodshed. For an agonizing moment, I have no idea what's real, what's fiction, and what's a grisly, terrifying nightmare.

Shock and disbelief steal my breath and squeeze my chest, causing my fingernails to slice the undersides of my palms. I feel dizzy. Lightheaded and sick.

Glancing down at my blouse, I almost hurl. This morning I was worried about a coffee stain, and now I'm bathed in my ex-husband's blood.

No, no, no... he's dead. Jeremy is dead.

I never wanted him dead.

"Indie?"

The man holding me, Dax, stops rocking and tilts my chin up with a finger, so he can see my face. His eyes peer down at me, and I focus on the brown one. The comforting one, rather than the one that makes me think of thunder in the veins and lightning beneath the skin. The brown one reminds of the limpid gaze of the Bassett hound I had as a kid, and chocolate. This close, I can see the striations of light and dark in the iris, and for a potent heartbeat, I feel myself sliding. Sinking. Relaxing into him.

Then the reality of our situation rushes back in, slapping me hard and causing every muscle to tense. I'm sitting in a stranger's lap, allowing him to soak up my sorrow, while a madman wields a gun mere feet from us. "I'm sorry," I whisper, this time to him instead of Jeremy, as I start to shift away.

His arm tightens. "No," he says simply.

There's a wealth spoken in that one word.

Stay.

Don't be sorry.

I'm sorry.

I'm here.

I've got you.

Despite the horror of the past five minutes, I marvel at how loudly those invisible words voice themselves, how perfectly I interpret every one of them. Maybe it's the physical touch accompanying them, the earnestness of his gaze. Maybe it's a form of extrasensory perception, something that's always made me scoff a little. Maybe it's simply the fact that after only three hundred or so seconds, circumstances have bound us together with more intimacy than any length marriage could achieve.

Whatever the reason, I allow his unspoken demand to seep into me, and I settle back into him. Daisy's body relaxes, and I realize she had tensed when I moved.

"Mother. Fuck. Is she okay? Holy shit." The man with Dax, who is on the slight side even apart from his more built companion, is at the other end of the small space beneath the courtesy desk, his hands clutching his once-meticulously styled hair. His eyes are wide, panicked, darting everywhere.

"Cover him up." Dax nods to his friend's jacket, and his eyes round even more.

"You want me to...?" He pulls the plackets of his jacket away from his body. "Aw, hell no. This is a custom, Dax!"

"I'll buy you a new one, damnit."

"You! Shut up!" Another gun-wielding terrorist bends over, glancing at the body. "And cover that shit up. Makes me want to puke."

Dax's friend holds his hands in a placating gesture and then slowly removes his jacket to lay it across Jeremy's upper body. Some of the tension seeps out of me at the action, and I'm able to skate my gaze around the lobby.

One of the men, not the one who shot Jeremy but one who wears a mantle of leadership, leans against the wall beside the double glass doors. He spares a glance at his watch, but keeps his eyes trained outside. They've lowered the blackout shades on each window, casting the lobby into an artificial fluorescent brightness. In the mornings, before I turn on the lights and open the shades, it's a shadowy and secretive feeling. If they cut the power, it'll be dark in here.

Another guy, the trigger-happy one, mills around the large room, his gun trained on the people cowering on the floor. The acrid scent of urine makes me wrinkle my nose. Someone, likely one of the people the gunman is hovering over, has lost control of their bladder. He makes a disgusted sound beneath the mask and walks away, while the others take up stations at the doors that lead to other parts of the building and various windows.

"No one talks," the man with the gun says. "Not even a fucking whisper. Keep your heads down and listen, and maybe you'll walk out of here." He looks at Jeremy and utters a little laugh to himself. "Maybe you won't."

I close my eyes. Working in a bank as I do, this is my nightmare given life. Worse, even, because Daisy is with me. My hand clenches on hers. I have no way of protecting her. I could give my life to save hers, would do so, in a heartbeat, but it could be fruitless. She could still die.

And even if she doesn't, even if we both, by some miracle, make it out of here intact... well, that's just the physical. The trauma this is likely to wreak on my little girl makes my breath catch on a sob in my throat.

The hand on my waist moves. It's barely noticeable, the fingers curling in to my flesh in a subtle movement, but it anchors me, nonetheless. I place my hand atop his and return the slight pressure. I'm abruptly aware of the press of this complete stranger's thighs beneath my bottom, their strength forming the perfect protective cradle.

Security. A glimmer of sanctuary through the madness.

Swallowing the sudden thickness in my throat, I turn my attention to Daisy, rubbing my thumb in a soothing circle on her wrist. I have no idea how long we've been there when in the distance, the wail of sirens sounds. It could be hours, could be minutes. All I know is that it feels like a lifetime.

I feel the room go still as we hold our collective breaths and listen to their approach. I can't think of another time I've ever been so happy to hear the sound of authority. They'll get us out of this mess. They have to. "Thank God..." I release the whisper with an exhale, more breath than sound.

"Showtime." The shooter at the door straightens and shuffles his gun into a more alert grip, his tone satisfied as he stalks away to confer with one of his colleagues.

Not long after, one of the phones at the desk rings. I wait, knowing this is the part where they talk to the cops and negotiators and tell them their list of demands. And after that, there will be a clever rescue, and we'll get to go home, and these monsters will go to prison where they belong.

Only, they don't answer the phone. They let it ring, once, twice, thirteen times. One brave soul, my elderly penny counter, lifts her chin and quavers, "Perhaps we should answer that?"

Trigger-Happy slams the stock of his gun against her skull, knocking her to the floor. She cries out sharply at the impact and then is still. Dazed, I hope. Not dead... please not dead.

"Perhaps we should shut the fuck up," the terrorist growls.

"Ronnie," the one in charge snaps. "Enough."

"You just said my name, you idiot!"

"Keep on, and I'll rip your fucking mask off, dipshit. This isn't why we're here and you've already made a big enough mess for me to clean up." He inclines his head to Jeremy. "From here on out, you keep your mouth shut and your safety on unless I say otherwise. Hear?"

Ronnie agrees, the set of his shoulders sullen.

There's a screech of feedback from outside, and we all tense. "This is Lieutenant Mike Fielding. I'd like to help you figure out how we can put a stop to this situation before it gets any more out of hand. To do that, I need to talk to you. I'm going to put the megaphone down and call. I need you to pick up the phone."

There's a huff from the leader. "Call away, mother fucker." As if in answer to his demand, the phone rings. He sighs and points to Tameka, who sits on the floor in front of the counter. "You. Answer it."

Tameka hesitates, and another one of the men steps forward to grab her by the arm and haul her to her feet.

"Oh, God. Tameka." Tameka is a firecracker. The chances of her doing as she's bid without a fight are slim, and my heart lurches in my chest, fear for her making it physically ache.

Please do as they say. Don't make them angry, I silently plead.

Our eyes meet and she slumps, allowing herself to be pulled without struggle to the counter where the phone rests. She presses her lips together before her tongue darts out to moisten them, and then picks up the receiver. "H-hello?" There's a pause, during which she listens, her gaze trained on the floor before her. "No, I'm a... I work in the bank. My name is Tameka—" She breaks off, listening intently, then lifts her attention to the ringleaders. Swallowing, she explains, "The lieutenant wants you to let a hostage go. An act of good faith."

An abrasive chuckle is his response, followed by a sneer. "No. Tell them no more calls, then. We'll call them when we're ready to negotiate."

"They said no more calls," Tameka repeats dutifully, her eyes glowing with defeat. "They'll call you—"

"Hang up."

"Wait, they're—"

A finger comes down on the disconnect, and Tameka lowers the receiver.

The fingers on my stomach tighten again, and I chance a look upwards and back at Dax. He returns my sober gaze. There's another odd, wordless communique between us, one that grieves and comforts and bolsters all at the same time.

Somehow, we both know.

We're not getting out of here anytime soon.

Chapter Four

Dax

"INDIGO CHASE."

The designated leader scrubs a meaty hand over his masked head, then strokes his chin as he cases the lobby. His eyes are alight with purpose, skipping from one horrified face to the next.

Fuck.

What does he want with Indie?

Indigo. Her given name swirls in my head, raising questions. It's an intriguing name, an unusual one. Does it mean something?

I'm not sure why my mind goes there, considering the circumstances—maybe some kind of defense mechanism to take me out of this nightmare.

The woman in question stiffens in my lap, clenching my palm inside hers. Her head tips up, and two bloodshot eyes latch onto mine, a silent question flickering in her aquamarine stare. This close, there are darker rings around the outer edges, the pale greenish-blue deepening to the shadowy hue of her namesake. She inhales a shuddering breath, gazing up at me like we've been intimate before.

Maybe we have.

Maybe fighting for your life with someone is the most intimate thing in this world.

All I do is shake my head—a small, subtle gesture, just enough to convey my answer.

Stay quiet.

"Miss Indigo Chase," the ringleader repeats with an air of dramatics, his strides casual as he paces around from person to person. "I was told you were the manager on duty here today. That makes you of great value to me."

Her eyes snap shut, her breaths turning uneven.

I shake my head again, then whisper into her hair, "Shh."

"Last call for Indigo," he says once more, tapping the firearm against his muscled thigh. "Otherwise, these bullets might start to misbehave."

She inches off my lap, but I tug her back down. The words are climbing up her throat, her identity nearing her lips, when another voice responds from across the room.

"It's me. I'm Indigo Chase."

Our heads twist to the left at the same time, landing on Tameka. Tameka lifts her chin with defiance, swiping both palms along her pantsuit as the gunman approaches.

Blake's hushed voice meets my shoulder blade. "Ooh, she's got gumption. I like her."

"No... Tameka," Indie murmurs, still making an attempt to slither free of my embrace. "He's going to hurt her."

"Hey, hey, stay quiet. It's okay."

It's okay.

My words of encouragement are countered by the blood smeared along her skin, staining her pencil skirt. They are discredited by the half-covered body lying near our feet, the body of someone close to her. A husband, boyfriend.

He's dead—crumpled in front of us, just inches away.

Indie is wearing pieces of him.

And I'm telling her it's okay.

The man closes in on Tameka, swinging the gun at his hip as he drinks her in, head to toe. A grin pulls at his lips. "Indigo, huh?"

"Yes, sir."

She stands strong, firm. Her bright red lips purse into a thin line, her eyes only skipping over to us for a split second before she meets the icy stare of our attacker.

His smile broadens through the mask hole. "That's so strange," he says, scratching the top of his head with the barrel of the gun. "I could have fuckin' sworn you called yourself Tameka when them po-pos called us up."

Tameka blanches, her tawny eyes flashing with fear. "Th-that was just—"

Her words are severed by the butt of his gun striking her upside the head with a sickening thunk.

Indie bolts from my lap, jolting to her feet before I can retain my grip. She lets out a pained cry and storms forward, shouting, "No! Please don't hurt her!"

My instincts are to grab her, pull her back, keep her quiet, but there's a terrified little girl clinging to me, her face buried against the side of my torso.

So, all I do is watch, my stomach pitching with dread.

"I'm Indie," she declares, continuing her bold trek towards the gunman. "I'm Indigo Chase. Leave her alone."

Indie falls to her knees beside her friend and co-worker, cradling the injured woman in a tender embrace. Blood pools from a deep gash carved along the top of Tameka's skull, rendering the woman unconscious.

The man stalks over to Indie, stuffing the weapon into the waistline of his pants. "Will the real Indigo Chase please stand up, please stand up…" He charges forward and fists a handful of Indie's hair, dragging her to her feet. "Please stand up."

She claws at his arm, broad and burly, etched with a sleeve of tattoos, and struggles to find her balance on her stiletto heels.

My jaw tics. My blood pumps hot with choler.

"Don't even think about it, big man," Blake whispers, sensing my urge to intervene. "They need her for something. They won't hurt her."

I swallow back the bile sticking to my throat, my whole body aching with an inherent need to play hero. To jump into the flames and save the girl.

Sabrina's words haunt me, whispering along my skin like a ghostly kiss.

"You can't save them all, Dax. Some of us don't want to be saved."

Daisy nuzzles further into the crook of my arm, her tiny cheek warming my chest. It's almost as if she can read my thoughts, wordlessly replying with her own.

Save me. Save her.

Another voice pierces through the anarchy, pulling my eyes to the scene unfolding. "Leo, man, the cops are everywhere. Ronnie just blew a guy away, and now we're fucked. Fucked."

Names. I listen eagerly, filing each name away with every detail and facet of character I can. Leo's the leader. The one in charge. The one with his hands in Indie's hair and the don't fuck with me attitude. Ronnie is the brutish, shaky one who shot Jeremy and seems to be entirely too on edge for something like this. Then there's the quiet one, attending to minutiae like cell phones and window shades, assessing everything. A details guy.

"Shut up, Trevor," The one called Leo barks back, his fingers laced through Indie's hair in an unwavering grip. "We're fucked, but we're not done yet. We're getting what we came for."

Trevor is the rattled one.

I soak up every word, barely conscious of Blake's hand on my arm. What the hell do they want? And what do they need Indie for?

"It's not worth it anymore, brother," Trevor counters. "This ain't worth our lives. Our futures."

"We're getting what we fucking came for." Leo spares a sharp glance over his shoulder, spitting out the words through clenched teeth. "If you're not with me, you're against me. If you're against me, you're dead to me, so walk the fuck out now and don't look back."

A moment of silence passes between the four men.

The unnamed assailant paces by the main entrance, watchful and quiet, while Ronnie observes eagerly with folded arms from the sidelines, almost entertained. I'm pretty sure he's tweaking. Trevor shakes his head, running a palm down the front of his veiled face. His sigh of compliance carries a different weight for all of us.

Relief for a few.

Terror for most.

Returning his attention to Indie, Leo releases her with an aggressive jerk of his hand, causing her to stumble back. "All right, Barbie doll. I'm going to tell you what to do, and you're going to do it. It'll be a cakewalk."

"Pl-please. Tameka..." Indie stutters, her chest heaving with panicked breaths, her hair knotted and cloaking her eyes. "She needs a doctor."

"I don't care about what she needs. I care about what I need."

Tears fall freely, and she licks them away. Indie glances in our direction, her lips quivering. "I have a daughter. Please, let us go."

Something brief, hardly even noticeable, washes over Leo's face as he follows Indie's line of sight, pinning his eyes on the little girl shielded in my arms. A frown follows. "Good. You have something worth fighting for. You'll be obedient."

Indie's defeated whimper is a dagger to my chest.

I wrap my arm around Daisy, pulling her even closer, letting Indie know that her daughter is safe.

Her eyes lock with mine, and something strange happens. Maybe it's simply empathy, two hearts speaking to each other. Maybe it's truth, zinging loudly between us.

I won't let anything happen to her.

I'm scared.

Trust me.

I don't know you, but I do.

Our voiceless conversation is cut short when Leo grabs Indie by the throat, ripping a small cry from her lips. He towers over her, all hulk and hostility, tugging her to him until their faces are only inches apart.

His breath causes her hair to flutter as he grits out his request. "The safe. I want what's in it."

She nods with acquiescence.

"And there's a safety deposit box. I want what's in that, too."

"D-Do you have a key?"

"No, but you do."

Indie's tone is careful, hesitant, unsure of how she should choose her words. "We... we both need a key. There's two keys. You should have received one."

His shoulders go taut, his stance tense. "It's not my box."

The nameless man near the doors finally speaks up. "What the hell else do you need, Leo? All you need is the safe. We're here for the money, to get the fuck out of here, to make Ace proud—"

"Fuck you, Garrett. There's more money in Ace's box."

Trevor growls his frustration, pulling off his mask in a fit of rage. "Jesus, man. This is crazy! We are so fucked. Up the ass, to the hilt, fucked."

He throws the mask to the ground, kicking it with his boot, revealing light brown hair, almost red, with a matching goatee. Trevor links his fingers behind his neck and spins around, huffing out his agitation.

I watch in disbelief and a dawning horror, my gaze meeting Blake's briefly and sharing the same thought. He took his mask off. Why did he take his fucking mask off?

Leo flings Indie backwards again, and she topples beside Tameka atop the dark blue carpeting, her skirt inching up her thighs, baring a flash of red underwear.

Ronnie notices. "You know, boss, I can take her in the back to collect the loot."

My muscles lock up, my hands balling into fists.

"The only thing you'll be collecting is broken bones after I'm done kicking the shit out of you for fucking this up," Leo snarls. He then nods his head at Garrett and orders, "Take his gun while I'm gone. I don't trust him."

"Whoa, hey—"

"Shut the fuck up." Leo spins back to Indie, flicking his finger at her. "Stand up. Let's go."

She scrambles to wobbly feet, knees quaking as she steadies herself, then glances our way through glassy eyes.

Please take care of her.

I promise.

"C'mon, Goldilocks. Don't got all day."

A strangled cry escapes before she turns away. "Mommy loves you, baby. Be a good girl."

The crack in her voice, the stark hitch of desperation, nearly guts me. In response, I thread my fingers through one soft pigtail, then graze my palm up and down Daisy's back. She doesn't reply. Doesn't flinch, doesn't speak.

She's in shock.

Indie stumbles away, Leo following, and I watch as they disappear into a back room while the three remaining attackers huddle up, appearing to evaluate the current situation.

Blake lets out a breath, shifting his back against the side of the desk to face me. We share a wary glance as he nods down at Daisy. "Poor kid. I see extensive therapy in her future."

"Assuming she has a future." I squeeze the child tighter in response to my own morbid thoughts, hoping she didn't hear them.

"The kiddo will be fine. It's me I'm worried about."

"I'm sure you'll charm your way out of this somehow, Blake."

"Are you kidding? I'm clearly the bungling sidekick in this scenario. The comic relief," he breezes, shuddering at the assessment. "We're always the first to go."

My eyes narrow in his direction, one eyebrow arching. "What am I, then?"

"The hero, Dax. You're the star." An encouraging palm slaps me on the back as he finishes, "No pressure."

Daisy nuzzles into me, delicate fingers fisting the fabric of my dress shirt. Her squeaky voice interrupts us. "Where's Mommy?"

Swallowing, I take in the blotches of blood stained along her Care Bears dress that features an image of a lion with a heart on its chest. A few locks of golden hair are sticky with remnants of the massacre, causing my heart to stutter. "She… she's working. Your mom will be right back, little lion."

A tiny chin inches upward until two blue eyes find my face. "There's a lion on my dress. His name is Brave Heart Lion."

"I see that," I say. "He looks very brave. Just like you."

Before Daisy can reply, a groan permeates our three-person pow-wow, and I skate my gaze over to where Tameka is lifting up on her elbows, a trickle of blood drawing a crimson trail down the side of her face. She places her fingertips to her head, her expression pained.

"She needs a doctor," I note, pressing Daisy's head back to my chest. "We have to figure these guys out. Negotiate with them."

Blake bristles beside me. "They don't strike me as the charitable type, Dax."

He pauses, lips pursing together while he ponders our options. We both drink in the room, attention floating from one worried face to the next. There's over a dozen hostages, a mix of employees and patrons. An elderly couple hold each other near the teller station, while a mother cradles two teenagers under each arm. An elderly woman sits amidst a scattered pile of coins near the desk, her expression bewildered. Everyone here has a story that demands telling. A future they deserve to live out.

This can't end here.

Filling his cheeks with an exaggerated breath, Blake bobs his head with a semblance of conviction. "We have one card we can play."

The three gunmen eye their surroundings every now and then, occasionally pinning their sights on me. I shudder, turning my attention back to Blake. "What's that?" I wonder.

Our eyes meet, and he replies, "You."

CHAPTER FIVE

Indie

OH, SWEET JESUS.

My breath hitches painfully as the man, Leo, drags me to the back of the bank where the vault and the safety deposit boxes are, and words stick in my throat. Swallowing, I try to speak.

Nothing comes out, adrenaline and fear keeping everything tied up tight. I needn't bother, because as soon as we cross the threshold into the back, he stops in front of the vault door and pushes me face first into its shiny metal surface, pressing in close behind me until I feel the gun's mouth caress the glide of my jaw.

"This is it, right, Barbie Girl? Where the money, the boxes, everything is?"

The muzzle bites harder. "Yes." The answer comes from somewhere deep. "It's all back there."

"Good. I want you to get me in there."

I pull a breath in and hold. One one-thousand. Two one-thousand. I hadn't realized how precious, how infinitely countable, each one is, until this moment.

This moment is a lynch pin. It will determine if the wheel stays in place, or if it all falls apart. Somehow, I know that, in the space of those two one-thousand beats of time.

I heard the sirens earlier. That tells me someone managed to hit the silent alarm. There's a lot that happens during a bank robbery when someone accomplishes that feat, a lot that's good for the bank, but not necessarily good for the people inside. It depends on who they're dealing with.

Hence the lynch pin.

And I hate, hate, that my daughter is caught in the crossfire.

"I'll do my best," I start.

The beefy fingers in my hair tighten, pulling at the strands. "Your best better—"

"Wait!" I cry. "Let me finish, please." To my surprise, he stops. My voice shakes, but I continue. "I will do everything I can to get you in this vault. This money... it's not mine. I don't give a fuck what happens to it. That little girl out there... she's all the fucks I have to give."

Leo relaxes his hold just enough for me to turn my head and look him in the face. What I can see of it, anyway, considering he's still masked. All I see is the pale grey of his eyes, ringed with dark blue. "Well, it sounds like we're on the same page, then, Barbie. Let's get on with it."

"There's a problem." My breath catches in my throat again, holding tight. He's not going to like what I have to say, and that's also a problem.

"How do you know there's a fuckin' problem when you haven't even tried yet?"

Leo taps the muzzle of the firearm against my chin, and I close my eyes against it. "Someone had to have set off the alarm for the cops to get here as fast as they did," I say, words spilling out one after another in my haste to make him understand. "When that happens, the vault goes on a timed lockdown. No one can access it from the bank. Not with a key, not with a code—it can't be done. I can put in the combination and turn my key, but I don't think it's going to open."

He jerks me around to face him, placing one thick, tattooed forearm against my throat and staring at me with shrewd eyes. "What's the combination?"

I fire the numbers off without hesitation, unblinking. It makes no difference. They'll be changed in twenty-four hours.

"Don't lie to me, bitch. If you're lying, I'll know, and I'll go out there and break every tiny bone in your little girl's body."

I let out a choked gasp, trying to push back visions of Daisy being subjected to this man's brutality. "I'm not! I swear to you, I'm not lying."

"Combination." I give him the alpha-numeric sequence again, and this time, he steps back and nods toward the safe. "Put it in."

I put the code in, standing back a little so he can clearly see every digit and letter I type, and when I finish, press the enter button.

My heart sinks when the green indicator flashes red, and a scrolling message appears: SECURITY MEASURES IN PLACE. VAULT PROTECTED

BY TIME LOCK TECHNOLOGY UNTIL 21:23 HOURS.

"Fuck!"

He paces a few steps away, the gun bouncing off his temple in agitation as he visibly tries to regroup. I wait tensely by the keypad, then turn and try the sequence again, unable to stand still and watch him unravel.

Please, God. Please work.

The same message appears. Behind me, I hear his frustrated rage in every clipped swish of his body as he moves. It's deafening in the small anteroom.

Nearing panic-mode, desperate to protect my baby girl, I try again.

And again.

My forehead dotted with sweat, I close my eyes and lean into the cold steel, shoulders shaking with a sob that wells up out of nowhere. "Please don't hurt her. Please... I'll do anything."

Nostalgic images sweep through me, memories of my life. My imperfect, precious life. Daisy pedaling her tricycle down the city streets, her pigtails floating behind her with the breeze, her giggles filling me with pride. Game nights with Tameka as we gripe about our workweek and laugh until our bellies ache. My mother stopping by unannounced to clean my house and blast Fleetwood Mac, for no reason at all... just because. Even Jeremy, despite his flaws, despite my resentment—I think about him, too, and those few happy years we shared together.

Now, he's dead. No more disputes or disagreements. No more bickering about alimony or childcare arrangements.

God, I'd do anything for one more petty fight.

It would mean that this was all a terrible dream.

Inches before me, Leo stops pacing and glowers down at me, his eyes glowing in the cutouts of his mask, as though he can compel me to make things different—as if I can somehow do the impossible and open this safe.

I force my spine straighter and bite down on my lower lip to keep it from trembling. Tension stretches between us as his mouth opens to speak, but before he can, another voice interrupts us from the doorway.

"Brother."

Leo whirls around. "What?"

"This fuckin' phone out here won't stop ringin'. You need to decide what you want us to do about it."

"Well, that's just great. Give me a fuckin' sec, Trevor." Leo, closes his eyes behind the mask and rubs the heels of his hands over them, the gun a forgotten accessory.

"What the hell is this?" Trevor pushes me aside to look more closely at the scrolling message on the vault. "Did you do this?"

"No! It's an automatic security defense. I swear, I—"

"Goddammit, Leo! What the fuck are we going to do? I told you we were fucked, and now we're not even walking out with the goddamn money! Hell, we shoulda just waltzed over to the fuckin' jail and asked them to lock us up in the first god—"

"Shut the fuck up, Trev." Leo's voice is tired, weary. He spares me a look, one that makes my chest squeeze and ice wrap around my spine. "We still have something we can use."

"Oh, yeah? What's that? Because it kinda looks like they have us ass up over a barrel, if you ask me."

Instead of answering, Leo takes hold of my arm. "Come on, Barbie. Let's go talk to the cops."

He drags me away from the vault, his fingers bruising my upper arm, and I try to keep up with his long, barreling strides. When we reach the lobby, my eyes dart immediately to the spot beneath the large courtesy table where we were all taking shelter. Blake and Dax are huddled together, while Daisy is tucked securely into Dax's lap.

As though she belongs there.

A weight I hadn't realized I carried lifts and I feel the first faint stirrings of something other than panic and fear. It's gratitude, but as Dax's steady multi-colored gaze catches mine, it's something more, as well. Something that makes my chest tighten, and not in fear.

It's brief, but it's powerful.

We're connected now.

I look away as Leo pushes me toward the desk phone, and as if on cue, it begins to ring. The gun presses into the small of my back, and he orders, "Answer it."

I obey, distantly impressed by how steady my hand is when I lift the handset. "Hello?" Leo leans over and punches the speaker button, and a calm voice fills the lobby.

"This is Bob Dunevan, head of crisis negotiations for the department. I'm going to be working with you to—"

Leo motions, impatient. "Get to the fuckin' point," he barks.

Bob stalls, then recovers. "May I have your name, please, ma'am?"

"Indie Chase."

"And are you a hostage, Ms. Chase?"

"I am."

"How many others are there with you?"

I look at Leo for approval, and he gives a small nod. My eyes travel the lobby, taking count of the clients and employees that I'm responsible for. I try to wrangle professionalism. "There are seventeen customers, including two teenagers and one… child. One man is dead. There are six employees, counting myself. Two women and a security guard have head injuries." My voice breaks on the last word, and I find myself searching for Tameka. She's upright, sitting a few feet behind Dax and Blake, against the counter. She smiles encouragingly at me as she holds a piece of fabric to her head, but the sentiment doesn't reach her eyes.

"You're doing good, Ms. Chase. How many people have taken control—"

"That's enough of that," Leo breaks in, his voice rough. "There are enough of us to be dangerous; that's all you need to worry about it. I'm going to tell you what we want so you can get on that. Soon as you get it done, sooner we get out of your hair. Sound fair?"

"We're going to do everything in our power to give you exactly that, Mr… ?"

"Nice try, Barney." Leo's voice is derisive. "We want money. That's why we're here. Of course, some dumbass had to be a hero and hit the fuckin' alarm, and now the safe is on a time lock. So, I need you to take care of that little problem for me, numero uno."

In the background, there are the sounds of Bob shuffling his grip on the phone as he dictates information to someone else. "How much?"

"Six million will suffice. Unmarked, untraceable, small bills."

"So… nothing too difficult." Bob's tone is wry.

"You'll make it happen, won't you, Bob. I sense you're good at your job."

"What else?" Bob asks.

"There's a safety deposit box in here I need access to. It's in that same vault I can't get into."

"Do you have the key?"

"No, I don't have the fucking key! Jesus, Mary, and Joseph, can someone just get another goddamn key already?"

The quiet brother, Garrett, cuts in. "Fuck the box, man. It holds pennies compared to six mil."

"I…" Leo sniffs, contemplating the suggestion, then shrugs his shoulders. "Fine. Can't be greedy now. Fuck the box."

For a long moment, there's silence. It's obvious that Leo doesn't easily relinquish his control, but he's backed into a corner. From Trevor's mask coming off earlier, to the names being bandied around, to the time crunch and desperation to get what he wants out of this… he's stuck.

I hold my breath, waiting.

"All right, sir," Bob says curtly on the other end of the line. "We'll try get your arrangements in place. Do you have any other demands?"

"Yes." Leo's eyes dance between all three men, his grip on the receiver tightening. "You guys arrested my brother, Ace, on something he didn't do. You can figure out who he is and how you fucked up on your own time. That shit doesn't sit right with us."

"Us?"

"His kin."

"Okay. I'm not sure—"

"I want him released. Today."

Several steps away, the brother named Trevor looks like he's about to go nuclear, his face red, a vein popping out on his forehead. "What in the ever-loving fuck, man? That's not why we're here, Leo—"

"Shut up!"

Bob gives a short, unbelieving laugh. "I'm not sure what you've been told, but I can't just release a guy from prison."

"I think if I start putting a bullet in the heads of everyone in here, you'll find a way," Leo says, his voice strong and devoid of feeling. He glances down at the black watch on his wrist. "So here's what's going to happen. You're going to get us six million dollars, you're going to get my brother out of that fuckin' cell, and you're going to get us a protected walk out of here. And maybe a plane." There's a pause, as if he's thinking it over. "Yeah. A plane. We'll spot you for the gas with the six mil."

"Jesus fuck…" Trevor mumbles, pacing with agitation.

"You're going to do all of that within the next four hours, and you're going to report in every thirty minutes with your progress. If I don't see progress being made, someone gets to taste a bullet." Leo's eyes are dead as they travel the lobby and land on me. "Any questions?"

Chapter Six

Dax

"I HAVE A QUESTION."

My head twists to the left to witness Blake raising his hand, just as Leo slams the phone down. Ah, hell.

Leo's eyes narrow with bemusement. "Go ahead, Pink Shirt. I'm all ears."

"Uh, well, my buddy here..." Blake fidgets beside me, smoothing out the wrinkles in his pink polo, then slaps me on the shoulder. "This big guy just so happens to be a renowned hockey player." He clears his throat when he's met with a slow blink of silence. "What I'm saying is, he's famous. Disgustingly famous. I'm talking bodyguards, fan clubs, money coming out the wazoo. He's got influence. You know... people. Possible mafia connections. Cartel, maybe..."

"Can somebody shut him up?"

"Blake, shut up," I ground out.

He throws his hands up, sweat glazed along his hairline as he continues to ramble. "Hey, okay, I'm just trying to keep you informed. You've got a celebrity as a hostage here." Swallowing, he adds, "And his highly respected manager."

The four men stare at us with a quiet intensity, causing my heart to jack-knife in my chest.

Leo finally replies. "So, what's your fucking question?"

"Can you let us go?"

Jesus.

I'm going to add, "How would you react in a hostage situation?" to all future resumes.

A gruff chuckle bites the air as Leo saunters over to us. He's about to speak when the loose cannon pipes up from the other side of the room, scratching the back of his neck. "Shit, yeah... I knew that guy looked familiar. He's right, boss. That motherfucker plays for the Seattle Fury."

Catching Indie's eye near the teller desk, I offer a quick nod. There doesn't seem to be any recognition there—only a flash of surprise glints back at me. "Dax Reed," I confirm, turning my attention to the ringleader. "Maybe I can help."

"Help?" More derisive laughter penetrates the space between us. "How the fuck are you gonna help me? All you do is skate around the ice with a fuckin' stick. Right now, you're no different than anyone else in this room. You're just as expendable."

"Am I?" I'm playing with fire, but I reach around to my back pocket anyway, holding out one hand as a silent request for permission. Leo's jaw tightens, but he allows me to fetch my wallet. I flip it open, then fish out a small key, dangling it in front of me. "Babe Ruth. Number nine. 1914."

"Talk in English, hockey boy. I don't speak sports."

"It's an extremely rare baseball card. You'll get an easy mil for it."

Leo falters for a moment, running a palm over his ski mask before he flashes me a grin. "I let you go, and you give me the card? Is that your angle?"

My gaze makes its way over to Indie again, noting the way she clings to the edge of the teller desk with white-knuckled fingers. Dried blood still stains her skirt and crusts her skin. Tearstains gleam along her high cheekbones as a flurry of unspoken questions float over to me. I shake my head, then address Leo through a cracked voice. "Not me. The children and the wounded."

On instinct, my grip strengthens along Daisy's waist, her fine wisps of hair tickling my chin. Indie's faint gasp of staggered hope echoes in my ears as I stare down the madman towering in front of me.

Blake coughs into his fist, "And Blake."

I jab him with my elbow, not breaking eye contact with Leo. "Let them go, and the card is yours. You still have plenty of leverage in here for the cops."

Trevor steps forward, landing beside the man I presume to be his brother. He shoves his hands into his pockets, rocking on the balls of his feet. "It's a good deal, Leo, man. Besides, I don't want no little kid blood on my hands if shit—"

Just as a wave of optimism floods me, it evaporates the second my peripheral catches sight of a man leaping from his place on the carpet and making a mad dash to the entry doors.

No, fuck, goddammit.

Four collective heads turn, matching the direction of my momentary distraction.

"Hey!" Leo bellows. "Get the fuck back here."

Garrett is the closest, so he jumps into action and tackles the man, just as he reaches the glass doors. They both go down, Garrett on top, caging in the frightened stranger with his knees as the room erupts with cries and whimpers.

"Let me go! Let me go, you son-of-a-bitch," the man demands, his voice strained and desperate as he lies flat on his stomach.

A scuffle ensues, the man twisting and turning, flailing his legs as he tries to kick Garrett off his back. Garrett shoves the hostage's face into the rough carpet, prompting a painful groan, and Garrett's smile gleams with victory when he feels the man has been subdued.

That smile dissolves the moment the man wiggles his face towards Garrett's opposite arm, then chomps down hard with his teeth.

"You fuckin' motherfucker!" Garrett wails, straightening on the man's back while he cradles his wounded arm, now impaired with a nasty bite mark. "Fuck."

The man utilizes his window of opportunity by flipping over, then launching Garrett backwards and mounting him with two hands curled around his attacker's neck.

Another crack rings out.

An earsplitting blast that has me shoving Daisy behind me, shielding her with my large frame. She lets out a scream, like a tiny mouse, while Blake covers his head beside me and the rest of the hostages duck.

Indie hits the floor, her chin darting up to check on her daughter, eyes shimmering with more tears.

"You stupid asshole." Leo rams his firearm back into the hem of his jeans, storming over to the scene of the crime. "Goddamn moron."

The man rolls off of Garrett, both hands gripping the fresh gunshot wound along his abdomen. "Oh, God. Y-You shot me... oh, God!" he cries, falling on his back, his features contorted with disbelief. Blood slicks his palms, oozing through the cracks in his fingers.

Shit. Shit.

The phone rings.

Leo halts his gait, cracking a bone in his neck as his shoulders go stiff. On the third ring, he fires an order to Indie. "Pick up the fuckin' phone, will you?"

She inhales a rattled breath, drawing to unsteady feet. Licking her lips, she reaches for the telephone, answering softly. "Hello?" A pause. "Yes. Somebody was shot." Another pause. "I-I'm not sure... it looks bad. He's in a lot of pain..."

In a flash, Leo is by Indie's side, yanking the receiver from her grip. "What?" he spits out.

The voice on the other end of the line is muffled. Only bits and pieces travel over to me.

Situation. Right decision. Work with you. Help him.

"No one comes in. No one leaves. I'll handle it." Pinching the bridge of his nose, Leo tosses the phone at Indie, and she barely catches it as she cowers back. Leo lets out a roar of frustration, then paces in a circle, his eyes wild and unhinged. "Who the fuck here is a doctor?"

My insides coil with anxiety, hoping someone speaks up.

Someone else.

But his question is only greeted with terrified silence, and I close my eyes, bracing myself for the inevitable.

"Someone in this room better fuckin—"

"I know a few things. I'll try to help him," I offer, my tone not giving away the fear lacing my bloodstream.

I'm not a doctor, but my father is. He's an acclaimed surgeon at UW Medical Center.

I've resented him all my life for it—resented myself for not wanting the life he wanted for me. I've resented the long hours, the family dinners caught in a cloud of his potent irritability, the emotional distance that always radiated off of him, and the condescending "pep talks" that reeked of disappointment.

I always wanted to be a hockey player. I wanted ice beneath my skates and brisk air in my lungs as I weaved through the rink.

I wanted the game. Rough, dirty, fun.

I craved that adrenaline in my blood, pumping hot and feral.

Sterile exam rooms were never my style. I traded scalpels and spreadsheets for a jersey and a puck.

But right now, I need to be the son my father always envisioned.

The one he wanted more than he wanted me.

"What the fuck r'you waiting for? Go save the stupid bastard," Leo barks.

Hesitation grips me when Daisy latches onto my dress shirt with eager fingers. I pull her off of me, gentle and careful, swiping away a loose strand of hair tickling her forehead. "Hey, little lion. My friend Blake is going to take care of you for a minute while I go help a man," I explain, forcing a comforting smile. "I'll be right back."

"Wait, wait," Blake splutters, freezing up when I pluck the child from my chest and haul her into his lap. "You know I'm not—"

"You'll be fine. Keep her safe."

Rising from my place on the floor, muscles tight and achy, I shoot him a reassuring glance.

"I killed my parakeet and eight out of eight house plants all in a single week!" he whisper-yells to my retreating back.

All eyes are on me as I make my way over to the groaning man who is writhing on his back, knees bent, face twisted with agony. Leaning down beside him, I assess the damage as he cradles his blood-soaked side. "Hey, it's going to be okay, old sport. What's your name?" I ask softly.

Perspiration coats his face, little droplets inching down his cheeks and temple. "Brian," he replies, the name splintering on his tongue. "You gotta fix me. I'm getting married next month."

My heart clenches.

The gunshot is low and to the left.

Hypovolemic shock, blood loss, and infection are likely. Perforated intestine possible.

Hopefully, there are no secondary missile injuries from bone or bullet fragments.

Without thinking it through, I tug my shirt over my head and use it to slow the blood flow, replacing his clasped hands with the fabric. I glance up at Leo, who hovers a few feet away, his boot tapping against the floor. "I need help."

"What do you fuckin' need?"

"An ambulance. A hospital," I bite out, grinding my teeth. "But I'll take a first aid kit. Maybe another set of hands."

Leo fixates on Indie, ushering her to do his bidding with a sharp nod of his chin. "You heard the man, Barbie doll. Fetch."

She flusters, disappearing behind the counter and reappearing a few seconds later with a first aid kit. When she hands it to Leo, he grabs her by the back of the neck and shoves her forward. Indie squeaks in surprise, falling to her knees beside me.

Leo smacks her on the backside with a leer. "Fix him up real good. If he dies, Ace loses his "get out of jail free card", and that won't go over very well for any of us."

Our eyes meet over the wounded man.

It's only a split second. There's no time for anything else.

But a flurry of emotions pass between us; a fellowship, a connection, a kindred duty.

And then I get to work, sifting through the medical supplies and doing the best I can with the limited amount of tools on hand. Gloves, gauze, tape, antibacterial wipes, antiseptic cream. I shake out a few painkillers and drop them into his mouth. "Take these. It's not much, but it's something."

Brian's skin is drenched in sweat, his complexion ashen. His teeth chatter with shock. "She picked out a black dress. For the wedding, you know?" he says as his body vibrates. "She thought it would be good luck."

"You'll walk down that aisle, Brian. Just hang tight." I glance at Indie, who looks frozen, her eyes as wide as saucers. "Hey. Indie."

She swallows, her head slowly turning to face me.

"I need you, okay?"

"I-I don't know what I'm doing… or how to—"

"You're doing great. I think I need moral support more than anything."

We share another quick look before I dip my eyes to the man's abdomen, noting how my shirt is almost fully soaked with blood.

"Is he… ?" Indie's question trails off, her voice catching.

"He's never been better," I reply, applying more pressure. "Right, Brian?"

Brian's eyelids flutter, his consciousness fading. My heartbeats stutter with worry as I take Indie by the wrist and press her hand to the bloody shirt. "Hold this here. I'm going to clean him up and find some bandages."

She fists the material, pushing down on the wound. "Are you a doctor or a hockey player?"

"Neither."

Indie blinks at me, her lips parting to speak.

I collect the antibacterial wipes, then gently move her hand away from the wound, allowing myself access. "I retired from the game a few months back. And my father's a surgeon, so I learned the medical basics over the years." Dotting at the blood, it continues to pool to the surface. I redirect my words to Brian. "Brian, hey. Stay with us, all right? Tell me about your girl. I bet she's pretty."

He's silent for a beat, his eyes closed. Then a single word escapes him. "Andrea."

"Andrea," I repeat. "Pretty name for a pretty girl."

"Tell her… tell her I love her," Brian rasps.

"Absolutely. She can't wait for you to tell her that you love her." My eyes lift, my hands still working. A smile hints on Indie's mouth as she watches me clean the wound, and I can't help but wonder what it would look like fully bloomed right now. Beaming and bright. "Talk to me," I mutter softly. "Tell me a story. I need something to keep me from unraveling here."

It's the truth. I'm pretty damn decent under pressure, but this isn't a tied score with ten seconds on the clock.

This clock is mortal, and time is ticking.

Blue-green eyes case me, from my bare torso, to my assortment of tattoos, to the glazed look of desperation I'm trying so hard to conceal. I can feel her thinking, trying to conjure up the perfect words to make this better. To pull some good out of the evil that surrounds us, clutching us in a vicelike grip.

Indie bites at her lower lip, her gaze dipping downward. "I'm sorry you were here today," she tells me, her tone gentle. Her eyes skip over to Daisy perched just behind my shoulder, and a glimmer of warmth captures her. When she pulls her focus back to me, the softness lingers. Something peaceful. "But... I'm also really glad you are."

Chapter Seven

Indie

"I'M SORRY YOU WERE here today. But... I'm also really glad you are."

My confession hangs in the air between us, an electric pulse that flickers before fading. His gaze widens on me for a moment, then his attention is back on the man between us, his big hands deft and capable as they replace his soaked shirt with a soft cotton jacket someone tossed our way. There's a small pile of random clothing articles, I see, none of it precisely sterile, but not important to our goal of keeping as much blood in his body as possible.

"Keep pressure..." Dax mutters, his hands covering mine and bearing firmly down. "We need to stop this bleeding." Leaving mine, his hands slip around Brian's torso to his back, prompting a low groan. "Sorry... okay, good. That's real good. There's an exit wound." Belatedly, I notice the blood seeping from beneath Brian's body and reach to grab another makeshift bandage. There's too much happening to process it all with any real efficiency. Daisy and Blake several feet distant have the bulk of my attention. And then Tameka, visibly in pain. All of my employees and customers, cowering and afraid.

This man beneath my hands, potentially dying.

Maybe it's a stupid thing to worry about, but I hate being inefficient. I hate being helpless. My breathing quickens as I ball my fist against the bandage, trying to hide the sudden trembling.

Dax touches my hand lightly, pulling my attention back to him. "How about that story?" he asks, reminding me of his earlier request.

"Oh, right... sorry." I clear my throat, forcing myself to stay calm. Dax's eyes hold with mine, the look he gives me commanding yet warm. His brown eye glows with encouragement, telling me that I'm doing just fine. I don't even look at the blue one. Swallowing, I hand him a bandage with the faintest smile. "Here you go."

Dax pushes the bandage efficiently into place and carefully eases his hands from beneath Brian's body. "Thanks," he says, his voice lower than before. He does something else to the man below us—trying to make him more comfortable, I presume. "Hanging in there, old sport?"

The outdated phrase lingers between us, calling to mind sailboats and Long Island sunsets. I can't help but laugh to myself, despite it all. When Dax looks up at me questioningly, I explain, "You don't really hear that term used anymore."

"'Old sport?'"

I nod.

"It's a throwback from my grandfather. It reminds me of him every time I say it," Dax says, his tawny eye glimmering with stories I'll likely never be told.

And just like that, my own story blooms.

"And 'so we beat on, boats against the current,'" I murmur softly.

Dax arches an eyebrow with curiosity.

"The Great Gatsby," I tell him. "Please tell me you've read it."

"I'm pretty sure I did, actually. Is that the one with the egg and the eye thing?"

A little snort escapes before I can stop it. "Oh, God. If that's all you remember, you have to read it again. It's only the best American novel ever written." My inner bookworm somehow shoves its way through the anarchy and fear, a tiny pocket of comfort swelling inside me. Something trivial to cling to when the world is crumbling down around us. "Please tell me you'll read it again."

He's looking down at Brian, but the corner of his mouth is crooked up in a barely-there smile. "Well, I like to read and all, but I may need a good reason for that one."

I glance over at Daisy—the little girl I named after my favorite book—making sure she's okay, and I mutter absently, "I'm realizing we're surrounded by a million good reasons to do everything we want." It looks like Blake is trying to braid her hair, while my daughter frowns at him skeptically. He gives her an exaggerated eyebrow waggle and holds his hands palms out, as if to say, just you wait, and the tiniest smile tugs at the frown.

It's enough, and I return to the story that immediately came to mind when Dax used the phrase "old sport."

"Gatsby always makes me think of sailing," I say, keeping my voice low. Leo and one of his brothers are feet away, talking to each other with tense expressions while their gazes rove the assembled group.

They aren't watching us, so I open my mouth to continue. "My dad —" My voice completely, humiliatingly cracks, and I stall out. The situation had let me forget for a moment that this isn't something I talk about, and certainly not to a complete stranger.

Dax doesn't feel like a stranger, though, so when he makes a quiet sound of coaxing, I keep going.

"My dad had this thing for boats. He collected vintage models and put them together. Raced in all the weekend regattas he had time for," I muse, the vivid memories a worthy distraction to our circumstances. "It was by craft that boats really captured his heart. He was a third generation boat builder here in Seattle."

Dax whistles low, perhaps recognizing the heritage bred into someone by the eternal scents of cedar and resin. As the son of a builder, Dad didn't stand a chance to be anything any different. Nearly a hundred years of artistry and seamanship was sewn into the fiber of who he was, ribboned into his very DNA.

"My mother wasn't that into it, though," I add with a sigh. I was young when I recognized and understood the intense polarity that existed between her needs and Dad's sacrosanct way of being. "She had a phobia of water, and my father did everything he could to respect it without giving up sailing. Despite him being a boat builder, I wasn't allowed in water deeper than the community pool until I turned sixteen. That would be the magic year, she decreed, when he could take me out."

Dax wraps his fingers around Brian's wrist, his lips moving as he counts and watches the old-fashioned watch on his own wrist. I wait until he's finished, not wanting to mess up his count.

"Every year until my sixteenth, Dad gave me a model sailboat he'd built for me, each named for a place we'd sail to when I was allowed to go with him. Bainbridge. Poulsbo. Bell Harbor."

"Those are the best kinds of gifts," Dax says. He sweeps his gaze back to me, a smiling lifting as he drinks in my nostalgic expression. "I was actually planning on sailing this week in Hawaii. I should be packing for Maui right now, can you believe it? Instead—" He stops and clears his throat, as if realizing that's probably not the best train of thought to pursue. Regrouping, Dax purses his lips and forces that smile back into place. "What was the boat named for your sixteenth? Was the sail everything you imagined?"

"No." My voice quivers, and I try to steady it before continuing. It was a long time ago and allowing myself to get upset about this now, in the middle of a bank robbery, would be the height of foolishness. "Dad went out for a sail one weekend before I turned sixteen, and he never came back." I smooth Brian's hair from his forehead, my eyes on Daisy as I perform the same small act of comfort I bequeath my daughter each night as she sleeps. "I didn't go sailing."

Dax doesn't respond. Everything's so fraught with tension, I half-wonder if he even heard me. We sit quietly on either side of Brian, watching his vital signs for any major changes. Dax begins taking Brian's pulse again, but this time a vertical line demarcates the plane of his forehead.

Leo remains a few feet away, speaking in low, clipped tones to a brother. Garrett, I think. There's a general hush over the lobby, an air of resignation blanketing all of us.

We have no idea how long we'll be here. No compass for navigating this ocean of regret and fear we're swimming in, other than the one crafted of silence—tempered with obedience.

"I'm sorry about your father," Dax finally whispers softly, his tone fused with grit and sorrow. Sorrow for me, maybe, and sorrow for Brian. Sorrow for all of us trapped inside this deadly prison that I once considered a safe haven.

I'll never feel safe again.

I sigh a little, shaky and terse, but my response is cut off by Leo's barked command. "Hey. Shut up over there. You don't need to yak to keep him breathing. How's he doing?"

Dax's demeanor shifts immediately, his posture going rigid. "He needs a doctor. A transfusion. Fluids. There's only so much I can do with a Wal-Mart first aid kit. If you don't—"

"When I want your opinion, I'll ask for it."

"You did ask." Dax recoils slightly, unable to mask his growing frustration. "I'm telling you—he's not going to last long in this state."

"Fuck..."

Dax continues, glancing my way before settling back on Leo. "Help me help you. Tell me the plan. What's the end goal?"

Leo is silent, seething a few feet away, and my fingers clench on the bloody rag clutched against Brian's belly.

My eyes find Dax, and I mutely beg.

Don't provoke him.

I got this, trust me.

I'm trying.

Tremors are beginning to wrack their way through me, and I don't know how long I can hold myself together.

Dax presses on, ignoring my wordless plea and pulling his attention back to Leo. "Do you want to walk out of here alive, or be carried out? Because I know what I want."

A charged silence hovers heavy in the air as everyone holds their breath, awaiting Leo's answer. He bristles near the desk with crossed arms, the corded muscles pulsing.

Tick, tick, tick.

Before Leo can reply, the phone rings, startling us. He looks at me, my hands on Brian, and then at Dax. "Answer it, hockey star."

Dax falters. His sights shift from Leo to Brian, then land on me, irises flickering with hesitation. But he complies, having little other choice, and rises to answer the phone. His stare turns hard and almost studious as he crosses the room, fixated on Leo, and I can easily see him on the ice, weighing his opponent with those odd eyes. Measuring every weakness.

The ivory receiver is coated with blood, and I know I'll never be able to use that phone again without wanting to be ill.

If I make it out of here, that is.

Dax picks it up, listening quietly. "He's alive. Barely hanging on."

My spine stiffens as I look over at Daisy. Blake is playing Rock, Paper, Scissors with her, miming theatrically whenever she wins a hand even though his features are haggard with worry. He glances up and catches me watching, then throws a thumbs up at me, as if to say, "don't worry."

Daisy giggles, the sound like sunshine and rainbows and unicorns all rolled into one.

I have to make it out of here. The alternative isn't an option.

"One sec." Dax's voice draws me back to the harrowing scene before me as I keep pressure on Brian's wound. Dax pulls the phone away from his ear, addressing Leo. "They have a deal for you: release the kids and the wounded, and they'll send in pizza, water, and let you talk to your brother while they're working on the other stuff," he explains, his words careful and steady. Licking his lips, Dax proceeds. "If Brian dies, or if anyone else is wounded, they're not sure what they're going to be able to do for you. He says you're backing them into a corner."

"Take the deal, Leo." It's Trevor, the mask-less brother who was freaking out earlier about how they were completely fucked. He's sweating profusely as he shoots off a demand. "And ask for some goddamn Jolly Ranchers. I'm about to die here."

Leo taps the gun against his hip, fidgeting where he stands. "It's just pizza and water. A fuckin' phone call. Probably hoping Ace will change our minds or some shit." He huffs out a laugh to Trevor, then shakes his head a little, dragging his focus back to Dax, who's still waiting on a response. "Okay, here's what's going to happen. We'll give them the kids and the wounded. And the dead guy, so he doesn't stink the place up. In return, I want delivery from Mel's Kitchen—not no fuckin' pizza. Just a bunch of different shit will do. And pop, not water. The Jolly Ranchers. The phone call."

My insides buzz with anxiety as he shoots off his list, my chest pinching violently. The lobby is dead still, none of us hardly breathing in the effort it takes to hear.

Dax finishes reciting Leo's seemingly never-ending list and softly replaces the receiver. "Fifteen minutes," he says. "The phone will ring, your brothers will stand guard while you talk, and we'll begin the exchange."

Leo gives a brief nod and paces a few feet away. Dax returns to his position beside me, placing his hands over mine and lending me some additional strength. "You okay?"

I nod. "You're good at that."

"At what?"

"Leading... mediating."

His shoulders shrug upwards a fraction. "I guess being team captain came in handy for something." Dax's hands press warm and reassuring over mine, even crusted over in a stranger's blood as they are. He sends me the hint of a smile when our eyes meet, then turns his attention toward Daisy. "You don't seem so different, you know."

Following his stare, I glance at my daughter, who is resting against Blake's shoulder. Her little face lights up with solace when I send her a wide grin of reassurance.

Looking back to Dax, the smile lingers.

Like recognizes like. We beat against that current, waiting for the riptide to drag us under.

Chapter Eight

Dax

9:58 AM.

I whip my gaze to the large, round clock perched on the far wall, the wands ticking like merciless time bombs. My heart beats in perfect sync, only adding to the air of trepidation that swirls inside my gut.

I'm used to manifesting anxiety into adrenaline, into thrill.

But there's no excitement in this room. There's nothing encouraging to latch onto. I can hardly see through the dense fog of blood, terror, and uncertainty.

A tiny hand squeezes mine, and I glance down at our interlocked palms.

Brave little lion.

Maybe there is something worth clinging to here. Something of value.

There's hope.

Hope that Daisy will play with her Care Bears again. Hope that Indie will climb aboard another boat. Hope that Blake will walk out those glass doors and post his life-and-death tale all over social media, and this will become nothing but a gruesome memory.

Hope that I'll feel Hawaiian sand between my toes as I stare out at the rippling water with a good book in my hands.

The Great Gatsby.

That's going to be the first book I read if I ever make it out of here.

I close my eyes and allow myself to drift away, drowning out the ticking of my heart before it detonates. The Maui sun glows bright over the horizon, heating my skin. The waves ebb and flow, washing away my fear. The calls of a Spotted Dove soothe my nerves.

"Wake up, hockey boy. Time's up."

The yellow-orange sun dissolves into a crimson flush, staining the water red.

And when I open my eyes, I see more red.

Blood still sticky on my hands, dappled across my bare torso. Jeremy lying in a pool of his own severed mortality. Brian unconscious a few feet away, his life fading with every second that passes by on the giant wall clock.

Tick, tick, tick.

Daisy tips her chin up, cerulean eyes meeting mine. "Are you taking me home?" she inquires, her voice small and lulling.

Ronnie stomps over to our position in front of the entrance, his dark eyes glowing wild behind his mask. "There's no place like home, eh, Dorothy?" he taunts.

"I'm not Dorothy, I'm Daisy. I'm a little lion."

He snorts. "A cowardly lion, like your mama, huh?"

Indie has been dragged back to the teller counter, a pistol jabbed into her side. Mascara tracks down her cheeks as she trembles in Leo's grasp.

I catch her gaze.

I'm getting her out of here.

Please keep her safe.

Trust me.

I do.

"All right, boys, let's do this." Leo starts firing orders, one palm gripping the back of Indie's neck as he digs the firearm into her abdomen. "Let these assholes inside. Hockey boy—you take the kid out. Try to escape, and Banker Barbie gets blown away."

A shudder ripples through me, my skin clamming up. Indie's eyes widen, a squeak of terror escaping her, and I nod my head with mute compliance.

Two EMTs stand waiting on the opposite side of the doors, carrying paper bags with a stretcher and medical supplies. Trevor and Garrett are positioned on each side of the entryway with their guns raised, while Leo keeps a firm grip on Indie down the middle center of the lobby. Ronnie paces around us, weaponless, but armed with violence and vitriol.

"I said, let 'em in," Leo repeats, his tone brittle.

Little fingers wiggle in my grip, and I spare a final look to Daisy, who shuffles on both feet, her pigtails swaying side to side.

I suck in a breath of courage, then pace forward.

Tick.

One step.

Tick.

Two steps.

Tick.

Three steps.

My hand curls around the door handle, leaving smeared blood behind when I tug it open.

"Daisy, baby...." Indie calls out, her words bleeding with devastation. "Please, please let me say goodbye."

Leo gives her a hard shake. "Shut your trap."

"I love you, babygirl! Mommy loves you!"

Daisy twists around to wave at her mother, her delicate features pinched with confusion.

I give her a gentle shove out the doors, muttering after her, "Run, little lion. Be brave."

She steps forward as police officers rush to meet her, and I back away from freedom, from sunlight and Blue Elderberry breezes, from the fresh air that teases my lungs.

I keep backing away, because Indie's life hangs in the balance, and because Blake is still inside, and because there are people in this lobby who are desperate for the same things I am.

This isn't over yet.

The medical staff push past me, while a middle-aged mother guides her two teenagers to the doors, saying goodbye through tearful kisses. When all three children are safe outside, I pull the doors shut.

Leo bellows from the back of the room, maintaining his grip on Indie and pointing his pistol with his opposite hand. "That idiot is dying over there," he says crassly, signaling at Brian. "And this one had an unfortunate encounter with my gun for running her lying mouth." He throws a cold glance to Tameka, who stands stalwartly a few feet away from her attacker, then looks down at the elderly woman he accosted earlier. "That old bat, too. Fix them up, give me what I asked for, then get the fuck out."

The EMTs move straight to Brian, by far the most critical, laying the stretcher beside him.

I startle when Ronnie grabs me by the bicep, his fingertips digging in hard, and yanks me away from the commotion. "It's not your time to shine anymore, asswipe. You might be a superstar out there, but in here, you belong to us."

"Them, you mean."

My words slip out unplanned.

His eyes flare, his grip on me tightening. "The fuck does that mean?"

"It means, you're not really one of them, are you? You're the black sheep. The misfit."

The clown.

"You got a death wish, hockey man?"

Ronnie reaches for a weapon that doesn't exist, then funnels his frustration into manhandling in me. He's a good five inches shorter than me, but he's stocky, well-muscled, and I don't put up much of a fight. I could knock him to the ground in less than a blink if I wanted to, but my plays have always been driven by strategy. Careful design. I know how to read my opponents.

Gritting my teeth, I continue to work my way under his skin as his fingernails bite into my own. Over his shoulder, I see one of the brothers—Garrett, I think—watching us, his face neutral. There's no neutrality in his eyes, though. A second before he catches me taking stock of him, I see naked enmity in their depths. Then our gazes connect and his is carefully blank once again. "I'm just speaking the truth, Ronnie. I get it, you know. I know what it's like to feel unwanted. Unworthy."

"Don't try to lecture me, boy," he snarls. "Know your goddamn place." His gaze shifts, landing on Indie, who remains obedient beside Leo as he collects the snacks and beverages. Ronnie's eyes glint with something sinister. "Want to know where my place is?"

Silence hangs between us.

He tugs me down until his vile breath beats against my ear. "Right between those milky thighs of hers." Ronnie licks his lips with a satisfied grunt. "Mmm. I'd tear that shit up, leave that bitch bloody."

Queasiness mixes with some kind of protective rage as I'm spun around to face Indie. She turns to me at the same time, and we hold for a long beat.

I don't know this woman—not really. I've only known her for an hour, but I know the inherent parts of her. I've witnessed her fear, her love, her devotion, her loyalty. I've learned her weaknesses, her strengths. I know that her eyes appear more green than blue when there's a barrel of a gun pressed into her belly.

Indie is a stranger, yet I know her better than I know some of my closest friends.

And she trusts me.

Swallowing, I keep my focus on her and mutter my reply to Ronnie. "Leo would never let you get close enough. We both know that."

"That what you think?"

"Yeah, I do. It doesn't have to be like that, though. You're just as strong as him. Just as smart," I lie. "You don't have to take his shit."

Ronnie strengthens his grip. "I don't take shit from nobody. And I don't take advice from fuckin' meatheads like you."

"You're just a pawn in his game, Ronnie. Don't you want to be the king for once?"

I see his wheels turning when I glance his way, but he tries to recover. "Just shut the fuck up and stop distractin' me."

Sighing, I let it go, hoping a seed was planted, so I can use it to my advantage at some point. My eyes case the room, from Tameka and the elderly woman getting their vitals taken, to Brian still unconscious as his wound is tended to.

It's a harrowing scene, but a burst of optimism claims me.

At least Brian has a fighting chance to walk down that aisle.

At least Daisy is safe.

I made good on my promise.

A voice cuts through my roving thoughts, pulling my attention to Brian, who's being strapped onto the stretcher. "He needs a transfusion. Now."

I'm about to glance back at Leo when one of the EMTs pins their eyes on me. A man, roughly fifty, with a salt-and-pepper beard. He's trying to gain my attention—signal me in some way.

I squint my gaze, and he offers a subtle nod.

Shit.

He's undercover.

A tingle of newfound hope runs through my veins as I trail my focus from Trevor, to Garrett, to Leo, wondering if they noticed anything amiss. Ronnie is oblivious as he continues to eye-fuck Indie, and the other men are too wrapped up in their own duties.

My heart stammers.

I look over my shoulder at Blake, who's been uncharacteristically quiet since the trade began. He's leaning back against the inside of the desk, knees drawn up, seeming more hopeless than I've ever seen him. He forces his trademark, lopsided grin when we make eye contact, and I return the sentiment as well as I can.

I need to get us out of here.

Returning my eyes to the undercover EMT, I watch as he cocks his head to the entry doors. I try to read him. I try to understand what he's telling me.

Clearing his throat, the man repeats, "We need to get this individual to the hospital immediately."

Leo grumbles. "Fine... fuck. Take that rotting corpse with you when you go." He gestures to a partially covered Jeremy. "And no funny business."

Goddammit, what am I supposed to do?

Does he want me to run? Fight?

Cause a scene to distract them while they usher more hostages out?

I shake my head, conveying my uncertainty. There's one armed police officer versus three armed maniacs—this won't work.

It can't.

Besides, Indie still has a gun trained at her hip. One wrong move, one misstep, and he's going to kill her.

The cop tilts his head to the doors again, then holds up three fingers, shrouding his hand with the stretcher, so only I can see.

My throat goes dry as I glance at Indie. I refuse to let her be collateral damage.

She trusts me.

One finger goes down.

Tick.

Two fingers go down.

Tick.

Three fingers go down.

Boom.

A pistol is drawn from the officer's hidden holster and pointed right at Leo. He shouts, "Lower your weapons! If anyone shoots, the deal is off."

Leo grabs Indie by the hair, shoving his own gun at her forehead. "Motherfucker!"

"No, please!" Indie pleads.

Trevor and Garrett draw their weapons.

An eerie hesitation, a dramatic pause, infiltrates the lobby... and I jump into action, headbutting Ronnie until he releases me with a howl of pain.

Chaos breaks loose.

The actual EMT starts dragging Brian outside as people run and flee, their terrified screams echoing off the walls, distracting the brothers, splitting their attention in multiple directions. I assist in ushering hostages out the door, Tameka first, then the old woman, Blake, the security guard. It's all a blur. It's pure madness.

Before I'm able to get to Indie, the barrel of a gun is staring me right between the eyes.

Trevor's hand shakes mildly when he points his weapon at me, and I catch Blake's indecision as he wavers just outside the doors, staring in at me with a look of horror.

"Go!" I yell at him, nodding my head. "Go."

Blake's eyes water as he backs away to freedom.

And that's when the gun goes off.

... Indigo.

Chapter Nine

Indie

THIS ISN'T HAPPENING. IT isn't real. Maybe if I close my eyes and open them again, I'll be back in my bed, snuggled up tight in my mound of blankets, still in my undies and t-shirt, dangerously close to being late for work.

I try. I really do. I squeeze my eyes shut and block out the sounds of chaos erupting around me, the feel of cold steel against my forehead. But then Leo's fingers dig cruelly into my hair, pulling what's left of my carefully crafted chignon loose, and he begins dragging me toward the back once again.

My hands latch automatically around his wrists to keep him from ripping my hair out at the roots, but it doesn't do much good. One of my shoes snaps free of my foot, my heel scraping against the rough industrial carpet and prompting a screech at the added torment.

It's not a nightmare.

I'm not that lucky.

The scene around me has dissolved in the space of one blink to the next into pure mayhem. The kids are out—I watched Daisy run out the doors. That's a small comfort, even as my hands itch to hold her. But Tameka? My other employees? Where are they? My eyes skate from one person to the next, trying to make sense of the madness. There's too much... I can't—

There.

Dax is pushing Tameka, Blake, and Marcus rapidly past him out the door, along with the elderly woman who was also injured earlier. Dax swivels, gaze roving the lobby, hands pushing one person after another out, but distractedly, as though he's searching... snap. His eyes lock on me and he freezes, hands stilling in the air when Trevor's pistol is aimed at his forehead. Blake is turning to stare, pleading without words for Dax to follow him. Dax is yelling "go" at Blake and pivoting, taking a single stride in my direction, his features hard and determined, communicating something instinctual I find myself believing in, even if I can't explain it.

It's a promise. Shelter.

Every cell, from those in my tortured scalp to the ones beating frantically beneath my dress shirt in my racing heart… they reach for him across the distance, leap to close every inch and bind themselves to that shelter. To that hope and strength.

And then the report of a gun sounds, first one and then a second ripping through the lobby with an explosion of sound far too familiar after just an hour's exposure. The sound rockets between us, carelessly dispersing the cells stretching between us with a shock of burn that blazes wet against my shoulder, sending them into frenzied retreat.

I'm bleeding.

The lobby shifts and spins around me as Leo drops me precipitously to the floor. I see his legs in my vision as he steps over me, gun extended, and fires again. "Fuckin' hero. Someone's always gotta be a fuckin' hero."

Oh, God. Please not Dax.

Hot tears spill from the corners of my eyes, and I struggle to sit. It doesn't hurt so much—just burns. Cocking my head, I try to scan down my neck to see the damage, but the wound is in an awkward place, and I can't see anything except blood running in rivulets down my torso.

It's a lot of blood.

"Let me help her," a voice begs, and I sag back against the floor in relief.

Dax.

He's alive. He wants to help.

He wants to help me because… I'm bleeding.

I've been shot.

Oh, my God.

"Take her to the back," Leo commands, voice cold. "Here—" Leo's hand starts to settle in my hair again, to drag me, I suppose, but Dax's arms come around me, one beneath my knees and the other beneath my neck. I bite my lip to suppress a whimper as he lifts, and the lobby spins again, causing my stomach to churn.

"I've got her."

He's got me. My shelter.

"Right-o. Carry the bitch, then," Leo grunts.

Dax's arms tighten around me, and I let my face loll into his chest. It startles me for a second—I forgot he took his shirt off earlier. His frame is hard, his skin hot against my cheek, smelling faintly of sweat and aftershave, and mingling with the salty tang of blood.

I don't know how I can even notice something like that right now, but everything feels hazy and dreamlike, and my senses are working overtime to keep me alert and tethered.

Each step bears us farther from the sounds of the now-subdued terror in the lobby, a fact for which I'm grateful. There's a click, followed by a thud as a heavy door hits the wall, and then Leo shoves Dax forward. I barely have time to register that we're in the bank's tiny break room before Leo is yapping at us again. It's an interior room, windowless and barely a hundred feet square, lined with cabinets, a sink, refrigerator, and a microwave oven.

"The two of you can sit your asses in here until we need you again. No fucking funny business." He shoves the butt of the gun in my face, and Dax turns me subtly just a hair's breadth away. "I know who you are. I know where you live. Remember that shit."

"We're good," Dax assures him. "We got it."

There's another long, measuring look, and Leo leaves, backing slowly out and closing the door behind him with a menacing snick of the lock.

I stop holding my breath, letting out a moan instead.

"Fuck. Hold on, honey." Dax props me on the surface of the countertop at the end of the small room and uses that arm to sweep mugs of condiments and assorted packets of plastic forks and spoons onto the floor before laying me carefully back. He tilts my head in the opposite direction. "Let me look at you."

I'm not entirely sure what happened, but I don't think the bullet entered my body. "I'm fine—"

"You're not fine, Indigo. Hold still."

Indigo.

I used to hate the sound of my full, given name, so artsy and pretentious. My mother came from a wealthy family of art collectors, the opposite of my struggling, boat-building father. She was never like them, though—she was a humble painter, never cavalier like my grandparents and gaggle of high-maintenance cousins.

She fell in love with a poor sailor, uprooted her life, and had no regrets.

Then, she had a daughter, and she named that daughter Indigo.

"Indigo possesses a level of beauty that no other color comes close to. It symbolizes structure, order. Integrity," my mother told me one day as I skipped around the backyard, whining because Jenny Thompson had teased me about my name. "You'll always be my anchor through the chaos, sweet girl."

I never looked at it that way. In a world full of Ambers and Jessicas, I hated being an Indigo.

Only... it sounds different right now. It doesn't sound so bad, spilling from his lips as he gazes down at me on the laminate countertop, inspecting my wound with gentle strength.

My focus fixes to his blue eye, and I go still.

Dax's fingers gently probe where the lash of pain is worst at the juncture of neck and shoulder. He makes a pained sound, and it's not anger pouring out of him, but sheer hopelessness. Desperation. He turns, and I hear the rip of a paper towel and water running before he's back, dabbing it with tender pressure against the wound. His eyes are pinned there, demarcated by a deep frown line. "Dax... it's okay. It missed me, mostly. You got Daisy out, and the others. We're okay." He doesn't reply, but removes one paper towel and replaces it with another. "What happened out there, anyway? Everything moved so fast..." I lift my hand to try to feel for myself what's going on with my neck, but Dax gently, without compromise, pushes it back down and continues patting at me.

"Those dumbasses sent in an undercover cop as one of the EMTs. He made a move, and everything went to hell. I think a lot of the hostages got out, but he raised his gun to try to shoot Leo. His shot was off, and he tagged you. And then Leo shot him." He presses down, and a flare of pain sends a hiss through my gritted teeth. "I'm sorry."

"It's not your fault."

"I should have done more. He could have fucking killed you. Is there a first aid kit somewhere around here?" Dax's motions are jerky with anger and frustration as he tosses the saturated paper towel to the floor. "It's not terrible, but it won't stop bleeding."

Swallowing down the surges of pain, I tip my chin up. "There might be something in the cabinet above the sink."

I watch him as he turns to look, the muscles in his back flexing smoothly as he reaches. For some reason, I start to shake. First in my legs, traveling up and grabbing hold of each intercostal in my ribcage.

"Here's something." From the corner of my eye, I see Dax pull a white tin from the shelf and return. "Whoa, you okay? Indie?"

"I-I think so. Help me up."

Almost died, but I didn't, so yay.

"Hold on." He holds up a roll of gauze, looking at me almost apologetically. "This is all I could find."

"That should work," I say through chattering teeth, lifting up on my elbows the best I can.

Still, he hesitates, chewing on the inside of his lip in a way that tells me he's feeling awkward about something. Dax averts his eyes, fumbling with the gauze. "It's going to have to run beneath your armpit and around your neck... kind of like an inverted vee, if that makes sense."

"Okay." I stare at him, blinking. Then it hits me. "Oh! You need me to take my shirt off."

Dax nods.

I look down and can't help it...

I start to giggle.

The shirt is covered in blood, first Jeremy's and now mine, the white material completely soaked through. It's disgusting. Horrifying. I can't believe I hadn't taken it off earlier, just to be rid of it.

And so, I giggle. There's no humor in the sound; it's more of a release of emotion I hadn't realized was all caught within me, battling to get out somehow. Dax squints, wondering, no doubt, if this is it. If I'm losing it.

Maybe I am. Maybe that would be the absolute best possible thing I could do right now. Just lose it. God knows keeping it together hasn't helped anything so far.

I raise both hands, cover my mouth with them, and laugh.

Hard. Helpless.

Loud.

And then the laughter changes to tears, the huge, gulping kind that come from the throat, the kind that are raw and scraping, and they fucking hurt, but they're going to hurt anyway, whether you hold them in or let them go, so I just let them out. Every one of them.

"Shit," I hear Dax mutter, and then he's scooping me up into a sitting position, until my legs dangle off the edge of the counter and he's standing between them. He holds me stiffly, my arms crushed against his chest with my palms still covering my mouth as I alternately laugh and wail and mutter curse words I never, ever say out loud, because Daisy's always around. But she's not here right now, and it feels good, so I cuss behind my hands.

And that feels good, too. I look for something to throw, but there is nothing, and I can't get my arms loose anyway, so I shift my hands down until they're clutching the skin just beneath Dax's neck, my nails flexing and digging into his muscle.

He flinches but takes it, which for some reason, makes me angrier. "Damnit! Fuck this—" My voice rises in pitch. "This is crazy! This is... absolutely crazy."

"Shit," Dax says again. He releases one arm to tip my head up to his, pulling our eyes together. "Indie, honey... you gotta keep it together."

"S-says who?"

"Says me."

I sniffle. "And why is that?"

"Because..." He hesitates, his brow furrowing as his gaze flits across my face, carefully choosing his words. "Because we both need to stay clear-headed if we want to make it out of here. And when we do, when we walk out those doors, I'm getting on a plane tomorrow morning, and I'm going to Maui."

My breath seizes. The words rising in my throat stutter to a stop.

"You and Daisy are coming with me."

Chapter Ten

Dax

AM I INSANE?

Maybe I'm insane. I'm clutching a bleeding stranger to my chest, inviting her and her daughter on a Hawaiian vacation with me come sunrise.

Sounds a bit certifiable, but I go with it.

I don't take it back, because the look in her eyes, the glimmer of blue hope staring back at me, is exactly what I'd hoped to see. This isn't about being smart or realistic.

This is about having something to hang on to when all hope feels lost.

Indie's body continues to shudder in my embrace, her fingernails carving half-moons into my skin. Her breath hitches, each word catching. "I… I don't even know you."

The adrenaline coursing through her begins to wane as I hold her gaze, my thumb caressing her chin ever so softly. It's a soothing gesture, maybe more intimate than it should be, but it seems to be working. She melts into me, her tremors mellowing into a faint tremble.

Forcing a smile, I pull back, dipping my head. "I don't think that's true."

A tapered breath steals her reply, and she fiddles with the white tin beside her on the counter. Knotted hair falls loose over each shoulder, a few golden pieces caked with blood, making her look like some kind of morbid angel. Indie's eyes cut back to me. "You protected my daughter. You saved her life," she whispers gently, her tongue poking out to moisten dry lips. "I guess… that's all I really need to know."

My forced smile blooms into something more genuine, something pure, and for an instant, I get lost in this strange connection. This link, forged in destruction.

Built with blood.

A loud clatter on the other side of the door startles us both, severing the moment, and I let out a quick breath, regrouping. Indie squeaks in pain when she inches forward on the counter, and I'm brought back to the harrowing circumstances in a flash.

She's wounded.

We're trapped.

I need to get us out of here.

I comb through the tin, looking for whatever tools I can find to patch her up. My eyes lift, noting how she bites her lip in an effort to block out the pain.

She needs a distraction, otherwise she'll break again.

I need her whole.

"So, Hawaii…" I mutter, untwisting the cap on the hydrogen peroxide bottle. "I've been there before. Just once."

Indie regards the bottle with wariness, digging her teeth into her bottom lip even harder. "Only once?"

"Yeah. Organized hockey isn't a thing in Hawaii, so I never traveled there for work," I explain. My fingers case the edging of her blouse, hesitation bringing my eyes to hers. "May I?"

She nods.

I keep talking as I tug the bloodstained blouse over her head, leaving her sitting before me, exposed both physically and emotionally. "I went to Maui with my parents when I was fourteen. It was the only vacation we ever went on together as a unit. All three of us."

"Really?" Her voice is a mere undertone as her skin pimples with goosebumps. Tangled hair lies in disarray over her collarbone, the ends dusting the swell of her breasts. "How was that the only family vacation you ever took?"

I scold my gaze for skating over the black lace of her bra and redirect my attention to the wound. "My father worked a lot. Too much. It was the only getaway he allowed himself to take, and those two weeks were some of the best days of my life." I swallow, dabbing the liquid onto cotton swabs. "He was different. Everything was different."

I'm speaking to her like she's an old friend, yet neither of us question it.

Indie hisses through a clenched jaw as I press the antiseptic to her wound and it fizzles in response. "How do you mean?"

"He was..." My mind fumbles for the right word, then I say, "Present."

"Present," she repeats softly.

I inspect the injury, relieved that it's only a flesh wound. Nodding, I gather the gauze and tape, then begin to bandage her up, wrapping it under her armpit and around her neck. My torso grazes her bare shoulder as I reach behind her, causing her to go still with a sharp intake of breath. "You okay?"

"I'm fine. Keep talking."

Somehow, she still smells like honeysuckles, despite the death that has seeped into her skin. I inhale her scent, letting it purge my own decay as I gather my thoughts, my fingers still working her dressing. "We spent a lot of time in the ocean. On the beach. We visited those little seaside fruits stands and ate fresh pineapple and coconut milk," I tell her. When I glance at her, she's watching me with curious interest. A softness. "I felt like he saw me as a real son in those couple of weeks, instead of... I don't know," I murmur. "A student. His protégé."

Indie's eyelashes fan over her cheekbones as she blinks back at me.

We speak at the same time: "A disappointment."

A despondent smile flickers on her lips, and I dip my gaze to the gesture, releasing a shaky breath. "You've been there, too, huh?"

"Sort of. My marriage."

"I'm sorry to hear that. Was he...?" My words trail off, the intent clear.

Jeremy.

"Yes," she confirms, glancing away. "We divorced eighteen months ago. He had a drinking problem, a communication problem, a responsible parent problem... which all ended up feeling like a me problem." Indie's eyes water, despite her effort to reel in her emotions. "It's not the same, but I understand feeling like a disappointment."

I nod my head as I finish securing the tape. "Well, it sounds like you deserve a vacation."

"Dax, I don't know—"

"I know. And maybe it's weird that I know, but I just do." Taking a step back, I observe my handiwork. The bandage should hold up until we find a way out of here. "I was going to Maui because it was the one place in the world I felt blissfully happy. At peace. And after a really shitty few months, I needed that. I needed healing," I tell her. "I think you do, too."

Indie considers my offer, her gaze flitting across my face, a thoughtful frown furrowing. "Will there be sailboats?"

A smile hints. "There can be sailboats."

Surrender lights up her face, but it's stolen away when another noise sounds from outside the break room, and we both recoil, our attention on the door. There's a clamor of commotion, and I try to visualize how many hostages were still left when we were ushered back here.

Did everyone make it out?

"Shit, we need to find a way out of here," I implore, soft yet firm. Indie inches forward on the countertop, an attempt to hop down, but her features twist with pain when she moves. My hands reach out to help, one arm snaking around her back while the other tucks underneath her uninjured armpit. "Here, honey..."

Honey.

I'm not sure where the term of endearment came from, as I've never been one for pet names.

Sabrina was always just... Sabrina.

But when her hair spun with nectar and honeysuckles tickles my nose, it's clear that the name fits.

Indie grips my shoulders, sliding down the counter to her feet. "Thank you," she whispers softly. "For everything."

Despite the havoc and bloodshed pulsing in the air, a calmness infiltrates me. Skin on skin, the pads of her fingertips linger on my shoulders until they glide down my chest. I clear my throat. "I'd give you the shirt off my back, but, well..."

"I think Brian is very grateful for it."

Our eyes catch with tenderness for a brief moment before the door flies open, and we jump away from one another.

Ronnie hovers in the doorway, a leer stretching through his mask. "Howdy. Leo wanted me to check on ya, make sure there's no tricks going on." He slides his eyes up and down Indie's half-naked figure. "I see a nice treat, though, I must say."

She quickly crosses her arms, trying to cover her chest. "Please let us go."

His abrupt laughter fills the room. "You two are the only cards we got left. Not gonna happen."

"Let her go," I try, taking a tentative step towards him. "I'm enough leverage."

"No can do, hockey man."

"She has a child."

Ronnie's eyebrows wiggle with suggestion. "I know. We got ourselves a real M.I.L.F."

"You're a pig," Indie spits out.

He grins wide, as if it were a compliment, then stalks closer to us, kicking the door closed with the heel of his boot.

Shit.

The room feels smaller and smaller as he gains on us, and I suffocate on the realization that we're utterly defenseless. We're stripped down and exposed. Vulnerable. My eyes scan the modest space, searching for some kind of makeshift weapon, some kind of protection.

Stepping in front of Indie and using myself as a barrier, I watch as he slows his steps just a foot away. "Leo's probably looking for you," I reason. "You don't want to piss him off."

"Fuck Leo."

"He looked a little frazzled out there. Unstable."

"That asshole's always had a few screws loose."

Indie pushes herself forward. "Must run in the family."

Another laugh rumbles over to us as Ronnie works his gaze over Indie's chest, running his tongue along his upper teeth. A groan of approval follows. "You got a smart mouth, Goldilocks. I'm lookin' forward to seeing what else it can do."

The threat is far from subtle, and a surge of dread pumps hot through my veins. Desperation crawls beneath my skin, causing my heart to skip with erratic beats.

"You're not going to lay a finger on me," Indie grits out, inching closer to Ronnie. She resists my attempts to pull her back, drawing her arm away from my grip. "I'd rather die than let you touch me."

"I could kill you first if you prefer. Makes no difference to me."

"You're sick."

"I'm a lot of things, sweetheart, but—"

We freeze when the door whips open for a second time, and Garrett appears, firearm waving between the three of us.

"What the fuck?" he demands. "Leo told you to check on them, not have a fuckin' tea party."

Ronnie huffs dismissively. "The bitch found her way out of her shirt; can't blame me for lookin'."

"You'll be looking down the barrel of Leo's gun if you fuck anything else up." Garrett's eyes shift towards me, a dark hazel, and he narrows them through his ski mask. "You and I are going to have a conversation later. Stay put."

My arm extends to shove Indie behind me. "A conversation?"

"So to speak."

"Listen, just let us—"

"I said, later." Garrett nods his head at Ronnie, clicking his tongue. "Let's go, asshole."

My gaze flickers between the two men, trying to get a read on them.

Garrett has hardly said a word this whole time—he's the quiet observer. Dangerous in his own right. He's built with more of a muted command than brawn.

Ronnie is the polar opposite. He's the powder keg. The wild card, all hard muscle and unpredictable aggression.

I'm wondering if I can take either of them right now, maybe catch them off guard, stab Ronnie with a fork the second he spins away. I saw an assortment of utensils in the sink. If I act fast, this could be our only chance. Maybe if I can blindside them, get the gun away from Garrett, and perhaps...

Indie tucks her hand into mine.

My racing thoughts quell, almost as if she could feel them. Predict my next move. When Garrett turns to leave, I spare her a quick glance beside me, and she finds my eyes.

Don't do it.

I need to get us out of here.

You will.

Swallowing, I turn back to Ronnie as he gives Indie a blatant last onceover, licking his lips. "Later," he drawls. He echoes Garrett, his intention clear. Before he stomps off, following his brother, he reaches for a broom perched against the back wall and curls his meaty fingers around the stick. "Don't want you two gettin' too creative in here."

With a quick jerk of his wrist, he thrusts the end of the broom upward, smashing it into the overhead light. The room blackens instantly. Indie squeaks in surprise, tightening her grip on my palm, and we both go still as the darkness swallows us up.

"Lights out," Ronnie quips.

My senses go into overdrive, my chest humming with anticipation. His heavy boots clap against the linoleum in slow, deliberate steps.

Clunk. Clunk.

I hold Indie behind me, thinking he might pounce. Attack.

Ignite.

Clunk. Clunk.

His footfalls mingle with eerie laughter, until both sounds are cut off by the door slamming shut. I wait for my eyes to adjust before letting out the breath of air trapped inside my lungs.

A whispered breath meets my shoulder. "I think he's gone."

Silence envelops the small room, only punctured by the echo of muddled voices from the lobby. Our breaths are charged with nerves, our futures dauntingly unclear.

"Shit... come on." I tug her forward, guiding her to the shadowy silhouette of the door frame. My leg kicks over a stack of boxes as we stumble to the opposite side of the break room through a wall of darkness. Trying the doorknob on a desperate whim, my chest deflates when its resistance jiggles back at me. "Fuck."

Indie's sigh of defeat only heightens my frustration. "There's got to be another way."

I work the knob, pulling and tugging.

"Maybe we can wedge something between the frame and force it open."

My efforts increase, and I yank harder, a growl rattling my lungs.

"Maybe there are tools in here. Something we can use to put a hole in the door."

Pull. Tug. Growl.

"They might hear us, though..."

I start pounding, maniacal and crazed.

"Dax."

Pound. Thump. Crack.

My fists pummel the wood, slivers biting at my skin. A line of sweat cases my brow, my heart threatening to detonate. "Fucking hell!"

"Dax, stop. You're going to hurt yourself."

Indie grabs my arm before it makes contact with the door again, trying to reel me in, trying to be that comforting presence I was so determined to be for her.

I'm losing it. I'm unraveling.

I let out a hard breath, my forehead falling forward against the oak door, and I pivot towards her, attempting to find her eyes through the shadows.

Cloudless skies, tranquil waters, blue-green hope.

I try to locate a twinkle of reassurance, something worthy I can cling to.

Indie inches closer to me, those teal-toned eyes brimming a hint of color through the black veil between us. She slides her palm up and down my bare arm, squeezing gently at the bicep. "When Daisy gets scared, I tell her that the one thing more powerful than her fear is her strength."

Swallowing, my eyes skate over the shaded lines of her face, her features soft despite the harsh reality of our predicament. I sigh, pulling my lips between my teeth. "I've always been the strong one. The leader. I don't give up until I cross over that finish line."

"This isn't a game, though, Dax. The finish line is unclear," Indie says in a whispered breath. "There's only this minute and the next, and hopefully the one after that, and how we get through them. Do we self-destruct and let ourselves drown? Or do we... sail?" She drags the pads of her fingers back down my arm, feather-light, and the barest smile tips her lips. "We gotta keep it together, remember?"

I let her words settle deep, right into my fear-laced bones. I told her to keep it together only moments ago, and here I am, breaking apart like fragile glass. Lifting up from the door, I nod my head, my chest humming with renewed strength. "Yeah..." I murmur, running my tongue along the roof of my mouth. "We've got that trip in the morning."

"Yes, we do." Indie holds my stare for a few weighty beats, then clears her throat. "You know, Tameka was always purchasing those candle warmers from one of our co-workers. Maybe I can find us a little light."

She steps away from the door, carefully guiding herself through the darkened space, and my own smile blooms to life.

I already found a little light.

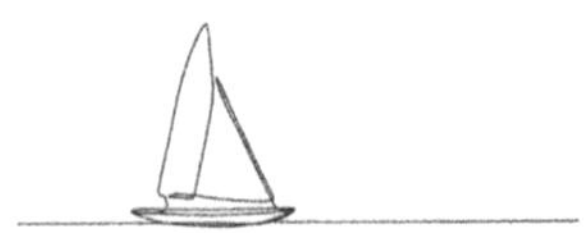

I'm not sure how much time passes by, but it can't be more than thirty minutes or so—even though it feels like a lifetime.

Indie and I sit side-by-side, our backs pressed up to the oak door, our legs sprawled out in front of us. A Halloween-themed candle warmer is placed between our thighs, the little bulb illuminating the ceramic, and a wax melt offering us a pleasant aroma. Something like butter pecan. The black cat warmer stares back at us as we try not to give in to the mind-numbing anxiety and "what-ifs" waiting for us on the other side of this door.

What do they plan to do with us?

How do we escape?

When will this nightmare be over?

None of those questions are productive or nerve-reducing, so I voice a completely different one. "What's on your bucket list?"

Indie glances at me, her curves bathed in a dim, yellow-orange light. Her hair is still in disarray, her skirt stained in blood, her skin bruised and dirty. Contemplative eyes flick over my face as she sucks in a quick breath. "I always wanted to learn how to crochet," she responds softly. She worries her lip, more thoughts trickling to the surface. "Go sailing, of course. Take a road trip around the country with Daisy. Make an entire Italian meal from scratch, including the pasta."

"Mmm. Now I'm hungry."

A smile stretches on her parted lips, teeth flashing white. "What about you?"

Our shoulders brush together as I rest my head back, all my hopes and dreams flashing through my mind like a movie reel. "Have two or three kids. Spend an entire summer up in the cabin my grandfather left me when he died. Make amends with my father. Shake Paul McCartney's hand."

"Really?" she says with an eager gasp. "I love him. The Beatles are my all-time favorite band."

"Mine, too."

Her eyes flicker by way of tangerine glow. "Looks like we have more in common than this... nightmare."

"Yeah," I swallow, nodding softly. "Looks like it."

I can't help but wonder what else we share in common. Foods, favorite places, sports, hobbies. I wonder if we'd be compatible, linked, beyond this shared tragedy.

We hold our stare, my eyes dipping to her still smiling mouth, my heartbeats thumping in time with her curious breaths.

"Hey, Barbie Girl! I need you and the hockey fuck!"

Leo's voice is like a viper sinking its fangs into our flesh. We fly to our feet, backing away from the door, from the venom seeping inside, and Indie almost trips over the candle warmer cord.

She whimpers. "Oh, God... no, no, no."

"It's okay. It's okay." I reach for her hand in the dimly lit room as we keep inching backwards. Leo's bulky boots sound closer with every breath. "It's going to be okay."

The doorknob rattles.

Indie tips her head up, meeting my fretful gaze. "Hawaii, right?"

"Hawaii," I echo.

Gunshots ring out on the opposite side of the door, causing my heart to gallop.

What the hell?

Leo retreats in haste, shouting, "Fuck!"

A barrage of gunfire continues to rain down from the lobby area, and our palms squeeze together as questions assault us, more nerves gather, and the cold touch of death hangs heavy in the air, filling our lungs with ice.

"We're going to die, aren't we?" Indie's voice cracks, her emotion palpable. "God... Daisy."

"Indie, listen to me..." I spin her around to face me, releasing her hand and cupping her jaw. My thumb dusts over her tearstained cheekbone, our gazes clinching with a kind of heady connection I assume can only be assembled in those life-or-death moments. "Strength is mightier than fear, okay? Your words."

She nods, her chin trembling.

"It's not over yet."

Another nod, and then, "What... what would you do right now, if this was your last moment on Earth?"

The weighty question steals my breath as our eyes hold.

Bullets blast.

Orders fire.

Shouting, cursing, yelling.

I block it out.

I block it all out, everything, and I move in on instinct, raising my opposite hand until both palms are cradling her face.

I kiss her.

Indie's mewl of surprise is snuffed out by my mouth, hungry and urgent, spurred entirely by desperation. This isn't love or affection. This isn't passion—or desire, even. She's beautiful, yes, soft and compelling, but this isn't that.

This is solace.

My fingers weave through her hair, tugging gently as she melts into the kiss, accepting it for exactly what it is and giving it right back. My tongue tears through her teeth, tasting her, drinking in her terror and worries and funneling them into something sweeter.

A reprieve.

Indie's hands grip my bare shoulders, then slide upward until her fingers are buried in my hair. A moan breaks free—hers, I think—and for a moment, I wonder what this would be in a different moment. A different life.

Because… fuck, she tastes so good. Ambrosia and warm honey. Her soft curves meld into my chest, her fingernails digging into my scalp as she leans up on her tiptoes to devour me. Our tongues dance to the rhythm of our petrified hearts, and I let a groan slip as I pull back to drag my lips across her cheek, down her jaw, until my face is nuzzled into the arch of her neck.

"Dax…" she rasps, out of breath, still clutching me close.

"I'm sorry."

She shakes her head, her long hair tickling my temple. "No, I—"

Her words are cut short when the door swings open, revealing Leo and Garrett, stained in blood spatter, weapons held high, faces twisted with fiery rage.

They both stalk towards us with menace and murder gleaming through their black masks, and Leo snarls, "Showtime."

Chapter Eleven

Indie

I SCREAM.

I can't help it. The sound escapes, pitched high and filled with terror, when Leo and Garrett burst through the door.

I know who it is, even with the masks shielding the defining features of their faces. We've been too close for too long. There's the length and structure of Leo's fingers, bony and claw-like as they reach for me and pull me away from Dax, toward the door. There's the breadth of Garrett's shoulders as he shoves Dax back, out of the way, when he instinctively reaches to hold me in place.

"No MVPs today, hockey boy," he says, pressing his gun into Dax's collarbone. "You're coming with me… and if you behave, Barbie and you will both be A-OK."

The arm around my neck is a vise, Leo's scent acid and fetid in my nostrils. "Dax—"

The arm tightens, clamping my vocal chords into helpless silence. "Shut up. You're coming with me."

He drags me toward the door. Beneath the arm around my neck, my hands reach. Why, I don't know. It's a gesture filled with futility; it's a boat against the current.

Dax fights to get to me, reaching for me, trying to grab for my closest hand. "Indie. Look at me, honey." I meet his eyes, Leo and Garrett fading into insignificance. It's only Dax in this moment. Dax and me and the tenuous thread stretching between us. "You're okay. We're okay. This is just a blip, and tomorrow there's Hawaii." His hand squeezes my fingers in a hard grip, even as Leo pulls me inexorably backwards. His eyes implore.

"Tomorrow." The word breaks loose, a sob full of heartbreak and conviction all at once. "Tomorrow there's Hawaii."

That's all we have before Leo rips me free of his grasp and out the door. He turns out the doorway and to the right, bearing me down the hall toward the rear of the building where the corporate offices are, Garrett following closely behind with Dax. To the left, behind us, the sounds of shouting and intermittent gunfire breach the door that separates the corridor from the lobby.

We're at the end of the hall when Ronnie bursts through the lobby door, arms a wild windmill as he runs right at us, and everything goes to hell at once. It happens in the blink of time it takes for the puff of gun smoke to rise in counterpoint to a deafening litany of rounds being fired. Ronnie's body jerks once, twice, three times before falling forward.

"Motherfuck!" Leo takes a quick step forward, half-tripping on my legs, and I choke at the added pressure on my windpipe.

Behind me, Dax makes an odd grunting noise, and Garrett utters a panicked "fuck."

A smoke bomb detonates.

Coughing and sputtering, I twist, frantic to see what's happening behind me, to find Dax's gaze once again. I know I'll see conviction on his face and majestic Maui waves rippling in his eyes. I need the brown one—I need that warm, brown eye, gleaming with hope. "Dax?" I can't see him. I can't find him. There's too much smoke. "Dax!"

He doesn't answer, and I bite my lip hard to keep from screaming.

"Put your weapons down and step forward with your hands raised. You are completely surrounded." The voice intones instructions with professional intensity, the speaker nameless, faceless behind a blank tactical mask.

"Dax!" I cry out, kicking my legs, trying to break free of Leo's death grip. "Dax, talk to me!"

My body shudders with panic, my lungs suffocating on smoke and sheer terror.

Where is he? Where's Dax?

"Quit your goddamn squirmin'," Leo hisses at me, then addresses the police with steadfast fury. "You stay back!" He creeps forward, the gun pressed against my temple, one eye on the men in S.W.A.T. gear flanking the doorway. He glances down at the crumpled body of Ronnie, and even his mask can't hide the anguish swimming in his eyes. Despite my horror, a strange sense of empathy tugs at me.

That's his brother down there.

And then, a sickening thought slices me, while time moves in slow motion.

Is Dax lying in the floor like that, blood pooling beneath him? All that vitality snuffed out, fading to gray in a Technicolor river?

I have to look… I have to see…

As Leo utters a sobbing curse beneath his breath and raises his gun, the one he had against my temple, I twist sharply and let my body go deadweight in Leo's hold.

He releases me, probably due to the smear of movement, trailing shadows of black I catch in my periphery, but I don't focus on them. Part of me knows it's the S.W.A.T. team swarming the narrow corridor. Instead, I fall to my knees and search the hall behind me, just in time to see Garrett disappearing around the corner…

Dragging Dax's bloodied body with him.

No, no, no.

I scream.

I still can't help it.

My hands rise to cover my mouth to hold it in, to cover my eyes to block out the awful sight, but it's memory, anyway. It's not going anywhere.

He was so still.

There's another wave of gunfire, the sound doing something violent and painful to my eardrums this time. Leo jerks beside me, falling to one knee, and as my gaze wrenches itself from one fragment of the terrible tableau to another, he lifts his gun, muddy eyes locked on me.

This is it.

I look to where I last saw Dax, tears falling freely.

Tomorrow, he told me. Tomorrow, there's Hawaii.

I close my eyes, position myself on that plane, and brace myself for takeoff.

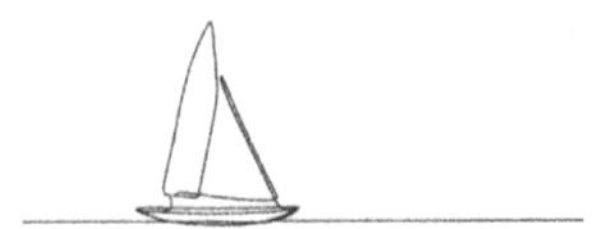

Hawaii is everything I imagined. Pale bronze beaches of volcanic sand, skies so vivid looking at them hurts, and the Pacific a cool, deep aquamarine. Somewhere distant, island music plays from a resort loudspeaker, a relaxed beat that simultaneously invites languor and limbo dancing.

I sit back in one of the hotel chairs, a morning mimosa in one hand, umbrella overhead, and watch Dax playing in the shallows with my daughter. He pretends to chase her while she squeals and leaps away, ribbons of water streaming from wet braids. Her high-pitched giggles and Dax's lower growls reach my ears, and a contented smile curls my lips.

I can't believe we're here. Paradise.

Dax looks up at me and smiles, and the sensuous edge to it makes my stomach clench and my toes curl on the lounge. We haven't taken things any farther than that out-of-nowhere kiss at the bank, but the promise is there. It's in the brush of his hand against my lower back when he walks me to breakfast, in the heated look he gives me over Daisy's head in the elevator.

It's here, all around me in this postcard-perfect scene straight from all of my favorite holiday movies, visible across ten yards of beach and the blinding sunshine reflecting off the water.

If the edges are a little blurry, the music a little tinny… well, that's just because I'm seriously exhausted.

Daisy tugs on my pantlegs, and I squint towards her.

Why can't I see her clearly?

Something shatters. A glass, a plate… I don't know. All I know is that I'm not on a lounge chair on a Hawaiian beach, but in my kitchen—my fucking kitchen—and Daisy is looking at the little counter television in horror.

Shit.

Pull yourself together, Indie.

"What is it, baby?" I start to walk toward Daisy, and the crunch of glass stops me. Looking down, I see the remains of my morning coffee splattered across the hardwood, mixed with the ceramic fragments of my "Some People Just Need a Hug" mug.

God, what happened? It's like I went blank for a minute.

When Daisy gives another insistent tug on my pants and points at the television, I step carefully around the glass and pick her up, then stand and watch the screen for whatever has her so agitated. It's clear in an instant.

"It was a horrific scene of murder and mayhem at Edgewater Bank on Fifteenth and Henley Streets yesterday morning. I was honored to be asked on scene to provide a much-needed look into the carnage left behind from the infamous Madden crew."

I knew that voice before I even looked at the screen: the news reporter from Channel 15, the one who'd been on scene as I was leaving the hospital. She was a smartly dressed brunette with a giant top-knot and bubblegum voice, and she'd basically accosted me as my mother reunited me with Daisy on the cobblestone sidewalk.

My blood boils. She was honored to be on the scene.

A microphone had been shoved in my face as my little girl ran into my arms. The woman had trespassed on my private moment—my small pocket of sweetness amidst the confusion, turmoil, and bloodshed. My arm was still tender and bandaged, the bullet wound painful. My eyes were still swollen from tears, and my heart was irrevocably shattered.

And there she was in her crisp, ironed shirt, perfectly coifed hair, and radiant smile, asking me personal details about the attack.

About the madmen, the survivors.

The victims.

Jeremy's face flashes to mind, and my stomach knots.

"The Madden gang's attack on Edgewater Trust and Reserve was regrettably not without its share of casualties, among them two of the assailants themselves, Trevor and Ronald Madden. Victims include Jeremy Wheeler, the thirty-two year-old devoted father of a four-year-old child. I was able to share a few words with Indigo Chase, one of our courageous survivors and Jeremy's ex-wife..."

Nausea sweeps through me when my image flashes to the screen, Daisy's face blurred out. I look like a wreck with my bloodshot eyes and chalky skin. My face is bruised, my hair limp and tangled. I'm clutching Daisy to my chest, shaking my head through the tears, trying to get away from the camera and lights.

"You survived a true nightmare, Ms. Chase. Seattle is calling you a hero. How do you feel about that?"

I watch the news report with limbs shaking, heart sinking.

"I'm not a hero. Dax was the real hero. No more questions, please."

The scene cuts away from me and back to the reporter, her bright smile fading into something more solemn.

I squeeze Daisy to my chest.

I haven't been able to stop checking the locks on every door and window since arriving home this morning from the hospital. I'm exhausted, but I can't sleep. I've called every hospital in a fifty-mile radius to check on Dax, but there has been no sign of him.

Unwillingly, I remember Garrett dragging him away, the low gurgling, grunting sound he'd made, the gush of blood pooling from his chest.

He was so still.

A pained sound escapes me as my Hawaiian daydream ripples through me like a wave.

Upstairs on my bed, there's a suitcase laying open, neatly packed with exactly seven pairs of underwear. Nothing else. I figure the underwear's the most important thing, as well as the thing I'm most likely to forget in a rush.

The suitcase is more symbolic than anything—my nod to hope. I don't really care if I go to Hawaii or not. I just can't stop thinking about the last glimpse I had of Dax. I want him to be okay. He did so much to help us, taking care of Daisy, getting her out safely, holding me together when I nearly broke.

Please, God...

He has to be okay.

On the television screen, images of the tragedy inside the bank play out, several bodies covered with white sheets or black body bags. The footage outside the bank shows the predictable police response to an event of this nature, cars skew-parked everywhere, several official looking vans, people in tense positions at various locations, ogling bystanders.

"... which brings us to a true hero who emerged during this tragedy: hockey star, Dax Reed, a young retiree who was well on his way to legend status. Unfortunately, he may be there sooner than expected, as his whereabouts are currently unaccounted for."

I set Daisy down in the doorway. "Go play, baby. You don't need to watch this."

Without protest, Daisy disappears into the living room, from where vague strains of Care Bears emanated, and I retrace my steps to the kitchen. Leaning on the counter, I glue myself to the small television, thirsty for details I wasn't privy to yesterday.

I must have blacked out, because when I came to, I found myself in a sterile white hospital room, hooked up to beeping machines and a plethora of cords. I couldn't find anything physically wrong with me, so I had pulled myself loose and stumbled wearily from the bed. Questions I didn't have answers for raced.

Where is Daisy?

Where is Dax?

How long have I been out?

The only thing I knew for certain was that I'd never made it onto that airplane.

Impatience surging, I had tapped the call button several times and waited for the nurse to appear.

"I need to go home," I told the fifty-ish year-old woman who appeared moments later. "I don't know why I'm here. Do you know where my daughter is? I need to go home."

"Shh... it's fine. You're okay, everyone's safe. Daisy—that's your little girl, right?" I nodded, allowing her to push me gently back into the bed. "She's with your momma at your house. Likely sound asleep right now, poor thing."

"She's... everyone's okay?"

"Yes, now you just lay on back and get your rest. You'll be discharged in the morning."

And I was. I was sent home this morning with no greater understanding of what had happened than I had to begin with. The afternoon has played out in a blur of disorienting flashbacks and dreams, more phone calls than I can count, and a giant ache in the center of my heart that won't subside.

Dax.

As if in concert with my thoughts, the reporter tucks a piece of hair behind her ear and looks gravely into the lens.

"If you, or anyone you know, has information into the disappearance of Dax Reed, please contact the Seattle Police Department. It's been a sad day for the city of Belltown as new details emerge..."

Her voice fades under the roar in my ears, covered over with the sprightly tones of cartoons from the next room.

My hands are shaking, and a glance tells me they're clutching the remote.

He's missing.

Dax is missing after being shot in the chest and dragged away by a monster.

There's no way he's still alive—oh, God, there's no way he...

He was so still.

I choke.

Knuckles white, I press channel down until I find another station, another reporter, her hand to her ear in a listening posture.

"Three dead in the Edgewater Trust and Reserve, and another unaccounted for: renowned hockey player, Dax Reed, who was apparently shot during the attack and presumed—"

Another channel, another reporter.

No.

An animal sound escapes me, and before I quite know what I'm doing, I've raised my arm and swept the television to the floor. It sparks once before going black, and the resounding silence hums in the aftermath.

In the heave of my breath that follows, I look up and see Daisy standing in the doorway, her little face sober. She turns and runs, and although self-pity tries to nail me to the floor, I follow.

My poor baby.

"Daisy... I'm so sorry," I murmur, an apologetic whisper. My eyes dance to her little frame bobbing up and down. Frowning, I shake my head. "What are you... ?"

Standing in front of the larger television in the living room, she places both hands as high as she can get them on the screen. She grunts and looks back at me as I stand, bewildered, in the entryway, and I realize...

She's trying to push the T.V. over.

"Oh, baby."

Empathy pours through me, then rage.

Rage at those bastards for picking my bank. Rage at Jeremy for not just taking our daughter to school, for being a total numb nuts. Rage at every media outlet out there for the calculating opportunity that hides behind every fake expression of grief and sympathy.

I stand beside Daisy, place my hands above hers, and count to three. "Push."

The television topples to the floor in a tangle of soulless wires, and Daisy and I look at each other. She doesn't speak.

She hasn't said a word since we arrived home this morning.

Tears rush to my eyes, but I mask them with a smile. "Want to do the one in Mommy's bedroom?"

Daisy nods eagerly.

"Alrighty, then. Let's go kill some T.V.'s."

Chapter Twelve

Dax

A MATTRESS SQUEAKS.

It's a muted sound, muffled and far away. Insignificant.

Yet it wakes me from the dead.

Squeak, squeak.

Tired muscles ache and burn, coming back to life, one strained breath at a time.

Holy shit... I'm breathing.

It hurts like a bitch to swallow down each mouthful of air, but I do. I do it once, twice, three times, each gulp greedier than the last. My chest screams in agony, the pain registering before the memories sweep through me. It's all a blur. A blur of chaos and anarchy and... her.

"Indigo."

Her name escapes in a parched whisper, my tongue like taffy. I'm shocked that I was even able to intake enough oxygen to expel those three syllables. My lungs rattle with rust as I blink rapidly, my eyes rejecting the tendrils of light pooling in from a partially cloaked window.

I must be in a hospital.

... Right?

A foul odor wafts across my nostrils when I try to shift my weight on the mattress. Mold. Decay. Searing pain follows, and I groan, my head falling back against a wooden headboard.

No... I'm not in a hospital.

I'm someplace else.

Forcing my eyelids open, muddy images take shape through the dimly lit room. It's a bedroom of some kind. Old and dilapidated. Dust clings to every surface, clogging my lungs with more filth.

When I attempt to move again, I realize that I'm bound. It's more than my weak, sick body tethering me to this squeaky cot—I've been restrained. Tape coils around my wrists, fastening me to the bedpost behind my back and causing my skin to pinch when I wriggle my hands. The gesture is enough to send another dose of fiery pain through my body, more groans crawling up my throat.

"Fuck... s-someone help me..."

My skin feels hot. Too hot. Infection poisons my blood, merging with fear, inciting chills to claim me from top to bottom.

Indie. Where is she?

I blink again, trying to recall what happened that would explain why I'm anchored to this rotting wood and box spring, trapped inside Lizzie Borden's bedroom, feeling like I've been killed and brought back from the dead at least twice.

"Dax!"

My mind replays her scream. I can almost make out the precise pitch—the way her voice cracks and shatters before darkness steals me away. I hear her scream more than I feel that bullet slicing through my chest, rendering me unconscious. Lost.

Hell, I'm still lost.

Is she?

I need to get out of here. I need to find Indie.

"H-Help..." With a stuttering voice, I beg the shadows for mercy, twisting my wrists against the sticky duct tape. The effort is futile, serving to only confiscate the little energy I have left. "Please."

I'm not sure if it's the infection, but I swear the shadows begin to take form, a black cloud closing in on me from the other side of the room.

A human-shaped cloud.

"Who's there?" I rasp out.

"You didn't strike me as a beggar, hockey boy."

Memories assault me. Flashes of light, a cacophony of noise.

"Motherfuck!"

"Dax? Dax!"

I can almost taste the gunpowder on my tongue.

There's smoke. The pungent smell of sulfur swallows me whole, acrid and thick. A smoke bomb. Ronnie drops in front of my eyes, just before my chest combusts with a single stray bullet.

And Indie...

She's searching for me. Trying to find me through the smoke.

Pleading and terrified.

I can't reach her.

"Took you long enough. Thought you croaked on me."

The voice is familiar. Garrett.

I squint my eyes through the bleary haze, a face slowly coming into view when he's caught by the shaft of light poking through the nearby window. Reddish-brown eyes scowl down at me, his jawline sheathed in rough bristles, the color matching his ruddy irises. He scratches at the stubble, then runs his fingers through a mop of shoulder-length hair. It's the first time I've seen him without the ski mask.

Swallowing, I continue to plead with him. "Please, I… I need to find Indigo. I…"

"Your Barbie doll is doing just fine. She's all tucked away inside her little Barbie dream house."

My heart lurches with relief. "She's… okay?"

"That's what I said."

A sigh leaves me feeling infinitely lighter.

Indie is alive. She made it out, just like I promised she would.

I glance back at Garrett hovering over my beside, dressed in a flannel and tattered jeans. His face is expressionless, the glint in his eyes full of purpose, not warmth.

He wants something from me.

My tongue pokes out to lick my lips, and I wince when another shot of pain radiates through my chest and down my torso. "I need… a hospital. I won't make it much longer."

That much is true. I feel death invading my bones, seeping inside the marrow, eager to drink up the last of my essence until there's nothing left.

Death wants something from me, too.

So, the question is… who wants me more?

Garrett puckers his lips, eyes narrowing as he takes another step forward. He remains silent.

"Listen, I'm dying here. I need—"

"You need to give me what I want. What I brought your dead-weight ass here for," he snipes. "Leo was an idiot, thinking his dumb plan was going to work. He's nothin' without Ace. None of us are, but I'm the only one man enough to admit it."

My subsequent plea is stifled by his palm slamming against my mouth as he shoves three pills inside. Sputtering, I try to spit them out, not trusting anything he gives me, but Garrett thrusts his finger inside, pushing them behind my tongue, nearly gagging me.

"Don't be stupid," he chides. "If I was tryin' to kill you, it would've been the easiest goddamn thing in the world to do. You were basically a corpse when I dragged you here."

I choke down the pills dry, feeling them slither down my esophagus with sluggish descent.

"Antibiotics." Garrett pulls his hand from my face, his stance straightening. "Should keep you bright-eyed and bushy-tailed for the time being."

An indignant glare meets with cool apathy. This asshole has me tied to a bedpost in an absolute dump of a bedroom, completely immobile, wrought with infection. I dip my chin, trying to assess the damage across my chest. White gauze and medical tape adorn the bullet wound, settled just beneath my right shoulder. Heat permeates the surrounding area as dried blood pokes through the edging of the bandage.

Heaving in a splintered sigh, I grit out, "Where... where am I? What do you want?"

Garrett's hands slide into two denim pockets as he steps away from the rickety twin bed. The light dances away from his face, leaving me staring at a looming shadow. "Welcome to Hotel Madden. You can check out any time you'd like, but—"

"Got it," I mutter, cutting him off. "How many bodies are buried under the floorboards? It smells like House of a 1000 Corpses in here."

"Nah, I ain't that creative. Ronnie, maybe... God rest his stupid, pathetic soul." Inhaling a bitter breath, he continues, tapping his fingers along his thigh. "It's an old house. Been in the family for years."

My eyes case the slew of cobwebs and debris before I realize I don't really care. I just want out. "And the reason you brought me to this shithole... ?" I wonder.

"Plan B, of course."

Thinning my lips, I frown. "Plan B?"

"Yeah, my back-up plan for when Leo's steaming pile of donkey shit idea inevitably went down the toilet." His head tilts through the dim wall between us. "You, hockey boy. You hold the cards. One card, to be exact."

"I don't..." My words trail off as my brain tries to register his implication through the fog of pain and drugs. Then realization stabs at me. "The baseball card."

His index finger raises with confirmation. "Ding, ding."

I shake my head, a grumble of apprehension slipping from my lips. "Nice play."

"I'm observant," he shrugs, the wood floor creaking as he begins to pace next to me. "I've always been the quiet one, staging my next move. Drove Leo nuts. He thrives on intimidation and force. Trevor's the pussy of the group, and Ronnie… well, that bastard had no self-restraint," he says. "Ace got me, though. He understood my value. Always knew I'd come in handy, you know?"

"Great. That's a sweet story. How about you take me to a hospital, and I don't turn you in?"

Garrett pauses his steps, peering at me over his shoulder. "I ain't dumb," he tells me, his voice bleeding with conviction. "Don't you think for a goddamn fuckin' minute that you can twist me up or give me second thoughts. I know exactly what I want, and you don't leave this bedroom until I get it."

"Fine," I grit out. "The key is in my wallet. Have at it."

"Not that easy… we both know that. You ain't dumb, either."

My body shivers with infection and hopelessness. I know that Garrett's shoddy patch job and outdated antibiotics aren't going to keep me alive for long. I'm going to die in his godforsaken room, fettered with duct tape, as the stench of death follows me into the dark void.

Fucking hell.

I tug at my bindings, grimacing when my chest throbs with hindrance. The fear only fuels my adrenaline, my desperation, and the physical strain it leaves behind causes my brain to cloud. I feel myself teetering, my head lolling side to side as a wave of dizziness claims me. "Fuck you…" I say, slurred and spent. "You'll never… never get away…"

Garrett leans over me, a frown pinching between his brows. "Don't underestimate me, hockey star."

His voice is merely a gurgled blur of sound as I fade out.

And then the cold, dark room is replaced with Hawaiian sunbeams beating along my skin as I stare out at a peachy horizon and lulling ocean waves. I feel her presence beside me like warm honey—a sweet comfort I never knew I needed.

I made it. I'm here.

There's sand between my toes and a beachy breeze melting the frost in my lungs.

Indie tucks her palm inside mine, her smile brighter than the first blush of dawn, then rests her cheek against my shoulder. "And 'so we beat on, boats against the current,'" she whispers gently, her words swept up by a warming wind.

I smile back.

I made it. I'm here.

And I can't help but wonder, as the dream drags me down, the mirage sinking its claws into my clammy skin...

I wonder if she's here, too.

Splash.

I'm doused with ice cold water, jarring me from another reverie.

"Wakey wakey, eggs and bakey."

My head rolls up from an awkward sideways position, and the cords in my neck pulse with discomfort. I lick the water from my lips, suddenly all too aware of how dehydrated I am.

"Kiddin'. It's actually three-year-old Spaghetti-O's. Don't think they really go bad, am I right?"

When my eyes adjust, I see Garrett perched on the filthy bedspread beside my taped ankles. There's a hint of an amused smile on his face that makes my fingers clench into fists behind my back. The movement sends throbbing shockwaves up my arms, straight to the hole in my chest. I hold my breath through the pain, then muster a response. "You're going to spoon-feed me?"

My voice is strikingly unfamiliar. Corroded and worn. I don't recognize the tone or inflection.

After three days locked inside his hellhole, I don't recognize anything anymore.

"Yeah, why not?" Garrett replies. "I've always been the nurturing type. A real gentlemen."

I stare at him through listless eyes, observing the way his straight face crumbles into laughter.

"Fuck, man. I'm a total asshole, actually, but I can't have you givin' up the ghost before I collect my payoff." He snatches my jaw with dirt-smudged fingers, forcing my mouth open. "Lunch time."

A metal spoon clanks against my teeth. Despite the way my stomach screams with need, I take in the mouthful of canned noodles and spit them back in his face.

Garrett stills. Tiny O's drip from his nose, spattering the expanse of my chest.

All I've eaten over the last seventy-two hours has been a few stale crackers. Garrett would shove a saltine in my mouth every now and then, followed by gulps of water from a glass cup that tasted like dish soap.

I'm hungry. I'm really fucking hungry, but my anger is hungrier.

I wait with bated breaths for him to retaliate. I wait for the inevitable smack or punch, maybe even a kick to my stomach. A jab to my poorly patched bullet wound.

Instead, he leans back, swiping a palm down his face with a long sigh. "Guess I deserved that."

A frown unfurls between my eyes as I swallow down the desert in my throat. "You deserve a lot worse than that."

"Fair enough."

We both go quiet, eyes locked amidst the partially lit bedroom. A ratty checkered blanket is secured to a curtain rod with bag clips, blocking out the natural light, save for a tiny crack. The luster illuminates Garrett's stoic expression, his face smeared with red-orange sauce.

He tries again.

This time I accept the spoonful, the emptiness in my gut replacing my defiance. My mouth waters when the metallic pasta touches my tongue, and I inhale it without chewing.

Then I scowl at him for good measure.

Garrett scoops out another sloppy bite from the bowl, his lips pursing together. "Do you think we all get what's comin' to us, hockey boy?"

I bristle at his attempt at cordial conversation, grinding my teeth together.

"Karma and all that shit," he continues.

My silence doesn't derail him.

"Fuck, man, Trevor always said we'd end up this way. Dead or in jail. Bad people who do bad shit get bad endings."

"Fitting," I murmur through another bite.

The spoon hits the bowl, sprinkling sauce all over the discolored bedsheets. Garrett shakes his head, pinching the bridge of his nose between his finger and thumb. "Ace is in jail. Leo's in jail," he says. "Ronnie and Trevor are in the ground."

"You'll join them soon enough."

"Yeah? You think so?"

He sets the bowl aside, my eyes trailing the sustenance I'm still craving. I watch as Garrett replaces the food with a half-full bottle of water and twirls it between his fingers, eyeing me.

"You strike me as one of those fuckin' do-gooders. A hero type. Always trying to do the right thing," he drawls, his gaze assessing me with a semblance of distaste. "But look at where that got you. Taped up in my gramps' old farmhouse, about to hop the twig. I thought heroes always got a happy ending."

My jaw tics, words slippery and hard to catch. I can't counter that claim. I can't poke holes in his theory because he's right... I'm fucking helpless, near death, and I know I don't deserve to go out this way. Just like Garrett doesn't deserve to be sitting before me, healthy and well-fed, his smirk weighing heavily on my last thread of hope.

His hazel eyes slant in my direction as he finishes with a wink, "Such a shame... you didn't even get the girl."

My breaths stall.

I should be thinking about Sabrina and our three epic years together. Her long, raven tresses, chocolate eyes, and bronzed skin. The pitch of her laughter, or the sweep of her nose.

Only... Indie's porcelain face flashes to my mind instead, drenching me in a quick shot of warmth.

Honey hair and sea breeze eyes.

The curve of her mouth. The way her tongue was sweet and pliant, giving me everything I desired in that moment.

Solace. Release.

The warmth flickers into a hot blaze, heating my blood, pulling something like a growl from my throat. But before I can fire back at him, Garrett shoves at my forehead with the heel of his hand, tipping my head back and bringing the spout of the water bottle to my lips.

"Drink up, hero."

Water trickles from the corners of my mouth, trailing down my neck and chest. I take giant sips, coughing and sputtering on the final swallow, until he pulls away and stands from the bed.

Garrett slams the near empty bottle onto the nightstand and pulls a cell phone from the pocket of his jeans. Wiggling it in front of me, he cocks his head, the gleam in his eyes wicked, and says, "Let's get started."

Chapter Thirteen

Indie

ON THE PILLOW BESIDE me, the phone chirps. I open my eyes and raise it so I can see the screen, squinting at Tameka's name.

I close my eyes again, snuggling more deeply into my pillow.

She's messaged every hour and a half, solid, for the past three days, except during the nighttime hours when I'm supposed to be sleeping. I don't sleep, but she doesn't know that. Doesn't need to know that. Doesn't need to know that I lie here most of the time, except when Daisy needs something, awake but not awake, caught in some weird space where I daydream about Hawaii and have waking nightmares about Edgewater.

Something nudges my hand and I open my eyes to see Daisy peeping over the edge of the tall bed. She's pushing her pink and white melamine Barbie bowl into my hand, and although she doesn't say a word, I know what she needs.

"Ready for breakfast, baby girl?"

She nods, and I swing my legs over the side of the bed, frowning at the bowl.

Maybe a different dish.

I chatter at her about nothing in particular as we walk to the kitchen, my hand smoothing her golden curls. I ask if she wants juice or chocolate milk. If she thinks her friend Ruthie will be over the stomach flu and back at preschool. If Ms. Shelby will pick the color pink today.

She doesn't answer as I seat her at the counter bar. Daisy simply points to the milk when I hold it up, inciting a wave of anxiety to claim me.

She's still in her jammies, her little feet plump and bare, and she's so, so quiet. I don't know what to do about the fact that she hasn't said a word since the incident at the bank. I don't know if it was the trauma of seeing her father killed just feet away from her, or everything that followed. All of it, surely. She seems perfectly fine otherwise, smiling at books that I read and responding non-verbally in the appropriate manner.

But my little girl refuses to speak.

So, obviously, she's not perfectly fine. Stifling a sigh, I pour Fruity Pebbles in a different bowl and set it before her with a spoon. I need to take her somewhere. She needs to talk to someone, or draw them a damned picture if she won't talk, and I'm not qualified.

I have my own trauma. When do mothers get to heal their own hurts, get to swim and wallow and fade into their own personal demons? Turning to the coffee pot, I wrap my fingers around the edge of the counter and breathe deeply through my nose.

In. Out. In. Hold.

Panic wells up within me, not for the first time, and I bite my lip hard.

I can't do this. I can't—

And then I hear his voice, as clearly as if he were standing in front of me.

"Indie, honey... you gotta keep it together."

My spine snaps straight, and I regroup. Renewed strength settles inside me as I address my daughter. "Daisy... Mommy's going to lay your school clothes out. Come get dressed when you finish eating, okay?" I wait for her acknowledgment—a small nod and flicker of the eyelids. It's enough. "I'll be upstairs in my bathroom."

Another nod, then I step away.

Upstairs, I stand blankly for a second in Daisy's doorway until I remember my purpose, and then pull a couple of outfits from the laundry basket on the floor and spread them out on the bed. I try to give her options as often as possible; it cuts down on the I-don't-like-this drama and makes her feel like a big girl.

Not that there's been much drama lately.

The clock on her bedside table reads 7:48AM, so I move it, knowing Mom will be here within twenty minutes to drive Daisy to school for me. She's been a godsend, taking her and bringing her home every day for the past week. I need to get out of these pajamas and into "real" clothes before she gets here. I want to look semi-presentable when she arrives, even if it does give the false impression that I'm ready to take on the world.

I think she knows that I'm grieving something, even if I haven't figured out precisely what, yet. There's Jeremy, of course. We weren't on great terms, but I would never have wanted the guy to die. And definitely not like that.

It's more than that, though.

It's grief and fear and anger all bound together in one vicious icy fugue, like that ice cream thrown on a marble slab, pounded and beaten and rolled into a single frozen entity. I grieve the things I lost that day: my daughter's father. My security in my workplace. My feeling of immortality.

My sense of shelter.

In my bedroom, I stumble over the suitcase that lies on the floor where it fell several nights ago. Lacy undergarments spill out around it, colorful spots on the neutral carpeting. Bending, I scoop it all up and carry it into the bathroom, where I open the closet door and toss it into the back.

Dax, my brain supplies as I stand and stare at it.

I think I might have lost him, too, before I ever had him.

The unfairness of it breaks me and I slump to the floor and cry—quiet, so I don't upset Daisy.

That's how Mom finds me a few minutes later.

"Oh, Indigo."

She stands above me, arms akimbo with hands on her hips, and it doesn't even occur to me to be embarrassed at being caught wailing in the closet like a crazy woman. I just wish I'd had a few more minutes to fall apart.

But that time is past.

I stagger to my feet and swipe at the tears on my cheeks, just as Daisy turns the corner. She eyes me up for a second before tugging on Grandma's shirttail and holding her arms out to either side. "Oh, look at you! Such a little princess. You're going to be the prettiest girl in school today." With a pat on her bottom, Mom shoos Daisy out and turns to me. "This isn't healthy, sweetheart."

"Mom, I know, I—"

"You can't continue to hole up in this house and ignore the fact that Daisy's not talking."

"I'm not ignoring that."

"You both need to see a psychiatrist. And get some fresh air. Some vitamin D will do wonders."

"Mom," I counter, my last thread of sanity splintering. This isn't a vitamin D issue. Sometimes that's easier to blame, of course—it's easier to blame than the messy stuff, for which there aren't any easy answers. Swallowing, I gather my remaining wits. "Can't I just be depressed for a little while? It's been a rough damn week, you know."

Tears begin to well again.

Her face softens as she put her arms around me, wrapping me in that place that is uniquely home. Uniquely Mother.

A small shelter.

"I know, darling," my mother whispers into my unwashed hair. "But you have to pull up those big girl panties, okay? Tomorrow is Jeremy's funeral, and you have to be there. You have to be strong, Indigo. Be strong for Daisy."

With a sniffle, I nod, then just as quickly shake my head. "I don't know if I can do it."

And I hate that that's the truth.

I've always been strong. Independent. I try to be a good leader, a worthy caretaker. But something inside me cracked that day, the day my life changed, and I'm not sure how to put my pieces back together and march forward with finesse and a smile.

I'm broken.

I feel my mother's lips press into my hair as her arms tighten around me. Then she pushes me resolutely away. "You remember when your daddy died?" Her eyes roll up, even as she asks. "Doh. Of course you do. You were reading that book in school and showed me that passage when I was having a hard time."

My heart squeezes. She would remember that. She has no idea—

"That boats against the current one. You remember?"

"Yeah." My voice is crusty, and I clear it swiftly. "I remember."

She shakes me just a little, her hands birdlike on my shoulders. "So, you know what to do, then. Just like the rowers do it. One stroke, one right, one left, until all of a sudden you're just... there." She shakes her head, her eyes distant. "Always hated that damn saying."

I laugh a little—I can't help it. "I love you, Mom."

"Love you, too, my Indigo Blue." She turns me out of the closet and toward the sink with a light slap on my backside. "Now, wash your face and get dressed while I take Miss Mini Me to school. I expect the dishes to be clean when I bring her home."

She sends me a wink, and I don't bother arguing, instead, moving to the sink to wash my face. I can only take so much motivation in one day, and sometimes it's easier to let that current take you where it will.

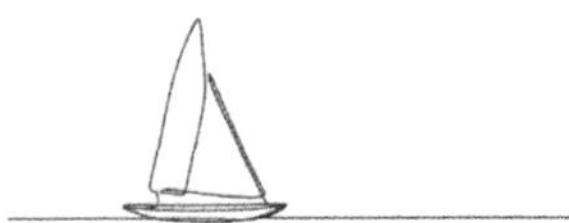

"What do you mean, you're not going?"

Tameka stands framed in my bedroom door, her expression a perfect blend of appalment and pity. I'm lying on the floor, my dress hiked over my hips and a pair of stockings clutched to my chest.

"I just tore them. They were my last pair," I answer, staring at the lazy glide of the ceiling fan above me. Tameka's face slides in between me and the fan, and I look at her briefly before closing my eyes.

"Are you... on something?" she asks, a faint note of incredulity in her voice. "You know, like drugs."

A smile touches my lips, but my answer is a noncommittal hum.

Maybe. Maybe not. Depends on how much trouble it'll get me in.

She seems to understand my tacit confession because a moment later her hands are beneath my armpits and she's tugging me into a seated position beside the bed. "You picked a fine time to get wasted, girl."

"I'm not wasted!" I retort in mock shock, a giggle negating my argument. I understand her surprise. I've never been really drunk, only mildly buzzed, always wanting to maintain control of every teeny tiny thing around me. But I was so panicky this morning at the thought of attending Jeremy's funeral that someone—his sister, maybe—slipped me a Valium. And I'd already had a glass of wine.

So, I'm officially feeling no pain now, and I don't care nearly as much as I did earlier about the crowd that will be there. The eyes watching. The curious whispers and intrusive questions.

"Indie, you're shaking."

Well, damn. She's right. The hands in my lap are shaking, a fine tremor coursing through them and traveling up my arms. I'm disconnected, though, the wine and the Valium doing their job so well that I didn't even notice my encroaching breakdown, the way I tiptoe that fine edge of chaos and apathy.

"Tameka, I don't wanna go see Jeremy and make my baby girl cry..." Reaching up, I clutch her hands in mine and stare with every ounce of pleading I can muster. "Please don't make me."

"Damnit... Mary!" She extracts one hand to stroke my hair, calling out for my mother, and mutters under her breath, "Mary, come in here and help me. Your child has lost her mind, sure enough."

In the next few minutes, my room fills with people. Mom. Christina, Jeremy's sister. His mother, Ellen. All of them staring at me with expressions ranging from confusion to sympathy to annoyance. Christina and Tameka help me to my feet and then onto the bed, Christina babbling something nonsensical about it only being one little pill. There's a keening sound that fills my ears, and then the mattress dips, Ellen sitting beside me to pull me into a loose embrace. The keening is me, wailing like a child denied a toy in the supermarket.

"Now, Indie. Hush, sweetheart," Ellen coos, brushing a kind thumb along my tearstained cheekbone. "Jeremy wouldn't have wanted this."

God... how do I tell her I'm not crying for Jeremy?

I'm crying for me, for Daisy.

I'm crying for Dax, damn him.

He was supposed to take us to Hawaii.

The room falls silent, the only sounds the muted thwap of the ceiling fan and my hiccupping sobs. Ellen's arms fall from around me, and she rises to walk stiffly from the room.

Tameka squeezes my shoulder and sighs. "You just did, Indie."

Horror claims me as her words sink in, and I freeze.

I said all that out loud.

Chapter Fourteen

Dax

"OH MY STARS AND glorious garters."

Blake's shellshocked voice sounds through the cell phone speaker as Garrett holds the receiver level with my mouth. "Hey, Blake."

His tone rises by at least three decibels. ""Hey, Blake" is the best you can do? That's all I get after mourning your untimely death for three straight days?" he balks, nearly screeching. "I hired another therapist just to help me cope with the guilt I harbored for leaving you there to die. Plus, another one to feed me cupcakes while I ugly-cried over our unresolved love story. That's four therapists, Dax. Four!"

Garrett's forehead wrinkles with confusion.

"Our love... ? Jesus, never mind." I can't help the shadow of a smile that forms upon hearing my best friend's voice. "Listen, I need you to do something for me. A big thing."

"Sure. Fine. I'll get right on that after I forgive you. Which will be never."

"This is serious," I tell him, my tone growing bleak. "I'm... I'm not okay."

A silence settles in—an eerie pause. I can almost see his eyes widening while he fiddles with the top button of one of his trademark pink polos. Before I can continue, Garrett pulls his arm back and finishes for me.

"Your buddy found himself in a bit of a pickle," Garrett explains, pacing in a circle. He lowers the phone from his ear, switching it to speaker mode as Blake's incredulous response rings through.

"Who the hell are you? Where's Dax?"

"None of that is your concern. All you should care about is keeping your friend alive."

"Is this a ransom call? I've watched Taken at least three dozen times. I'm fully prepared to outsmart you."

Garrett's eyes roll over to me, an eyebrow arching. His reply is braided with annoyance. "You ain't gonna outsmart me, kid. Pull any tricks and Daxy boy gets put to bed with a shovel, got it?"

Blake blows out a hard breath, his nerves evident. "He's a celebrity, you know. Extremely famous."

"Yeah, yeah, I know who he is. I also know the whole world says he's presumed dead."

Another wave of silence infiltrates the room.

Everyone really thinks I'm... dead?

No search parties, no scent hounds?

Just...

Dead.

Garrett continues. "I've been watchin' the news," he sniggers. "I should send all them reporters a fuckin' fruit basket or something."

"Well, now that I know he's alive, things will change. The police are going to—"

"The police aren't going to do shit," Garrett cuts in. "They have no idea where we are, and neither do you."

There's an audible gulp on the other end of the line. "Fine. What do you want?"

"I want that baseball card, pretty boy. The Babe Ruth, number nine."

"That's in a locked security deposit box inside of a bank that is now a grisly crime scene... likely because of you," Blake says, flustered. "You're one of them, aren't you? One of the vile cretins who murdered innocent people and ruined my custom jacket?"

"You're ripping my heart out, Pink Shirt."

"This is absurd." Blake grows more panicked, calling out, "Dax? Dax, are you there?"

An ache stabs at my chest as I try in vain to loosen my limbs from the duct tape. Garrett begrudgingly waves the phone at me, and I grit out a reply. "I'm here, Blake."

"God..." Blake grouses, then inhales a big breath. "Okay, okay. Tell me what to do. I'll try to get it."

"You'll do more than try." Garrett brings the receiver closer to his lips, hesitating briefly to collect his thoughts. "You're his power of attorney. Any signatory in possession of the key can access the box."

"You've done your homework. Wonderful," Blake replies. "Except that I don't have a key."

"You will soon enough."

A sigh of distress filters through the speaker. "What about the bank? It's all roped off with murder tape."

"We wait until it reopens."

"That could be weeks!"

"Good thing I'm patient."

I glare across the room at Garrett who stares right back at me, stony-eyed. Jaw clenching, I drop my head to the headboard, refusing to believe that I'll be tied to this goddamn bed for weeks on end. Garrett's been giving me rope—literally—enough to use the bucket in the corner of the room, but that experience is awkward and restrictive and non-conducive to escape, especially as weak as I am. I have to think of something else, or I will lose my mind. It's a given.

My fingers tingle with numbness as sweat dots my brow, skin slick from the breaking fever. I've always been good at reading my opponents, but Garrett is difficult to assess. I don't have an angle, or a weakness to manipulate.

Not yet.

Blake murmurs his reluctant acquiescence, filling the space with my only shred of hope of getting out of here alive. "Tell me what to do."

Three more days pass.

Garrett dropped off the safety deposit box key for Blake, leaving it at a secure location arranged during that first phone call. Now it's just a waiting game until Edgewater Bank reopens its doors.

The hours pass by in a slow blur of random fever spikes, itches I can't scratch, uncomfortable bouts of sleep, and the occasional visit from Garrett who feeds me an assortment of expired pantry staples, such as canned chicken, spam, and beans. My body is weak and tired, but my mind is a continuous wheel of anxious thoughts, nostalgia, and a future that feels woefully out of reach.

I can't sleep. I can't do much of anything but stare at the mauve and mint green wallpaper, now yellowed and peeling. Ancient pieces of furniture are home to families of cockroaches that keep me awake with their hisses and chirps and scurrying legs.

A fever claims me that third night, and I welcome it. I welcome the accompanying exhaustion that will inevitably steal away my despair and take me somewhere else.

Anywhere else.

Garrett shuffles inside the small room while my body shivers with sickness. More antibiotics and pain relievers are shoved down my throat by dirty fingers, water following. I cough and spurt, the actions riddling me with pain.

"Don't fuckin' die on me yet, hero."

My brain flares with irritation, and I want to lash out. It's his fault I'm in this state. You don't want me to die, then fucking do something about it. Hydrate me. Stop sticking your bacteria-laden fingers down my throat. Take me to the fucking hospital.

But I don't say it.

My eyes are hooded, vision cloudy. Garrett looms over me with an expression I can't read as he taps the empty water bottle against his thigh. I run my tongue along dry lips. "Y-You have the key. You don't need me anymore..." I'm not sure if my statement is a fever-induced cry for mercy, to put me out of my misery, or a futile request for release.

Whatever I intended, Garrett sniffs his rebuttal. "It ain't that easy. Your buddy needs proof of life, or he won't cooperate."

Blake.

I wonder what he's doing right now—how he's coping. He's always been high-strung and neurotic under stress. I'm the level-headed one.

Tremoring from chills, my teeth chatter through a response. "Tell him..." A final farewell filters through my mind like sludge, and I have no idea what to say. It should be profound, epic. Just like our friendship. "Tell him—"

"None of that "last words" bullshit. It's just a fuckin' fever. You'll be good as new once the drugs kick in."

Garrett's face flickers in and out of focus, his voice morphing into something like static or waves. Almost as if I placed a seashell to my ear.

And then I'm gone.

I'm not sure if I'm dead or possessed by fever dreams, but relief washes over me when sunlight pours in from a tall bay window, warming my bones. The chills disperse into tiny tickles when little fingers poke my ribs.

"I'm a lion. Roar!"

Two honey blonde pigtails bounce and sway as the little girl dances around me, tickling my sides. Her Brave Heart Lion dress pulls a smile to my lips. "What are you doing here, little lion?"

Daisy giggles. "I live here, silly."

Another voice, booming and familiar, catches my ear, and I look up to find my father sitting at his desk, lost in a sea of paperwork. "I always knew you'd manage to impress me one day, son."

"You did?" I frown, stepping towards him, wondering why the floor teeters as if I'm walking along the deck of a boat. "My years as a successful, renowned athlete just didn't cut it for you, huh?"

"Superficial folly."

He doesn't glance up, adjusting the wire-rimmed glasses along the bridge of his nose. My eyes narrow, wondering where the hell I am. Glancing out the sun-streaked window, the tree branches shimmy to a lyrical breeze, and I find myself entranced. Lost… but not really lost. Perhaps I've been found.

"Fate is a funny sort of thing."

I'm met with milky white skin and turquoise eyes, a smile brightening her already radiant features. Indie scrunches her nose up at me, the gesture flooding me with a strange kind of magic. "Where are we?"

She takes my hand in hers, linking our fingers. "We're nowhere. We're everywhere."

"I don't understand."

"But you know." Indie's palm squeezes mine with surety. "The understanding comes later."

Thunder cracks outside the window, followed by violent bolts of light, causing me to flinch. The sky turns black as raindrops pelt the glass like angry daggers. I frown. "It didn't look like rain…"

A sigh carries over to me. "It always looks like rain, Dax."

The hold on my hand feels different. Sharp and severe. The scent of honeysuckles fades to amber and spice.

Sabrina. Her long nails dig into my hand, her witchy eyes reflecting the storm.

My frown deepens. "How did you get here?"

"I never really left. You know that." Sabrina's smile glows with a hint of sadness as she brings my palm to her flat belly. "I thought we could try again. Maybe we can overcome the storm this time."

Painful memories assault me when my eyes dip to her stomach.

The loss. The emptiness. The permanent scars.

I couldn't quite reach her after that, and everything unraveled.

Blood seeps through the cotton of her dress as thunder claps in the distance. It slicks my hand, my breath hitching. I pull back, looking down at the red smears along my skin, the grisly stains, my heart slamming into my ribs with every strike of lightning. When I glance up at her, she's gazing over my shoulder with a wistful expression.

"Or... maybe not," Sabrina mutters solemnly. "You can't save them all, I suppose."

As the sky illuminates with another flare of light, the room brightens to glittering gold. I follow Sabrina's stare, landing on Indie and Daisy sitting together atop a colorful rug, legs crossed, books in hand. Their laughter replaces the festering dread swimming through my veins.

Turning to Sabrina, I suck in a breath, my insides rattling. "It's all chaos," I murmur.

"Look within the chaos..."

I shake my head through a swallow. "I don't understand these riddles. I—"

Her image morphs into something haunting, stopping my response. The blood stains swell along her stomach, blooming all across her chest and torso, encompassing her in crimson death. Fear weakens me, and my legs shake as I stumble back.

Sabrina closes in on me, inching closer, a blade appearing in her fist. She raises it with a grin. "Look inside, Dax."

"No..."

With a shrill howl, Sabrina slams the edge of the blade into my chest.

I awake with a start.

I'm soaked in my own sweat, hair sticking to my forehead as I try to catch my breath. My bullet wound smarts and stings, the pain radiating with every thrum of my pulse.

A presence hovers beside me. That single sunbeam pokes through the window, illuminating swirls of dust and two tawny eyes fixed on me.

Garrett sits in a folding chair with crossed arms, his face pensive. "Welcome back, hero."

I'm spent and drained in every possible way. Eyelids heavy, heartbeats sluggish, the will to fight depleting with every tick on the grandfather clock.

I'm not a hero.

I'm just a slow-dying soldier.

My silence weighs heavy in the room, but there's nothing left to say, and Garrett doesn't speak again. He just sits there, watching me. Studying his target.

His sacrificial lamb.

And when he finally leaves the room and returns sometime later with food and water, his hands aren't full of rusted canned goods. Instead, he sets a box of piping hot pizza on top of the folding the chair and sits beside my fettered legs, the mattress creaking beneath his weight.

I remain mute, and so does Garrett.

But he feeds me three slices of sausage and green pepper pizza that day, and it's fucking good, and it's exactly what I need to rekindle the fire in my blood that had been doused with infection, rot, and utter hopelessness.

Garrett isn't the stone cold monster he appears to be.

He's human, and humans have flaws.

Humans have vulnerabilities.

Humans have cracks.

As he crudely wipes pizza sauce from my mouth and pours more water down my throat, his eyes hold mine, pupils dilating and flashing with something that resembles... guilt.

I may have found my way in.

Chapter Fifteen

Indie

TWO WEEKS GO BY, and I'm taking a much-needed nap when the doorbell rings, loud and insistent. I'm on the couch, at least, covered over with a worn afghan my mother crocheted for me when Jeremy and I got married.

Ducking my head beneath the blanket, I wonder if I can just ignore whoever's at the door. Unfortunately, the answer comes a second later when they press again and lean, so the sound continues tinkling through the house, a merry middle finger to my mood.

Grumbling, I get up to answer its call.

"Tameka." The bane of my existence stands on the small covered porch, leaning an elbow against the doorbell without apology.

"Oh, great, you're awake," she says, pushing her way past me. Her arms grip two sacks that are bulging with groceries, which I side-eye with equal parts shame and appreciation.

"You didn't have to buy me groceries." I follow her to the kitchen, where she sets the bags on the counter and begins pulling items out one at a time. Like me, Tameka is currently on paid leave while the bank remains a closed crime scene.

Unlike me, she's anxious to get back into the swing of things.

I'm dreading the day I get the call that we'll be reopening.

"Did you leave the house this week?" she asks, sliding a pointed glance at where the T.V. still lies on the floor in shambles. "Maybe you just forgot to tell me."

The Greek yogurt she sets down in front of me is faintly enticing, so I pull it to me, ripping the foil lid off. "Spoon." I watch as Tameka plucks it from the right drawer without having to search, well-acquainted with my house from our regular weekend wine and game dates. "Don't judge. You know I didn't."

"That's convenient, considering I made you a therapy appointment."

"What? Therapy? You can't just do that, Tameka—"

Panic roars through me at the thought of leaving the house, of even placing one foot over the threshold. It's stupid, I know. But things happen all the time—crazy, unpredictable, awful things. We're living proof. It was bad enough that I had to release my fear long enough to let Daisy go to school, but on an intellectual level, I knew I couldn't subject her to the chaos of my own maddening phobia.

"Relax." Tameka sets a hand on my shoulder and squeezes gently. "Online. It wasn't expensive, and you can pay me back if you want. If it's awful and you don't want to, you don't have to. But you need to talk to someone, Indie. This isn't healthy. You know that."

I swallow the lump in my throat and nod, focusing on the hardwood floor. I do know that. "Today?"

"Today." Tameka consults her phone. "I scheduled a chat for you in t-minus twenty minutes. Let's get you set up."

I've never had therapy before. Pretty sure I needed it after my father died, but my mother fully believed in the power of inner resilience, of putting ourselves back together with self-love and determination. I also likely needed it after my divorce from Jeremy, but at the same time, I had an incredible support system who fed my soul and gave voice to all the feelings I couldn't express. I made it through that at-times hostile divorce and managed to remain whole-hearted and positive throughout the experience.

This is different, though. This feels... harder.

No one I talk to, except Tameka, has been through the same harrowing experience as me. And even Tameka's experience was drastically different from mine. Not lesser.

Just different.

Sometimes I daydream about following up with my fellow co-workers, or even the patrons who'd been caught in the crossfire. Mrs. Captain and her coins, Damien, that middle-aged mother and her two frightened teenagers.

Brian.

I think about Brian a lot, wondering if he ever made it down that aisle. Maybe Dax saved his life that day. Maybe I did, too.

Only, I never manage to pick up the phone or do that Google search, and I don't know why. Perhaps I'm afraid of the answer.

Perhaps... his life wasn't saved. Maybe Andrea is grieving and alone, falling asleep every night in the wedding dress she never got to wear.

And that's another weight I simply can't bear right now.

I settle in front of my laptop screen and chew my thumbnail as I wait for the therapist to show up. Tameka selected a live chat rather than a video chat, guessing correctly that it would make me feel more comfortable. There's a little box at the bottom of the screen that invites me to share any preliminary thoughts I have with my therapist.

Drawing in a deep breath, I start typing.

Indie: I'm scared. Of everything. Sirens in the night. Unlocked doors. Stepping outside to get the mail. When I try... it feels like I can't breathe, like I'm going to pass out.

I pull my hands back from the keyboard, look at the words, and wait. Am I supposed to feel different? I just feel vaguely anxious and fatigued.

Felicity: Hello! It's so nice to meet you here. I'm Felicity, and I'll be your therapist. I'll assume you've had time to read through my bio, so I won't repeat my credentials.

I didn't, but I trust Tameka to have found the best person for me.

Indie: Hi. Sure, yes.

Felicity: Great! Give me just a moment to read through this... Okay. Tell me why you feel frightened, Indie. Is this a new development, or something you've always dealt with?

My lip curls. I'm not certain I'm going to like this Felicity.

Indie: Didn't you read my bio?

Felicity: Yes, but I need to hear it from you.

Indie: I don't like to talk about it.

Felicity: And the reason for that, right there, is what we want to explore. What are you afraid to face?

Thunder sounds like gunshots.

My lavender wax melts remind me of that lobby.

Strange men on the street might as well be Leo, escaped from jail and hunting me down.

Police sirens cause a panic-attack.

Daisy is broken.

Everything is broken.

God... what am I not afraid of? The question pops immediately into my jumble of thoughts and after a hesitation, I go with it.

Indie: I'm afraid of everything. Talking about it makes it real, of course. It makes me remember really shitty details I'd rather forget. I'm afraid of getting sucked into that place and staying there. I'm afraid of revealing things to people who can't understand what it was like.

Felicity: Give me an example.

Dax. His face swims in the tears that crowd my eyes.

Indie: There was this man.

Felicity: Yes?

Indie: He was heroic.

Felicity: Was?

Indie: I don't know where he is. He was shot right in front of me, and then he... disappeared. I think he's dead.

Felicity: I'm sorry, Indie.

Indie: It's foolish. I only knew him for those few hours we were stuck there together. But there was this sense of something beyond our circumstances, you know? A fated connection. A glimpse into what could have been. I feel like I'm mourning something I never really had, and I know it doesn't make any sense...

It hurts to tell that to someone. It's an admission not just to her, but to myself, that I hoped for... something. Something more than those few hours. Something more than Hawaii, even.

Wetness tickles my cheek, and I realize for the eleventy-seventh time that week, I'm crying.

Felicity: It's not foolish. What you're experiencing is a bond formed by shared trauma. It's very natural.

Indie: But he's likely dead now, and I can't walk outside without freaking out. So, what do I do about it?

I can feel the smile in her reply, and feel my lips twitch in response. Maybe Felicity isn't so bad, after all.

Felicity: One step at a time, young Skywalker.

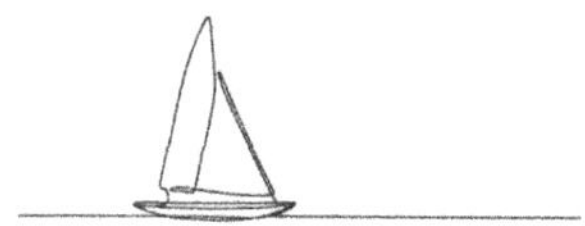

When therapy is over forty minutes later, I have an assignment and a renewed sense of hope. The best therapy, Felicity explains, is exposure, so my assignment is to do something every day that forces me outside the house, even if it's only for one foot and one minute at a time.

I decide to start with the backyard. I have a garden there, a walled refuge I painstakingly created with pergola and wicker, plants that could last into cool weather, and a trickling fountain. If I can make it back to my garden, perhaps I can recapture some small piece of my serenity that I've lost.

Tameka stands behind me as I stand in front of the French doors that open from the dining room to the covered portion of the patio, where the grill sits along with a table and several chairs. At my hip, I open and close my fist before reaching out to open the door.

The breeze is warm, fused with late-summer humidity. It curls into my nostrils, carrying the scent of lemon goldenrod and Mardi Gras sneezeweed. I close my eyes, then inch forward.

Just a toe. When I feel my stomach start to tighten, I stop.

One foot. One minute.

I can do this.

I feel Tameka's hand curl around my palm, a sweet encouragement, and taking a deep breath, I step out into the sunlight.

Chapter Sixteen

Dax

BLAKE'S DEMAND FOR PROOF of life is a welcome relief as the days drag into the second week.

The sound of his voice is the only certainty I have in this nightmare.

"You'll be pleased to know that I've reconnected with Casey, despite the fact that I'm still holding out hope for you, big man."

Garrett looms a foot away, having released my right arm from the duct tape. My fingers struggle to grip the cell phone as pinpricks of feeling slowly return to the appendages, but the sensation of giving my hand something to hold, something tangible, is a promising reminder that I'm alive and breathing. I'm not sure why Garrett provided the small courtesy, but it's likely for the same reason he fed me the pizza, and for the same reason he'll get this look in his eyes every now and then—almost like he wants to say something.

Confess. Cleanse his conscience.

He never does. He's hardly spoken a word to me over the past week.

But I'll take what I can get.

"Casey, huh? I thought that wasn't a thing," I reply to Blake, my tone low and full of gravel. I'm always so fucking thirsty.

"A sordid web of lies, Dax. My specialty."

A smile, natural and unprompted by any agenda, teases my lips, assuring me that I haven't lost my sense of humor. "I'm glad you're good. I'm glad you're... okay."

The humorous banter ebbs, replaced by my cruel reality. There's an alarmingly high chance that we'll never see each other again. I'll never get to hug my best friend one last time, and he'll never sit across from me at the coffee shop, rattling off his ridiculous, grandiose tales in that manic tone I've come to embrace.

There may never be another game of Scattergories, or late nights at the winery, or weekend binges of Chopped, where Blake would get inspired to cook colorful meals that usually tasted like spoiled Brussel sprouts.

As my stomach aches with hunger pangs, I know I'd give anything to eat his stinky-tofu-glazed-beet-surprise right now.

Blake sighs, the sound reeking of melancholy despair. "I'm not okay. I'm probably the least okay I've ever been, which is saying a lot, considering I basically run on fashion and anxiety… and Mango Tangos." He falters, clearing the catch in his throat. "I'm a mess. A dignified mess, but a mess none-the-less."

"You've always been a dignified mess."

"Fair. Very fair."

Garrett twirls his finger beside me, ushering me to hurry it up.

My jaw tightens. "So, ah, the bank reopens Tuesday? You have the key?"

Tuesday, Friday, June, December. Time is nothing here.

"I have the key," Blake confirms warily. "Right along with my noose to hang myself with after I hand over your death sentence on a silver platter."

A chill sweeps through me, my eyes lifting to Garrett who stares blankly from the shadowy corner of the room. "We don't know that." I heave in a breath, forcing out one more question before our time is up. "Uh… hey. Do you know if, um, Indie is okay? And her daughter?"

"The bank teller?"

"Yeah."

She still haunts me.

Indigo.

Indie and her brave little lion. Two golden strangers carved into me with directionless daggers, branded into my soul by a single shared nightmare.

I need to know that they're both okay. That my silent promises did not go in vain.

"As far as I know. She wasn't one of the confirmed deaths," Blake replies, then pauses to add, "But I can try to find out."

"Thank—"

Garrett interrupts, yanking the phone from my hand. "You got your five minutes, pretty boy. Time's up," he barks. "And if you go runnin' your mouth off to the Barbie doll about Ken, we're going to have some problems."

"You're just going to kill him anyway," Blake says, his words flaring over the speaker with a clipped edge of grief.

"I guess we'll find out."

Garrett disconnects the call, stuffing the phone into his pocket and pinning his stare on me. He has the amber eyes of a wolf. Predatory. Cold. I return the look with a warmer one, hoping to melt some of that ice. "It's the truth, isn't it?" I probe. "You'd be a fool to keep me alive, and you said it yourself—you're not dumb."

His lips draw into a thin line.

"I don't think you're a killer, though," I continue, stretching my fingers to shake away the remaining tingles. I resist the urge to scratch at my itchy chest wound, running my free hand through my mess of unwashed hair, crusted with old blood and numerous night sweats. "You want to be. You've tried."

"What the fuck do you know, hero?" Garrett takes a purposeful step forward, his features twisting with outrage, stance defensive. "All you do is skate around with a fuckin' stick while people cheer. You sign your name on nice tits and smile for all the pretty cameras. You've probably never suffered a day in your life until now."

I don't mean to indulge him, but my own defenses ignite. "You don't have a damn clue," I whisper, almost a hiss. My response isn't strategic or carefully thought out. It's pulled from an authentic place, brimming with a lifetime of demons and penitence. "Being tied to this shit-stained mattress has been a cakewalk compared to some of the hands I've been dealt."

"Bullshit." Garrett eyes my free hand with cautious apprehension, likely debating if he made the right call. "I'll bet you were an over-privileged Mama's boy turned frat douche. New girl every week. Hit in the head too many times with a football, but at least your face made up for your scrambled brains."

"Interesting theory."

His arms cross, shoulders shrugging with indifference. "I ain't wrong, am I?"

"Just a little." My lips twitch, thoughts reeling. "You were right about the Mama's boy part."

"I fuckin' knew it."

"I was a Mama's boy," I confirm. "Because no matter what I did, I couldn't get my father to love me. So, I took what I could get."

There's a shift in his certitude. Garrett's jaw tics as he stares down at me with mute regard, his biceps pulsing beneath the cropped sleeves of his t-shirt. He forces out a weak, "Boo-hoo."

"Yeah." I nod my head, maintaining eye contact, trying not to let old ghosts possess me. "I was a geek in school. I hated football, and girls petrified me. My adolescent life was studying and hockey."

"A real sob story," he mutters tersely.

"The inferiority I harbored in the eyes of my father turned me into a workaholic with an assortment of different complexes. I always had to be the best at everything to make up for the fact that I was a subpar son." I pause, noting the peculiar glint in his eyes that tells me he's relating to my spiel in some way. "I worked myself to physical illness a lot of the time, fueled by desperation. And then when I made it, when people finally recognized and glorified me, all I felt was... empty. The lights were too bright, the fame too suffocating. The person they saw on their television screens wasn't the person I saw in the mirror every day, and it sure as hell wasn't the person I wanted my father to see."

Garrett stands wordless beside the bed, arms still crossed tight.

I continue. "Then, she came around. Sabrina."

"You can't save them all, Dax."

My muscles seize with violent memories. I took her words to heart that day—I took them as a challenge. I couldn't save them all, but I could try.

I tried so hard, I smothered the kindling of life that still sparked between us, until it became nothing but black smoke and ashes.

Garrett sniffs. "She sounds like a peach, but unless you're gonna go into nice detail about her tits and ass, I'm not all that interested in your fuckin' Hallmark story."

"You ever been in love?"

A severe frown unfurls between his eyes, a gruff chuckle following. "Yeah. My job."

"Being a bungling criminal?" I probably shouldn't goad my kidnapper, but I don't exactly have much to lose at this point.

"That wasn't us, what you saw back there. That wasn't me."

"I'm relieved to hear that you murder and pillage much better than that."

"Fuck you, hero. I don't even know why I'm humoring you," Garrett bites out, taking a step forward. "Yeah, we do heists for a living. Been doin' it for years. I fucking love it, too, the thrill, the adrenaline rush. But when Ace got caught and took the fall for us... we all fell. This was our last gig. Biggest mistake was bringing Ronnie on board—that fuckin' halfwit."

I listen intently, both disgusted and intrigued. "Sounds like you should've been in charge. Not Leo."

"Fuck yeah, I shoulda been." Garrett's eyes light up with conviction. "Ace knew it, everyone knew it. I'm good at that shit, with taking lead, but Leo never saw it. He never saw me."

There's earnestness in his tone, despite the fact that he's trying to garner sympathy for his very illegal career choices. There's emotion laced into his words.

I listen.

Garrett shakes his head, huffing as he looks away. "We never killed anyone, you know. Not once. We weren't about that shit. It was all about the money, and it was fuckin' Leo's call to bring Ronnie into it after Ace got put away." He scuffs his shoe against the floor. "I knew this would happen."

"Why didn't Ace put you in charge?" I wonder absently, oddly curious.

"Like he had a damn choice, rotting away in that prison cell. Leo took charge like he always tried to do, pushin' me to the sidelines. This was our last snatch before gettin' the fuck outta dodge and leaving the country," he says, a vein in his neck dilating. "Looks like it'll just be me, all alone with my piña-fucking-colada on a beach somewhere."

My insides pitch. "After you get rid of me, you mean."

Garrett rolls his tongue along his teeth, hesitating. His gaze narrows in on my hand as it massages my opposite shoulder, loosening the taut muscle. A wave of impasse washes over him—a moment of indecision. He's debating if he should tie me back up, or let me have this tiny freedom.

Assessing my situation in a few quick beats, he paces back, away from the bed. "I'm gonna go find some food to keep your worthless ass alive for a few more days. Hope you didn't get used to the pizza because it's stale crackers and well water from here on out."

I watch with a straight face as he continues his backward trek. He's still eyeing me. Still debating his next move.

A sigh of relief escapes when Garrett finally decides to leave, spinning around to the bedroom door. I grit out in a low breath, "See you soon, killer."

He falters for just a moment, the muscles in his back stiffening.

Saying nothing, he leaves.

Tick, tick, tick.

The grandfather clock counts down from the opposite side of the room, the seconds sounding hopeful instead of anxious.

I wait five minutes.

And then I get to work.

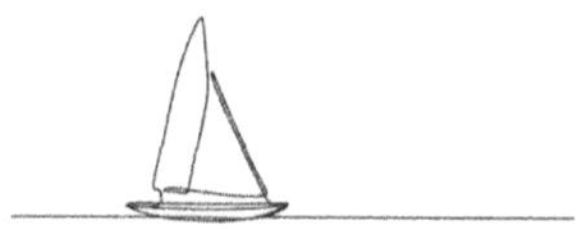

"Rise and shine, hero."

I feign sleep, lifting my head from my right shoulder and blinking slowly until Garrett's face comes into view. Dark circles rim his ruddy eyes as he stares down at my hunched over position on the bed. Licking my lips, I reply, "I was dreaming about that mouth-watering cuisine you were preparing for me."

"Fresh from g-ma's rat-infested pantry," he quips. Garrett holds up the cardboard box, then snatches a few stale crackers, shoving them between my teeth. "Yum."

I cough back the crumbs. "Tastes like five years ago."

"Give or take a year."

Forcing myself to chew, I try not to retch as the disgusting crackers dissolve into mush inside my mouth. I choke them down with a hard swallow, then reach for the box with my loose hand. "I got it."

Garrett scoffs, appearing to regret his decision to keep me partially untethered. "Look at you, all capable and shit. You'll be scootin' around the rink again in no time, eh?"

"In a casket, I presume," I mumble through another cracker.

"Yeah, well, that'll make for an interesting game."

There's a hint of humor glimmering back at me, and my left arm twitches behind my back. Lowering my eyes, I press my lips together with a long sigh through my nose. "How are you going to do it?"

A beat. "What?"

"Kill me."

The mood shifts, charged with melancholy, as if gray storm clouds just rolled in. Garrett wrinkles his nose, the only outward expression of his inner flicker of doubt, but he covers it with a mask of detachment. "How do you want to go, hero? I'll let you pick."

I blink. "How generous of you."

A half-smile curves on his lips as he slams his hand to his heart. "There's hope for me yet, huh?" Garrett shakes his head with a derisive chuckle, then hesitates. His eyes squint in my direction, mouth pursing with thought. A few seconds pass, and then he's sitting beside my bound ankles, glancing around the room before his sights land on me again. "My Ma used to tell me that. There's hope for you yet."

My breath stalls as I try to read the room. The new tone in his voice. Swallowing, I nod. "Relatable."

"Parents can be a real pain in the ass, you know? It shouldn't matter what they think, but they have this way of molding you. Shaping your future, your whole goddamn identity, and it's utter bullshit. They shouldn't hold that much power."

We share a glance, my chest tightening. "You didn't get along with your mother?"

Garrett shrugs. "She was all right." Blowing out a breath, he tents his hands, elbows to knees. "I mean, she wasn't a total asshole. She just... didn't see me the way Ace did. Ace was the golden child, and Leo was his lapdog, second in command. Trevor was the baby, the pathetic pet. And Ronnie..." Crude laughter tears from his lips. "He was the fuckin' clown. She called him that, too—a clown. He was never taken seriously. He knew his place, though."

"And you?"

He hardens, muscles contracting, teeth grinding together. "I was just there," Garrett says, staring off into the cobwebbed shadows. "Watching. Observing. Tryin' to think fast, think ahead, formulate these grand ideas before someone else figured it out first. But no one ever listened—it's like they never wanted to involve me. I swear Leo even went out of his way to keep me out of the family business, especially the dangerous shit. It's like he thought I was inept. Then he brings Ronnie into it... fuckin' asshole." Garrett sighs, looking away. "Don't know why I'm spillin' my guts to you. Guess it feels okay to be heard for once."

My throat feels dry, my emotions scattered like chaff in the wind. Unsure of how to proceed, I nod in agreement, murmuring under my breath, "We all want to be heard. Seen and appreciated."

Our eyes hold, a common thread linking us in some morbid, fucked-up way. We're nothing alike. We're not carved from the same stone.

But we're buried in the same dirt.

"Ain't that the fuckin' truth." Garrett clicks his tongue, head swaying side to side. A few somber beats pass before he slaps his palms to his thighs. He glances my way with a hard exhale. "You thirsty, hero? I could use a beer, myself."

The query causes my heart to stutter. A beer?

Tongue-tied, I simply nod.

"I suppose I owe you a worthy send-off, eh?" Garrett rises from the bed, the slightest smile tipping his mouth. "Be right back."

When the door creaks closed, I fall back against the headboard, gathering my wits. My courage.

Tick, tick, tick.

Two full minutes pass by before Garrett returns, and in that small window, I manage to use the rusted pruning shears tucked underneath my back to cut through the spool of duct tape restraining my ankles. I found them earlier, after I'd successfully released my left wrist from the bed post, then hopped and hobbled around as quietly as possible, scouring the filth-laden room to find something sharp enough to cut through the tape. It was drawn too tight, too thick, and I couldn't get it loose without a tool.

A shot of adrenaline courses through me when I'm finally free.

My legs are stiff, hardly mobile, but I pull myself upright from the bed and maintain my balance as my feet touch the hardwood floor.

Then, before I can make a move, the bedroom door swings open.

"I'm more of a scotch guy, but beer—"

Garrett's words stop short when his eyes lift, and he finds me standing unfettered beside the bed. He holds a beer in each hand, dangling the bottles at his thighs while his whole body goes rigid. All I can do is stare, unprepared for my next play. I haven't had enough time to strategize.

I think he's about to pounce on me. His eyes are flaming with hot coals, wild and worried. But he doesn't move from his place in the doorway.

He just watches me.

He waits.

And as the grandfather clock ticks away like a harrowing scoreboard, I collect my balance and pace forward, inhaling a giant breath before whispering, "Hey, killer."

Chapter Seventeen

Indie

A MONTH SOARS BY, and even though the late summer heat is muggy and sweltering, I can't help but feel a frost deep inside my bones. I shiver, tucking myself further into my afghan. Glancing up from the expense account I'm working on, I catch sight of Daisy as she pauses at the French doors of the kitchen and peers out, waving. My mom steps behind her and tugs her gently away.

I sigh a little. My stomach rumbles with hunger pangs, but I don't want to go inside just yet. This afghan and I have become permanent fixtures on the patio daybed swing, nestled into a cozy nest of pillows and blankets to offset my permanent chill. This is where I work now, having found a new job working from home as an accountant for a local ad agency.

The fact that I want to be out here like this, even if it is only in my backyard, is surreal, but I'm grateful for every small bit of progress I can claim. It's twelve steps from the door to this swing, and ten more past the swing to the boundary the tall fence provides. I remember the victory of each step forward, jaw clenched, a cold sweat dotting my forehead.

Each step was a birth. A rebirth, really. A stretching of a metaphysical birth canal, a physical pain that gripped and squeezed and stole my breath.

"Breathe through the pain," Felicity had encouraged in our chat, and I did just that, closing my eyes and latching on to the words in my head. I didn't know what Felicity sounded like because we had never spoken, and somehow, her imaginary voice became Dax's soothing tones whispering in my ear. His hand curling around mine.

One blue eye, one brown.

It felt like his warmth surrounding me, and I forgot, for the expense of energy it took to shift one foot forward and then the next, for the space of time that lapsed while I stood and breathed in stillness… I forgot he wasn't there.

I forgot he wouldn't ever be there.

Now I sit and revel in the triumph of each step, paltry to most but unimaginably huge to me. Now I make it a point to be outside most of the day, if only to give a big "eff you" to the agoraphobia that still holds me prisoner on this side of my front door.

One step at a time, young Skywalker.

Felicity's words flow through me, Dax's voice singing loud.

It's the courage I need to pull myself out of this blanket fort and head inside, start supper for my silent child, and put on a brave face.

I'll come back outside tomorrow, treasuring these little triumphs.

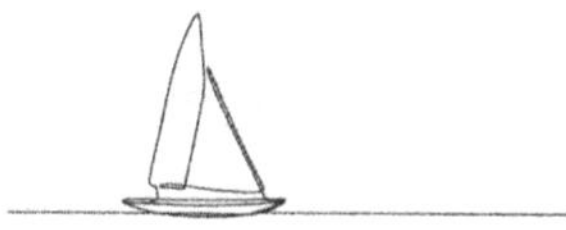

"Daisy, I really like that shirt you're wearing. That's one of those Caring Bears, isn't it?"

From my spot on the stool at the kitchen counter, I watch as Daisy peers down at her colorful shirt, then back up at Marie, the child psychologist recommended by her preschool. She's still not talking, and after trying everything I could think of to inspire speech, to bring magical words to her little lips, I gave up a week ago and scheduled an in-home appointment.

Even though the psychologist gave the wrong name, intentionally trying to draw out a response, Daisy only gives a slow nod and returns her attention to the piece of paper in front of her. She colors carefully, her forehead puckered in a tiny frown, her mouth pursed in what I recognize as her thinking expression.

"Is he your favorite?" Marie wonders softly.

Daisy doesn't respond this time, and after a moment, the psychologist makes a notation on the yellow legal pad beside her.

I pick up my coffee and take a sip, gripping it tight to keep my hand from trembling. The outfit my daughter wears is not the same as the dress she was wearing the day everything went down—that one was stained by her father's blood—but it's similar. Brave Heart Lion, her favorite of all the bears. I remember Dax paying attention to it, trying to distract her with his gentle smiles and easy strength. The psychologist requested something that might help to subtly jog her memory and help her delve into the triggers for her refusal to speak.

I didn't want her to put it on. I don't want her to remember.

Maybe that's the problem.

"Daisy, can you help me draw some pictures? I love making pictures, but I need some help. I bet you're really good at it."

Daisy pushes a piece of paper toward Marie and waits.

"Thank you, sweetie. The first thing I want to draw is a hero. Will you help me draw a hero?" Without waiting for an answer, Marie picks up a red crayon and begins to draw. Even from a distance, it's obvious she's drawing a fireman. Daisy sits quietly for a moment, her turquoise eyes observing gravely before flickering to the crayons in front of her. After another moment of deliberation, she picks up the pale green, and I feel my heart stutter in my chest.

Dax was wearing a green shirt on that fateful early-summer day.

I watch for a few minutes as they draw together, Marie's low tones soothing even to me across the room. I find myself battling the disturbing desire to tell her everything, so I force myself to a standing position and walk on bare feet to the sink. Biting my lip, I dump the remains of my coffee down the drain and stare out at the backyard through the kitchen window, the place that has become my unlikely haven over the past couple of weeks.

My thoughts are full of Dax, which is why the anomaly that greets my gaze goes unnoticed at first. My eyes move past the image, pause on the Japanese maple at the corner of the stone patio, then abruptly return.

Wait a minute.

There's a man in my backyard.

For a painful second, adrenaline directs my impulses and panic overtakes me.

Intruder! Run!

I drop the mug, the rubber mat at the bottom of the sink the only thing saving it from bursting into a thousand pieces. Visions of ski masks and firearms assault me, stealing my breath.

Scream!

I open my mouth, but sound sticks in my throat like a peanut butter sandwich chewed to paste. I close my eyes, fingers clawing at the sink while I try to force rational thought past the flight reflex.

Breathe, Indie. Just breathe.

Finally, my brain catches up, my heartbeats subduing to a less concerning pace when I realize the man is...

Dax's friend.

Just like that, my emotions settle, lulled by the fact that it's... Blake.

Yes, he's undeniably skulking outside the window of the dining area where Daisy and Marie sit, pushing up on his tippy toes and pressing his nose into the screen to try to see into the room... but it's Blake, a familiar and friendly face, dressed in a pair of pressed blue jeans, a paisley shirt, and a scarf I'm kind of envious of.

A sob rises to my throat, a second wave of emotion climbing, and when I stifle it swiftly with my fist, it turns into a giggle as I process the absurdity.

What the hell is he doing? Why is he here?

I find myself moving toward the door, feet still bare. I have no idea if he intends to come inside, to speak to me, but I can't let him leave without doing so. I have to see him, talk to him, hold his cheeks between my hands. I have to know. Is he struggling, like I am?

God, what utter crap. Of course, he is.

I have to hug him. Dax was his friend—for how long, I don't know—but I know they were close. And if I miss him this much, after only a few hours with the man, I can't even fathom what Blake is feeling.

At the door, another idea, equally absurd, hits me, and without giving myself too much time to think about it, I tug my slipper shoes on over my feet and swing the door open without so much as a glance in his direction. My spidey-senses register the jump he makes as I breeze by him, making a beeling for the table at the edge of the patio, as if I have some purpose there. In my periphery, I see him make himself small against the side of the house, then slowly slink behind the boxwoods that leave around a foot of space between them and the siding.

"Where the heck is that... ?" I grumble, loud enough for him to hear, then root around near the table, finally lifting a delicate tin ladybug that we use to hide our extra key. "Ah-ha!"

I make a big production of returning to the door, opening and closing it, but instead of going inside, I stand and wait beside it for Blake to stand.

When he does, approximately six seconds later, I lob the ladybug at him, nailing him in the chest.

"Ow! Christ on a cracker, what'd you do that for?"

I cross my arms over my chest. "Why do you think I did that, Blake? What are you doing sneaking around my house? You scared the crap out of me!"

"Well, you scared the caca out of me, and that's infinitely worse."

I rub at my temple, where I feel a headache coming on. "I'm pretty sure they're the same thing, actually—"

"Just take my word for it, missy. And no more murder-y ladybugs, please." Tugging at the scarf around his neck, Blake gestures inside the house. "How's the little lass?"

"How's—" My words clip short as I blink in his direction, shaking my head. "Blake, what in the world are you doing here? Not that I'm not happy to see you, but..."

I stop again. Studying his face, sudden tears rush to my eyes as time stands still. Unable to help myself, I step forward and wrap him in a firm hug.

"Oof." He nearly stumbles backwards, heisting briefly before his arms lift to encircle me, his hands awkwardly petting the small of my back. "An aggressive hugger. My favorite kind."

My smile meets his shirt collar, and I inhale a deep breath before stepping away. "Now, kindly tell me why you're creeping around my bushes."

Blake shifts, uncomfortable, straightening his shirt. "Oh, you know, I just wanted to check on you and the mini-Indie. Make sure you guys were doing okay."

It's both the right thing to say... and the wrong thing to say.

It's right because it makes me forget, for the few seconds it takes him to back away toward the gate that leads around to the front of the house, that we weren't victims of a hostage attack not long ago. For just a moment, we're merely old friends, catching up.

But it's wrong because it makes tears run like Pavlov's mice down my cheeks as I search for words. Words that reveal the truth, forcing me to remember the cruelness of our reality.

Swallowing, I shake my head, dipping my gaze to the grass. "No," I admit. "No, we're not okay. We're both messed up. I can't go any further than my backyard, and Daisy..."

A frown wrinkles his brow, his eyes wide with worry.

"She won't talk, Blake."

"What do you mean she won't talk?" He stops, hand poised on to open the gate, and narrows his eyes at me.

"I mean, she won't freakin' talk. If she wants juice, she brings me a cup and the bottle. If she's tired, she takes my hand and leads me to her bedroom. She's using an invented sign language to communicate, she rarely smiles, and it has me so freaked out, I have a psychologist in there with her right now."

My words spill out in a tearful confession, a cry for help, and I cross my arms over my chest as I push back an ugly-cry breakdown.

Blake's gaze darts to the window and he bites the corner of his lip, nodding to himself. "Okay."

"Okay?" I bring my eyes back to his, anger surging. "Blake, what on Earth—"

"Look, I have to go. I have a thing." Blake inches backwards again, lifting his hand in a flustered little wave, nearly tripping on a loose stone. "I'll be back, though. Next week, probably. And I'd like to see the little lion. Are you on the book of Faces?"

I nod dumbly.

"Great, I'll look you up. Adios!"

With that, he leaves me standing with my hands raised in supplication, wondering what the hell brought the friend of a ghost to haunt me to a madness I'm pretty sure I've already reached.

Chapter Eighteen

Dax

WHEN I WAS FIVE years old, my father asked me what I wanted to do with my life.

There was subtle intimidation in his tone. Not "what do you want to be when you grow up?" Even then, as a small boy, I knew the answer he sought.

The answer he expected.

But my mother's voice had filtered through my scattered brain: "Always follow your heart, Dax. It will never steer you wrong."

Her warm wisdom filled me with conviction, and I replied, innocent and sure, "I want to be a hockey player, Dad."

I think that was the turning point for us.

For me.

His eyes flared with amber and embers, glowing with what I recognized at the time as something bad. Something that made me want to cower and take those words back, storing them inside me forever.

As the years pressed on, I became very familiar with that look. Those eyes, the color of almonds and hardness of stone, watching me slide around the hardwood floors in my socks with a plastic baseball bat and invisible puck, cheering myself on as I scored goal after goal. Those eyes, narrowed in my direction behind wire-rimmed glasses as I sat glued to the television screen, clapping and booing the players as they shuffled along the ice.

Those eyes, never once in the stands after I finally made the hockey team.

I knew that look better than I truly knew him.

Disappointment.

And so I wonder what he'd be thinking right now if he saw me standing here, drenched in rainfall, my bones shivering thanks to the cooling night and a lingering fever that just won't relent. My body feels weak and strange, my legs hardly my own. They don't feel like the same legs that carried me to two Stanley Cups.

So, I wonder.

What would he think?

If I don't recognize myself, would he? Would his eyes shift from disappointment to relief that I'm someone... new?

I'm a blank slate he can mold and shape into exactly what he wants. Maybe I can finally become what he's always expected from a son.

Or would he feel smug and self-satisfied that he's been right all along?

My heart thumps with restless pitter-patters in time with the falling rain, and my fingers ball into fists at my sides.

No.

Wishful thinking.

I know exactly what he'd see, and it would only be more disappointment.

A breeze sweeps through the quiet street, causing my teeth to chatter as I remain perched on the sidewalk, hidden by an ebonized sky. The house I face is not a familiar one, but the occupants inside haven't left my mind for a long, lonely month.

And maybe I'm bordering on crazed stalker at this point, delirious on adrenaline and pain medication, as I stare at the quaint blue bungalow with seven steps leading up to a mahogany door.

Maybe I've lost my damn mind.

But when the window fills with warm tungsten, and gilded honey hair floats by, my breath stops. My muscles relax, my fists unclenching. Calm dances along my sweat-slick skin, soothing the residual tremors.

She looks good. Alive and well.

Safe.

Bright, happy—just like that moment I first saw her. Before our worlds collapsed, tumbling us into wreckage and ruins.

Before I changed.

Inherently. Eternally.

Indie bends down to scoop Daisy into her arms, their smiles wide, their hair a matching halo of gold. They parade around the living room, and I think it must be fate that I'm privy to this intimate moment. This sweet dance. The image almost pulls a smile from my lips as I envision this exact scene playing out on a Maui coastline.

Waves crashing, birds singing, a perfectly painted sunset dappling the ocean water in crimson and coral.

I'm there, too. I'm right there with them, basking in our unsullied dream.

But that's all it is—a dream—and if I know anything about dreams, it's that...

They always die.

Daisy slides down from her mother's grip, then prances away from the window, likely bound for her own naïve daydreams and whimsical fairytales. I watch her skip out of sight, the skirt of her nightdress trailing behind her. Indie watches, too, her eyes glimmering with love and affection, and maybe something else.

Yes... definitely something else.

Fear.

And I only know that because I saw it firsthand, shining from those same stunning eyes, as we fought for our lives together, strangers turned kindred soldiers.

What are you scared of, Indigo?

I swallow. My throat feels tight as I drink her in, branding her into my memory. She's all warm ivory light—something I know I'll crave during the cold nights ahead when my demons take over and darkness overwhelms.

Indie paces to the bay window, her hand stalling as she lifts it to the curtain. She pauses, eyes canvassing the unlit street. A small frown furrows, wrinkling her perfect porcelain skin, and I slink back, out of sight, dipping behind an adjacent tree.

Then, the curtains draw tight, and she's gone.

I close my eyes, exhaling slowly. My legs teeter from standing so long after weeks of being dormant. My chest wound pulses as it desperately tries to heal. My mind races with questions and unknowns.

But... I know what I have to do.

My own curtain closes, and I swallow down a deep, calming breath, turning from my place on the sidewalk and taking unsteady steps to the car that's waiting for me.

When I pull open the passenger's side door, I slip into the vehicle, greeted by a cloud of mourning and squeaky windshield wipers. I grit my teeth. "I'm ready." My voice echoes through the small space, filling it with more bleakness.

A sigh breaks through, forcing my attention to the left.

Blake stares over at me with misty eyes. He shakes his head back and forth, his doleful expression illuminated by the single street lamp. “Are you sure?”

“I’m sure.”

There’s no hesitation there. No reconsideration or doubt.

After all, the entire world thinks I’m dead.

Who am I to disappoint?

Chapter Nineteen

Indie

EIGHT MONTHS LATER

March has settled into Seattle, and it's not the balmy, southern kind.

It's a cold, dreary day, with the weather channel predicting a blizzard later this morning as the temperature continues to plummet. Except I'm tired of being cooped up inside, while wet snow has covered the ground all winter, so I'm sitting on a park bench beside Blake, clutching a cup of hot coffee between my gloved palms. The threat of the impending snowstorm is eerily present in the atmosphere this morning, Seattle's constant gray sky more leaden than usual, the air more expectant and crisper. People pass us on the sidewalk, bundled to the max, walking hurriedly to their destinations.

So, maybe we're crazy for attempting this outdoor coffee date, but I was desperate for the reprieve from the constant constriction of four walls.

"It's been a hell of a year," Blake says, settling back onto the park bench with a sigh of contemplation. Nostalgia swept through us like the late winter draft, bringing an assortment of memories to mind and spinning our conversation into one of fond reminiscing. He sticks his hands in the pockets of his long coat, a puff of vapor dancing before him on the wind as he cuts his eyes over to me and grins. "You've come a long way, buttercup."

I snort, burying my smile in the gator around my neck. "You sure know how to build me up," I tease, watching as his shoulders shake with laughter.

Bad joke. Very bad joke.

It's true, I have come a long way... even if it doesn't always feel like it. Daisy has, too. Despite the fact that she still isn't talking, she's happy. Social and smiling.

It's enough for now.

I continue on, deliberately making light of the situation to avoid going too deep. That's how I roll these days: I keep things light—just beneath the surface. "I can finally go out and buy my own milk and tampons, instead of having you and Tameka bring them to me."

Blake shudders. "I'm so glad you're over that."

We share another chuckle before a contented silence stretches between us, during which we watch a few brave toddler moms run herd on their red-cheeked babies at a nearby playground. The stone bench we sit on is damp and cold beneath our blue jeans, a reminder that winter is clinging fiercely, loathe to be gone just yet. Just beside us, though, hope springs in the long red stems and creamy yellow chains of the early blooming stachyurus.

"Daisy has a spring recital coming up," I tell him after a long draw on my latte a few minutes later. "I know she'd love to see you there."

Daisy has come to adore her "Unkie Blake," as he calls himself. What other man would let her paint his toenails and apply lipstick? Blake has been pivotal in our healing process, always making us giggle and showing up at just the right moments.

Daisy even drew a picture of herself on stage with two people standing in the audience. One was me, evident by the yellow hair, and the other was clearly Blake—scribbled onto the paper with his stick-figure arms raised high, shirt bright pink, and his favorite scarf around his neck.

"What's she going to be doing?" Blake perks up in his seat, his eyes brightening at the revelation. "Ooh! Will she wear sequins?"

I can't help the laughter from pouring out of me. "Of course. Purple ones," I confirm, spinning the latte between my fingers. "And get this —she has an actual speaking part in addition to the dancing. Her instructors were so proud of everything she's done in the past few months, they wanted her to do more. It's just one phrase..." I trail off, a sadness seeping in, unwanted. I shouldn't expect a miracle. I shouldn't allow myself to hope that my little girl will utter those four words on stage, breaking her eight long months of silence.

But the hope is strong.

"What is it?" Blake cuts into my fretful thoughts, his hand landing on my knuckles, hovering gently. "What's the phrase?"

"And so they loved," I murmur.

His fingers flex on mine as he ducks his head. "Damn."

"Yeah."

"Indie—"

I shake my head at him, averting my eyes. "Don't."

He removes his hand and settles back against the bench, going quiet once again. The nascent feelings I had for Dax are no secret between us. After our first reunion outside my house all those months ago, Blake became a fixture in my and Daisy's lives. He began joining Tameka and me for our Saturday night wine and whines, and when I was ready to step outside the front door of my house, he was there to walk beside me... all the way to the car and back again.

But the one thing we don't discuss, aside from one drunk Saturday night when I poured my heart out to him and Tameka, is Dax.

After that tequila-infused conversation, the one where I started blubbering about our fated connection, our severed potential—"There was something, I know there was something there. If only we'd had time to really explore it, to figure out what it was, whether we could have been something together, or if we would have fizzled. He was my what-if. He was my freaking green light, you know. Like in Gatsby. All those hopes and dreams, just across the way..."

We didn't talk about Dax again.

I woke with my face pressed into Tameka's hip and Blake wound around me like an octopus, my head banging with liquor regret, my tongue fuzzy with word regret, and my mouth as dry as the turkey Mom ruined seven Thanksgivings ago. I extricated myself carefully, groaning at the movement, and when Blake peered up at me and opened his mouth, all it took was a hissed, "Not one word" to establish the fate of Dax in any future conversation.

Dead.

The topic was as dead as he was.

"So." Blake attempts a new direction after a few quiet minutes, though, not necessarily a better direction. "How did that guy work out? The one you were talking to online with the long, shiny hair and the tattoo of his Tibetan Mastiff?"

I stifle a snicker, then grimace. "It didn't."

At Blake's urging, I'd finally taken the plunge into online dating and set up a profile on a popular website. It had been a dizzying, overwhelming experience from hour one. The men who'd swiped, commented, tagged, messaged... it made my head spin and my heart ache to even consider them. I've never dated much, save for a few blips pre-Jeremy. I was young and foolish then, and all I cared about was what movie we were going to see, or how cool their car was.

Now I need to consider their co-parenting abilities. Their credit score. Their love language and Enneagram.

The whole process has been daunting.

I had finally settled on one guy to focus on, and we had "talked" for a solid month before agreeing to meet at a local coffee shop. Something easy and harmless—no pressure.

Only, I bailed at the last minute.

Sighing into my coffee cup, I close my eyes now, thinking back on my moment of panic. I had stood in front of my grandmother's full-length mirror, eyeing my reflection and considering my outfit: a loose sweater dress that hit at the knees, a pair of tall boots with a scant heel, and my hair pulled back in a loose pony. It sent all the right messages—pretty and subtly sexy, but nothing overt. I felt good.

And yet, I felt all wrong. I didn't want to be pretty for this man, this stranger. I didn't want to be pretty for anybody, except maybe my little girl.

A frown creases the space between his eyes, and Blake questions my response with cautious confusion. "What do you mean?"

"I mean... I didn't meet him." I watch as my friend narrows his gaze at me, and I continue, trying not to sound defensive. "It just didn't feel right, you know? We weren't vibing."

"All you were doing was chatting online. Don't you have to actually meet to know if you vibe?" he asks wryly, eyes still slanted as he tries to read between the lines.

I cross my arms. "I had to explain all of my jokes." Shifting on the bench, I add, "Twice."

"In his defense, you are not a very good teller-of-jokes."

Rude.

I force back a grin, pouting instead. "Okay, that's enough abuse for one day, thank you very much," I tell him, the toe of my boot kicking at the dead grass below me. "He just wasn't pushing my buttons. I didn't see a reason to let it go any further."

Blake shakes his head and prisses his mouth, the picture of disapproval. "Dax won't like—" He stalls.

"What?"

"What?" The color drains from Blake's face, and he shifts focus across the park, pointing randomly. "I require your opinion on that diaper bag. It looks like a Prada, but I didn't think they made diaper bags."

"Blake, since when do you give a rat's ass about diaper bags? What did you just say?"

"Hmm?"

Frustration weaves with awareness—a strange feeling that causes my skin to break out into goosebumps. And not from the cold. "About Dax."

"Nothing. I didn't." Blake chuckles, letting out an awkward huff under his breath, then redirects his attention the other side of the park again. "Whoa, what's that? Look over there."

"What?" I say again.

"Is that a hamster?"

Blinking, I shake my head, gaze searching the park and only coming up with squirrels and dogs on harnesses. "What the hell are you talking about?"

"A chipmunk. It's just a chipmunk. Hey, I gotta go, I've got a car full of groceries for..." He falters again, swallowing hard, his eyes widening comically. "For my mom."

"I thought your mom lived in Nevada."

"My other mom." He stands quickly, blowing me a kiss. "Same time next week, buttercup!"

"Huh?"

I've never been more confused.

I watch him stumble away with a flustered little wave, bumping into a passerby as he backs up, apologizing with animated arms.

What was that?

Suspicion blooms, tendrils spreading like southern kudzu through the memories of every conversation we've ever had. A thought strikes me, pinching my gut.

I never saw his grave.

Dax's grave.

I was too chicken at the time to attend something so final, so terminating, so I didn't even ask about a service. Was there one?

A vigil, or a funeral?

Was his... body ever recovered?

I almost choke on the thought, then realize I would have heard if they'd located his body. Dax was a celebrity, a public figure. A discovery like that would have been all over the news and social media platforms.

God, is there something I don't know?

No.

I shake my head at the mere thought, at the notion that Dax is alive and well out there, hiding from the world. Hiding from... me.

That's crazy.

And yet, I'm distracted as I sit frozen to the park bench, my heart thrumming inside my chest, my mind racing with fantastical scenarios. I'm distracted as I cling to the coffee cup so hard, the cap pops off and warm liquid splashes my thighs. I'm distracted as I watch Blake walk swiftly down the opposite side of the street to a nearby parking garage, disappearing from my view.

And then… I'm not distracted anymore.

I'm determined.

My own car sits streetside, calling to me. Beckoning me. I climb behind the wheel and wait, heart still beating wildly, my eyes trained on the exit of the parking garage.

Blake pulls out a few moments later, checking once, twice—six freaking times—before finally turning out into traffic.

Jesus, Blake. You drive like a grandma.

Heaving in a deep breath, I pull out after him, plucking my sunglasses from the cupholder and settling them on my face for extra camouflage.

I won't rest until I know for sure there's nothing there. Not until I know that Blake's use of the present tense was nothing more than an honest mistake, some weird wishful-thinking slip of the tongue.

Not until I know for sure that the man who haunts me is a dead man.

Chapter Twenty

Dax

WEAK EARLY MORNING SUNLIGHT breaks through the tall trees, a welcome antidote to my foul mood. The corded muscles in my arms stretch and pull with every lift and thwack of the ax as the pieces of birchwood split in half.

I run the back of my arm along my forehead, perspiration dotting my skin. It's a brisk thirty-two degrees out here on my mountain, but I've been working since before the first hint of daybreak crested the horizon. There was something in the air when I woke this morning that hinted at a departure from spring's tease. A late season snow shower, maybe. So I'd rushed coffee and skipped breakfast in favor of work.

I'm always working. Learning. Exhausting myself with chores and general busyness to keep my mind from drifting away to another life—a life that's long gone, sealed up tight.

Buried.

I've learned a lot over the last eight months after deciding to disappear into the Oregon wilderness with little knowledge of how to survive or live off the land.

I've learned that dying is easy.

Staying dead is much harder.

My stubborn ego has kept me focused and determined to make it out here on my own, only accepting the occasional grocery haul from Blake. The truth is, I'm pretty terrible at hunting and catching my own food—and not because I'm incapable of learning.

It's because they all remind me of Skittles.

Skittles, the rabbit Blake named, who I somehow managed to capture that first week after days of unsuccessful attempts at finding worthy meals. I survived off of roots, wild greens, shoots, and flowers until I discovered fresh berry bushes to keep my hunger tamed before I eventually learned how to catch fish in the nearby river.

But I tried to hunt. I tried to kill and skin.

Only, Skittles was really goddamn cute when I caught her. Fluffy and soft. She felt like a small comfort as she squirmed between my hands, her tiny heart beating out of control, a desperate pardon. I'd been clumsy and inept at the time, still healing from my brush with death, and I think the fight for food had weakened my resolve.

Instead of sealing her fate with the edge of my blade, I brought her inside my cabin and claimed her as a pet, while quickly shutting down the idea of ever slaughtering my own meat with my bare hands. Now it's mostly tart berries and fish, as well as Blake's impromptu visits with giant paper bags from Whole Foods.

I inhale a deep, crisp breath, glancing skyward. I'm bathed in watery sunlight as dawn struggles to kiss the treetops through a gray cloud canopy, and I toss my ax to the earth beside my feet, finished with my wood-cutting for the time being. A snowstorm is absolutely on the way, and I need to get the fire going.

Running a hand over my overgrown bristles, I stretch my arms with a sigh... and that's when I hear the telltale sign of car tires rolling down the long dirt road.

Shit.

No one has ever bothered me out here, tucked away from civilization in the deep forest of Mount Rainier, right at the edge of the park—well, aside from the occasional black bears. It's my personal sanctuary, the only spot I can trust my secret to remain safe. Only Blake is privy to the truth.

Eight months ago, after licking my wounds on Blake's couch for two tortured weeks, I made the decision to disappear. Run. Escape from the spotlight, questions, news reports, and droves of fangirls who would inevitably follow my every move. There's no Twitter out here in nature's palm. No aesthetically appealing Instagram feeds or constant TMZ articles breaking apart my life and stealing a little bit of my soul with each classless word. There are no cameras. No responsibility.

Unfortunately, there's no forgetting either... but I'll take what I can get.

This old cabin has been in my family for years, left to me by my grandfather after he passed away seven years ago. I'd only visited once since acquiring the little slice of seclusion, having been too busy with my career. But that one visit called to me. It followed me around, beckoning my return.

Whispering to my yearning for a simpler life.

Things seemed to fall into place during those two weeks, rooted to Blake's neon orange couch, staring at his assortment of colorful, quirky canvases lining the walls. Everything made sense. The pieces fit. And even though Blake could never understand my desire to fully retreat, to remain a ghost, it all felt… right.

And so, I haunt.

I haunt these woods and knowing skies.

I haunt the streams and slow-dancing trees.

I haunt myself.

Squinting my gaze toward the expanse of dirt road, I breathe in a sigh of relief when Blake's shiny red Miata comes into focus with the license plate 'MEOWTA.' Sunlight gleams off the windshield as he closes in on the cabin, driving exceptionally slow to avoid rocks and stones from denting the frame.

It's early, but Blake is always up early. I know this because I was woken up at four A.M. every morning for two weeks by his enthusiastic shower singing of Rick Astley's Never Gonna Give You Up. The only time this wasn't the case was when he'd belt out Britney Spears instead. Then, he'd whistle as he made breakfast in the adjacent kitchen, destroying any hope I had of falling back to sleep by blasting the smoothie blender, while his two miniature poodles clicked their pink-painted toenails across the walnut flooring, eager for their taste of avocado toast.

I love Blake.

I could never, ever cohabitate with Blake.

"Good morning, big man!" he shouts from the half-opened window, his sunglasses hiding his smiling eyes. "I brought you more food. There were sales, and I love sales."

The car comes to a stop a few feet away, and I massage the base of my neck, my tanned skin glinting with sweat beneath the diffuse light. "Morning," I reply, far less chipper.

Blake hops out, pushing his sunglasses up over his head and eyeing me from toes to top. His lips purse. "Starting the day off bare-chested and brooding, I see."

"I'm not brooding."

"Hey, I'm not complaining. The lumberjack look kind of suits you."

I scratch at my beard. "You came all this way to drop off food? You know I'm capable."

"I know that's what you tell yourself," he sing-songs, skipping around to the passenger's side and scooping two bags into his arms. "The proof is sitting in your living room, nibbling on those little crunch sticks. Your dinner is called Skittles, Dax."

"Once you named her, I couldn't eat her."

"That's why I've got your back." He breezes past me, scarf tails trailing behind him. "I picked up tons of gluten-free pastas, Italian sauces from the farmer's market, grass-fed beef, and your very favorite: chicken pot pies. Plus, a few other goodies, including beard oil."

Blinking at his retreating back from the edge of the lawn, my legs sprint into action. "What the hell?"

"The pies are organic, don't worry."

"The beard oil, Blake." I follow him into the unadorned cabin, trailing his heels. "Why?"

The bags meet my tabletop with a clatter, prompting Skittles to stomp her feet from the wire cage Blake gave me. My friend sends me a quick look over his shoulder. "Why? Because you have a beard, Dax. Just because you're Grizzly Adams now, doesn't mean you should let yourself go." Blake swipes groceries out of the bags, setting them onto my kitchen table. "Besides, it was one of those sponsored ad thingies on Instagram. They're really catchy these days. It sucked me right in."

I watch him from a foot away, hands planted on my hips, eyebrows arching to my hairline. His chirpy humming noises disable my bitter retort, and I try to melt a little. I know Blake cares. I know he's trying to help, trying to keep a tether between me and mainstream society, but he's missing the point. I don't want any of that. I don't want politic updates or celebrity gossip, and I don't want beard oil.

Running a palm down my face, I step forward. I come up beside him in front of the wood table I made myself after finally getting sick of eating my fish on the dusty floors. The old cabin had been mostly furnished, but for some reason had been missing the old family-style dining table I remembered from my youth. One of the cousins had probably stolen it.

My eyes case Blake now, taking in how happy he looks from his peach-colored polo to his unyielding grin. Old memories wash over me, and for a striking moment, I miss those days. Our inside jokes and easy banter. Our lunch dates and team events. Our unique friendship that isn't quite the same anymore, no matter how hard he tries.

Everything changed that day at Edgewater.

I changed.

She springs to my mind right then, and the words escape before I can catch them. "How is she?"

Blake falters, his light brown eyes dancing up to me. "You're welcome to ask her yourself."

"You know I can't do that." My jaw tics, teeth grinding. "Don't act like this is just a phase or an early midlife crisis. I chose this, Blake. Indefinitely."

He flinches. "Aren't you... lonely?"

I try not to let him see my honest reply.

Yes.

I'm lonely. Bored. Emotionally stunted. Sexually frustrated.

But there's magic out here, too. There's peace in these deep woods. In the woodland critters and quiet nights. In the bonfires, the earthy breezes, and the sky full of stars that looks infinitely closer from where I stand.

This is home now.

My head shakes side to side as I swallow through my response. "No."

"You're a terrible liar, Dax," Blake groans, returning his attention to the grocery haul. "Better than me, definitely, but still pretty bad."

I press my palms to the table and lean forward, exhaling slowly.

After a few seconds pass by, Blake finally answers my original question. "She's doing good. Better."

Glancing up, our gazes meet. "Better?"

"She's getting out of the house more. Our coffee dates really helped with that. Daisy still isn't talking, but she has this recital coming up, with sequins, and..." He notices the strain on my face and clears his throat. "They're strong, you know? Fighters. Indie's job is going well, and I think—"

"Is she seeing anybody?"

Something in my heart stutters, the air in my lungs swelling and thick.

Why the hell does that matter?

"Sorry, I don't know why I asked that." I look away, avoiding Blake's curious stare. "It's irrelevant."

He taps his fingers along the lid of one of the pasta sauce jars. "It's not if you cared enough to ask."

"I don't. I just... want to make sure she's safe. She's been through a lot."

"Or you want to mentally murder the guy who's keeping her bed warm because you're not there to do it yourself."

My defenses flare, only quelling when a strange feeling of anxiety replaces them. "Wait, so there is a guy? She's dating someone?"

"I thought it was irrelevant."

"Blake," I warn, hackles rising.

Choler heats my blood, and I don't know why. I have no business caring about who Indie sleeps with—no right. We were never together, and as far as she's concerned, I'm dead. We shared a single kiss and a few fear-based promises, but that's where it ended.

We ended there, amidst gunfire and bloodshed.

It was far from a beginning.

Blake clicks his tongue, sighing what sounds like submission. Twirling around, he leans back against the edge of the table and crosses his arms. "She's single, okay? The poor thing can hardly step out her front door, let alone hop into the dating scene. She's all yours if you want her."

"That's not going to happen."

I spit the words out low and deep. Quickly—before any fanciful illusions can dilute my rational thought.

"Okay, okay, jeez," Blake mutters. "All I'm saying is, it's only been eight months. Not eight years. Not twenty. It's not too late to change your mind and go back—"

"Will you stop? I'm not going back." The bitter edge in my tone causes us both to wince. "It is too late. It was too late the moment those bank doors busted open."

Heavy silence infiltrates us.

I feel like an asshole.

Straightening with a quick cough, I scratch at the back of my head, mussing my mop of untamed hair. Blake's gaze darts away as he busies himself with the array of pasta boxes, lining them up in a row. "Look, I'm sorry," I backpedal. "I just—"

"No worries, big man." Blake slaps on a bright smile, then pats my shoulder as he folds the empty bags. "I'll get out of your hair now. Your... considerably longer, oddly attractive hair."

I let out a huff-veiled laugh.

He reaches over to ruffle said hair, but I shoe his arm away, my grin widening.

"Okay, I'm outta here," Blake says, stepping back from the table. "I've got a client call at ten. Enjoy the goodies, my friend. There are some little bunny delicacies for Skittles, too."

My eyes cut to the assortment of food, noting a few packages of organic hemp treats. The image warms me, despite my frosty disposition.

Damn you, Blake. Just let me freeze here.

Before he disappears from the cabin, I stop him, calling out, "Hey."

Spinning on his shiny shoes, he greets me with a smile.

I swallow, glancing down at my feet. "I hope you know, I do..."

"Yeah?"

"I, um..." The words hover on the tip of my tongue, but I can't spit them out. "I do appreciate you coming by."

His smile falters, just slightly, before he sends me a little wave and shuffles out the front door.

My shoulders deflate, my heart sinking.

I miss you.

I miss my best friend.

But I don't say it, I don't confess, because...

Clearly, it's not enough.

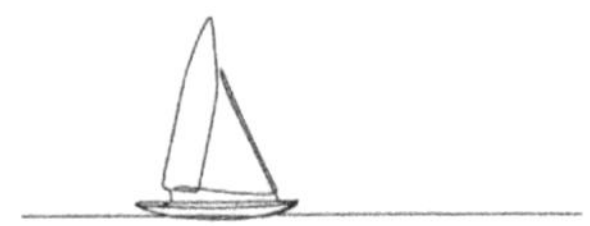

Skittles takes up residence in my lap a little while later as I stare blankly at the table still bestrewn with Blake's collection of food items. I know I should get the pot pies in the freezer. I know I should put everything away, but there's a weight inside me, holding me down.

I carry a lot of weights.

The rabbit hums and vibrates atop my thighs, signaling her contentment. I'm envious of it. I can't quite remember what it feels like to feel so... at peace.

Leaning back with a hard sigh, my eyes transfix to the small bookshelf across from me, stocked full of my grandfather's favorite novels.

One, in particular, stands out.

The Great Gatsby.

I haven't read it yet. Eight months out here, all alone, and I've never once picked it up off that shelf. I've never dusted it off and grazed my fingers along the spine, or inhaled the musty pages. Despite the fact that it was the first thing I'd planned to do after escaping from that bank, from that old, rotting house... I never have.

And maybe that's because I never really escaped.

I'm just hiding.

Indie floats through my mind then, a golden goddess, sweet and bright. My eyes close as I try to envision the curve of her jaw and the softness of her hair. Her image is foggy now, overshadowed by things far more gruesome. Nightmares. But I cling to her out here in the vast wilderness—Daisy, too. My brave little lion.

Blake said they're doing better. Not good, but better.

I suppose there is solace to be found in that, yet I can't help but hope for more. I'm better, too. I'm not taped to a grotty mattress with infection coursing through my bloodstream, waiting for death to finally claim me. That's... better.

But I'm not good, I'm not okay, and there's a difference.

Tap, tap, tap.

Skittles darts off my lap at record speed when a soft knock punctures my dreary haze.

A knock. At my front door.

I can't help the amused smile that stretches when I wonder what Blake forgot. More groceries. Comical stories. Updates on his love-hate relationship with Casey.

Pulling myself to my feet, I traipse to the front of the quaint cabin, the floorboards squeaking beneath my footfalls. I don't even hesitate as I reach for the brass nob, pulling it open in swift swoop. "Let me guess, you—"

My words are cut short.

Frozen to the back of my throat.

Suspended in time.

I can't even muster a breath as my heart short-circuits inside my chest, my sights fixating on what must be a mirage standing on my front stoop.

She's not real. She's only a dream angel.

Indie's eyes widen, spearing me with blue bewilderment. A little sound escapes her trembling, parted lips. It's a gasp. A strangled gasp. She cups one hand over her mouth, inching backwards and almost stumbling. Those eyes blink back at me, glowing bright with wild disbelief. She looks like she's staring at a ghost.

That's because she is.

Her chest heaves with panicked breaths, another sound breaking free. It's still a gasp, a purge of utter confoundment, but it's laced with something else. A single word.

My name.
"Dax."

Chapter Twenty-One

Indie

FROM WHERE I HAD pulled off and parked behind a copse of trees, I watch with sweaty palms as Blake enters the driveway of a small, rustic-styled cabin tucked back in the woods, pulling behind the property. A sun dulled by heavy clouds and newly spitting snow manages to peek through the lacery of tree branches reaching skyward, still mostly naked in their late winter dresses. A pair of squirrels chase each other through the crackle of brown leaves that covers the forest floor, already beginning to attract a thin layer of snow. They stop and peer curiously my way, wondering, no doubt, what I'm doing there. I'm a stranger. Uninvited. Unexpected.

I'm wondering the same thing, and look nervously heavenward.

This is dumb. The weather report I listened to on the way said to expect snow for the next two days, and the weight of it is anticipatory in the atmosphere. It's headed our way. Maybe I should just leave. There's nothing here for me, anyway.

Maybe this is Blake's mother's cabin.

His other mother?

Stepmom, maybe.

It's possible.

My finger is on the ignition button when Blake's car reverses in the gravel driveway ten minutes later, causing me to hesitate and ponder my next move. Rather than press it, I step out of my car and hover, waiting for him to leave. Truth hammers in the flow of blood through my veins and I want to vomit.

I know, I think I know, before I take the first step leading toward the small porch, what I'll find when that door opens.

God, it can't be true.

Can it?

Part of me doesn't want that door to open. Part of me wants to remain in this stultifying land I've dwelled within for the better part of the past year, this landscape of tonal apathy and neutral feelings.

But that would be too easy. I need to know the truth. Ever since Blake's slip in the park, followed by his bungling coverup, everything's been out of sync. Unraveling. Everything I've worked so hard to reorder, to reorganize… it's falling apart, right in front of me. And Blake has been central to this collapse. The traitor.

My heart is numb with a flush of emotion I can't take time to identify at the moment. I only know that it's a dizzying range of feeling that makes no sense when sealed together.

Fury.

Hurt.

Helpless hope.

I have to reorder my world. I have to make this right.

So, I march through the veil of trees until I reach the stony walkway, only stopping when I'm perched on the front stoop.

This is it.

Lifting my hand, I knock.

The footsteps that supersede the tapping of my knuckles thump in time with my racing heart, and then the door whips open, rendering me speechless.

"Let me guess, you—"

His words fall off, just as my heart falls to the bottom of my stomach.

Even though I had a feeling, even though some part of me fucking knew… I still manage to be sucker-punched when that door swings open and he's standing before me, flesh and bone, inky skin and shaggy hair, eyes wide—brown and blue.

I feel my mouth open and work, the words catching for a second before his name rasps out like sandpaper against wood. "Dax."

His expression, in that microscopic span of seconds while he's caught off guard, runs a gamut of emotions he can't hide. Despair. Guilt. Elation. "Indigo…"

An electrical charge hangs heavy between us, laced with confusion, with disbelief, and I have no idea what to say.

Dax has no idea what to say.

But just as swiftly as that door flew open, a mask descends over him, and all I see is a stranger. He's slightly scruffy now, his hair longer, his body a bit leaner, but overall familiar in form. There's something strange in essence, though. An aloofness. An isolation.

I falter, confused.

His voice grumbles in his throat, and he clears it before continuing, his tone turning oddly formal. "Indie," he corrects. "I, uh… wasn't expecting you."

"No, I don't suppose you were." My words are a rough whisper, gritty with emotion.

Dax doesn't reply. He simply stands before me in living, breathing color, his chest bare and gleaming with sweat as if he's been doing something manly. The faint scent of green wood and a neat stack of firewood on the porch hint at what that might be, and I'm seized by the sudden desire to see him in action, witness the pull and flex of each muscle as he hefts the ax and lets it fall. I want to observe his movements, his strength.

His lifeforce.

Clenching my jaw, I push away the thoughts.

What is wrong with me?

Dax lied to me. He lied to the world, to all the people who watched him play hockey and adored him. To his family and friends.

He's a liar.

I push my shoulders back and stand straighter. Between us zips lightning, but it's not the same spark that I felt in the bank, the one born of fear and kismet tangled irrevocably together. This lightning is anger.

I draw on it, feeding strength to my voice. "So, that's it?" I press, swallowing down the remnants of my hope. My relief. "You didn't expect to see me."

At his side, his hand clenches and unclenches. I wouldn't have noticed if I hadn't been watching him so intently, soaking in every slight change that's manifested since the couple of hours I spent in his presence at a bank months past.

Dax dips his eyes to the cement beneath my feet, then sweeps them back up, drinking me in. "You look well," he finally offers, his tone stilted.

"I look well," I parrot, scoffing out a laugh and turning to look out over the small patch of cleared yard around the house. "Well, I guess that's all I need to know. I'm glad to see you're so… healthy, Dax. Being alive suits you." I loathe the catch in my voice, the evidence of my rising emotions.

"Indie, listen—"

I manage to turn around without falling, noting that there are five steps to the ground, and I eye them with vicious certitude. I will take each one without wavering. "You know, if you didn't want to take Daisy and me to Hawaii, all you had to do was say so."

Step one.

"Indigo—"

Step two.

"Spare me, Dax. Please."

His eyes flash with wounded surprise, taken aback by the hostility in my tone. "Let me explain."

Step three.

"I think you've had sufficient time for that. What has it been… ? Eight months?" I grit out through clenched teeth. "Just… go back to your wood chopping, or whatever it was you were doing. I was never even here."

Dax sighs wearily, glancing upward, the breath leaving him in a plume of frigid smoke. "I didn't think it was a good idea. To tell you the truth."

I look down at my feet, which remain stubbornly still on the second step from the bottom. I didn't think my heart could hurt like this again. I thought I had broken that part of it, and I was done.

Move, Indie. Two more steps.

"Let me make you some breakfast," he tries. "I'll explain as much as I can."

On the railing, my fingers tighten. I want to leave, march away without a backward look. On the other hand, though, I want to know why he's here, scruffy and half-naked, chopping fuel like a mountain man when I'm reasonably sure he's fairly well-off. I want to know why he said the things he did, made me feel the way I did, and then abandoned me.

Because that's how I feel—abandoned.

Betrayed.

I lift my chin with defiance, yet my shoulders deflate with submission. "Fine," I relent, the word a mere breath. "Ten minutes."

Without making eye contact, I climb the three steps and brush past him on my way inside the cabin, ignoring the heat that pours off him in waves in favor of looking around. His hideout is small and quaint, with rag rugs scattered over a scarred wooden floor and comfortable furniture framed in heavy lines, softened with broken-in cushions patterned with duck and deer. It's a single room broken into different regions, a kitchenette, living room, and space for sleeping separated only by the barest excuse of a wall.

One wall is covered with framed photos in black and white, and as Dax moves into the kitchen, I wander over to it, shoving my hands down deep in my pockets as I study the images. They're mostly of men, some in waders, strings of fish held proudly up for posterity. An elderly man I recognize from one photo to another, one a bit younger with wire frame spectacles and an austere, haughty appearance.

Dax.

As a gangly teenager, different but recognizable still, those unusual eyes still noticeable in variant shades of black and white.

I feel his presence as he comes to stand beside me. "This is my grandfather's hunting cabin. My father was never into the nature scene, so Grandad left it to me when he passed," Dax explains quietly, his shoulder just grazing mine.

Turning, I tilt my head to look up at him. Is it my imagination, or is he standing too close intentionally? It's making it difficult to draw in a breath without smelling that sweaty-clean scent of him. "So... you needed to get away and think?" I force myself to keep my voice even and impassive, the opposite of the emotions roiling through me. "For eight months."

"It's complicated."

He takes a step to the side, and I can almost breathe again, except he's still too close. I tell him that, just not in those words. "The eggs are burning," I murmur, my gaze fixed on the wall of frames. Then I spare him a glance, hoping I'm covering up the tears brimming in my eyes with the firm set of my jaw. "Nine minutes."

Dax sighs, something like frustration and apology and guilt all rolled into a single sound. He wants to say more, I see it on his face, but the eggs are burning, so he backs away, rounding the corner into the kitchen.

Closing my eyes, I don't allow the tears to fall as I compose myself, hesitating another moment before following Dax into the kitchen. I seat myself at the tiny table in the kitchenette, watching as he works to dish up breakfast, glancing at me over his shoulder in between tasks. We both remain silent until he's sitting across from me, our knees flirting beneath the surface of the small table, and I self-consciously pull mine to the side.

The simple meal placed before me is made up of sliced tomatoes, fried eggs, and Canadian bacon, and I find myself I'm hungry for the food and for answers. I pick up my fork and slice into the egg, letting the yolk run before speaking. "Tell me what happened to you." My eyes skate to his, and he pauses mid-chew. "Make me understand."

Dax looks back down at his plate, speaking in between bites, his voice trying to remain monotone. "I was shot."

My fork clanks against the plate when he doesn't elaborate. "Thanks, Dax. I remember."

"Sorry, I..." He keep his eyes trained downward, smashing the eggs with the tines of his fork. Following a long breath, he finally continues. "Garrett, one of the brothers, saw me as a back-up plan and abducted me. He kept me alive with the goal of having Blake bring him a collector's card I had stored in a—"

I can't help a sound from escaping at his mention of Blake.

I knew he had known this whole time, from the moment I saw him pull out of Dax's driveway. This wasn't a recent discovery. I knew that he had lied to me for the past eight months, but Dax's casual mention of his duplicity winds me up again.

Dax looks up sharply at the sound of my gasp. "Don't be angry with Blake. He was doing what I asked him to do."

I wipe my mouth, leaning back in the chair and giving myself a moment. There's something... off with the way Dax is acting. Not that I knew him long, but I don't remember this coolness. It was all warmth and concern. "Did you ask him to be my friend?" I question, needing the truth. The whole truth. "Did you ask him to become my emotional support animal? To become indispensable to me on so many levels I couldn't begin to identify them?"

His head is shaking before I finish. "I asked him to keep an eye on you and make sure you were doing okay. You and Daisy," Dax insists, pushing his plate aside. "If you became friends, it's because you were meant to be friends."

I eye him warily.

"Believe it or not, Indie, I've thought about you every single day since that bullet entered my chest."

My heart stutters. I watch the different emotions play across Dax's face, and at first there's truth. There's raw confession shining back at me, only snuffed out when the silence stretches on too long. He puts the mask back on, his features hardening, then reaches for his plate and stabs at the eggs.

Sucking in a rattled breath, I nod. "Right, okay," I reply softly. "So, Garrett kidnapped and kept you alive."

Chewing, he responds in that unemotional voice I'm beginning to loathe. "Barely, but yes. Eventually, I got away and came here. I needed... space. I needed time to process everything, figure out what I really wanted out of life." Beneath the words, something simmers. His eyes gleam with things I don't understand—untold stories. Horror stories. "It seemed like a good idea to get away from all the media, the people, the attention."

"Okay," I nod slowly, drinking in what he's telling me. "I get that, I do. There were times I wanted nothing more than to disappear. But why did you feel like you needed to keep this a secret from me?"

He doesn't reply for a long minute, and when he does, it's after a sigh.

Another unambiguous sigh.

This one holds regret, and I think I know what he's going to say before he even says it. "I may have said a few things at the bank that I shouldn't have said. I was just trying—"

"You mean when you invited Daisy and me to Hawaii, and then you kissed me?"

Penitence creeps into his gaze. Dax fixes his eyes on me, this time holding firm. "We were both in a state of heightened emotion. I needed to keep your head in the game, keep us both from panicking —"

"Let me guess," I interrupt. "It seemed like a good idea at the time."

"It was a good idea. Indie, you were this-close to completely losing it."

"So, you fed me fairytales." I swallow down the hurt, hating that it hurts. He's right, in a way—it did help. It filled me with hope. Something to look forward to.

Except... I never stopped hoping.

Rising from the wooden chair, I walk to the window and stare sightlessly out, dimly registering that the snow has thickened, moving from threat to certainty. I hug myself against a chill. How did I get to a place where I allowed myself moon over a man who wasn't feeling the same things I was feeling? Sure, I thought he was dead, but I also thought he felt the same way before his supposed demise.

I rub my arms, trying to erase the goosebumps.

"Indie?"

Squeezing my eyes shut, I speak with my back to him. "I can admit when I'm wrong, Dax, and I know I was a wreck that day. What you did helped." He makes a small noise that I speak over, finally turning and opening my eyes, so I can see his face. "It did. It might make me pathetic, but it's fine."

"You're not pathetic. That's not what I meant."

I keep talking. "You may have said those things because you wanted to hold me together... but you and I both know that's not all it was." I capture his eyes with mine, holding that unique brown and blue gaze prisoner. "I felt it. I felt it in your words, in your kiss."

A muscle in his jaw tics as he stares at me, wordlessly.

I walk to the couch and pick up the jacket I discarded earlier, shrugging it on. "You need to stop lying to yourself and everyone around you. Be honest about what you're doing here, and get back out there, into the world again." Flipping my hair out of my jacket collar, I finish, "Get back to the man you were, Dax. The man I saw in that bank."

Dax frowns, hesitating, then stalks closer to me. "You know nothing about me."

With a sharp intake of breath, I square my shoulders. "Maybe. I know the man you showed me during two of the most naked hours I've ever spent with another human being, though. That has to mean something."

"Does it?" He moves in further, his shell hardening even more. "I was terrified, just like you. I wasn't myself."

"Keep telling yourself that."

His nostrils flare as he bends down, our faces inches apart. "You have no idea what I've been through, Indigo. None."

"Tell me, then." I stand firm, resolute. "Enlighten me."

"You wouldn't understand."

His words slice and slash, prompting heat to climb my neck. They feel like an insult—a slight to my intelligence. "Right," I say, an indignant whisper, my fingers curling into my palms. "I wouldn't understand. Just like I didn't understand that your invitation to Hawaii was a grand fabrication, and your kiss was nothing but a lie."

"No, that's not—"

"Time's up, Dax. Maybe I'll see you around."

Stepping away from him, I lift my hood and move angrily to the door. I fling it open, gasping when a gale of wind and snow gusts against me.

"Shit." Dax storms up behind me, reaching for my elbow. "Indie, you can't leave in this mess."

I shrug him loose and step out onto the porch, but my dramatic exit is halted by Dax grabbing my hand and tugging me back inside the cabin.

"It's not safe."

"Let me go—"

He kicks the door shut, pulling me against his chest. "I can't."

Then his face is blotting out the light as it descends, and his mouth is blotting out all sense as it lands with uncompromising demand against mine. My eyes close with no direction from my brain, my lips part, and that small, shriveled part of my soul unfurls and whispers against his tongue.

Yes.

Chapter Twenty-Two

Dax

YES.

Her mouth is the warm bliss I didn't know I was missing for the past eight months. It's the memory of a forgotten life.

It's a spark.

And for a beautiful, aching moment... I can feel.

It wasn't even that long ago that I felt so much—loss, fear, betrayal, regret, hope. But chaos seeped inside me, poisoned me, ruined me. I'm not the same man she met inside that bank. I'm just a tainted copy.

But I feel something when her lips press to mine, and I want more of it.

I fucking crave it.

Renewal threatens to puncture the hard walls I've been painstakingly assembling as I swallow her gasp and take her face between my palms. I push it aside. I funnel that nostalgic warmth into white-hot anger and come at her with teeth and claws instead. My fingers leave little bruises on her cheekbones. I nip at her bottom lip, tugging it with a deep growl.

Indie's back arches against me as her squeak of surprise, her mewl of pain, sends a rush of electricity straight to my groin. She pulls away with a sharp breath. "Dax... we shouldn't."

"Why not?" I don't wait for her response and yank her right back, until she's flush against my torso. "Don't overthink this."

Her face twists up and our mouths crash together once more, our hums of pleasure a symphony. She's lulling waves of deep blue, a contradiction to my turbulent waters. My tongue pushes past her lips, dipping inside to taste her salt and sweetness, desperate to cling to this temporary release.

Spinning her around, my hands slide downward until I'm fisting the hem of her sandy-toned blouse. Indie's back slams against the wood planks of my cabin wall, and I pull the blouse up over her head in a quick swoop. She falters. "Wait, Dax... please."

My forehead falls to hers, a long sigh escaping. "Okay."

"Okay."

Her breathy reply kisses my mouth, and my eyes lift. Emerald and indigo swim together as one, drenching me in clarity.

I want this.

She wants this.

Our bodies continue to mold and press, despite her words of wavering. Her fingers climb up the planks of my abdomen, dancing along the skin until she drags her nails back down. A groan escapes as my pelvis thrusts into hers, my hands coiling around her slim waist and gripping with a fierce need to claim.

Fuck.

I want. She wants.

We take.

Indie inches up on her toes, palming the nape of my neck until our mouths collide once again. My tongue possesses hers with urgency as I reach for any part of her I can grasp. Her hips, her breasts, her hair. Indie's leg lifts, curling around my upper thigh as her fingernails pierce the base of my skull. Whimpers mingle with a sharp cry when I tug on her golden mane of hair, forcing her head to the side so I can taste her deeper. I only pull back to breathe her name. "Goddamn, Indigo..." I grit out, stealing her back, eager to recapture the heat.

Then it's belts, buttons, and bra clasps. Indie shoves my blue jeans from my hips while I unhook her navy lace bra and discard it, dropping to the heap of clothing. Her own jeans follow, until we're nearly bare before each other, her frame steadied by my cedar wall, my arms planted on either side of her, caging her in. I dip my chin to my chest, gazing down at her trembling hands as she teases the waistline of my boxers.

Swallowing, I clench my jaw, breathing heavy. "You okay?"

"I..." Indie finds my eyes, her words hitching as she licks her lips. "I've never made love to a ghost before."

The air feels charged as her statement registers, and for a striking beat, a tidal wave of peace washes over me. That same fleeting comfort I felt the moment our lips brushed together. I'm not sure if it's the vulnerability scribbled all over her face, or the soft gaze of her eyes, or the way her words wrap around me like a hug.

Whatever it is, I repel it.

My hips push forward, my cock jabbing the juncture between her legs, and I groan at the contact. "This isn't love, honey," I say in a harsh breath.

This is something far more essential.

Before her frown can fully unfurl, I kiss her again, one palm slinking around her throat, and the other drawing the slip of underwear from her hips until it pools around her ankles. Indie gasps into my open mouth when the air skims her fully nude skin, and I reach down to lift her by the thighs, wrapping her legs around me. Hoisting her up high, I suck her breast into my mouth as she clutches my overgrown hair, tugging at the mess with taut fingers, her neck craning back.

Her moan is electric when I nick her pebbled nipple with my teeth. "God, Dax..."

"Fuck, you're beautiful," I murmur around her breast. "So sexy."

I carry her through my living room, down the short hallway, and toward the bedroom. The intention is the full-sized bed centered along the far wall, but when Indie reaches between us to cup my erection through my boxers, squeezing it in her fist, my breath stops, and I pivot just inside the doorway to slam her up against the wood paneling.

Her cry of surprise is cut short by my hungry mouth, and then two hands are pushing the boxers down my legs until we're both bare.

Exposed and vulnerable.

I feel the need to counteract this feeling with rebellion. With steadfast resolution. There is no room for weakness here—not after I've spent the last eight months perfecting my defenses. Sex has always centered around intimacy for me, but I can't risk that now.

I can't risk letting her in.

I can't risk feeling what I felt that day.

"Dax—"

"No." My mouth silences her once again as my tongue plunges inside, replacing her words with moans. When I pull back, I say, "Embrace the chaos."

Indie makes a breathy sound when my cock spears her inner thigh, and she grips my shoulders with sharp nails. Then she nods, a barely perceptible motion of her head.

Permission.

Gripping her waist with a virile growl, I drag my mouth down her jaw, biting and nipping, allowing the frenzy to fester. She arcs against me, grinding, needy, slicking me with desire, and it amplifies my madness until I'm right between her thighs, teasing her heat.

I haven't had sex in almost a year. Not since Sabrina. I always imagined myself hitting up the bars and clubs if I ever became single again, indulging in cheap thrills and one-night stands, but I was too broken when she left. Too ripped open and torn apart.

Instead, I wallowed. I simmered in my misery, my feelings.

And those feelings threaten me once again as I hold Indie up against the wall, a heartbeat away from thrusting inside her. She's magic, somehow. Lucidity amidst disorder.

A reminder of what I've lost and what could be.

As much as I try to force it all away, it's enough to cause me to wrap my arms around her and spin her around, marching her toward the bedside. Indie falls atop the mattress when I let her go, and I take a moment to drink in her milky skin and hidden curves. She looks good lying below me, perched on my sterile bedspread, adding her vibrant colors.

My jaw tightens, fighting against the softness that tries to invade.

Indie reaches for a blanket with pinkening cheeks as daylight filters in from the adjacent window, spotlighting her beauty. I climb over her, one knee on each side, then push away the covering. "Don't do that," I say softly, draping her with my body—a far better shield. "We can't both hide."

I don't allow her to respond. My mouth descends, and my hands roam, her thighs spreading involuntarily as I situate my hips between her legs. Her tongue tangles with mine, spurring surges of hot arousal, and I reach down to grip my cock, jerking it as I position myself at her entrance. Chemistry bubbles between us, a telltale pull, and it's the same draw I felt the moment I laid eyes on her in that bank lobby. I don't know what it means, I can't explain it, but I let it guide us through whatever the hell this is.

I let it lead.

Indie bucks her hips, a straightforward request, and I groan when the tip of my dick nudges her heat. Maybe I should be gripped with hesitation, and perhaps she should second guess this, and I suppose we should both consider the fact that this might be a colossal mistake.

But all I do is thrust inside her.

No deliberation, no questioning, no regard.

I just feel.

And I'd like to say that all I feel is her pussy tightening around me, and her nails carving into my shoulder blades, and her breasts flush against my chest. I want to say that all I feel is sex and sweat and emotionless passion.

Only, when her eyes lock on mine, widening and glazed with something like genuine affection, my heartbeat quickens. My chest flutters. My throat draws tight in response.

I feel something else.

It's when her body starts to move, and her lips release my name, that I rein in the wayward sentiment and void my mind of the intrusion. I manifest it into carnal rage and unleash my demons instead.

My thrusts are wild as I sink deep inside her, over and over again. I bury my face into the arc of her neck, pulling the delicate skin between my teeth, leaving my mark. She wraps her legs tighter around me, the mattress squeaking in time with her own whimpers, and she holds me close—for dear life. Almost as if I'm not real. I'm just a dream, a mirage... a ghost.

Maybe I am. Maybe this is all a fucked up fantasy, and my dream angel will fade, just like she always does. The thought drives me, a fierce desperation, and I grunt and groan against her warm skin, breathing in her scent as I fuck her with no mercy.

"Oh, God..." Indie mewls, her teeth finding my shoulder and biting hard. "Dax..."

"Fuck... fuck," I grit out, weaving my fingers through her hair and tugging. It's been so long—too long—and I won't last. I feel my body tensing, peaking, and I nibble the shell of her ear, whispering in a gravelly breath, "You're going to make me come, Indie. You feel too damn good."

"Yes. Dax, yes."

Yes.

Jesus, I'm pathetic, but I can't hold back. Three more thrusts and I pull out of her, lifting to my knees and releasing onto her stomach, my tapered moans drowning out the sound of my fucking conscience telling me what an asshole I am.

Goddammit.

The shockwaves subside, and my uneven breaths bring me back to reality—the reality of how I just fucked Indigo, after lying to her for eight months, didn't bother to get her off, then came all over her like she was nothing more than a cheap lay.

Fucking hell.

Indie tries to mask the rim of tears that pool and spill, but her emotions are unmistakable. She wears them as expertly as I hide mine.

She turns her head to the side, biting her lip, her breath catching as she whispers raggedly, “I thought you were dead.”

Her body glistens below me, sprawled out and exposed, naked and trusting. The evidence of my release glares back at me, branding me with shame.

She’s more than this.

We’re more than this.

I collapse beside her on the mattress, her gaze still firmly fixed away from me. My arm envelops her as my drawn-out sigh tickles the curve of her shoulder, and I lean down to graze it with a kiss. Swallowing, I close my eyes and murmur back, “I am.”

We drink in the silence, believe the lie.

Chapter Twenty-Three

Indie

I LAY THERE, THE scent of sex and regret hanging heavy between us. Bitterness burns the backs of my eyes, and I blink rapidly before swinging my legs over the side of the bed. His hand catches my bicep.

"Where are you going?"

"To clean up." Barely keeping myself from jerking loose, I break free and shuffle swiftly across the floor to the bathroom, closing the door behind me.

The bathroom is small, with a pedestal sink, toilet, and shower enclosure rather than a tub combination. I twist the taps and pull the curtain, letting the water heat, then lean on the sink and raise my eyes to regard myself wearily in the mercury-flecked mirror.

Jesus. I look like I've been rode hard and put away wet, Dax's cum roping my stomach and the pale skin of my torso bruised with fingerprints like beacons.

Neck.

Collarbone.

Breasts.

Jaw.

Marked.

And I hadn't even come.

My eyes flicker with an emotion I recognize as a mix of irritation and despair, and I step away from the sink and into the shower. Vapor clouds the small enclosure as I tip my head back into the steamy flow, closing my eyes against the shampoo and body wash in the tile basin before me. It smells like the skin that was just pressed against me, I have no doubt.

The reminder triggers that obnoxious pulse between my legs, the one currently bitching because she didn't get her resolution, and with a disgusted sound I slap a hand hard between my folds. "Shut up," I mutter, unsure if I'm talking to my clit or my heart, my stupid weak heart that I worry I left back in that bedroom. "We've been flying solo for years, no need for a change-up now."

Dax did something to me, and I don't know if I'm ever going to be the same. I'm not crying, but a sob escapes anyway, and I fall forward, one hand reaching out to brace against the cold tile, the other working in counterpoint between my legs. My forehead lands against the wall and I watch the water swirling around my feet.

Ripples.

It ripples outward, like everything has done since that day in the bank. One event setting off another, the violence of the robbery inciting the sweet torment of Dax, his absence murdering my peace. "Damnit."

Another sob. My elbow hits the shower curtain, so close in the tiny space. I need to come. It's a physical pain at this point. Dax worked me up, but didn't let me fall, and now I can't focus long enough to find my release.

I can't even be angry with him—that's the real kicker. He tried to hide it, but I saw every thought, every emotion as it flitted across his handsome face. He was feeling something, and he absolutely hated it. For whatever reason, he decided eight months ago that it was better not to feel the way he had that day in the bank, and somehow, he managed to turn that part of himself off.

Until today.

Me.

A little hum of hope stirs, but I shove it down because I know, deep down, I need more than that. It's all or nothing.

"Sexy thoughts," I murmur. Think sexy thoughts.

My thoughts invariably go to him, to the intensity of his expression when he yanked his cock from within me and spent himself on my stomach. Full of self-loathing, there'd nonetheless been something tender and baffled secreted away behind those eyes. There'd been a second when I'd wanted to latch my legs around his hips and hold him deep inside, claim him as he had done me.

You just wanted to come. My vagina throbs in protest as I circle and rub. That's not the way. Carry your ass back in there and ride that —

I growl.

At the same moment, the curtain swings violently open and I jump, my hand jerking away from my body. Dax stands before me, still gloriously nude. I try and fail to keep my eyes above where his cock swings heavy between his legs, already hardening.

"What are you doing?" His eyes travel me as if he has the right —as if I'm his—and anger flares. Deliberately, I turn my back and replace my hand.

"Finishing what you started," I answer briefly. "Do you mind?"

"I mind," Dax murmurs, his voice hardly audible over the showerhead. "Like you said, I started this, I need to finish it."

"Not necessary. I'm more than capable—"

Before I quite calibrate to what's happening, he steps into the shower behind me, jerking the curtain into place. He places one hand on my hip, pulling me back and into him even as I twist.

"What are you—"

I yelp as his hand comes down on my ass in a firm swat, and the other takes hold of my jaw, angling my face upward so his mouth can reach mine. "Shut up, Indie." He kisses me then, deep and wet, the water of the shower mixing with lips and tongues and words unsaid between us.

I fall silent. I don't know what this is. I'm not sure I want to know. I feel him lowering himself behind me, angling my bottom until it's right in his face. Hands on my hips to hold me in places, he drags his nose along one cheek and then further, into the cleft of my pussy. I jerk when his tongue spears into me, the sensation odd from behind, strange, but... good.

So goddamn good.

A noise escapes me, and I feel his lips curl against me, satisfaction evident in the movement. "Dax, you don't need—" My words of dissent change to a moan when he plunges a finger without warning into my channel and begins to move it in time to the thrust and swirl of his tongue. The angle should be all wrong, and yet he's hitting a sweetly sensitive spot that invokes a gasp each time he touches it.

My knees go weak, damn him.

In one smooth movement, Dax straightens and twists me to face him. He lifts me up, propping me against the wall, the chill of the tile prickling my flesh. My legs curl around his waist, notching us together perfectly, and as I loop my arms around his neck, my eyes lift and cling to his.

His blue eye. Electric blue sex.

Just as we have so many times before, we speak in silent communion, some empathetic telepathy of our souls allowing us to understand each other without a word crossing our lips.

I'm sorry. Dax apologizes with a featherlight kiss to my mouth.

It's okay. My lips part, but he retreats, his hands coming to cup my bottom and pull me closer.

Let me make it up to you. His cock nudges at my entrance, the fingers of one hand parting my folds to grant him admission.

Please. With an indrawn breath that fades to a sigh, he slides home. We rest, locked together, our mutual breaths soughing hard as we take a beat to simply feel each other... every point of connection, every flare of heat, every bit of his hard pressing into my soft.

I lift my chin, my head falling back against the wall with a thump. Water splashes over the barrier of his shoulders and onto my face and chest, tiny needles magnifying every sensation. From beneath my lashes, I look at him, and begin to move, tiny shifts of my pelvis against his. This is mine. This is for me. I smile when his jaw goes tight, and the fingers clamped around my ass constrict.

That electric blue eye narrows fiercely. Do your worst, his expression says.

And so I do.

I am selfish when I put my hands on Dax's shoulders and use his strength to punch myself up and down as though it's the last night at the carnival and he's the ride a magician created just for me. I swivel my hips and grind against him and rock myself to madness, but ultimately, I whimper when I can't quite grasp that explosion I seek. "I can't—"

"It's all right, honey." One of Dax's hands rises to brush my hair from my face, and then he's turning us, shutting the water off, and holding me close as he carries me from the bathroom back to the bedroom. Every step makes need throb through me like agony; I've been so close for so long... it hurts.

"I need to come."

"I know."

Dax lays me on the bed, coming down on top of me and pushing back inside, but with tenderness. He kisses me, slow and deep, like lovers do, his tongue moving hungrily with mine before he moves to my jaw, and then my neck. I'm so full of his mouth on my skin, the little fires he stokes into blazes, that I can't focus on the movement of his hips against mine as he spears me with fevered strokes. I can't sort one wave of rolling pleasure from the next, can't identify where it starts or try to predict when it will end. I have no control over my own body, and for once, for the first time ever, it's utterly, completely... okay.

I hold on, and let it take me where it will.

The first orgasm catches me by surprise. It's stronger than anything I've ever felt, bringing actual tears to my eyes. I close them, unwilling to let them fall, unwilling to let him see what he's done to me.

It's just sex, I tell myself, knowing it for a lie even as I think it.

Only when the ripples fade, only when he feels the pulses of my body around him diminish, does Dax allow his second release. My body shudders at the drag of his cock against my sensitized flesh, and in seconds, another orgasm bears down upon me, prompting a strangled scream. Dax's face, buried in my throat, moves with what I'm certain is another arrogant grin, but I can't address it. All I can do is throw a weary arm over my eyes and do my best to hide as he collapses atop me, carefully keeping most of his weight from crushing me, and places both palms on my cheeks.

"Hey." His voice is low, so low and gritty. "Don't do that. Don't hide, Indigo."

I don't answer. I can't. If I open my mouth, I'll cry, or tell him I want his babies, or something equally foolish. I bite my lip.

"Indie." He tugs at my arm, finding my face, and his expression shifts to worry. "Shit, why are you crying?" Rough thumbs rub gently at the corners of each eye to catch the pooling liquid.

"I'm not."

"Jesus. I know you... I felt—look, I'm sorry about earlier," he tries to explain. "I was just—"

"No, Dax, wait." I place two fingers over his mouth and struggle to find the right words. "It's okay. Earlier, I mean—I understand. And I came. It was good. It was so good. Better than anything I've ever felt before." I feel my lower lip start to tremble and squeeze the sheet with my other hand, where Dax can't see.

His frown is subtle, his eyes searching.

"It's just... you're sitting up here in this cabin like a hermit and I'm... I'm only barely able to step outside my house, still. We..."

I don't have to finish the sentence. Dax is pulling away, rolling off of me to settle on the other side of the bed. He gathers me to his chest, kissing the top of my head once before tugging the blanket over both of us. "Yeah, I get it," he finishes at length.

"But it was so good," I reiterate, cuddling into him. I can take this day, enjoy the warmth and comfort of a man's body for once in a long, long time. I deserve it, surely. It's not a forever kind of thing.

And it really was good. Incredible.

The crescendo in a song; the climax in a movie. Fireworks and orchestras.

So, I leave him with those hopeful words, and I smile through my tears, allowing him to think they are fused with joy and magic and the start of something wonderful.

But I know, I know... this shouldn't happen again.

And that hurts.

Chapter Twenty-Four

Dax

WAKING UP ENTWINED WITH another human being is something that feels almost… like a promise. Hopeful. It's like that first hint of daybreak when morning blush swallows the sky and paints the treetops, filling me with the possibility of a new beginning.

A do-over.

Indie teases me with those tempting prospects, and I soak it all up, ignoring logic and rationale. I allow the dream to take life, trailing my fingertips along the arch of her shoulder as the bedsheet dips beneath her breasts. I revel in her soft curves. Her warm skin. The rise and fall of her sun-kissed chest, marbled with streaks of blue light from the prism windchimes dangling just outside my bedroom window. She's an indigo overture.

I bask in the allure of her, in her way that is so much more than just physical.

I savor… all of her.

My chest tightens as my brain slams on the brakes, a hard-wired reaction to the idea of peace. To the idea of a future beyond my self-imposed isolation.

You're dead, Dax. This is the life you chose.

That inner voice drags me back down into the empty void, ice to my slow-thawing heart. The son-of-a-bitch.

Sparing Indie's sleeping form a final glance, I roll onto my back, rubbing my eyes with both palms. A sigh spills out of me, a defeated sort of sound, and I realize I have no idea what the hell we're supposed to do now. Snow continues to accumulate outside the window as the windchimes work overtime through the harsh gusts of wind. She's trapped here, with me, with the ghost of a man she thought she knew after having sex with me, twice. This whole situation is backwards and bleak.

Indie is going to wake up thinking we're about to ride off into some kind of picturesque sunset together. That smile she left me with; those happy, godforsaken tears—damnit, and maybe there's a small part of me that wants that, too. There's a part of me that still craves the life I never got to experience with Sabrina.

A part that wonders if maybe, possibly… I do deserve more than this.

I could get used to this reality, after all. Mind-blowing sex and midday naps with the gorgeous woman beside me—a woman who hasn't strayed far from my mind since the moment I laid eyes on her in that bank lobby, smiling away in a coffee-stained blouse.

My heart frosts over when images of that blouse, sullied with blood and brain matter, decimate the appeal.

Goddammit.

Happy endings don't bloom from grave beginnings.

Indie stirs beside me, nuzzling her cheek against the pillow. I bite my lip, already knowing that pillow will smell like honeysuckles long after we've said our final goodbyes. The thought warms me before it hardens me, and I throw off my covers and toss my legs over the bedside with another long sigh.

I'll let her sleep. I'll let her dream of that white picket fence and happily-ever-after.

And when she wakes, I'll make her food.

I'll apologize for everything—for what's been said, what's been done, and for what will never come to be.

Then… we'll say those final goodbyes.

I don't even hear her bare feet shuffle into the kitchen as I place the family-size chicken pot pie into the oven. I'm not sure how long she's been standing there in her wrinkled shirt and sleep-mussed hair, staring at me from across the island with some sort of wary affection.

We lock eyes.

What is this, Dax?

It's nothing.

Don't lie to me.

It's nothing, Indie. Trust me.

I thought I did.

The oven alerts me of its 375-degree temperature, causing us both to startle, severing the moment. Clearing my throat, I glance away and pretend to set the timer that has already been set.

"Dax."

I stiffen. "You hungry?"

My gaze stays fixed on the incredibly fascinating stove clock.

Tick, tick, tick.

Another scoreboard. A countdown to our inevitable demise.

"Dax, please," she murmurs. "We should talk about..."

When I finally pull my focus back to her, she's wringing her hands together, one knee bobbing up and down with fretful desperation. The look in her eyes has me swallowing back an abrupt wave of emotion. "It was fun, Indie."

Her frown is like a dagger. "Fun?"

"Yeah... fun."

It's not a lie. It was fun. It was really fucking fun being inside her, feeling alive for the first time in almost a year, tasting her with my tongue, and hearing my name expelled from her lips like a euphoric hymn. It was fun playing make-believe—sheltering from the storm, while we created our very own.

It was so much more than that, too, and she knows I know that.

But all storms pass, so I lift my chin with conviction and dig the blade deeper. "It was just sex, Indigo. Something I haven't had in a long damn time."

The fury that skates across her features has me questioning if this storm will actually pass, or if it will take us both out instead. Regret stings the back of my throat.

"I'm going to let that one go because I know you didn't mean it." Indie's arms fall at her sides, her fingers clenching into fists as she fights back tears. Heat blotches her collarbone, climbing up her neck and staining her ears red. "I know you felt something, Dax. You might be able to hide from the world out here, isolated and alone, pretending to be a ghost, but... you can't hide from me," she says in a shaky breath. "I felt it, too."

She stalks towards me, circling around the island, and I want to run. Bolt. I've reprogrammed myself to flee instead of fight. My battle cry is nothing more than a pathetic whimper, and my weapons have disintegrated into dust.

I'm not a hero anymore.

I'm a coward.

Only, Indie doesn't give me a chance to crawl away. She reaches out, linking our hands together and tugging me towards her, and hell—she sure doesn't feel like my enemy. She doesn't taste like warfare when my body molds into her, my lips dipping forward to kiss her hairline.

She's surrender.

I choke back the ashes and gunpowder, finding her through the smoke. My hands raise, cupping her face, her cheeks soft and delicate beneath my calloused thumbs. "Fuck, I'm sorry... I never meant to drag you into this mess. You're not supposed to be here."

She lets out a cathartic sigh as I pull her against me, the top of her head level with my chin. Her breaths beat along my neck, a warm comfort. "Maybe I am."

No.

She's too pure, too sweet.

I'll poison her.

"Indie..." My palm curls around the base of her neck as I inch back, meeting her gaze. "Listen to me, I—"

"No, you listen," she says in quick breath, cutting my words short. Chewing on her bottom lip, her stare is more blue than green as she fixates on me. Melancholy blue. "Maybe I am supposed to be here, Dax. Not for some sweeping romance, or the start of a picture-perfect future... but for closure. I think we both needed a little resolution after all that madness."

I study her, my thoughts clipping to a stop. My mental essay on how this could never work dissolves, right along with the obnoxious swell of hope that had been blooming in my gut from the moment I opened my front door this morning.

Stupid.

Indie's right. This is nothing more than comfort—just like that kiss, that glorious, heart-stopping kiss that almost made me forget we were barricaded in a break room, serenaded by bullets, and hunted down by death.

I find myself nodding and backing away, my grip on her weakening. "Yeah... closure," I force out, looking down at the gap between us. "We deserve a worthy send-off."

"We do. It's not a Maui beach, but I'll take it."

Glancing back up, my lips twitch with apology. "We're not exactly the storybook type, anyway."

"We're really not, are we?" Indie chuckles despite the grim mood. "This is more fitting. Caught in a blizzard, trapped inside this old cabin. I'm pretty sure I saw a bear outside your window."

My own laugh follows as I take another step back, letting her go. "We have a lot of those here."

"Yeah... I'm more of a city girl, myself. I belong in Belltown with my little lion, and you seem to be doing okay here with your brooding and bears."

The humor of her words is overshadowed by the finality of it all.

In other words:

This is it.

We're not meant to be.

Goodbye.

I hate that the thought prickles my skin, making me feel itchy and uncertain. Sighing, I slip my hands into the pockets of my gray sweatpants and rock back on my heels, stealing a look out the kitchen window. The swiftly falling snow has finally subsided, the evidence sparkling beneath a sunny sky. A solid foot of white is the only thing keeping her here now.

When I turn back towards her, she's smiling softly in my direction. "Stay a few more hours," I offer, the words spilling out unplanned. Part of me longs to beg for more time—days, weeks, a lifetime. But I push the absurdity aside and finish, "Stay for dinner. Then I'll dig your car out, and you can get home to Daisy."

Indie worries her lip between her teeth again, still swollen from my violent kisses and love bites. She nods, squaring her shoulders. "Okay. I already texted Tameka that I'd be stuck here until the snow died down. I can stay for dinner."

"Good," I smile. "Great."

And it is great—those final five hours with her, catching up over chicken pot pie, falling into easy banter and conversation. There's no talk of the robbery. No mention of my escape from Garrett or my brush with death. We don't discuss Jeremy or Sabrina, or the dark stain that equally tethers us and keeps us apart at the same time.

We talk about our dreams, our childhoods. We talk about Daisy and how strong she is; how brave and kind. I tell her about my temporary living arrangements with Blake, and how he has a different colored toothbrush for each day of the week, just because.

She tells me about Tameka and their silly game nights, and how she's been there for Indie, more than anyone else.

More than me.

But... we don't talk about that.

It's light and comfortable and effortless. It's the opposite of how we began on that fateful Monday morning at 9:03AM, and I hate that it gives me a glimpse into what could be—into what we might become if we were carved from a different beginning.

If I were more than just a ghost.

The notion haunts me as I plow through the snow hours later, cleaning and warming Indie's car. And when the sun begins to set, coloring the snowfall in shades of burgundy and blush, the time for second-guessing and daydreaming is over.

It's time to say our final goodbyes.

I fidget in the living room, peering up at the wall clock as Indie slips into her peacoat and winter boots. She adds layer after layer, while all I long to see is her naked and bare, sprawled across my bedcovers like she was this morning.

Something inside me aches.

"I'm really glad you're okay, Dax."

Her words steal me from the reverie, and I pull my lips between my teeth, nodding. "You, too. I'm glad we did this," I say through a tense jaw. "Closure."

"Closure," she parrots softly.

I'm not sure whether to shake her hand and see her off as a friend, or kiss her like a lost lover, staking my indefinite claim.

I decide on neither, pulling her into a hug instead.

Indie is soft and warm in my embrace, and she deflates against me, letting out a little gasp. Something almost painful. "Goodbye," she whispers into my chest.

Closing my eyes and breathing in her sweet scent, I squeeze her tight and mutter, "Goodbye, honey."

We hold each other as I spare another look at the clock over her shoulder.

Tick, tick, tick.

Time's up.

She steps away, keeping her eyes lowered while she gathers her wits and spins around, heading to the front door.

"Indigo."

Indie halts, her steps pausing as she slowly turns to face me from across the room. Her eyes glow with curiosity and... something else. I swear it looks like yearning. "Yes?"

My heart stammers in my chest, matching the look in her eyes. "Maybe someday we'll be the storybook type. Maybe..." I swallow down the lump in my throat, hating the way it tastes. "Maybe someday we'll take that trip."

Her eyes flare with a glimmer of hope. "Will there be sailboats?"

"There can be sailboats."

The familiar exchange echoes all around us, and we both smile at the sentiment—the vision. The far-off dream. Indie breaks the spell first, pulling her eyes from mine and sucking in a slow, uneven breath.

One more beat passes, and then she's gone.

I flinch when the door shuts tight, a gust of cold air forcing its way inside and slicing my skin. Or maybe it's her absence settling into my bones, chilling me straight to the core. I can't help but shiver as my shoulders sag and my legs go weak.

Moving to the recliner against the far wall, I have every intention of collapsing into the brown leather and wallowing in my loneliness.

Only, something catches my eye.

There, perched atop the seat cushion, is a book.

The Great Gatsby.

Glancing to the empty space on the bookshelf where it previously resided, my heart gallops at the notion that Indie placed it here for me to find. To read.

A little piece of herself.

A reminder.

Don't forget me, Dax.

I reach for the well-worn book, the spine weathered, pages creased. My thumb flips through the yellowed paper as I take a seat in the chair and settle in.

Maybe someday.

Maybe someday there will be sailboats.

For now, there are only currents.

Chapter Twenty-Five

Indie

"YEAH… THIS IS A no for me, my dude." Tameka shakes one of her brilliant pink claws in Blake's face while I give him a measuring look over the rim of my wine glass. I've been mostly quiet tonight, allowing Tameka to fight my battle for me.

When I'm angry I cry, and I really don't feel like crying anymore.

I think back to the last time I cried.

Tears.

So many awful tears.

I bust through my front door, a sobbing mess, after my snowy cabin interlude with Dax. I kick off my boots and peel off my heavy layers, until I'm nothing but blubbering bare bones, face down in the couch cushions. Tameka stops by with two hot teas and sheltering arms, and she lets me fall apart against her. She doesn't say a word as I blurt out the entire wretched story through my hiccups—she simply sways me back and forth with a motherly kind of comfort.

When I finish, she holds me at arm's length, dries my face with the dishcloth she snatched from the kitchen, and asks me, with disturbing seriousness, if I want her to go chop his balls off.

"No!" I protest.

So aggressive.

"Because I can," she shrugs, tone casual. "Or, if you don't want that, I can at least give them a good twist. I had brothers, you know. I'm good at it." She pipes up then, alight with another brilliant idea. "Oh! I have this aunt who lives down in Louisiana, too. I can call her up, get her to put a spell on the little man."

I laugh helplessly by the time she finally runs out of ideas, sliding down the front of the couch to sit my ass on the floor. "No more," I beg. "It's fine. I'm fine. It was just a shock."

She slides down to sit beside me, slipping my fingers through hers. That warmth is back, comforting me like the herbal tea still clutched in my opposite hand. "I know."

My breath shudders through a sniffle. "I'm so damn happy he's alive."

"I know, Indie."

The tears try to start again, so I close my eyes and will them away. Swallowing, I shake my head. "I'm so mad at Blake for letting me grieve the way I did."

Tameka sighs, squeezing my palm. "Yeah, we'll handle that on Saturday—don't you worry."

I rest my head atop her shoulder, a smile hinting when I imagine just how Tameka will "handle that." My sigh matches her own. "I mean, I suppose I underst—"

"Hey." She swats at me, her lilac shampoo softening the command in her tone. "Shush. No more trying to figure it all out or understand. Just acknowledge it, and then move on," she says, placing a small kiss along the top of my head. "You got this, girl."

Deep breath in.

Deep breath out.

"Thank you, Tameka."

So, now we're here, wine Saturday, and Tameka isn't letting Blake skate by with anything. She's a dragon.

My dragon.

Blake tries again. "You don't understand. I was sworn to secrecy," he says, flustered, hands waving with vivid animation. "Do you know what that's like? To be trusted with such a thing? The enormous responsibility. The guilt. The stress!"

Tameka rolls her coppery eyes. "Mmhmm."

Gulping, his gaze flickers from the dragon to me.

He knows where the real danger lies.

"And it wasn't until later that I really understood the extent of..." Blake trails off, fiddling with the scarf coiled messily around his neck. "You know... that I realized how much you cared, Indie."

"You mean, until you realized she could fall in love with him," Tameka provides.

Blake and I both shift uncomfortably. The color drains from my face, while he drains his wine. Changing direction, I glance at him with imploring eyes, trying to express my feelings without breaking down again. "You were my friend."

At last, I've managed to form words.

At the sound of my voice, Blake looks up from the bowl of his wine glass to me, his eyes wide and glinting. "I am your friend, Indie. I swear that to you." He leans forward, conveying his truth. "I hated like hell being caught in the middle, wanting to tell you and ease your suffering, but knowing that doing so would hurt Dax. I just... I just couldn't hurt him anymore than he had already been hurt," he finishes, exhaling slowly.

I cock my head the way Daisy does when she's curious about something, intent on figuring it out. A frown follows. "The gunshot wound?"

"No, not just that. It was more than that. He..." Blake places a fist gently to his chest. "It has to come from him, Indie, but... let's just say he had a lot of soul-searching to do."

Tameka and I are both quiet, taking a moment to let the words sink in. "Fair enough," Tameka finally offers. "It doesn't mean anything if he doesn't tell you himself."

Maybe it's the wine, but I don't understand at first. I want to know what happened to Dax. Why he hurts, what broke him—what made him think that disappearing was the only way to cope. If he won't confide in me, I want someone else to do so.

I just want answers.

But as I sit there with my glass of wine and heavy heart, trying to process everything, that truth is illuminated like a shaft of light upon the water. I think I understand.

I can't fix him. I would have tried, of course, but I would have failed, and we both would have suffered in the process. The only person that can fix Dax... is Dax.

He needs to be his own hero.

I take a thoughtful sip of my merlot, fixing my gaze on my reflection in the window. A woman, slim, a mass of bright gold hair shining in the light of the lamp she sits beneath. Her eyes haunted and expectant, even to me.

She'll wait.

I'm good at waiting.

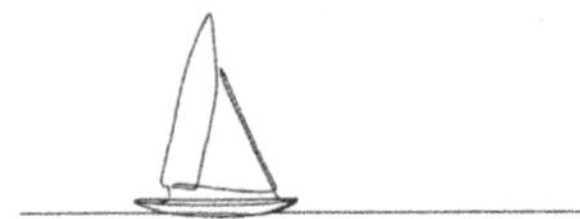

Felicity: How did you feel when that door opened, and you discovered he was alive?

The question rolls around my head as I poise my fingers over the keyboard and ponder my response. Somewhere else, in another room behind another screen, Felicity waits patiently for my answer, knowing I have to think about the tough ones.

How did I feel?

I close my eyes, letting the emotions drift back from the other day at the cabin. The chill of the air, that recognition of impending weather. The visceral awareness of every small thing around me—the occasional leaf floating to the ground, the scent of wood smoke in the air, the quietude and peace. And then the door creaking open, Dax's chest bare before me.

I open my eyes.

Indie: Shattered.

Felicity: I need more, Indie.

More.

I only have so much left to give.

Sighing, I try to dig deep and find the right words.

Indie: I was... caught off guard, but it was as though part of me knew. Intuition, maybe. Or it could have been the little things Blake had said over the past few months. Slips and hints. I was angry, too. Bewildered. Frustrated. Why did he do that to me? To Daisy? I mean, did he really need to go to such extraordinary lengths to escape my attention? It was... insulting.

Felicity: Good.

I breathe heavily, panting as if I've been running miles rather than sitting at the kitchen counter with a laptop in front of me.

I continue on.

Indie: Then I thought... maybe it isn't about me at all. Maybe he's fighting a battle I don't even know about. So, my anger bled with compassion. Sympathy. A yearning to help him.

Felicity: Also good. Did you tell him any of this? Let him know how you were feeling?

I think back. Had I told him?

The details are fuzzy.

Indie: I think so.

Felicity: Great. How did he respond?

Indie: He made me breakfast and then he fucked me.

At first, I think I only thought the response. My own internal dialogue.

But when I glance at the screen to phrase a more graceful reply, I realize my evil twin fingers informed Felicity of their own accord.

Damnit.

With a sigh, I sit back and wait to be chastised. Felicity's little dots that indicate typing are already chasing each other at the bottom of the screen, telling me her answer is in progress.

Felicity: Ahem. In that case, I need more details.

I squint. Coming from Tameka, this would not be an unusual request. But from an anonymous mental health professional... ?

Indie: Details...?

Felicity: As in, how are you feeling about this now? Do you feel that it resolved things between you at the time, or are you planning on seeing each other again? Those details.

Indie: Oh! Okay. I thought... never mind.

Felicity: Nope. Only when you're released from treatment.

I snort. There she is. I knew there was a Tameka hiding somewhere behind that screen. Shaking my head, I get myself on track.

Indie: I'm okay with it, in all honesty. A little blue, maybe, but I think it fits somewhere in the category of closure? And I guess that answers your next question. It's done. It's resolved. We won't be seeing each other again. There was this... chemistry... that we needed to explore. Unfinished business we needed to take care of. We took care of it, I got some things off my chest, and he explained his reasons, kind of, and now we're just... done.

It rings true. Kind of. The thing that I don't get into, the thing I don't give myself time to think about... is that I miss him. I miss him in the unhealthiest, most obsessed of ways.

Even if I never really knew him, I miss him as if we had been lovers all our lives. I lay in bed last night and wept salt rivers into my pillow, pressing a fist against my mouth to muffle the sound of my cries. Seeing him again, feeling for scant hours what it could be like to be with him—it fucking hurt afterwards. It ached later, like a phantom limb post-amputation. I wanted to itch it, to tear at it, rip it from my body—only, it had already been ripped away.

It wasn't there.

So, I tell Felicity good-bye and rise to start tacos for the Taco Tuesday I instituted a month or so after the bank incident, determined to put a smile back on Daisy's face. She helps me in the kitchen, carefully grating cheese with the kid-friendly grater, while I brown and season the beef.

"Chips or shells?" I hold up a bag of tortilla chips, along with a box of taco shells. Daisy's eyes light upon the chips, and she points, nodding playfully. "I know, I know. As if there's any question," I smile.

I'll never not ask, though, hoping that one day she'll decide to answer me with her voice instead of her eyes and hands.

"Can you set the table for us, kiddo?" I prompt her, holding out the bag and her plastic plate. She takes them willingly, and is back seconds later for more Daisy-proof offerings to carry to the dining table. "Such a good helper. Thank you, baby."

I'm finishing the last couple of tasks in the kitchen, giving Daisy time to finish setting the table, when the doorbell rings. Forehead wrinkling, I start heading to the front of the house with my hands in a dishtowel. My daughter sprints ahead of me on two eager legs, and I freeze, calling at her to stop. "Wait, Daisy. Don't—"

It's too late. Oblivious to the hazards posed by opening a door without first checking what might be on the other side, Daisy flings the door wide. My heart lodges in my throat and stays there, thick and painful, when my sights land on two familiar eyes, one brown, one blue.

He's on my porch.

Beneath the cover of the dishtowel, I pinch myself. Tall and lean and propped somewhat awkwardly against the doorjamb, hands in the pockets of a pair of jeans, Dax stands beneath the yellow light of the porch globe, his gaze fixed purposefully on me, then my daughter.

As I free myself from the shock of seeing him, I realize that tears are spilling their way down Daisy's face, and I bend to scoop her quickly up. I'm shocked when she twists away from me, when her arms fly open to Dax instead, and when she falls forward, trusting that he will catch her.

And he does.

He catches her.

Dax holds her tight to his chest, rocking her back and forth in a hug that does nothing to curb the tears I can feel streaking down my own cheeks. He finally steps over the threshold and shuts the door behind him with the heel of his shoe, then sniffs the air with dramatic appreciation. Pulling back slightly, he looks at Daisy and speaks, voice gruff.

"Hey, Little Lion. Is that tacos I smell?"

Chapter Twenty-Six

Dax

OVER A WEEK GOES by in Indie's absence, and the transition is as jarring as the early spring snowfall melting by way of seventy-degree temperatures.

She was only here for a day.

One day.

It feels like longer. It feels like she's always been here, her scent on my pillow and her voice lingering in these hollow hallways.

The snow only lasted one day, too.

But if I've learned anything over the past year, it's that a hell of a lot can change in a single day.

When the eighth day hits me with warm sunlight and a tepid breeze as I open my front door, something feels different. The sky is a rich blue, the grass a verdant green.

I can't help but think of her eyes.

I'm not sure why the correlation angers me, but I chop my wood that morning through fiercely gritted teeth, the veins in my forearms popping, muscles tight. Even my sweat feels angry as it tracks down my bare torso, glistening beneath the rising sun.

Bright, like her smile.

Chop, chop, chop.

I've tried to force her from my mind over the past week, but the attempts have proven fruitless. Mostly, because every time I read a chapter of that book, I think of her.

I think of sailboats.

But I don't fucking deserve sailboats, and I sure as hell don't deserve her, so maybe that's why I'm pissed off and spiraling this morning. I'm sick of wanting something not meant for me. I'm over these exhausting daydreams that haunt me every waking minute—these fantasies.

Chop, chop, chop.

I'm just done.

Tossing aside my ax with a final growl, I rein in my chaotic breaths, stepping away from the wood pile and staring up at the too-blue sky. I'd like to say that I've spent the last week soul-searching, reflecting... maybe even reconsidering my decision to disappear.

I haven't.

I've filled my days with mindless routines and back-breaking work, just to distract myself from those very things. Blake stopped by over the weekend with tubs of paint and supplies after I texted him that I was itching to do cabin renovations.

He also came by with floral drapery, an abundance of quirky knick-knacks from Home Goods, and a fucking kitten.

A kitten with a polka-dotted bow he'd panic-adopted from a local shelter and named Pickles.

Pickles.

I slow-blinked at him so long, completely silent, he rambled his way into a tangent about cats, and how they are ninety-five-point-six-percent tiger, which makes them ideal pets to have in the deep, dark woods, and how the bowtie was a custom, made in Milan.

Needless to say, I turned down the furry orange gift. My wild rabbit and personal demons are enough responsibility at the moment.

Running a palm down my sweat-slicked face, I breathe in the open air, resenting it for the very first time. It's so crisp and clean. Peaceful. It's a carefully crafted lie. Even out here in the dense forests, all alone and surrounded by quiet, my heart is restless. My skin crawls with unease. My mind races with doubt.

If I can't find peace here, of all places, where else is it?

Frustration fuels me as I gather the logs of birchwood and carry them to the porch, drop the pile beneath the covered awning, and storm through the front door. The door claps shut behind me when I slam it with my sneaker, causing Skittles to stomp her feet beside my recliner.

"Sorry," I mutter, as if the animal might understand. "Just one of those mornings, you know?"

Skittles just stares at me, ears flattened back against her head.

Rabbit, Dax. You're talking to a rabbit.

Fuck, I'm lonely.

The one-sided conversation with my pet jackrabbit frazzles me further, so I kick my shoes off, one by one, letting them fly across the room and hit the wall. My fingers stretch, curling into tight fists as I march across the living room, where Skittles scurries away, taking cover from my wrath inside her bunny cage.

I'm fighting the urge to apologize again when my eyes drop to the wood floor, landing on my book beside the reading chair. I squint. The pages have been torn and shredded.

Chewed.

Oh, hell.

My skin heats as a new surge of anger roars through me. I haven't finished it yet. I've been taking my time, soaking up the words, fearing that when I reach the end, she might leave me. Indefinitely. And I guess I'm not ready for that.

Bending down, I pick up the chewed-up novel, watching in horror as pages slip from the spine and float to my feet. Splintered, inky words stare back at me.

Champagne and the stars.

Let myself go.

The green light.

Boats against the current.

I realize my hands are shaking as I try to stitch the jagged pieces back together, knowing it's futile. Knowing some pieces are irretrievably lost.

And then it hits me.

As I'm fending off a rage-infused breakdown, a devastating collapse over this goddamn book that has millions of prints available to repurchase… it hits me.

Just because a few pages are lost, doesn't mean the words cease to exist.

My breath catches.

Struck with revelation, I straighten and place the tattered shreds of paper back inside the book before setting it down beside my leather recliner. Skittles watches as I cross into the kitchen and fetch a pen and notepad, then situate myself at the table.

I scribble away. The words fall carelessly onto the lined paper, words stored away for far too long, words I'm desperate to purge and expel. This is a cleanse.

It's not redemption—it's release.

I think about Gatsby and his green light, his hopes and dreams, and while I can't remember how the book ends, I'm not sure it really matters right now. This isn't about the end. This is about the middle, the defining moments that shape the end, and I realize that I have a say in that. I have control.

Just because some of my pieces are lost, doesn't mean I'm beyond repair.

I'm here, still standing amidst the chaos.

Glancing at the wall clock with a ball of epiphany lodged in my throat, I rise to my feet, tucking the sealed envelope into my pocket.

Tick, tick, tick.

It's time.

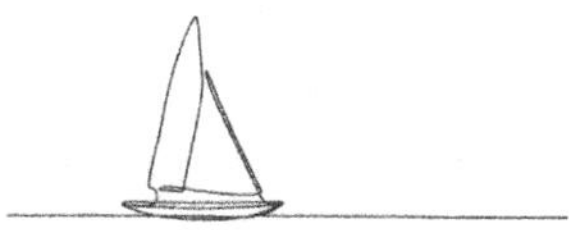

I find myself standing on her front porch later that night.

The lantern of light illuminating her mahogany door isn't green—more of a pale yellow—but it calls to me, nonetheless. I don't even hesitate in pressing my finger to the bell, then leaning against the doorjamb as a flurry of clunky footsteps move closer.

Daisy.

I'm surprised when the door flies open, and my little lion is standing on the other side of the entryway, her golden hair bouncing right along with two tiny legs. There's a moment of shock, a second when tears—my God, fucking tears—spill over her blue eyes and down her cheeks; then she's dancing. Backwards, forwards, back again.

My smile edges the corner of my lips up, then stalls when my gaze lifts.

She's there suddenly—clutching a dishtowel, her tresses piled into a messy bun, her eyes misting the moment she locks them on mine. There's confusion and promise and disbelief glowing back at me, and the sight of her, the breathtaking sight, sends a current of credence straight to my heart. She reaches for Daisy, who twists away and grabs wildly for me, instead.

Me.

I look away from Indie. I have to because Daisy is reaching for me, still crying those damnable silent tears, and I have no choice but to scoop her up, no desire to do anything but that. She falls against me as if my arms are a beacon of shelter, as if I'm… some kind of missing piece she finally rediscovered.

I rock her back and forth.

Side to side.

And then I push my way through the threshold, hugging her to me, accepting the invitation I'm not fully convinced I even received.

But Indie doesn't stop me. She doesn't force me out.

She just stands there, frozen, her own tears tracking down her cheeks.

I sniff the air, the aroma of cumin and cilantro making my mouth water. "Hey, little lion," I murmur against Daisy's temple, then set her back down with my own grin. "Is that tacos I smell?"

"Dax."

Indie finally speaks, her steps slow and uncertain as she approaches me from her perch in the kitchen. Her irises flicker like a storm, but I'm unsure if I'm witnessing the eye or the aftermath. I decide that caution is best, I shouldn't assume, so I falter in the foyer and slip my hands inside my pockets. "Hey. I, uh… didn't plan on showing up like this. I just—"

"I'm glad you did." It's almost as if her response caught her off guard. Indie's eyes widen, just slightly, and she ducks her head. "We just… didn't expect you."

No, she didn't expect me. Not tonight, not ever.

I didn't give her any reason to.

Nodding, I do my best to explain something I have little explanation for. But… I have a place to start, at least. "I read the book," I say softly. "Gatsby."

She swallows. "You did?"

"Yeah. I mean… I read most of it before my rabbit got bored and started eating it."

The hint of a smile tickles her lips.

"Something happened today," I continue. "A feeling. Enlightenment, maybe. I'm not really sure, to be honest, but somehow… I just knew. I'm done hiding."

Indie worries her lip between her teeth, still fisting the coral-toned dish towel with white knuckles. Her steps cease a few feet away from me, just out of my reach.

And yet… she feels closer than she ever has.

Glancing down at her bare toes, then back up, she stretches a smile. "I'm still kind of mad at you," she admits, fidgeting with the fringes of the towel.

"You should be."

"I don't even know what to say."

"I understand."

A somewhat comfortable silence falls between us as Daisy leans against my thigh, hugging my leg. Beach-themed décor surrounds me, the interior of their home sprinkled with seashells, sailboat canvasses, and aquamarine walls.

It's comforting, serene.

It feels... peaceful.

The truth is, I'm not sure what to say either. Indie left my cabin with acceptance in her eyes and closure in her heart—closure that we were over. And here I am, standing in her living room, giving her hope that maybe we're only just beginning.

Are we?

I can't answer that right now. Only hours ago, I was chopping wood for my nightly fire, reasonably content with my solitude. And then, as if an invisible coin had been tossed, I was in a taxi, on my way to Blake's high rise condo with a single bag of clothes and an unhappy rabbit.

A temporary arrangement, of course.

I haven't given any thought to my foray back into society. The cameras and lights, the breaking news reports, the endless questions that are sure to be asked. People are going to want to know my story. They'll want to know where I went, how I escaped, and why I ended up over two hours away in my grandfather's cabin, wallowing in seclusion as a lonely ghost.

I'll need to tell my family.

I'll need to relearn a lot of things, like living again. Truly living.

But for whatever reason... she came first.

They came first.

Indie takes another careful step forward, her eyes fixed on mine. She's only focused on one eye, though, the brown one, and I wonder why that is. When she's close enough to touch, she extends her hand and reaches for Daisy's.

Daisy reaches for mine.

We stand there in her living room, holding hands through her daughter, not knowing what the hell we're doing, or where we're going, but embracing the uncertainty anyway. Daisy sways between us, squeezing my palm and shuffling her feet, her joy evident despite her silence.

She's not speaking yet, but neither are we. I'm not sure what Indie is thinking, or if she'll ever forgive me for disappearing when she needed an anchor… but the soft look in her eyes, the look of pure solace, tells me all I need to know. Words will come later.

For now, we stand strong, facing the currents together.

I think there's a green light at the end of this dock.

CHAPTER TWENTY-SEVEN

Indie

"AND WITH A SWORD in her paw, the warrior lion princess led all the other lions to victory over the wicked Spider Queen and her followers, leaving them trampled in the dust."

From the doorway, I hear a snort of amusement. Keeping my expression straight and eyes on Daisy, I tuck the blankets in around her neck. "I love you, sweet girl." As always, I pause and wait a moment for her response. It hasn't come in the form of words in months, but her eyes twinkle up at me, her arms tucked snugly beneath the covers.

The smile is enough.

Bending down, I press my cheek against hers and inhale the baby powder and lavender scent of her skin. Love you so much. Even if I never hear your voice again. "Night, baby," I whisper.

One last lingering touch of my hand to the rise and fall of her tiny chest beneath the pile of blankets and I stand, closing the door softly on the dim illumination of the nightlight behind me as I leave.

Dax waits in the hallway, a little smile playing around his lips. "Left 'em trampled in the dust, huh?"

Heat touches my cheeks as I walk ahead of him toward the den, where we've been reconnecting most of the night. "She needs stories of strength. Tales where the girl is her own hero."

"I get that."

I push away the reasons for why that is, far removed from the usual reasons for such tales. In the den, we stand and look at each other, a little awkwardly, a sudden tension stretching between us. I realize now that Daisy has been a buffer for most of the evening.

Determined to act natural, I sit on the couch in my usual spot, folding my legs beneath me. After a second, Dax follows suit, sitting down beside me and stretching his arm out along the back of the sofa.

His long fingers just brush my shoulder. If I shift the smallest amount, they'll be buried in my hair. Part of me wants to do just that, while the other part screams at me to run.

I sit there, tight and rigid, as every cell in me cries at the memory of how his hands felt on my body, bruising my skin and memorizing my curves.

Sin. Sustenance. Shelter.

"So."

"Um..."

We start and stop at the same time, Dax waving a hand in gentlemanly fashion for me to proceed.

I clear my throat. "So, you've been reading Gatsby."

His shoulder lifts in a little shrug, the gesture making his fingers dance way, then return. "I had to. It's... it's hard to explain, but the little I was able to read made me do some thinking. Reflecting, I guess."

Sending him a rueful smile, I say, "Before the rabbit ate your homework."

"Something like that, yeah," he chuckles.

Rising, I walk to the bookcase across the room and peruse the shelves with a finger before pulling a book from one. It's my own copy of The Great Gatsby, used and tattered, a finger-sized hole worn through on the back cover from where I've held it and rubbed absently.

This book carried me once upon a time. When Dad never came back to take me sailing, when all of Mom's worst fears about deep waters became truth, Gatsby somehow held me together. It was required reading for school, and the repeating images of water and sailing and boats held a resonance that carved me hollow and made me whole at the same time.

I carry it to Dax.

"Here," I murmur gently, handing him the copy. "If you can keep it from Bunnicula, take mine. It's all scribbled in, but still mostly readable—"

"Indie." His hand covers mine on the book, a spark of warmth flickering in his eyes. The brown eye glows with specks of gold. "Thank you," is all he says.

I watch as Dax flips through, pausing occasionally to linger over an underlined section or note in the margin, then clears his throat.

His gaze flits to mine. "So, there's this thing..."

Watching me steadily, he motions back and forth between us with his free hand, his other hand moving to encircle my wrist.

My heart, my stupid heart, starts thumping in my chest.

Please don't break me. Not again.

The evening has done a lot to shift my lingering anger to a state of cautious hope. I don't know what I'll do if he spoils it now. Lifting my chin, I wait for his words.

As if sensing my skittering unease, his thumb strokes small circles on the flesh of my wrist. "I think circumstances had us leaping, hard and fast, without a lot of thought," Dax begins, biting on his lip. "Which is exciting... but it's kind of like jumping off a cliff in the darkness, you know? Your heart is beating fast, partly because of whose hand you're holding, but mostly because you have no idea of what's beneath you."

I force a nod, my stomach unsettled.

This... this sounds a little like good-bye. Only, why would he come by to say good-bye a second time? It's cruel, and regardless of the internal battle he's dealing with, I don't think Dax is cruel. But he's still talking, so I still listen.

"I like you, Indie," he continues. "I like you a hell of a lot, and I don't want to leap headlong over a cliff with you, not knowing where we're headed. You—we—are worth more than that. I like the idea of taking things slow and steady."

For once in my recent existence, I can't think of what to say. I squint at him.

Slow and steady. Slow and steady.

"If you want to, that is?" His expression uncertain, Dax begins to pull his fingers from around my wrist, bringing me to my senses.

"No! I mean... yes. I'm sorry. It took me second to figure out..." I slap a palm to my forehead, inwardly cursing my own idiocy, then draw my gaze back to Dax. "Slow sounds good, Dax. Steady sounds... really good."

"Good."

His smile does funny things to my insides, and I have a sudden vision of how slow and steady might work. Having him close, having these little glances and touches and nothing more...

Torture. Complete and utter torture.

I smile brightly. "Okay, then. Slow and steady it is."

We got this.

Dax pats the sofa cushions before standing, his eyes twinkling with relief. "Okay."

I mirror him, walking to the door and facing him when he swings it open and waits expectantly. "I guess I'll see you later, then." I don't have anything for my fingers to fiddle with, so they find the hem of my sweater, stretching it nervously.

"Yeah, you will."

Rather than rushing out, Dax reaches down and grips the point of my chin between two fingers, tilting it up for a sweet, too-brief kiss that he presses to my lips. Then he's gone, leaving me standing in the doorway with my sweater hand pressed absently to my mouth.

All the better to hold his kiss in place.

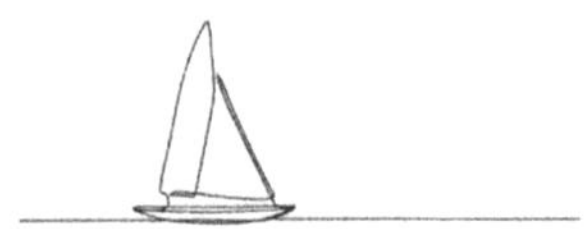

Mom pauses as she mixes together her Sunday mimosa, glancing over at the picture that Daisy is showing her. "That's lovely, sweetheart. I want one of those for my gallery wall for sure." Turning her attention to me, she wonders, "How long has she been drawing these, Indigo?"

From across the kitchen table, I peer over at Daisy's scattered pile of drawings. The subject is largely the same in all of the sketches. A line of marching lions, which in many cases, look more like laughably vicious kittens and figures that resemble Tameka, Blake, me, and Dax in various stages of battle.

My nose crinkles with adoration.

She's only four, but somehow Daisy's art transcends age and the simple psychological exercise it began as. They're not sophisticated drawings, but there's a gravity about them that speaks of weight, of sadness—even in polka-dotted lionesses and princes with spiky hair and purple trousers. It's a human weight, the kind no child should know but everyone suffers at least once.

Loss. Suffering. Fear.

Emotions I am all too familiar with.

I should have realized that Mom, with her background in art, would sink into Daisy's pictures immediately.

And that's fine, of course. But she can't have them.

"They're private," I blurt.

Mom gives me a measuring look. "I'm not planning on selling them, Indigo. I just want one for the house. But... goodness. Look at these." Her gaze is avid. "Her use of color and movement. The composition. It's..."

"I know, Mom. I've looked at them." I see them. Daisy's gaze travels from her grandmother to me, confused and watchful. I smile away her doubts. "Anyway, you can pick one to take home. Daisy would want you to."

"I don't want to upset you—"

A knock on the front door interrupts our discussion, and I bounce up from the chair. "Coming!"

A quick peep through the glass reveals Blake and Dax standing on the stoop, arms full of a box that jerks when I open the door.

I blink. "What in the world?"

"Hello to you, too, buttercup." Blake swoops in for cheek kisses and sails past me, while Dax follows more slowly, appraising me with vigilant eyes.

"Hi," he offers.

"Couldn't stay away?"

Dear God, I've forgotten how to flirt.

He doesn't seem to mind, if the slow smile inching up the corners of his mouth is any indication. "No. I really can't," he replies, a little sheepish, ducking his head and stuffing his hands into denim pockets. "I can't stay long, though. I just had something I wanted to drop off for Daisy... if it's okay with you. If it's not, I can take her back."

Her?

I narrow my eyes, lips puckering. "I'm not fond of rabbits."

"Not Skittles, I promise," he says with a grin, then adds, "Much to Blake's dismay."

Curious, I watch as he sets the box on the floor and opens the top a scant inch. Immediately, a tawny nose tipped with black pokes through, whiskers questing insistently. "Mrreow."

"Oh, my God." A kitten. He brought a kitten. "Daisy is going to flip."

"Her name is Pickles, and Blake found her at a shelter. She hates me." Dax sighs, gaze lingering on the tiny tabby. "I've always sort of preferred dogs. And rabbits, apparently."

I snicker, wondering how this little ball of fur could hate anybody. "Let's get Daisy. I can't wait to see her face."

I'm about to stand to fetch my daughter when Daisy skips into the room, Blake and Mom following behind her. Two blue eyes pop open, fixed to the box that seemingly moves on its own. She points, glancing up at me, as if asking for permission.

"Go ahead, baby," I encourage gently. "Look what Blake and Dax brought for you." Daisy approaches the box warily, her chin held high as a way to peer over the top. "Go ahead, open it up. Slow, though."

Settling beside me, she opens the box with careful motions, an indrawn breath her only audible reaction to seeing the kitten waiting within.

Her face, though. Her face transforms.

Daisy's curious eyes grow huge, welling up with tears. Her mouth carves crescents into her cheeks with the smile it makes, and her hands flap with endless excitement.

The kitten sits in one corner of the box, staring up at the humans above her with a mix of confusion and suspicion. She's an ochre ball of fluff, most of it forming, appropriately, a haze of fur around her face.

She looks like a baby lioness.

A little lion for my little lion.

I look over at Dax, my own eyes filling with emotion, and find him watching me.

We speak in silence.

She's perfect.

You're perfect.

Thank you.

His face softens as he averts his eyes, drinking in the moment. Then he places a big hand on Daisy's head, ruffling the strands of gold. "I hope you like her, Little Lion," he says, crouching down in front of her, hands dangling between his knees. "I know you'll take good care of Pickles. Just like your mom takes good care of you."

My heart erupts with adoration.

Daisy flings her arms around Dax's neck, holding him tight and pressing her face into the arch of his neck. She doesn't speak. She doesn't say a word, but maybe she doesn't need to. Maybe Dax understands her the same way we understand each other, because he simply whispers, low and tender, "You're welcome."

Chapter Twenty-Eight

Dax

"DAX! YOUR RABBIT ATE through my Aunt Mabel's vintage armoire!"

My eyes ping open.

Sunlight pours in through the giant, uncovered windows, causing me to blink and shift my weight on the orange couch.

Or "Tart Tangerine," as Blake has corrected on numerous occasions.

I'm used to being woken up by the smoothie maker, or by Lolli and Pop, Blake's two miniature poodles, jumping up onto the sofa and deciding that my legs make better dog beds. Sometimes it's the bustling sounds of Seattle city life, rousing me from my dreams.

I have to say, though… Aunt Mabel is a new one.

"Skittles, you absolute terror," Blake scolds from the opposite end of the long hallway. "Bad bunny! Naughty little scallywag."

Filling my cheeks with air, I blow out a frazzled breath, then lift up on my elbows. Four sleepy, ebony eyes stare back at me from the narrow gap between my ankles.

This is my life now.

"Dax!"

"Hell, I'm coming," I muster in a sleep-laden voice, my limbs stiff, muscles achy. I've been sleeping on Blake's couch, again, for only three days, but it's three days too long. I've been working up the mental courage to call my parents and let the world know I'm alive and well—sort of—but if anything is a kick in the ass, it's Blake yelling scallywag at six A.M.

With a final grunt of surrender, I pull myself up from the sofa and rise to my feet as Lolli and Pop hop down, scurrying away. I scratch the back of my head and stretch, then shuffle down the hall, my bare feet cold against the hardwood flooring. When I enter the second bedroom, Blake's office, my eyes land on the corner of the space, where Blake is holding Skittles in a cloud of resentment. His gaze narrows in my direction when I appear in the doorway.

"This beast is the bane of my existence, Dax."

I sigh. "It's just a rabbit."

"On the outside, it's a rabbit. On the inside, it's the diabolical incarnation of Audrey II from Little Shop of Horrors."

My lips pucker. "I'm not familiar."

"Feed me, Seymour!" he bellows dramatically.

Amusement mingles with exasperation as the heels of my hands rub the sleep from my eyes. Shaking my head at my flustered friend, I respond, "We'll be out of your hair soon. I need to get the ball rolling on… well, everything. Seeing my parents, getting my finances in order —"

Blake's snort of laughter cuts in. "Hare."

I blink.

He holds the rabbit up, her button nose wiggling, feet scampering in his grip. "Hare."

"Jesus."

Blake rises to his feet, plopping Skittles back into her cage as he brushes pieces of hay from his grey slacks. "It's fine, big man. There's no rush—mi casa es su casa."

"No offense, but your casa is kind of…" I fumble for the right word.

"Enchanting. Delightful," he provides. "An unimaginable oasis."

A smile pulls on my lips. "We'll go with unimaginable."

We share a laugh, and Blake slaps my shoulder as he moves past me, likely heading to the kitchen to make his morning smoothie and egg-and-spinach-surprise.

With extra spinach.

The past three days have been a whirlwind of planning, trying to dodge the public eye in my sunglasses and overgrown beard, as I'm not quite ready to announce my sudden reincarnation. I want my parents to know first. I want to see my father's face when I step inside my childhood home in Hawthorne Hills, and I want to see what he sees when his eyes land on me. Living and breathing.

Will he hug me? Will he slam the door in my face? Will he sigh in that specific way that he does, the long sigh of disappointment that has followed me around all my life?

I guess I'm a little terrified to find out.

My words to Garrett stumble through my head as I lean back against Blake's marble work desk: "We all want to be heard. Seen and appreciated."

The problem with my father is he's always seen right through me.

I've always been a ghost to him.

The sound of the smoothie machine startles me into an upright position, and I ruffle my hair with my palm—my too-long hair, currently flattened on one side by Blake's Marilyn Monroe designer throw pillow. My mind races with a to-do list, making mental bullet points of the things I want to accomplish today.

Get a haircut.

Find a place to live.

Trim Skittles' nails before she ruins Blake's luxury floors, and he ruins me.

Ask Indie out on a date.

Maybe.

She might just want to stay friends.

I should probably ask her that first.

Anxiety blooms in my gut as I push up from the desk and step out of the office, adding a final task to my list.

Tell my parents I'm alive.

Gulping down my trepidation, I meet Blake in the kitchen, just in time for a plate of green eggs to be thrust at me, while he bends down to feed his dogs two pieces of avocado toast, humming Rick Astley under his breath.

I start with finding a place to live.

The familiar home looms atop the tall hill, bathing me in vivid childhood memories. Some good, some bad. All an inherent part of me.

It's vastly different from the sterile condo I just settled on in Bellevue—a twelve-hundred square foot high-rise overlooking the city with white walls and grey wood floors.

This house is all cozy brick and burgundy shutters, a welcoming red door, and lush landscaping I can envision my mother lost in with her gardening gloves and wide-brimmed hat. Visions of running through the hedges, playing hide-and-seek with the neighbor boy, bring a smile to my face.

The smile fades when I remember what I'm doing here.

I swallow.

My steps are slow and faltering as I make my way up the cement walkway, my heart in my throat. I have no idea what to expect when that front door opens, but I hope she opens it. I hope it's Mom on the other side of the threshold because I'm not confident I can face him yet. I'm not ready to hear that sigh, to see that pointed look spear me behind his dark-rimmed glasses.

Apprehension tries to steal my courage, but I know... ready or not, it's time.

So, I knock.

My knuckles rap along the chipped red door as I fidget on the welcome mat, my eyes peering through the crack in the curtains, searching for movement or shadows. It's not long before I hear the approaching footfalls, and my insides spike with dread.

Please be her.

Please be Mom.

The door swings open, revealing the haggard stance of my father, his eyes sunken-in, complexion pasty. His normally tanned skin and jet black hair, evidence of his Russian descent, are blended with ash and white. He gapes at me, completely silent, one hand gripping the door frame, while the other whips his glasses from the bridge of his nose, as if that will help him see me better.

I want to melt into the concrete—pretend I was never even here at all. I want to run, go back into hiding, live like a ghost until the end of time. But I don't really want that... I only want that because he's looking at me like he truly sees me, and I have no goddamn clue what to do with that. I'm not sure how to react to something so foreign.

My father says nothing, the sentiment in his dark eyes unreadable. I also don't speak. I just stand on the front stoop with tendrils of nerves winding their way through me, tongue tied, words elusive.

And then he's ridden with strain, the angry kind. His jaw sets firm, his grip on the door turning white-knuckled. He squeezes his eyeglasses so hard in his opposite palm, they shatter in his fist. Either he doesn't notice, or he doesn't care, because he continues to stare at me with a narrowing gaze, steely and punishable.

"Who's there, Ivan?"

He remains eerily silent, even when Mom's voice cuts in.

Even when her scream tears through the tension mounting between us.

Even when she's throwing herself into my arms, wailing and weeping, loud enough to incite a grouping of neighbors to gather on the sidewalk.

"Oh, my baby boy. Oh, my son!" she sobs, dampening the front of my shirt with her tears of relief. She only pulls back to eye my father, perched behind her in the entryway. "Ivan, get over here and hug your child!"

My own tears threaten to claim me as I hold my petite mother in a tight grip, my attention aimed at my father over her shoulder. He doesn't hug me. He doesn't speak.

He just storms away.

Mom pulls me inside the house that will forever smell like apple pie, unable to let me go, even when we're seated side-by-side on the worn sofa. Her blue eyes are heavy with grief and shock as pieces of light brown hair frame her face. "Dax," she murmurs in a fractured whisper, clutching my hand between both palms. "What happened to you, sweetheart?"

There's so much to say. So much to tell. So many details to explain.

The events of the past year spiral through me, from the bank hold-up, to my near-death experience, to my captivity with Garrett, to Indie and Daisy, to my selfish decision to disappear.

It's right there, on the tip of my tongue, desperate for release.

But all I manage to say is, "He doesn't even care."

My mother's eyes glow with more tears that spill down her brightly rouged cheeks. She squeezes my hand as she shakes her head back and forth. "He cares, Dax," she tells me, her breath catching on a wave of emotion. "You have no idea how much he cares."

I look away.

Clenching my teeth together, I stare straight ahead, my focus on the empty space where my father once stood.

She's right. I have no idea.

He's never bothered to show me.

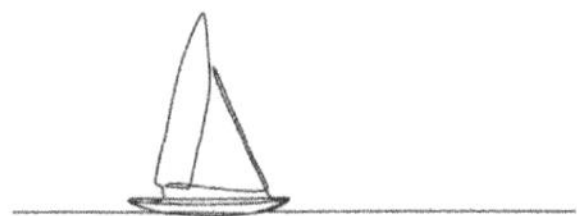

When night falls over the city, I'm back at Blake's condo, eating Thai food out of little white boxes. My friend sits beside me, with Lolli and Pop sprawled lazily between us.

"The Golden Girls. Utterly timeless," Blake says through a mouthful of curry.

His contentment doesn't seem to rub off on me. I force out an ingenuine chuckle of agreement, my mind elsewhere, and my heart despondent. The long, hard discussion with my mother this afternoon weighs heavily, and the absence of my father throughout the entirety of it weighs even heavier.

Sucking down a bite of noodles with my chopsticks, I zone out from the television laugh track and think back to my internal to-do list, needing a better distraction.

I cut my hair. I trimmed Skittles' nails, much to her dismay. I put an offer in on a new place—all cash, stored up in my multiples savings accounts. I unveiled myself to my parents, leaving their house with a promise to return tomorrow.

A promise to my mother.

She tried to cover for my father's glaring absence the way she had throughout my childhood: with an outpouring of maternal affection and excuses that rang hollow.

"He cares," she told me. "Trust me. He just doesn't know how to show it. He's gone to process all these messy emotions. Next time will be different."

"I'll come see you, Mom, but he doesn't need to be here. Tell him that."

She was already shaking her head, pushing the cookies she'd insisted on baking toward me. "I certainly will not. You need to make that first move, sweetheart. Swallow your pride because his runs too deep."

I snorted and brushed at some crumbs on the counter. "Mom. I've been swallowing my pride since I was five years old. I can't keep doing it. I don't even understand..."

"Don't you?" From her seat across the kitchen table, she eyed me closely, forcing me to examine my relationship with my father.

I shook my head. "Not sure what you mean."

"You were the one thing he couldn't control, Dax. His only child—a son, no less. His pride. You were never disrespectful or dismissive, but you had no interest in the things that he loved. Medicine. History. His ancestry. That you chose hockey over these things was a knife to him."

"I..." I wasn't sure how to reply, and I knew I'd be processing her analysis long after our visit. It was a reason, sure, but did it make it okay? Not at all.

At least I could understand him better.

"It's okay, Dax. We must all choose the things we love, the dreams that choose us. He has yet to figure this out." She sighed and sipped her coffee. "He will, though. He's a smart man."

I chuckle to myself as I remember how she had arched her eyebrow and tapped her temple, adding, "it was why I married him, after all."

Despite my father's greeting, it had been a good day.

A busy day; a long one.

And now, there's only one thing left to do.

Pulling out my cell phone, I scroll through my list of contacts until I find her name.

Indigo.

Dax: Hey :) I was wondering if you wanted to go out on a date. Dinner or something.

I click send, then frantically add,

Dax: With me.

Only a few moments go by before her response dings in my hand.

Indie: Hi! I'd love to. Let me know when. I'll see if Tameka or my mom can watch Daisy.

Dax: Great. If you want, I can find out if Blake is up for the job.

Indie: ... I'll see if Tameka or my mom can watch Daisy.

Laughter rumbles in my chest, a smile stretching through my reply.

Dax: Fair enough. Tomorrow at 7? I know a good place.

Indie: In public?

Hesitation fuses with a pang of nerves. I've been in isolation so long, I don't even know how I'll react to public scrutiny or overly aggressive fans. Even my incognito Uber rides have made me twitchy and uneasy.

Drawing in a deep breath, I message her.

Dax: Yeah. In public.

She texts back right away.

Indie: I'll hold your hand.

My heart fills with warmth at the sentiment as I send my thanks and slip the phone into my back pocket. I'm not used to anyone holding my hand—I've always been the strong one, the leader. The hero. But Indie's words trickle through me, softening my dauntless exterior and offering shelter from my self-inflicted storm.

And it feels good.

It feels really good to share the weight.

I'm not sure how I'll react tomorrow night, sailing headfirst into uncharted waters, but the notion will be far less intimidating with Indie's hand held tightly in mine.

I have an anchor now.

I have her.

Chapter Twenty-Nine

Indie

WARMTH UNDERSCORES THE BRISK evening air as we stroll past the Seattle Spheres. They loom above us like illuminated cat toys filled with foliage, snagging my attention for a moment. The restaurant Dax scored a reservation for is somewhere in this area, but he parked a couple of blocks away, wanting to walk. I'm glad for the distance, if only because his hand brushes mine periodically as we walk.

An accident, or with intention?

Holding my breath, I turn my hand ninety-degrees, so my palm faces behind me and my pinky finger is closest to Dax. It's the first thing his hand will touch, and it would be only natural, if his hand were oriented the same way, for both our pinkies to clasp each other.

If only for a breath.

God, I'm ridiculous.

I'm about to relax my hand when he does it again, and his pinky doesn't hesitate. It catches and tangles securely with mine for considerably longer than a breath. Then he turns his hand and twines his fingers with mine, all of them, enveloping my palm securely within his own.

I smile.

"Is this all right?" His voice is low in tambor, yet cuts through the busy sidewalk noise, nonetheless.

"More than." Feeling unaccountably shy, I sneak a glance up to find him peering down at me with a bemused expression. "What?"

"You look nervous."

Oh. My poker face is not on point tonight. Clearing my throat, I reply, "I am nervous."

"Why?" Stopping in front of a restaurant with a discreet sign that reads 2120, he waits before entering, pulling me to the side to avoid traffic. "We've been held at gunpoint. Avoided death. Had sex. What is there to be nervous about?"

I manage to meet his gaze, holding my own steadily as I put what I've been feeling for the past couple of weeks into words. "All of that feels like a prequel, somehow. It's like we're just getting started, and we're moving on to the things that actually mean something, you know?" I swallow, wondering if that made any sense at all. "The important stuff."

His expression, which had been teasing, sobers as his hand tightens on mine. "Yeah," he admits gently. "I know exactly what you mean. But there's still nothing to be nervous about. This is a test you've already passed, honey."

"Test?" My eyes widen, eyebrows arching to my hairline. "When did I pass a test?"

Moving his hand to the center of my back, Dax steers me inside the restaurant and gives his name to the suddenly very starstruck hostess. He looks down at me, solemn-faced, before letting his eyes travel the restaurant. "When you smiled at me without having the first clue who I was," he says.

The admission startles me at first. I nibble my lip, still tacky from lip gloss, and follow his gaze throughout the busy restaurant. There is already so much attention on us, so many curious stares, and I realize Dax deals with this sort of thing on a daily basis. Or... he did. Before he disappeared.

And now he has to deal with it tenfold, as a man back from the dead.

I can only imagine the relief he must have felt to not be... noticed. By me. Something so backwards in today's society, but so important to Dax.

As the hostess leads us to a table in the back, I'm aware of an ebb and flow in conversation around us. Gazes dart toward us, then away. A buzz claims the air, almost electric in intensity, and I know it's because of him. The public announcement of his non-death has clearly made the rounds, and his appearance isn't going unnoticed. The touch of his hand on the small of back has shifted from a subtle support, to the use of me as a prop.

Shifting subtly, I take hold of it and offer a squeeze as we're seated. "You okay?"

His indrawn breath is deliberate, and he withdraws his hand to raise his water glass and take a sip. "I'm good."

"We don't have to—"

"I'm good, Indie," he insists, and I'm unsure if he's trying to convince me… or himself. "There's nowhere else I'd rather be."

Despite his words, I can't help feeling like he's retreated somewhere—somewhere far away, a place I can't reach. A silence settles in, and I fidget with the plastic edging on the menu as I peruse the selections.

The dishes are interesting and mouth-watering. Pork belly porchetta, grilled octopus, braised oxtail and duck. Dax and I order drinks and an appetizer and lean in to wait, the intimate, cozy atmosphere of 2120 winding itself around us like a lazy cat.

Dax's eyes dip to my mouth for a brief moment, then slide up to meet my soft stare. "Talk to me."

"Okay." Clearing my throat, the day's antics come to mind, and I cross my arms atop the table. "Pickles got into a loaf of bread that we'd left on the counter today. I managed to rescue it before the situation progressed too far."

"Oh?" he chuckles.

" I know. Who'd have thought a cat would like bread? Daisy was on the floor in a fit of giggles." A smile unfolds as I muse over the kitty shenanigans. "Pickles is good for her."

Dax's expression is sheepish as he reaches for the water again. "I… uh, sorry about that. She may have been a little wild at Blake's place, too. I was hoping she'd calm down once she settled in."

I huff, then beam him a playful eye roll. "Yeah, no," I tease, drawing out the word. "She's a psycho kitty. She thinks my feet are whack-a-moles for her claws. She terrorizes the couch. The drapes are vines that she swings from. I'm dying. Every day, I'm dying, and it's all your fault."

Dax's shoulders are shaking with laughter while he takes in my tirade. "I'm so sorry. Did I say that yet?"

"You did." My grin broadens, and I reach across the tabletop for his hand, dusting my thumb over his knuckles. "And… I'm not sorry."

He raises a curious eyebrow.

"She's a pretty awesome snuggle buddy," I inform him. "I kind of like her, and Daisy adores her. So… thank you."

His eyes twinkle back at me, the blue just a little brighter than the brown, but before he can reply, a commotion to the left jerks my attention away.

"Miss, we really can't—"

"Dax! Oh, my God, Dax! It is you! Can you autograph me? Please? I'm so happy you're alive!"

"Miss—"

An apologetic waiter is shoved aside by a trio of young women in their early twenties. They're glammed-up to the max, decorated with makeup, hair extensions, and push-up bras lifting their breasts.

One pair of those breasts is now pushing in Dax's face, and her plunging cleavage, further revealed by the red nails tugging at it, hovers over our table. "Right here would be perfect," she says giddily.

I stare at Dax in horror as the scene unfolds.

Is this... his life?

Somewhere behind me, a flash goes off. Pictures. Someone's taking photos. The intimate sound of dinner conversation is the angry buzz of busy bees now, insistent and clamorous.

This. This right here. This is why he retreated to that cabin and planned on never returning to polite society. It's because society is anything but polite. It's carnivorous, intent only on satisfying its own greedy urges and desires.

I want to cry as Dax visibly grapples for control across from me. I want to yell at these diners-turned-hyenas, bare my teeth and force them back. I want to yank on those extensions and send these little girls home to mama for a few lessons in propriety and class.

Dax declines the offer to sign the girl's cleavage, scribbling his signature onto her arm instead. He's eerily quiet, and while he remains calm and professional, I can feel the tension rolling off of him in waves. His mouth is in a taut line, his jaw ticking. He breathes heavily, his shoulders drawing back to showcase his stiff, rigid posture.

He's uncomfortable.

He should be.

A finger taps my shoulder. I half-turn to see a man with a professional grade camera and a flash of white teeth, squatting near my chair. "Ma'am? Justin Carroll with Seattle Buzz. Mind if I ask you a few questions?"

"I..." I glance back at Dax, but he's involved with another swooning fangirl. Another autograph. Another tight smile.

"Great, thanks," the reporter breezes. "What's your name, sweetheart?"

"My name? Indie, but I don't—"

His eyes narrow. "Indie? As in, Indigo Chase?"

"Yes, but—"

"From Edgewater. I knew you looked familiar," the man says, slapping his knee. "Oh, this just got a lot more interesting."

"She's off-limits." Dax cuts in, his hard hand covering mine atop the table with sudden possessiveness as he pulls me to my feet. "We're done here."

The reporter's face falls, his expression turning grim, but he doesn't question—he simply steps out of the way and pulls his camera into readiness as Dax tows me after him. The crowd parts, as if commanded by an unseen force, and we're outside in seconds. We breathe in the fresh air that smells of seafood and impending rain, almost like we've been deprived rather than merely sitting in a restaurant only moments ago.

I didn't realize, though, until we're standing out here on the sidewalk, the city humming around us and the night clean and cool, that it felt like that inside.

Suffocating. Dense. Choking.

Dax walks a few steps away and runs his hands through his hair, disrupting the stylish mess he adorned at the beginning of the date. "I'm sorry," he says, his back to me. The muscles beneath his polo flex with tension. "I didn't realize it would be like that."

My heart aches for him. "It's okay," I mutter gently, my purse hanging from my fingertips as this flood of melancholy hangs between us.

He whirls to face me, one finger extended toward the entrance. "No, damnit, it is not okay. "That bullshit is never okay. It's invasive and entitled and..." He stops, closing his eyes and intaking a long breath. When he regains control, swallowing hard, his posture deflates. "Come on. Let's walk."

I nod, and we walk.

We walk without speaking for half an hour. At first, I think we're going to the car, severing the night short, but when we stroll past it and keep going, I relax into my shoes. Oddly, I'm not ready to go home just yet. Despite Dax's barely tethered temper, the ambush of crazed fans and reporters, and my discomfort with being out of my house, it feels good to walk beside this man, smelling his aftershave and feeling his hand occasionally brush against mine.

When we come upon a stand selling pretzels and donuts, I tug on Dax's sleeve and nod my chin. With a smile of submission, he orders a pretzel and two coffees, and we continue our journey, sharing the treat as we go.

Swallowing down a bite, Dax finally speaks, his tone far more subdued. "That's partly what I didn't feel I had the bandwidth to come back to."

I understand, bobbing my head and glancing up at him. "I get that."

His anger has dissolved into contentment, and I'm not sure if it was the salty pretzel dipped in honey mustard, or the hazelnut latte warming him up, but I hope...

I hope it was me.

Our hands find each other's once again, and in accord, we turn and begin a slow stroll back in the direction of the car.

"It's different now," Dax muses, stealing a quick look down at me. "I used to be able to compartmentalize, you know? Carry on a conversation with Blake, while I sign a girl's—" He breaks off, an adorable flush staining his cheeks.

"Boob, Dax. You can say it."

"Whatever." A laugh escapes him as he ducks his chin to his chest. "Anyway, now it just... really, really pisses me off. Especially when you're involved, subjected to this madness. And that pisses me off, too, because I'm not an angry person, Indie. I don't want you to think that I am."

"I don't." I shake my head quickly, hoping he sees my truth. "I think you handled it perfectly. You have a good grasp on your self-control."

His eyes flare before turning contemplative. "But things have a way of changing people."

This wipes the soft smile from my lips, and all I can do is nod stiffly in reply.

Yes, yes, they do.

I'm living proof, after all. Edgewater changed me. It changed Daisy.

But...

No. That's not altogether true.

I halt Dax mid-stride and stare up at him, placing both palms on his cheeks to ensure I have his full attention. "Yes, things change people, Dax... but they change the way we react to things." He's silent as he watches me, a flurry of emotions skating across his handsome features. "But... you know me, right?" I continue. "Am I changed? Did Edgewater change me, fundamentally, as a person?"

A thoughtful moment hovers heavily between us, passing cars and city life the only sounds infiltrating our silence.

"I'm still the same person, Dax. A little bruised, a little scarred. I was disoriented for a while, dazed and uncertain, and it's taken me a while to get my bearings. But I'm finding myself again," I tell him, dusting my thumbs along the bristles of his jaw, watching his eyes dance with revelation. "The real me. I'm still here."

Stretching up on my toes, I press a kiss to the tender skin just below his earlobe.

"And so are you."

Chapter Thirty

Dax

"HEY, HERO."

A familiar voice filters its way through my ears as I try to pull myself into a sitting position, but I'm hindered by the rope around my wrists. Grumbling, I let out a sigh of frustration. "Really?" I draw my gaze to Garrett, who looms over my bedside. "This again?"

"Can't have you trying to bail on me. Your hero antics are gettin' old, hockey man."

I tug at the restraints. "This is stupid. You don't need me anymore."

Garrett approaches the tattered mattress with languid steps, his hands stuffed inside his pockets. He pulls his lips between his teeth with a shrug. "Sorry, no can do. You're stuck with me," he says, his light eyes glimmering by way of the singular crack in the window covering. "But I think you already know that."

"Dax! Come look at this."

Indie's voice captures me, far-off, somewhere I can't pinpoint. She's close, but not close enough. My hands curl into fists, yanking at the bedposts, my legs trying to kick their way free.

"Dax, hurry!" she calls again.

"I-I can't… I'm trapped." A low growl rumbles through my chest, my muscles sore and strained. When Garrett takes a seat beside my tethered ankles, I spear him with a look of desperation. "Please. She needs me."

"She'll wait." Garrett runs a dirty hand through his hair, smoothing it back, then meets my pleading gaze. His features soften, a frown of contemplation settling into his forehead. "I guess I was wrong about you. Looks like you got the girl, after all."

Daisy's little feet run past the door, causing my heart to lurch.

"A happy ending for a real fuckin' hero."

"I'm not..." Swallowing, I squeeze my eyes shut.

I'm not a hero. I'm not a hero.

My head starts to pound as flashes of light infiltrate my mind.

Light, noise, images.

Memories?

Garrett rushes at me.

Broken glass.

A struggle.

Jumbled words.

My bullet wound throbs, drenching me with weakness.

I'm not strong enough. I can't take him.

I'm going to die here.

Everything goes silent, and then... I'm somewhere else.

"I always knew I'd end up here one day."

When I open my eyes, my breath stalls. I'm bathed in sunlight, perched seaside on a lawn chair, staring out at the rushing waves. Birds sing overhead, and I squint my eyes through my sunglasses, wondering how the hell I got here.

Pivoting to the right, I discover Garrett sprawled out in his own chair beside me, a cocktail in hand. "Where are we?"

"I think you know," he replies, tone evasive. Garrett holds up the glass of frozen slush, accessorized with a colorful umbrella. "Got my piña colada. Good shit. Totally underrated."

I shake my head, trying to rid myself of the strange fog. It feels peaceful here, but something's wrong. This isn't right. It's a fabricated perfection, false, hollow.

Where's Indie? Where's Daisy?

How did we even get here?

"Think there's redemption for an asshole like me?"

Blinking through the bright rays of sunshine, I return my attention to Garrett as children and strangers move past us along the beach, splashing at the shore. The scent of coconuts wafts through the air, mingling with Hawaiian melodies from across the coastline. I'm fumbling for a response, unsure of what to say, how to answer that, when something new steals my attention.

A red stain.

Garrett's shirt blooms with crimson, growing larger by the second.

I point at his chest, my words catching. "You're bleeding."

"Yeah?" Unfazed, he takes a sip of the cocktail, slurping it through a narrow straw, then leans back in his chair with a sigh of contentment.

"So are you."

"What?" My eyes drop to my own chest, where a similar stain stares back at me. So much blood. So much red. My gunshot wound must have come unstitched, and now I'll bleed out.

Right here in the Maui sand.

Frantic, I pull my shirt over my head, searching for the open wound, desperate to stop the bleeding. I don't want to die. Indie needs me.

They need me.

"You know what really grinds my gears, hero?"

Garrett's interruption calms my bout of panic as he leisurely sips his drink and stares out at the water in front of us. He's not worried. I guess I shouldn't be, either. When our eyes meet across the chairs, I slow my frenzied motions and murmur quietly, "What?"

He sends me a melancholy smile, then returns his attention to the rippling currents. "We never got to have that beer."

Something crashes, and I startle awake, soaked in sweat.

Shit.

Another fucked up dream.

Blake's voice bellows from down the hallway, following the ominous clatter. "Dax! Your rabbit knocked over my Grecian statue of Dionysus!"

What the hell?

I stare blankly out the window, the sky still deep with morning dusk.

It's way too early for this.

Pulling myself up on the couch, I settle back against the cushions, choosing to let Blake deal with the mess until I clear my head. The dream is still stark and vivid in my mind, leaving me unsettled. The remnants of it prompt me to reach behind my back, into my wallet, and sift out the wrinkled envelope with a letter enclosed.

A letter I wrote that final day at the cabin.

A letter unsent.

Unfolding it, I stare down at the pen strokes through the dim light.

"I had no intention of writing you this, but here we are..."

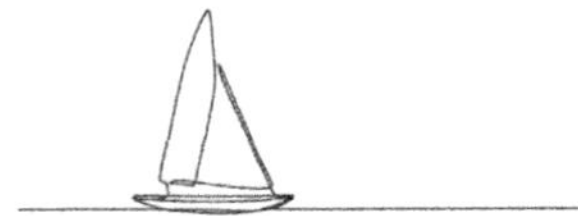

While Blake is out for the evening, on a date with Casey, a knock sounds at the front door. I'm not expecting company in my boxers and white t-shirt, so I race to throw on a pair of jeans, then head to the front of the condo, pulling the door open.

"Surprise."

Indie stands on the other side of it, holding some sort of tin-foiled casserole dish in her hands, accompanied by Daisy.

And Pickles.

My heart races.

Daisy holds the kitten up in two tiny hands, proudly showing me her new friend, while Indie shoots me an apologetic smile. "I hope it's okay that we brought the new addition. They're inseparable these days."

"Of course…" I'm still processing the fact that they're here, with food and a naughty kitten, and with big, happy smiles, that I still haven't invited them inside. Shaking away the daze, I step aside. "Of course. Shit, come in. It's great to see you."

Ducking her head, Indie moves through the threshold, her daughter skipping behind with a grin. "Sorry to stop by without notice. I…" She bites her lip, her gaze skating around the living area before settling on me. "I thought we could finally have that date. You know, minus the aggressive audience."

My smile is automatic as I take the dish from her hands, a warmth settling into my bones. "Yeah, that was kind of—"

"Terrifying," she provides.

"Thoroughly."

The humor lingers as we stare at each other, blending with something else. Something heavier. Something soul-deep. Our previous date flashes to mind, and while it was a total shitshow at the restaurant, the real date came afterwards. The pretzels and coffee, the wanting looks, the sweet kisses. She held my hand, just like she said she would.

"I'm the same person, Dax. I'm still here. And so are you."

Her words prickle my skin, puncturing me with that familiar, lingering doubt.

No.

Not tonight. Tonight there is only belief in something better.

I push it all aside and clear my throat, glancing down at the casserole. "This is really thoughtful, Indie. Let me go change," I tell her, eyeing her long, black dress and loosely curled hair. I look like a bum, and she's a vision. "I wasn't expecting company."

"Don't you dare. You look perfect."

Arching an eyebrow, I question her claim.

"I mean, you could use a few more stains on your shirt—then you'll definitely look the part for a Chase dinner party."

Laughter rumbles through me, and I nod my head, the tinfoil crinkling in my grip. I move to set the dish down, catching her watching me when I sneak a peek over my shoulder. She wrings her hands together, bracelets jangling, looking unsure.

I don't want her to be unsure.

Do I make her feel unsure?

I wonder if she noticed the flicker of apprehension that crossed my face—if she's been reading me like her favorite book, absorbing my torn pages and unsaid words. I wonder if she sees a green light, or if there is only red.

Daisy darts past us, chasing Pickles as the kitten prances in circles with mewls and purrs, and the image softens me. It overshadows my misgivings; my haunted thoughts. My gaze meets Indie's again as she soaks up the scene, and her lips curl up, her eyes shimmering with affection.

They look greener than they ever have.

And in that moment, I know, without a doubt... I'm sure.

I'm sure about her.

I'm sure about them.

Indie made me chicken pot pie from scratch, having been told by Blake that it was my favorite. We whipped up a salad and dinner rolls to accompany the dish and sat at the glass-topped table that overlooked the city to eat our meal, the scene cozy and domestic. Daisy played chaperone between us for the few minutes it took her to consume the four bites it took to fill up her tummy, and now we're sipping on red wine as I tidy the kitchen.

I feel her saunter up behind me as I start the dishwasher, so I twist in place, my gaze zoning in on her flushed cheeks. She fingers the stem of her wine glass, a flirty smile teasing her lips. I drink her in, from her painted toes to her hair spun with gold. "We've done everything a little backwards, haven't we?" I ponder, unable to keep my focus from slipping to the low-cut neckline of her dress.

She notices, flushing harder but standing firm. "I think the first dates are supposed to come at the beginning," Indie confirms. Heat dances in her aquamarine eyes.

"Do you think that's bad luck?"

"That our courtship started during a hostage situation?"

My mouth twitches despite the harrowing memories. "Is that what this is? A courtship?"

Indie ducks her head, somewhat bashfully, then sips from the rim of her glass. She takes a few steps closer to me, swallowing as she lifts her chin. She's close now—so close I can smell the honeysuckles in her hair. I sweep my gaze over her a second time, remembering how she felt tangled in my bedsheets, skin slicked with sweat, moaning my name. My pillow smelled like her for days, and I can't help wanting all of my pillows to smell like her.

I feel stirring from down below.

Damn.

Orchid-tinged lipstick leaves a kiss on her glass as she sets it on the counter beside the dishwasher. Braving a final step towards me, Indie sucks in a breath and replies, "I'd like it to be more."

Her warmth invades me, as does her words.

More.

She wants to be more than shallow promises to Hawaii and hopeless kisses. More than a one-night stand in my cabin of ghosts. More than this strange limbo we're in, caught between a tentative friendship and something bigger than us both.

And hell, I want that, too.

I move in, my hands gripping the curve of her waist and pulling her forward. Indie squeaks in surprise, her own palms rising to plant against my chest. Pressing my forehead to hers, I murmur back, "Me, too."

Indie's breath catches—a hopeful little sound. "You do?"

"Yeah, I do." I slide one hand up her body until it lands along her neck, my thumb dusting the soft skin. "I can't promise I won't fuck this up. I'm still a little... broken."

"We're all a little broken, Dax," she whispers to the narrow space between us. "We're all navigating rough waters."

Currents again. I grip her tighter.

"But we beat on."

How is it that she seems to know exactly what I'm thinking?

My internal chaos seems to dissipate the moment I crash my lips to hers. My waters calm, the storm breaks. Her tongue is my anchor as it sweeps along mine, causing me to cradle her face in both palms, tugging her as close as I can. Indie's body presses into me with surety and surrender, her arms circling around my back and gripping my shoulder blades to steady herself. The heat blossoms between us. The room evaporates until it's just us.

This kiss isn't a distraction, like we shared in that break room. It's not a reprieve from my loneliness back at the cabin.

It's a renewal.

My fingers weave through her loose curls, holding her to me as I tilt her head to deepen the kiss. Her whimpers fill my mouth, her fingernails digging into the planes of my back. She pulls away for a quick gulp of air, but that's all I allow. My teeth nick her bottom lip before I steal her breath, my tongue plunging back inside, until she's spun around, her back to the countertop as a means to steady her shaking knees. We don't break the kiss when my hand travels down her thigh, inching beneath the hem of her dress, or when her leg lifts to curl around mine, our pelvises grinding together and forcing a groan from my throat.

I only break the kiss to inch back, breathing heavy, heart racing, and whisper raggedly, "Think Blake will mind watching Daisy tonight?"

She smiles at me through swollen lips, her eyes glazed with lust. Indie tightens her hold on me, preparing to answer.

But before she can speak... someone else does.

"I'm a lion. Roar!"

We untangle ourselves, tearing apart in a flash, and Indie whirls around until we're both peering out into the living room where Daisy has been playing quietly.

I glance at Indie, noting the rush of tears to her eyes as her hand clasps her chest with a startled gasp.

Holy shit.

Daisy stands tall before us, grinning wide, holding the orange tabby kitten high above her head.

CHAPTER THIRTY-ONE

Indie

"OH, MY GOD." Ohmygod, ohmygod, ohmygod. She's talking. I flash a quick look at Dax as I stumble past him and fall to my knees in front of Daisy.

We both heard that, right?

Play it cool, mama.

Ohmygod.

I feel the tears on my cheeks, but I can't give them credence at the moment. "Daisy… baby…" I can't remember what the psychologist said I should do when—when, not if—this happened. Ignore it? Play it off? Talk about it? God, I don't remember. "You're a lion?"

Daisy nods, holding Pickles out to me. "Nan ya mama ban—"

I can't help but laugh through my tears as she butchers the iconic Lion King line, then I bury my face in Pickles' soft fur as my daughter skips back to the living room to continue watching the film Dax set up earlier.

Dax's hand settles on my shoulder and I turn, pinning the kitten between us when he wraps his arms around me and holds me in the protective circle of his arms. "Go on," he murmurs. "Let it out."

And I do. The desire that flamed between us minutes ago is forgotten momentarily, pushed aside so I can gasp and sob out my relief and lingering fear, let it vanish in trails of salt and snot on his t-shirt. When everything is gone, I discover us on the kitchen floor, our backs to the cabinets built into the island. A room away, the closing credits of The Lion King play, and I know my daughter will be hunting for me any second. I stir from my limp position against Dax's chest, loathe to move.

"I'm so sorry—"

"Don't." Dax's hands cup my cheeks, and he pulls my mouth to his for a tender, fierce kiss. "I'll deny it until I'm gray, but I shed a few myself when she busted out with 'I'm a lion!'"

Sniffling, I nod. "I'm just so happy. So relieved."

"I know, honey. I am, too."

"Everything's falling into place, Dax. It feels like we're finally..." I lift one shoulder, searching for the right expression. "... almost home, you know?"

Although there's the faintest hint of trouble in his mismatched eyes, he kisses me again, lingering on my bottom lip. "Yeah. I know."

"What you guys doin'?" Daisy's voice, high and bright and so familiar, even after this long stretch of silence, pierces the bubble. I startle against Dax, and we burst into giddy laughter.

It's clearly time to go, but my heart is light for the first time in months.

I know we're just getting started.

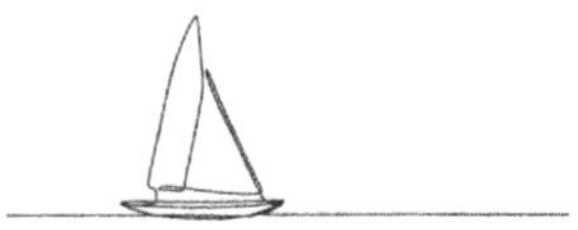

Several days later, I'm pouring a second cup of coffee and preparing to sit down to a little work when a knock sounds on the front door. It's Dax, leaning with sheepish hope against the doorjamb, a brown paper bag in his hand. As he holds it up, delicious scents waft my way, invoking a full belly growl that makes him grin.

"Hungry?" he wonders, smile lingering. "I thought maybe we could try 2120 again... in private this time."

"Are you kidding? I'd be down with Bob's Burger Joint, but this smells amazing." I open the door wider, and he steps in, pausing next to me. Our chests are the expansion of a breath apart, and this close, the subtle aftershave he wears, something citrusy with a hint of spice, fills my senses and makes my mouth water.

"I want to kiss you," he murmurs, his mouth hovering just beside my ear. "But I'll wait."

As he moves further into the house, I close the door, releasing my breath with a whoosh. Damnit, man. Now I don't know which I want more…

Food or a kiss.

Since the days have been getting progressively milder, we sit outside to eat, moving to my swing when we finish to laze against each other and enjoy the sunshine for a little longer. I've forgotten little pleasures like this. Simple things, like the warm strength of a man's body against mine. Conversation. Enjoying a meal together.

Daisy will be home from preschool in a little while, but for now it's just us, a pseudo-date in the middle of the day, and it's bliss.

I don't want to get too accustomed to it, though. Despite how comfortable I feel with him, and how good he makes me feel, I don't know much about Dax except the inexplicable pull I feel toward him. The way my heart speaks to his. I've already had one undeniable experience in heartbreak; if my marriage to Jeremy taught me anything, it's that I'm too fragile for putting my heart out there to be trampled on over and over again.

Pulling me into him so my back is to his chest, Dax links our hands and pulls my palm to his lips for a quick kiss. He's quiet, so much so that I search for something to say to fill the silence, something I don't typically worry with. Silence has never bothered me.

"Would you rather… eat a dirt sandwich or a worm pie?" I ask.

I feel him chuff against my hair. "Worm pie."

"Eww. Would you rather… have no kids or ten kids?"

"Ten."

"Really?" I twist to look up at him in surprise.

"Absolutely," he says back with no hesitation. Amusement glints down at me. "Kids are the real deal."

I wrinkle my nose, remembering Jeremy's distaste for all things baby. "Dirty diapers, spit-up, crying, tantrums—"

"Every bit of it."

My fingers find my empty ring finger, and I twist the blank space on my skin, my gaze vague as I look across the yard. "Jeremy did not want kids, you know. He wanted me to have an abortion when he found out I was pregnant with Daisy."

"Mm." Dax's tone is noncommittal, but there's a wealth of distaste in the single syllable.

"I was so angry with him for the longest time after he… after he was killed. It was like this part of me saw it as him just wiggling his way out of his responsibility any way he could, you know?" My own words slither through me, causing my insides to clench with disgust. "No, no… that's an awful thing to think. I'm sorry."

Dax is quick to squeeze my hand. "Don't be sorry. Grief is a senseless beast."

Swallowing, I bite down on my lip, choking back my irrational train of thought. "I appreciate that, but… I think I really need to let it go. If I'm going to move on, I have to forgive him. Not just for dying, but for everything that came before."

My revelation surprises me. How do I go from contemplating the hurt he leveled me with to this, all in the space of minutes? I'm not certain, but it feels authentic.

The backyard is quiet following my statement, as if not only I, but the springing blades of grass and the new budding trees are also processing my truth. A gentle breeze ripples the softly swaying pink bells of the stachyurus several feet away, and I close my eyes, listening.

And then I let go.

I forgive you, Jeremy.

A thousand heavy weights lift from my shoulders, and inside, I float.

Behind me, Dax releases a slow exhale, but he's stiff. Without even looking, I feel the tension pouring off him, so I fidget in place as I speak his name. "Dax?"

"Yeah?"

A beat rolls by, and I ask, "What about you?"

"What about me?"

"Will you tell me about what happened with your ex?" I wait with bated breath, hoping I haven't overstepped. It feels only natural to discuss relationship history with Dax—the people who have shaped the way we love, good and bad. Sometimes ugly.

We all have our baggage.

"I don't like to talk about that."

The reluctance in his voice has me treading with caution, but still, I persist. "Nobody enjoys talking about their exes," I tell him, shifting within the circle of his arms so I can see his face. "Sometimes it's necessary, though… so we can move on. Heal."

"You trying to psychoanalyze me, honey?" There's teasing in his tone, but I'm not teasing. I genuinely want to know. So, I shake my head, mute encouragement for him to keep going, and Dax sighs. And then… he caves. "Sabrina was…" He looks at me briefly, then out at nothing. "She was everything I thought I wanted. Gorgeous, successful, funny."

I ignore the ridiculous stab of jealousy and focus instead on what he's telling me. She was then.

I am now.

"Long story short, she ended up pregnant. We were thrilled," Dax says, pausing again to reflect. "It wasn't planned, but that was okay. We talked about getting married, I bought a house, she started picking out all this stuff for the nursery..."

A black cloud looms ahead, and I brace for the storm.

"And then... she miscarried."

No. Emotions sweep through me, and I interlace our fingers together, holding tight. "God, how awful."

He nods, a clipped movement of his head. "She was devastated."

"I'm sure she was," I concur. "But..."

"But what?"

I hesitate, and his eyes meet mine for the first time since beginning his story. "But what about you? Weren't you devastated, too?"

"Of course, I was." Dax frowns, shifting beneath my weight. "That was my baby. I want babies. I want children."

"But the way you said it... it was like her devastation was more significant than yours."

Dax draws his bottom lip between his teeth, thinking. His eyes turn contemplative. "In some ways, it absolutely was. I grieved on my own. I tried to help her... but ultimately, I think I smothered her." He retreats for a moment, his features pinching with guilt and regret. "I was always asking if she was okay, if she needed this, if she wanted that. She just wanted space. Needed space. Time. I don't know why I couldn't give it to her."

"You needed to fix it," I say, knowing him better than I probably should at this point.

All he gives me is a nod.

I wonder if I should let it go now, continue the story another day, give him a reprieve from these ugly memories. But the words slip out anyway. "What happened?"

His shoulder moves in a barely noticeable shrug, but his fist is a coiled serpent in my lap. "I caught her in bed a month later with one of my teammates."

"Oh, Dax..." Tears rush to my eyes as I lean into him. "What did you do?"

"There wasn't much left to do." He shrugs again, trying to downplay the trauma of it all. "I yelled. Threw things. Put a fist through the wall of the house we'd just bought. Then I tossed her clothes out on the lawn because I knew... we were done. We both knew it." Dax spares me a solemn glance, his eyes haunted. "She was gone the next day."

I loop my arms around his neck and stretch myself along the expanse of his chest to offer my mouth in a gentle kiss. "I'm sorry," I whisper. "I'm so sorry she hurt you, and I'm sorry you lost your little one."

The tension slips slowly from the taut musculature beneath me, and he relaxes, burying his face in my neck. "I need to forgive her," he mutters. "I know she was a mess, and the hormones..." Shaking his head with a long exhale, he finishes, "I just need to let it go."

"You do," I agree. "We can let go together."

"Okay," he murmurs into the arch of my shoulder. "As soon as I'm finished hugging this beautiful, sexy, amazing woman on my lap."

I grin, grazing my fingernails along his scalp, relishing in the feel of his soft hair mingling with his warm breath along my neck.

"Mommy!"

I jerk upwards at the sound of my name on Daisy's lips as she bolts toward us in her Frozen dress—it's a sound I still can't get used to. I drop a light kiss on the corner of Dax's mouth and whisper, "Let it go." Then I clamber off him to greet my daughter. "Daisy!"

Daisy is halfway across the yard with my mother in tow. Mom's curious eyes are fixed not on me, but on the man rising from the swing behind me. "Hello, hello," she says, her brow arching with intrigue. "Who do we have here?"

"Mom—"

"Dax Reed, ma'am," Dax intervenes smoothly, extending a hand.

"Dax Reed," she echoes, taking his hand and holding it as she regards him with a narrowed gaze. "That's a familiar name."

"He was in the bank, Gram," Daisy says off-handedly, bouncing up and down in her sandals.

Mom's eyes flare with recognition, then soften. "Well... it's a pleasure to make your acquaintance, Mr. Reed."

"Just Dax, please," he smiles fondly. "And you, as well."

Mom waggles her well-defined eyebrows at me in approval and hurries after Daisy, who is skipping towards the door.

Chuckling after them, I half-turn to Dax. "I'd better get in there and help out. Daisy will convince her she needs half the carton of fish crackers, a million grapes, and an entire slice of cake all to herself."

"Definitely a girl after my own heart."

I elbow him with a snort as we walk through the grass, side by side. "I thought that was me?"

"Like mother, like daughter, I suppose," he teases.

"Aren't you the smooth talker."

"Just the truth."

My heart gallops with affection as I duck my chin to my chest, cheeks glowing pink. "Thanks for bringing lunch today, Dax. I enjoyed it."

He catches my arm when we near the French doors, and we simply watch for a second as Mom and Daisy flutter around the kitchen, wreaking havoc from one cabinet to the next. Then he draws my chin up to his, searching my eyes for a moment before seizing my mouth in a kiss that is neither gentle nor sweet.

"Not as much as I did," he mutters, then yanks the door open and disappears within.

Chapter Thirty-Two

Dax

"THAT WAS FUN."

Indie swivels in the passenger's seat, reaching for my hand that rests atop my thigh as I stare out through the windshield. The sun has settled behind the horizon, replaced by stars and moonglow. Glancing to my right, I spare my date a tender smile. "I'd consider it a success. Only two autographs, one crying girl, and minimal cameras."

She chuckles lightly. "And no boobs."

"No boobs."

My eyes dip to Indie's chest on instinct, the deep V neckline of her dress causing me to shift in my seat with a new wave of pent-up tension.

We still haven't had sex.

Not since the cabin.

I'm a patient guy, and I've gone far longer than a few weeks before, but constantly being in Indie's presence, breathing in her scent, feeling her soft curves beneath my fingertips—fuck, I'm going out of my mind.

Her eyes glimmer knowingly when we lock gazes, my thoughts tangible. She knows exactly what I'm thinking about, and if the way she squirms in her seat, the hem of her dress riding up her thighs with blatant intention, is any indication of what she's thinking about...

I'd say the night is just beginning.

After Tameka agreed to watch Daisy for the evening, planning a fun trip to the zoo, as well as a big girl sleepover, Indie and I braved the restaurant scene again, dodging eager fans and curious onlookers. While it wasn't nearly as bad as my first foray into the public eye, I'm certainly still adjusting. And I'm confident the best part of this date is yet to come.

Pulling my hand from her grip, I reach over the console and find her knee, cupping gently until my fingers trail upward, landing along her inner thigh.

Indie sucks in a sharp breath, the air charged. "How much longer until we get home?"

I grin. "Too long."

We exit off the main highway and head towards Indie's home in Belltown. We've spent the last few days together, our afternoons filled with lunches and tea and coloring competitions with Daisy. Park dates and long walks have filled our hours, the weather warming considerably as springtime blossoms all around us. We're getting to know each other. We're connecting on a new level, a level that surpasses our trauma bond.

Opening up about Sabrina on her backyard swing was a pivotal moment for me. I saw the tears in her eyes—I felt her compassion and warmth, from the way her voice cracked after my confession, to the way she touched me. Held me. Soothed my demons until they quieted.

Indigo is not Sabrina.

And I think that's been part of my block; my heavy walls. I'm waiting until that ball drops, until something tears us apart and rips her away from me. Until my need to fix—my inherent desire to repair and restore—suffocates her, and I find myself all alone again.

But she's here now. She's right here, smelling like nectar and sweet promises, looking like a goddamn angel beneath the brilliant starlight.

And she's already been through hell and back... with me.

I sigh, contentment filling me as I turn down a familiar street that is still busy with bustling nightlife. When I glance at Indie again, inching my hand further up her dress, between her thighs, her lips part with a gasp. She spreads her legs further, allowing me more access. I can't help but groan as my cock stiffens in my dress pants. "Careful," I say, low and dangerous.

The lustful glint in her eyes matches mine. Her lip catches between her teeth as she faces the windshield, leaning back in the seat, those thighs parting wider. "Dax, I have to say—"

Indie's words evaporate, replaced by a scream.

"Look out!"

I cut the wheel to the right when two blinding headlights plow right at us, the vehicle crossing into our lane.

Fuck!

For a moment, I'm in that bank again.

Glass doors plowing open in a glaring haze of sunshine, weapons blazing, masked men storming in and stealing away our sense of safety. Our peace.

Forever.

But the images fade into bright lights and squealing tires.

We swerve right, the car spinning out and coming to a full stop in front of an alleyway, as the opposing vehicle nearly clips us and drives off into the night.

Silence infiltrates the space, only pierced by our heavy, fearful breaths.

We both stare straight ahead, processing the near-hit, trying to regain our composure. I wonder if she went to the same place I did. I wonder if she returned to that bank.

Adrenaline courses through me as I turn to Indie, watching her eyes slam shut as her body trembles with the aftermath. I blow out a breath, reaching for her hand. "Are you okay?"

She squeezes me through a nod.

Then she shakes her head.

"Indigo—"

With a small cry, Indie opens the car door and jumps out onto the sidewalk, prompting me to do the same. A few bystanders ask if we're okay, and we say that we are; we lie and say we're just fine...but as Indie wanders off into the alley, hugging herself through a rush of tears, I know we can't pretend for long.

"Hey, hey..." I soothe, coming up behind her and encircling my arms around her waist. "You're okay."

She twists in my embrace, smashing her face against the front of my button-down shirt and releasing her tears into the pin stripes. "I'm sorry."

"Hey," I say again, pulling back to find her eyes. I tip her chin up with one finger, and our hearts do the rest of the talking.

Just like they did on that very first day, on a fateful Monday morning.

I've got you, Indie.

I'm scared.

Trust me.

I do. I always have.

I'm about to pull her into a hug, but Indie inches up on her tiptoes, finding my mouth instead. She grips the front of my shirt in two shaky fists and shoves her tongue into my mouth with no warning, only desperation. I'm taken off guard for a moment, nearly stumbling back on the pavement, but I regroup quickly, snatching her face between my hands and devouring her with the same passion she's giving me.

It's carnal. It's angry. It's volatile and fucking hot.

And it escalates. Quickly.

I walk her backwards through the darkened alley, housing only a few gated garages, and push her up against the brick wall beside a dumpster. Neither of us seem to care where we are right now, who could be watching—all we care about is satisfying this need. This craving.

This ache.

Indie whimpers, arching her back and pulling the dress up over her hips. She fumbles with my belt as I rip her underwear down her thighs, not breaking the kiss. My tongue slides over hers, our teeth crashing together, my pelvis thrusting with want. I reach under her thighs to lift her up, dropping one arm to help her with my belt and zipper.

We're still kissing. Still moaning and burning and breathless.

My pants fall to my ankles, and I pull my cock through the hole in my boxers. I'm harder than ever, my blood pumping fast, the tip wet with arousal.

Indie reaches down to fist my erection, both of us groaning as we pull back and lock eyes for a striking moment.

I need you.

I know.

Please.

Fuck, you're killing me.

With a sharp cry, hers and mine, I shove my way inside her. I'm not gentle. Nothing about this is gentle or romantic. It's primal and dirty, and it's exactly what we need.

Indie wraps her legs around me, throwing her head back. I pump into her, hard, rough, violent. One hand grips her right beneath her ass, the other rising to fist her hair, tugging at the golden strands. Holding her head back, I bury my face into her neck, my teeth nicking the flesh as I fuck her against the wall with little restraint.

"Dax... oh, God, don't stop..." she moans, digging her nails into my shoulders, her legs holding me tight.

My cock slides in and out, fast and brutal, my orgasm building with each thrust. She's wet and perfect and so goddamn sexy, shoved up against this wall, making these sounds, and begging me not to stop.

Reaching a hand between us, our bodies slapping together, slick and needy, I press my thumb against her clit and rub her into a frenzy. "Come for me, Indigo. I need you to fucking come..."

Her mouth hangs open, features pinched with the onset of her release. Desperate little gasps climb up her throat, culminating into a violent crescendo of shockwaves and currents, prompting my own release to erupt.

"Fuck..." I grunt, pounding into her two more times before I explode. I come hard, burrowing into the arc of her shoulder, inhaling her scent as I fall apart.

And then... I fall apart.

I'm not sure what happens, what triggers me, but I fucking break. I break right there in the dingy alley, still inside her, our combined releases spilling down her thighs.

I can't even remember the last time I cried.

Indie freezes, her breaths still coming quick and uneven as her hands move from my shoulders, up my neck, her fingers landing in my mess of hair. We hold each other, her nails lightly scraping my scalp, providing a sweet comfort while I purge the entire last year of blinding madness. I release again, only this time, it's a cleansing.

"It's okay," she whispers, mimicking my words from only minutes okay. "I've got you."

I know she does. I feel safe and protected, and... loved.

And when I pull back to find her eyes, mine still wet with remorse, I'm overcome with the urge to release once more.

Inhaling a shuddering breath, I remove a piece of sweat-laced hair from her forehead, replacing it with a kiss. "I need to tell you something."

It's time.

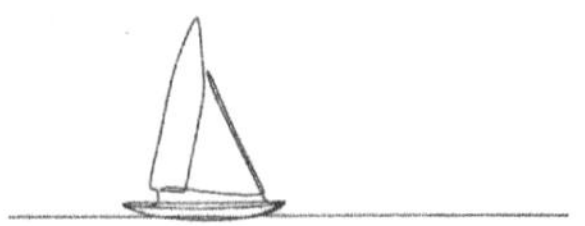

Eight Months Earlier

"Hey, killer." I pace forward, feet unsteady, my eyes trained on my opponent. He fists the neck of both beer bottles, his stance drawing tight as he stares wordlessly at me. "Thanks for the beer, but I really can't stay."

Garrett watches as I approach with subdued caution. "Look at you, all functional and shit." He sniffs, then brings one of the beers to his mouth, taking a swig. His eyes roll over me, from my chest wound to my shaky legs. "Barely."

"I don't want to hurt you."

"It's fuckin' adorable you think you could. You can hardly stand, hero."

He's not wrong.

My fingers curl around the rusty pruning shears, my only defense, as sweat trickles down my temple. I'm already exhausted from freeing myself—from the energy spent simply trying to stand and hold my weight up.

I inhale a flimsy breath. "You don't want to hurt me either."

Garrett sets his jaw, eyes narrowed in my direction and gleaming with an internal battle he's trying not to project. He doesn't reply.

Taking a risk and braving a new angle, I toss my weapon to the floor beside my feet. It clamors to the old wood planks, causing Garrett to flinch, just slightly. I raise my hands, palms forward, my white flag of surrender on full display. "See? I don't want to fight. I just want to walk out of this room, get to a hospital, and put this behind me," I tell him, keeping my voice even and infallible. "I won't turn you in. You can walk out, too, and find that beach somewhere."

His sharp laugh pierces the air. "You think it's that easy? I don't have a bunch of big ass bank accounts to go home to. I don't have shit."

"I can help you. I'll still get you the baseball card."

"Bullshit. If you think I'm some kinda idiot—"

"I don't," I cut in, and I mean it, and I hope he knows I mean it. "Two of your brothers are dead, and two of them are in jail. You're the last man standing, Garrett. That says it all."

Garrett goes silent again, shifting his gaze to the left, the beer bottle tapping against his thigh as he works through his options.

Let me go, or fight to the death.

It's not a matter of who will win. We both know which one of us will walk out of here alive if weapons are drawn and blood is shed. It comes down to one, simple question:

Can he live with himself afterwards?

I don't think he can, so I run with it. "Are you a killer, Garrett?"

"I'm sure no fuckin' hero."

"That's not what I asked." I take a cautious step forward, hands still raised. "Are you a cold-blooded killer? Like Ronnie?"

"I ain't nothin' like Ronnie."

"No, you're not. You're not crazy like Ronnie, or impulsive like Leo, or weak like Trevor," I blurt, still moving forward, still remaining calm. My right leg gives out a little, and I pause to regroup. "Leo never wanted you involved because you were a threat. You were smarter than him, and he knew that, and that pissed him off." I watch his micro expressions with bated breath, trying to read him, trying to figure out his next move. "If you're as smart as I think you are, you'll see that I'm not lying. I'm going to help you."

Silence dangles between us, like the two beers in his hands. Garrett studies me, irises glowing with a blaze of confliction. The truth is… the smart thing to do, for self-preservation, would be to kill me. Riddle me with more bullets and bury me out back.

Trusting me is a risk.

Trusting me would not be smart.

All I can do is hope that his humanity trumps that.

Garrett's lips twitch with indecision, his chest heaving up and down with labored breaths. Rolling his tongue along his teeth, he glances at the grandfather clock, cruddy and cobwebbed, perched against the far wall. Nothing works in this antique of a house, but that clock does.

Tick, tick, tick.

"Maybe you'll help me, maybe you won't," Garrett finally says, fracturing the fraught silence. Tick, tick, tick. We stand roughly four feet apart—just enough space, that if one of us were to pounce, it could be deadly. Garrett inhales another long breath, lets it out, then takes a purposeful step forward. He finishes, "But I can't bank on maybes."

Fuck.

Garrett rushes at me, the beer bottles falling from his hands, the glass splintering.

Just like my last shred of hope.

He tackles me, and goddamn, it hurts like hell, and it takes every ounce of strength I have to keep his hands from coiling around my throat and squeezing the life out of me. I use my knees as a barrier, holding him just far enough away, trying to blindly reach for the pruning shears that I foolishly abandoned. Garrett notices my attempts and swats them across the dusty floor.

"You're not a killer," I grit out, my gunshot wound pulsing as the stitches pop, staining the front of my chest in a gush of scarlet. My hand is curled around his neck, the other joining, and Garrett twists and turns in my grip, his own hands slinking around mine. My knees quiver with weakness as they try to push him backwards, but my strength is draining with each passing second.

Tick, tick, tick.

His face is beet red, muscles corded in his neck, veins distended. He spits through his teeth, "Are you?"

I manage to gain the upper hand and kick him off me, just barely, just enough that I can roll over and snatch the pruning shears.

But Garrett is on me again, stepping on my hand with his dirty boot, until I growl out with pain. He spins me onto my back and mounts me, caging me in with both knees, his hands going back to my throat.

I claw at his wrists, trying to prevent him from strangling me. "Y-You… don't want to kill me…" I manage to force out, vision bleary.

"You're right, hero, I don't," he says, applying more pressure.

I twist my head to the side, scanning my surroundings. If I can just find something to knock him out, to daze him, maybe I can make a break for it.

Garrett chokes me harder. "I just want you fuckin' unconscious, tied to that bed again, until I get my hands on th—"

Thwack.

My arm flies out, a stone bookend tucked inside my palm, and I collide it against Garrett's temple with a sickening crack.

He crumbles.

We both go still as the blood rushes back to my face, my eyesight clears, and my breaths slowly steady.

Shit… how hard did I hit him?

Garrett lies motionless atop my chest as I lie frozen with dread.

Shit, shit, shit.

Gathering my strength, I roll him off me, until he's on his back, his shirt stained red from the pool of blood seeping from my bullet hole.

He groans.

Thank God.

"Garrett… fuck, I didn't mean…" I rise to my knees, wincing with pain, then lean over him to inspect the head wound. I know I should book it, make my escape, but guilt eats away at me as I take in the deep gash along his temple, oozing crimson. It looks bad—really bad. Fuck. Realizing I'm still fisting the bookend, now painted in blood spatter, I drop it like a hot poker.

Garrett lets out another feeble groan, his eyes flickering. When they ping open, squinty and bloodshot, he stares up at the ceiling, hardly noticing my presence. His head lolls to the side as he mutters, "Tell Leo…" His eyelids flutter again, his words trailing off.

My heart stutters.

No, fuck, no.

"Whoa, whoa, wait… you're going to be fine," I say, the panic eclipsing the pain. I search the room for a towel of some kind, settling on an old t-shirt and pressing it to his bleeding temple. "No last words, remember?"

He swallows, his breathing shallow. "Tell Leo… I made it. I got out. He can't know that I…" Garrett wheezes through a cough, his eyes rolling up. "I'm on a beach somewhere. I fuckin' made it."

Emotion laces with disbelief. I'm drenched in sweat and blood and profound regret, holding the blood-soaked t-shirt to his temple as I watch his life slip away. My throat is tight, stinging with bile as I nod my head, my body shivering. All I can muster is, "I'll tell him."

I swear a smile tips his lips as his head falls to the side, and two final words break free. "Thanks, killer."

Garrett goes still, his eyes half open, his last words branding me to the bone.

I fall back on my heels.

In shock. Horrified.

I just killed a man.

Lifting my hands, they vibrate in front of me, coated in blood—the physical evidence of my crime. And when I numbly sift through Garrett's pocket, locating his cell phone and calling Blake, I go someplace else. Somewhere far away.

I disconnect.

Blake finds me sitting on the front stoop of the deserted farmhouse an hour later, overjoyed and elated, enveloping me with hugs and words of relief.

But I hardly notice him.

I find no joy in my rescue.

And I think… I think that's because it's no longer a rescue mission.

There's nothing here worth rescuing.

Indie's tears wet my hair as she holds my head against her chest, our bodies perched side by side against that same brick wall. My confession weighs heavily between us, sounding louder than the streams of traffic at the opposite end of the alley.

She holds me tight, rocking me back and forth. "It's okay, Dax. You're okay. It was just an accident," she murmurs, bathing me in her sympathy. "You didn't mean it. It's okay."

Her words flow through me, sweetness and solace.

And when I glance up, I notice that we're sitting behind an old Irish pub, huddled beneath a dim lantern.

It glows green.

With Indie wrapped around me, her kisses on my skin and forgiveness in her voice, I inhale a deep, purifying breath, staring up at the green light as I exhale slowly.

Maybe there is something worth rescuing, after all.

Chapter Thirty-Three

Dax

I HAD NO INTENTION of writing you this, but here we are.

I'm sitting in a secluded cabin in the middle of the woods. I've been here for eight months, ever since I escaped from your old family farmhouse that Garrett kept me captive in for weeks. I'm not sure if you knew that. You were too busy waving your gun around, terrorizing the woman I've managed to fall for, and altering the course of all of our lives.

I'm leaving, though. I'm finally getting the hell out of here and facing the currents—the ripple effects from that day.

Have you ever experienced profound chaos? A downward spiral. True, blinding madness that keeps on spinning, plummeting you further and further into a black hole you can't seem to claw your way out of. It infiltrates everything. It seeps into every choice, every thought, every relationship… every awful misstep.

I have. It started the day you walked into that bank.

Fuck, no, that's a lie.

It started long before that. But it's been really damn easy to blame you for everything.

I'm not exactly sure what this letter is supposed to be—forgiveness? Acceptance? Deliverance? Maybe I'm letting go. Or maybe I'm embracing.

Either way, there's something I'm inclined to tell you.

When I was near-death, trapped inside that farmhouse, I got to know your brother. Garrett. This may sound ridiculous, and I'm going to blame the fever, but I saw another side to him in those few weeks.

I saw the same side I see in myself.

Because of this, I had to let you know... he made it. He got his hands on my Babe Ruth baseball card, traded it in for cash, and made a successful escape over the border. He's probably on a beach right now, sipping on piña coladas and watching the waves roll in.

Anyway, I'm going to try and pick up the shattered pieces of my life and, one day, maybe I'll be doing the same. Sitting on a beach, finally at peace. Or maybe a boat.

Yeah. A sailboat.

I'm finding that chaos comes easy. Peace is a hell of a lot harder to hold onto.

But maybe this letter will bring me one step closer to it.

Dax Reed (The Hockey Guy)

A few weeks go by, and as I'm aimlessly sifting through Blake's pile of mail on the countertop, a return address catches my eye:

Washington State Department of Corrections.

My stomach pitches.

I pluck the letter from the stack, the ink smudged, the handwriting messy. I'm caught in a cloud of disbelief as I blink at the muddled letters, taking a moment to process it all. My fingers start to tremble, so I squeeze the envelope.

Hell.

Sucking in a deep breath and mentally counting to three, I tear it open, pulling out a piece of lined notebook paper scrawled with blue pen.

I read.

Hockey Boy —

This was a fucking surprise.

Never thought I'd hear from that famous athlete I tried to gank.

Only reason I'm even replying to you is because I'm bored as fuck, and this gives me something to do aside from listen to my cellmate read his pretentious books out loud.

Pretentious. Good word, huh? I'm learning lots of pointless shit in here from Gibson. He's like a motherfucking poet. A real Steinbeck. That guy's a poet, right?

Ah, fuck if I know.

But yeah… so here we are. Sounds like you've got a lot of crazy shit on your mind. I think there's people for that— you know, one of them crazy doctors who give you crazy pills to cure your crazy shit. You should look into that. I bet you can afford a good one, and I sure as hell don't have any brilliant advice.

But I do have a word for you. Gibson fills me in on all kinds of fun words. Who would've thought a prison cell would be more educational that that preppy ass boarding school my Pa tried to put me in?

Anyway…

The word you're looking for is entropy.

Entropy signifies a state of disorder or chaos. A measure of uncertainty. How's that for a fancy definition? I bet you never even heard of that word before.

(If you want more interesting facts and grandiose words, just hold up a bank. It's a real fun way to land yourself in a jail cell, and maybe you'll get stuck with a guy like Gibson.)

Grandiose. Another good one.

Not as good as entropy, though.

And hey, maybe that's where you'll find your answers. Right in the center of the chaos. Sometimes you gotta embrace the chaos in your life in order to find the peace in it, ya know? Something like that.

Oh, and one more thing.

If you ever see my brother again… tell that fucker, I'm happy for him.

Our Pa put me in charge of that kid when we were still playing with our fucking Lego blocks. Said he wasn't meant for this kinda life. He was better than it. I made a promise that I would, so I had the burden of keeping his ass out of trouble all these years. Away from the danger. Away from all the bad shit.

It never turned out that way, of course. Garrett's always had a way of involving himself— of figuring shit out when we couldn't. He's been pretty fucking invaluable.

Hey, do me a favor. If you ever share a pussy cocktail with my brother on a beach somewhere, tell him he's invaluable. He'll get a kick outta of the fact that I even know that word, and maybe he'll start liking me enough to try and bust me out of here.

So yeah… tell him I always knew he'd be the last man standing.

Always knew he was the best of us.

Anyway, hockey star, it was great catching up.

Ha… not really.

I think that's just what people are supposed to say in sappy-ass letters like this.

I don't wish you well, and I don't really care what happens to you.

Have a mediocre life.

Leo

My legs give out, and I slide down the side of the kitchen island, back pressed up to the maple siding, a ball of emotion slicing my chest.

The memories roar inside me, the guilt bubbling back to the surface tenfold.

But as I grip the letter in my fist, the paper wrinkling in a tight hold, I'm overcome with… something else. A new feeling washes over me, forcing out the ugliness. Replacing the poison.

I feel free.

My head falls back against the island as I imagine Garrett on that beach with his cocktail. Maybe he really is there. Maybe he's free, too—free of the madness, the violence, the uncertainty.

Maybe he found his peace.

I let out a cathartic breath as the harrowing memories begin to dissipate, traded in for visions of rippling waves, sunny shores, and absolution.

Smiling, I wonder if perhaps we'll meet again one day.

I'll tell him he was invaluable.

To Leo. To his family.

In a lot of ways… to me.

Someday, maybe,

We'll finally get to share that beer.

Chapter Thirty-Four

Indie

BACKSTAGE OF THE AREA elementary school where recitals are held, nerves twine freely through the adults straightening tutus and reapplying lipstick and blusher, English ivy everywhere it's not supposed to grow. The kids are oblivious to their parents' undercurrents of anxiety; their eyes gleam with excitement and they chatter like magpies, even Daisy, who, once she found her voice, hasn't stopped talking for thirty seconds.

I squat in front of her, my fingers fidgeting with the straps of her pale purple sequined costume. "You ready, baby?"

She nods. "Uh-huh. I'm gonna do the twirl with the girls, then the fifth position in the middle of the stage, and then I get to say my big finish."

"Your big finish," I echo tenderly, my heart squeezing with pride. "What's that again?"

"You know. I've told you a thousand million times," she reminds me.

"I do know." I smooth her bun. "I'm just nervous."

"Why are you nervous, silly? You're just watching." She skips from one thought to the next. "Can I have more lipstick? Marley's mom just gave her more lipstick."

"Sure, baby." Obligingly, I apply more vivid poppy color to Daisy's lips, then step back as the dancers are called to group with their classes. Giving her a little wave, I conceal my reluctance to let her go with a bright smile and make my way off stage.

Dax has an entire row reserved front and center, filled with Blake, Tameka, and Mom. I sit in the empty seat they saved for me between

Dax and Mom, grabbing the hand he offers. "She's fine," I whisper to my mother as the music begins. "Not nervous at all."

"Not like you, huh, babe?" Tameka laughs from further down the row.

I make a face at her. "I feel like I'm going to be sick," I relent, pulling my camera out of my bag. I took thirty-seven photos backstage, and we took group photos before we ever came inside with every variation of people and pose I could think of...

But I need more.

I realize it's just a spring recital. They take place every year for hundreds of little girls and boys all over, some of whom will go on to dance every year thereafter—others of whom it's simply a fun activity to pass the time with.

It feels big, though. It feels significant. Maybe it's because it's the first big event since Edgewater, and the first event where we've all been in public together since that day. We've all been through so much, warrior-ed our way through to the other side in our own ways. Blake and Tameka coped by reaching out and making themselves indispensable parts of other people's lives. They wove their way into the fabric of my life, and Daisy's, and Dax's lives, in such a way that removing them would create a permanent, irreparable tear.

Daisy coped through silence and art. She withdrew into her own thoughts, refusing to speak until she knew exactly what she thought about everything. Until she had worked out every emotion, every complex thought.

Dax did the same thing, closing himself off from the world so he wouldn't have to speak to anyone, or give life and shape to his experiences.

And me?

Sometimes I don't even know how I coped. I think it was the tears and copious words to Felicity when the dark beyond my doorstep threatened to eat me whole. I think it was allowing myself to fall apart, always knowing someone would be there to put me back together until I had the strength to do it on my own.

Selfish, perhaps. But maybe that's why we pick certain people to occupy places in our lives that we don't give to anyone else. We know they've got it. They've got us.

As I zone out, lost in my thoughts, music begins to play. It's a bright, happy tune, sprightly and joyful. The curtains part slowly, pulling back to reveal a tableau of brightly dressed tiny dancers in various poses center stage.

My hand grips Dax's so tightly, I'm surprised I don't break every bone. But then, he squeezes mine back.

There she is. My baby girl.

My little lion.

As the music plays a tune of spring showers and flowers blooming, she squats low and leaps high, runs and twirls and worships the cardboard sun hanging in the corner of the stage with all of the other little flower ballerinas. She and the other ballerinas dance a story of parent and children flowers, drawing them close to them in a communal hug before allowing them to decorate a field in gay abandon. The parent flowers preside over them proudly, swaying back and forth on a slightly taller dais before they grow still. Daisy moves to the front, center stage, and kneels amongst her "children."

When she speaks, her gaze fixes on me, and her voice is strong and clear.

"And then they loved."

The audience breaks into immediate applause, but it's not until Dax pulls his hand from mine to clap that I realize I haven't taken a single photo, too mesmerized to do so. Tears are streaming down my face, and when I hear a sniff and glance sideways, I realize that Blake is having the same problem.

"Damn sequins," he mutters. "Get me every damn time."

He wipes his eyes with a purple paisley tie, and startled, I giggle. It's exactly the impetus we need to stand and burst into undignified whistles and cheering, and I manage to get a few amazing photos of Daisy's wide grin at the sight.

Later, the season-end reception is held at a small park down at the water's edge. Normally, the number of people and the open area would make me jittery, but I calm my nerves for Daisy's sake. I stand near the concrete barrier wall with the bay a soothing flush of waves on one side, and Daisy playing with her friends a few feet away on the other. Dax and Blake are at the buffet, picking up plates for us, and Mom wandered off somewhere away from the water, ever cautious where that's concerned. The sun is just beginning to set, and it's magical, the city lights aglow all around us, the conversation a peaceful hum.

Giving myself permission to relax into the moment, I turn more fully toward the water and stare off at the distant shores and far-off lights of boats.

Minutes later, a hand touches my shoulder, and my mother settles in beside me, her hands clutching the concrete of the barrier wall in a tight grip.

"Indigo."

My eyes widen. "Mom? What are you doing… "

"Oh, I wanted to talk," she says simply.

Pulling back from the wall, I usher her away. "I can come and sit beside you at one of the tables, Mom. I know you don't like to be this close—"

"No, no. I'll be fine." She tugs me back with a steadying breath. "That was one of the things I wanted to…"

I stare at her, lips parted, gaze searching.

"Indigo, I'm so sorry, sweetheart."

Shaking my head, I continue to look at her dumbly. "I don't understand."

Slowly, glancing down at where our hands rest on cold stone, she picks up my hand with hers. "I shouldn't have held so tight. Shouldn't have wrapped you in my fears, held you back from experiencing the thing that made your daddy happiest. I thought it was fine, really, until all of this business happened with the bank, and I watched you shut yourself up in your house."

"Mom—"

"No, let me speak." Her hold on me is firm. "This is something I need to say. I should have said it a long time ago."

I nod, my throat choked with tears. Over Mom's shoulder, a large vessel—some kind of tug, maybe—toots a mournful song that echoes through the bay. We wait for the sound to fade, and then she continues.

"You shut yourself up, afraid to step over your threshold and live life outside your doors, and I can't help thinking that was partially my fault. I instilled fear in you. It was always, 'be wary of those deep waters. You never know where that current is, or when it's going to drag you under.'"

"You weren't wrong, Mom."

"I wasn't right, either. Life isn't for the faint of heart. It can't be lived without risk." She hesitates, then strokes her thumb over mine. "I understand that now." Drawing a deep breath in, she exhales it swiftly and releases my hand, then turns back to the water.

"It wasn't your fault, though. I was just scared, period," I insist, struggling to put that part of my life into words. "I had absolutely no control that day, and the worst thing was that Daisy was there. I couldn't protect her. Couldn't reassure her. Couldn't make her feel better." I smile wryly. "Dax did all of that. When it was all over, it was just easier to stay home, not worry about what I would do if anything happened again, you know? It was a non-issue. I was in control… and I needed that."

After a moment, she nods her head. "I guess I can understand that," she admits through a sigh, glancing my way. "Anyway, I'm sorry I didn't let you go out on the water with your father while you had the chance."

My eyes water. "Mom… it's okay. Really."

"Really? You forgive me?" Her glistening stare mirrors my own before a splash captures our attention. A fish flops along the surface, then disappears. "That water looks really nasty."

We look down together. The water does look gross—a dark greenish-black in the deepening twilight, with filmy bracken atop. It is not at all inviting. "I agree," I reply. "And yes, I really forgive you."

"Thank you, my darling. My Indigo Blue." She flashes me a smile, then twists her neck over her shoulder when commotion heads our way. "Oh, there's Dax and Blake. They've got their hands full."

I turn to look in the direction she indicates, and sure enough, Dax and Blake are strolling toward us, while Daisy and Tameka dance together just beyond them.

I smile, but feel it slip almost immediately from my face as their expressions change in counterpoint to a sound behind me.

An odd shushing sound. Almost like…

No way.

Swiveling, I'm just in time to see my mother climbing atop the concrete barrier wall and then, with a mischievous grin in my direction, gracefully leaping into the cold Seattle waters below.

"Mom!"

I don't think.

Gathering the filmy skirt of the pale yellow dress I'm wearing, I vault over the wall and into the black water, gasping as it closes over my head. The wall is not high, and the water's not deep. It is cold, though. My feet hit the rocky bottom and I spring back to the surface, sputtering filth and already shaking uncontrollably. "M-m-mom! M-mother!"

"H-here!" I hear her a few feet away and find her. Our eyes meet, and we swim to find each other. I reach for her and she for me, and we cling, foreheads touching. "W-why did you do that, you idiot child?"

"I-I'm the idiot?" I demand, my voice a mask of horror.

"What the hell are you two doing?" Dax's voice comes from above, confused and horrified.

His face peers over the edge, and we both look up, then at each other, and start laughing uncontrollably.

"G-get us out of here, Dax," I beg. "P-please!"

"I ought to leave you crazy women in there," he grumbles, though, his tone is laced with teasing. Laughter follows as he climbs over the ledge. "Hold on."

Dax manages to gets us out in record time, and someone produces blankets and hot drinks to subdue the chill. Mom and I smile foolishly at each other the entire time.

Maybe we'll both take a sail one day.

Together.

Chapter Thirty-Five

Dax

MY HAND LIFTS, KNUCKLES hovering over the red door.

It's not any easier today, standing on this front stoop, heart pounding, thoughts in disarray. Part of me still wants it to be her.

Mom.

Please don't be him.

Please don't be him.

But I need it to be him.

I need to look my father in the eyes and make him see me.

I need to fix this.

Heavy footfalls approach from the other side of the threshold, and I already know it's him. My father. Dad. I haven't called him that since I was ten years old, and I'm not sure why that bothers me… but it does. "Dad" always felt too personal for the shaky relationship we've shared. Too intimate. He's simply been "my father"—the authoritative figure, the barely-there guidance, the invisible man I've desperately tried to please since I was a small child.

I hold a breath in my lungs when the door swings open, just like it had the first time I showed up, fresh from a grave the world thought I'd met.

My father's eyes flare when he sees me, his body stiffening beneath the foyer's chandelier. He plucks the spectacles from his nose, his Adam's apple bobbing with some sort of emotion as he studies me, mutely.

"Hey," I manage, my muscles locking. It takes a moment for me to collect more things to say, as my brain seems to have locked up, too. Swallowing, I inhale an uneven breath. "Can I come in?"

His silence is heavy—it's always been louder than his words.

Cleaning his eyeglasses with the hem of his polo, he issues a curt nod. "Of course you can come in. You lived here for twenty years, after all."

He turns his back to me and spins away. An invitation.

I step into the familiar home, the scent of apples and spice filling me with warmth.

As if on cue, my father mutters, "Your mother is out doing her riff-raff. Something with her hair. There's leftover stroganoff in the refrigerator if you'd like to wait—"

"I came over to talk to you," I interrupt, watching as he stalls his feet, back still facing me. "If you're not busy." Something stirs inside me, loud and bold, and I correct myself. "Actually, even if you are busy. We need to talk."

My father goes rigid, his shoulders taut. He stands perfectly still at the edge of the hallway, his office only a few doors down, likely a beacon of reprieve from this potential shitshow. It takes a few moments for him to respond, and when he does, the words aren't at all what I expect.

"I suppose that would be wise."

He doesn't look at me as he pivots away from the hallway, taking long strides toward the living room sofa. I'm frozen in the entryway, temporarily tongue-tied, as my eyes follow his retreating form until he takes a seat on the far side of the couch. He sits up straight, gazing down at his loafers, both hands propped along each knee.

I join him.

Taking my place beside my father, there's a good amount of space between us, which is nothing new. I glance in his direction, observing the tension on his face, carved into his age lines and wrinkles. He doesn't make eye contact, silently waiting for me to speak.

With a quick cough into my fist, I proceed. "So, I figured—"

"I almost didn't survive it."

Silence infiltrates us again, only this time it's laced with confusion. I allow a few, startled beats to pass before I inquire. "What?"

My father grips his knees, his fingers curling around the kneecaps. He looks vulnerable, out of his element. Maybe even a little bit... scared.

Lifting his chin, he whips his glasses off again and rubs at his eyes. "When I thought you were dead, I..." Another long minute stretches between us as he shakes his head and finally looks my way. "The pain nearly killed me. The guilt. The apology I never got to give you."

My lips part to speak, but nothing comes out.

I'm speechless.

"I hold a lot of regret in my heart, Dax." He places his palm to his chest, eyes brimming with tears I've never witnessed before. "I've made many mistakes in my life, but nothing comes close to the mistakes I've made with you."

Emotions climb my throat. My father looks worn and weary, his frame more withered than I've ever seen it. His eyes are tired, his hair thinning. In this new light, he's no longer the terrifying influence I both feared and revered all my life.

He's just a grieving, haunted man.

His brown eyes gleam with atonement as his chest rises and falls with each labored breath. "I don't expect you to forgive me, son. I know it's too little too late," he says raggedly. "But I want you to know... that vacation we took—that trip to Maui, just you, me, and your mother—it's always been here." He slams his fist into his chest, more tears blooming. "Sometimes I pretend that we never left. That I'm still that man, that father you saw drinking milk from fresh coconuts, laughing with you on our balcony as we forgot about the real world. My pride fell away. My need for control, for power, washed away with the waves, and I wish... I wish the tide never brought it back."

I stare wordlessly at him, leaning back and processing his confession with a tight jaw and clasped hands. A single word slips out. "Son."

My father purses his lips into a thin line, a questioning frown following.

"You've never called me that before. I never thought you ever... saw me as one. Not really."

"I've always seen you, Dax." More sadness fills his eyes, the years of remorse shining prominently in his ruddy irises. "It was me I failed to see. My toxic behavior. The consequences of my nasty pride. Your mother always told me you'd wind up hating me one day..."

"I never hated you," I tell him, my heart seizing with sentiment. "That's what made it so hard."

Bringing a hand to his mouth, he clasps it over his jaw, his shoulders beginning to shake with grief. It's a profound sight. An image that will be ingrained within me forever. It's my father, walls down, bare-boned, fully exposed in front of me, spilling regret into his palm and purging his soul of every misdeed. It's something that has me forcing back my own tears as I inch my way down the couch and pull him to me, encircling my strong arms around him and gripping tight. I say nothing, afraid my voice might break.

"I'm proud of you, son. I'm so very proud."

Goddamn. I squeeze him tighter, patting his back with my palm as my mind races. "I've done things you wouldn't be proud of," I admit, my tone somber. I pull my lips between my teeth and close my eyes.

My father moves back, wiping the wetness from his cheeks and gathering his control. He returns the wire-rimmed glasses to the bridge of his nose and faces me once again. "We all have, Dax. And if I've learned anything from this ordeal, it's that forgiveness comes from within. We can never truly heal until we forgive ourselves," he tells me with a sharp breath. Leaning into the couch cushions, he continues. "Your mother told me that it helps to look around and take in all the goodness. The bright spots. The rare moments of peace. Perspective, perhaps..."

Peace.

Leo's words ring inside my head: "Sometimes you gotta embrace the chaos in your life in order to find the peace in it, ya know?"

My lips twitch with irony. The man who brought the utmost chaos into my life is the one encouraging me to find my peace. And somehow...

Somehow, there's fucking peace in that.

A smile breaks through. "Only entropy comes easy," I murmur. "We need to fight hard for all the rest." I observe the way my father studies me—but not like I'm his student this time, not like a science project, or his protégé. Like he's trying to learn. I let out a sigh, leaning beside him and placing my hand over his. "There's peace within the chaos. There's beauty in the ugly. There's goodness hiding inside the bad."

He goes quiet for a moment, a reflective glimmer dancing in his eyes. He nods at me, encasing my hand with both of his. "I know you more than you think I do, son," he says gently. "Look around you. I'm certain you'll see that your goodness far outweighs the bad."

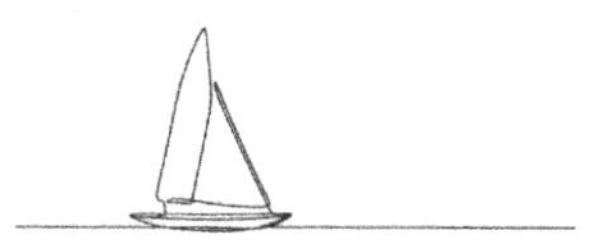

My feet still at the edge of the garden.

The last stop of the day.

I untuck the floral card from my pocket, scanning the words and corresponding image before lifting my eyes to the celebration before me.

Laughter rings loud. Music sings. Smiles are wide and magical.

I spot him instantly, his arm tucked around his wife in her black dress, whose dark red hair is spilling over her shoulders in wine-infused waves. They are both chatting with guests, sipping cocktails, and taking it all in.

Taking each other in.

Brian's attention hasn't left his bride in the small amount of time I've been standing here with charmed, watchful eyes. When I discovered the wedding invitation hidden inside the assortment of advertisements and gossip magazines Blake tossed onto the kitchen table, I was both confused and... elated.

I thought about Brian a lot during my months in isolation, wondering if he'd made it, wondering if he ever got to walk his fiancé down the aisle.

Andrea.

A pretty name for a pretty girl.

My search results upon my return hadn't given me anything conclusive, considering I didn't even know his last name.

But he knew mine.

And somehow, he found me, leaving the invitation in Blake's mailbox, with a little handwritten note scrawled onto the back: "Thanks for fixing me. I'd be honored to have a hero at my wedding."

I recall bristling at the term hero, still bitter, still processing my long, lonely months in hiding and the trauma that had triggered them. I had no intention of coming today—simply knowing Brian had survived was a worthy solace, and I was happy he was getting his happily-ever-after.

Only, as the days went on, something told me I had to be here.

I had to witness it for myself.

My father's words filter through me as I watch the scene unfold. The stolen kisses, the clink of champagne glasses, the joy and blessings heavy in the air. Maybe my good deeds don't outweigh the bad. Maybe a life saved doesn't make up for a life taken.

But it means something.

For Brian and Andrea... it means everything.

Standing off to the side, I lean my shoulder against the white wood house that hosts this intimate backyard celebration, drinking in the happiness that surrounds me. My heart fills with something hopeful. Something peaceful.

Something I want for myself.

Before I can slink away unseen, Brian glances up from his guests and spots me. Surprise washes over his features, widening his eyes, straightening his stance. He stares at me from across the yard, still holding onto his wife as she mingles with friends and family.

I'm not sure what to do, so I lift my hand in a little wave.

Hey, old sport.

The surprise on his face softens to relief, to gratitude, stretching his mouth into a wide, watery smile. Brian raises his glass to me, a friendly salute.

A hello.

A thank you.

I smile back at him. You're welcome.

Then I walk away, filled with that same relief. That same gratitude. The realization that, no, I can't save them all... but I played a hand in saving one.

And that feels really damn good.

As I drive back towards Belltown to spend the evening with Indie and Daisy, I make a quick stop. There's one more thing I need to do.

It's time for my own happily-ever-after.

Chapter Thirty-Six

Indie

INDIE: Hi, Felicity. It's been a while.

I tap my fingers nervously on the laptop while I wait for Felicity to respond. Three dots jump and dance on the screen, indicating she's mid-reply.

Felicity: I wondered what was going on! Tell me how you've been.

Indie: Things are good. Really, really good.

Even as my fingers type the words, I look around for something wooden to knock upon. I awoke this morning feeling like I needed to tell Felicity, needed to close my therapy chapter, but it almost seems like tempting Providence to do so.

It's true what they say. When something seems too good to be true, it usually is.

Felicity: Tell me more. What's good?

I hesitate, pushing my sleep-and-sex tangled hair behind my ear, and settle more comfortably into the mass of pillows on my bed. From the bathroom, an off-key version of "I'm Too Sexy" sounds, and I can't help the grin that tugs at my lips. Maybe it is too good to be true. Maybe it'll all fall apart tomorrow.

But right now, it's as real as real can be.

Positioning my hands, I go for it.

Indie: Well... as I type this, my friend Tameka has Daisy for a sleepover from last night. Dax is using my shower and singing, and he has an awful, wonderful voice. He left coffee on my nightstand, and when he gets out, I'm probably gonna jump his magnificent bones. For the third time. Good enough?

I feel laughter in the dancing dots, then a simple,

Felicity: I'm happy for you.

At that moment, the bathroom door opens, and steam pours into the room, heralding Dax's entrance.

Indie: Thank you, Felicity. For everything. Gotta go. :)

Swiftly, I place the laptop on the nightstand and pick up my coffee, managing to look demure just in time for Dax to notice me.

He pauses in the act of pulling on his boxers. "What's that look for?"

"Nothing at all," I say, drawing out the words. Then I wink. "But you won't need those."

Dax grins, tossing them aside with obliging haste, and stalks toward me. "I won't?"

"Nope."

"And why is that?" he prompts.

Stretching my arms out, I welcome his warm bulk as he slides in against me. "Because I decided I don't want to get up yet."

"Mm." Our kiss is a conversation, me listening as he tells me with tongue and lips and teasing nips how much he appreciates that idea. When he pauses, I reply, telling him with the slide of my own tongue and lips, every little thing I've come to adore about him.

I adore him.

The smattering of freckles on his shoulders that I decorate in sweet kisses, the thick curls of his biceps and flat planes of his pectorals—all of his physical magnificence is a beautiful accompaniment to the soul that lies behind those mismatched eyes. Rising slightly, I kiss each eyelid, then the slope of his cheekbones.

"Mommy?"

"Oh, God," Tameka's voice cuts in. "Daisy, sweetie, come with me —"

"Jesus, Tameka—"

Everyone talks at once, Dax springing up from where he lay partially over me to grab the blanket, ensuring it covers all the important bits. I stare at the ceiling and wish I could sink through the mattress to the floor.

"Mommy."

Startled at the sound of Daisy's voice so close to my ear, I turn my head to see my little lion inches away from my face. She's looking at me curiously. "Hi, baby."

"What are you doing?"

"Um. We were just playing a game."

"It looked like you was kissin'."

Beside me, Dax clears his throat, and I pin him with a brief glare before continuing. "Well… what would you say if we were kissing?"

Daisy tilts her head and scratches her neck but doesn't answer. "If… maybe kissing was part of the game?"

She narrows her eyes. "I don't think kissing should be a game. You should kiss when you's in love." Looking over my shoulder, she nails Dax with the same stare I just did. "You love my mommy?"

"Ah…"

Oh, dear God.

Flustered, I stammer, "Daisy, we really shouldn't ask questions like that…"

"Why not?"

"Because those are very special words, and maybe Dax isn't ready to say them right at this moment, young lady. Please, go find Tameka, so I can get dressed."

Her eyes widen. "You mean, you're playing games nakey?"

Panic button. It's time. "Tameka!"

Tameka barrels in, clearly having been standing just around the corner, hand covering her lips to muffle her laughter. "C'mon, kid. Let's leave your mom to it for a minute."

Gripping Daisy's hand firmly, Tameka begins to take her from the room. It doesn't, however, prevent my sudden chatterbox's last words. "Mr. Dax?"

Dax clears a tickle in his throat as he fidgets beside me. "Yeah, Little Lion?"

"It's all right if you want to love and kiss 'er. I give you permits."

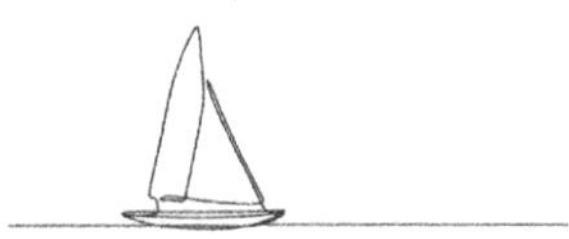

"Where are we going?"

Dax and I have been walking for a while through downtown Seattle, strolling slowly through the twist and hum of scooter and passerby with, I assume, no particular destination in mind. No agenda than simply enjoying each other's company.

But that's before the buildings, the signage, the scents and sounds —the homeless man in front of Valla's, for God's sake—begin to infiltrate my consciousness, pulling my attention from the man by my side to our surroundings.

"Dax, is that...?"

I stop, digging my heels in next to a coffee shop and crossing my arms over my chest. Dax circles to stand before me, placing his palms on my shoulders and rubbing soothingly.

My skin prickles with unease. "Why are we here?"

Roughly a block past the coffee shop, on the opposite side of the busy road, Edgewater Bank sits back within a sidewalk cul-de-sac, bordered on either side by a low stone wall, the bank opposite the road. Wooden benches curve around several trees that offer shade—trees I'd always found to be the perfect spot for lunch or a coffee break. If I sat in just the right spot, I could look down the perpendicular street and watch the waterfront.

Only... I don't want to be here, now.

The distant sight of those benches sends tendrils of panic creeping along my spine. Shifting my gaze, I look at Dax.

His words are a soft plea, his tone pure comfort. "I need you to trust me, Indie."

"I do trust you." I tip my chin down the block, swallowing hard. "But I've done all the facing of my past in a figurative sense, so I don't feel any need to do so in a literal sense, you know?"

Without waiting for an answer, my feet lead the way, fear digging into me, and I begin to walk back the way we came.

"Indie..."

My feet keep walking.

One step. Two steps. Three steps.

"Please."

The vulnerable hitch in his voice freezes me. I close my eyes, breathing courage into my lungs, and with a massive sigh, stop and turn back to Dax. "I hope this is good."

The corner of his lips quirk in his signature grin. "I promise."

We close the remaining distance to the bank in quiet, and when we reach the shady gathering area, I walk forward with more boldness than I feel. I'm unaware that Dax has fallen back until he speaks low behind me. It's just my name, but it rings with conviction and command, and I swing around immediately, curious.

He's on one knee.

My heart flies in tandem with my hand to my throat, where I clutch it all together with everything I am.

Oh, dear God, wait. I can't... I'm not ready—

"Dax—" My voice is a rusty nail on stone. I can't let him do this. He went to Brian's wedding yesterday, and it must have done something to him. It must have given him ideas about happy-ever-afters and forever wedded bliss.

I don't think I can do that right now.

Jeremy's memory is still raw, his presence tempered by the violence of his death, but still alive. When I think about marriage, I think about being unhappy. Trapped and lonely.

"It's okay, honey. Breathe." Dax smiles, as if he knows I'm about to completely lose it right there in the middle of the sidewalk in front of Edgewater Bank. He smiles, as if he's perfectly okay with picking up my pieces of crazy and putting me patiently back together.

Just like that, my throat relaxes, and my heart returns to its rightful location, because I know.

That's Dax.

Here he is, Seattle teeming all around him and me having a mini freak-out at what appears to be a proposal in progress, and instead of getting upset about it, he's smiling and telling me it's okay. Reminding me to breathe. He's been doing this for me since day one. Calming me. Soothing me. Patiently waiting out my crazy, like normal is boring, and he wouldn't have me any other way.

He's not Jeremy. He's not an emblem of the past, nor a reminder of the single most terrifying day in my personal history. He's the man that I...

God. I think I love him.

And he's speaking. He's swiping at the tears dripping off my chin, and I make myself pay attention to his words.

"...Indie. All our memories of this place are mixed up, but one thing is certain. This is where everything started for you and me, and I think that might make it one of my favorite places. Here's what I want you to remember going forward."

Making a fist with one hand, I press it to my mouth and jerk my head in a nod, waiting. Reaching forward, he takes hold of my other hand and separates one finger. "One. This is where I fell in love with a little lion girl. A girl with eyes like her mother and a spirit that roars. She took one look at me, and I was gone."

I nearly choke. "Dax..."

He draws another of my fingers up to join the first. "Two. This is where an incredibly wise woman told me I had to read Gatsby again, and I did. I get it now. All of it, Indie. We're fighting currents, but I can see our green light."

My head keeps bobbing up and down, emotions consuming me.

A third finger. "Three. It was here, in this place, that we were forced to dance with the demons that made us weak," he says. "Our parents. Our exes. Our pasts. We had to let them go. We had to trust each other to see us through that door, one way or another."

Fourth finger.

"Four. It was here that I took a chance on my tomorrows and offered you something that felt like a lot. Then I got stupid and disappeared... but hopefully, we can put that behind us."

His regard is hopeful, and I move my fist so he can see the acquiescence in my smile. "Forgotten," I whisper.

Dax moves my last finger to join the rest and holds my hand loosely. "And five. Edgewater is where I met and fell in love with one of the strongest, most compassionate women I have ever known," he murmurs. Kissing my fingertips, he finishes, "And beautiful. You're beautiful, Indie, soul to skin."

I should probably say something in reply, but I'm too busy sobbing. I try to pull my hand loose so I can at least hug him, but he holds it firmly, so I content myself with flinging my other arm around his neck and bending to bury my face in his hair.

It's then that I feel the slide of metal on my finger.

Jerking back, I inspect my hand. There is a ring in place on the ring finger of my left hand—something dainty and petite, but thankfully, not looking too much like an engagement ring. It's silver or white gold, with an emerald and diamond sailboat set into the band.

A promise ring.

It's perfect.

I don't realize I've breathed the words out loud until Dax's mouth lands on mine for a long, satisfied kiss. "I want to marry you one day," he tells me, for my ears alone. "But we're not there yet. Until then, though, I figure we can make our way together."

"I love you, Dax," I against his lips, returning the kiss.

Then we're rising, clinging to each other as we set off along the Seattle sidewalks and the swirling currents of our future, eyes fixed on the horizon, and the green light glowing brightly at the end of our dock.

Epilogue

Dax

CURRENTS.

Ripples and gentle waves undulate beside me as Blake adjusts my blush bowtie.

Blush. Not pink.

"This bowtie is a custom, Dax. I take my duties as your best man very seriously," he notes, smacking me on the shoulder, then steps back to inspect his bow-straightening abilities. His lips purse. "Off-center."

I groan. "Indie won't care if my tie is crooked."

"She will. I've trained her well over the last three years."

My head shakes through a chuckle as his words sink in.

Three years.

It's been three years since I sauntered into Edgewater Bank with my best friend, a chip on my shoulder, and dreams of a Hawaiian reprieve forefront in my mind.

In a flash, everything changed.

Gunfire.

Bloodshed.

Anarchy.

Her.

It's funny. She's what I remember most about that morning. Her hair tickling my chin as she sat perched in my lap, leaning into me for solace. The smell of honeysuckles on her skin. Her blue-green eyes communicating the things we couldn't say.

That kiss.

I recall promises of Maui—an invitation borne out of desperation, but woven with something deeper. A knowing that she was more than just a fellow hostage, in a random bank, on a fateful Monday morning.

Three years later, I finally fulfilled the promise of that invitation, and I will be fulfilling many more such promises before the sun sets.

Blake sends me a smile as he makes his final adjustments with the bowtie, sighing somewhat dreamily. I arch an eyebrow. "Are you done? It can't be that hard."

"Oh, it's not. I lied about it being crooked," he breezes. Then he sniffs me. "I just wanted an excuse to savor that delicious cologne you're wearing. God, is that Jean Paul Gaultier?"

"It's whatever you bought me for Christmas last year, and said, 'Wear this. It's delicious.'"

"I've got your back, big man." He slaps me on the shoulder again, grinning wide, before his smile slips into something more tender. "You know I'm proud of you, right?"

His easy affection causes my heart to clench.

I'm not sure where I'd be right now if it weren't for Blake. From standing by my side through all my years in professional hockey, to rescuing me from the single worst moment of my life at that farmhouse, to bringing me groceries and laughter when I'd never felt more alone, to giving me a place to stay, to being a good friend to Indie...

To right now.

Standing with me on the beach as my best man while I wait for my bride to stroll through the sand.

With a rabbit.

Blake swats the water from his eyes and bends over, scooping Skittles out of her small cage that's been decorated with vines of ivy and baby's breath. She's already chewed through most of the foliage. "It's not too late for Dax to change his mind and marry me instead, right, Skittles?"

I laugh.

Ah, yes. The most unexpected love story to come out of the last few years of chaos is, hands down, Blake and this mischievous rabbit.

After I canceled the deal on my high-rise condo and moved in with Indie and Daisy, I came back one night to collect Skittles, eager to rid my friend of the bane of his existence.

Only... to my surprise, I caught the two of them sound asleep on his tangerine sofa, the bunny sprawled across his chest, all rolls of fur and floppy ears, as Blake drooled into his Marilyn Monroe pillow.

They've been inseparable ever since.

Blake even created an Instagram account titled, "Lolli, Pop, and Skittles," featuring the lovable adventures of his three quirky pets. The account already has half-a-million followers.

I watch as my friend kisses the rabbit's ebony nose, and I shake my head, still chuckling. "I hope Indie didn't hear you say that."

"Indie? Yeah, right... it's Tameka I'm worried about." He visibly shudders. "That woman is a dragon."

Can't say I disagree with that.

As if on cue, the dragon herself glides over to us in a peachy-pink slip dress, revealing her claws in a playful threat. "Someone called?"

Blake holds Skittles out at arm's length. "Take the rabbit as a sacrifice."

"Absolutely not," Tameka says, sashaying beside us and tsking her tongue. "You're far more valuable. You knit me scarves."

He shrugs after a moment of contemplation. "Fair."

My lips twitch with an amused smile, and I stuff my hands into my dress slacks as a breeze rolls through. Indie should be coming out of the little beauty tent at any minute for our intimate beach ceremony, followed by a big send-off.

A sailboat departure into the sunset.

I had the boat custom-made for our post-wedding sail by a company here in Maui, somehow managing to keep it a secret from Indie. She has no idea. I can't wait to watch her eyes light up when she spots the sleek little sailboat tethered to a distant dock.

Never having been a big sailor, I wasn't sure what to do, but found a family-owned business that listened to my story and was able to design the perfect seaworthy sailboat for our little family. With our joint inexperience, our maiden voyage will be skippered by a licensed captain, as well.

No sense in tempting the providence that brought us together.

It's been decorated with a giant "Just Married" sign that Blake created, appropriately named Indigo Blue, and waits only for our feet to climb aboard as husband-and-wife.

I can't wait for her to see it.

Music starts up as the officiant takes his place next to me, Blake on my opposite side, and Skittles near his feet. Tameka skips over to where Indie will eventually be standing.

My breath stalls in my throat when realization sets in that I'm about to marry the love of my life.

Damn.

Fidgeting beneath the Hawaiian sunshine, I swallow hard, clasping my hand over my wrist and keeping my eyes trained on the beauty tent across the beach.

Our mothers step out first.

Arms linked, both women stroll through the sand in modest pink dresses, stopping to issue me words of endearment, along with a plethora of cheek kisses. I hug them both, my nerves only heightening.

Daisy follows next, her arms filled with Pickles. She said she didn't want to be a flower girl—she wanted to be a "Little Lion Girl." So, that's exactly what she is. Her dress is bright white, made of tulle and lace, and it floats along with the breeze as she skips down the makeshift aisle with her lion ears headband and a tiny tail poking out through the back of her skirt.

Blake starts to cry.

When Daisy trots up to me, petting Pickles right between the ears, I kneel down in the sand until we're face-to-face. My own tears threaten as I look into her wide blue eyes, our smiles matching. "Brave little lion," I whisper gently, kissing her forehead.

Daisy's grin broadens. "You're brave, too," she murmurs back. "Little lions only learn from the bravest of lions."

My heart leaps.

Blake cries harder.

Wrapping her up in a final hug, she spins around to place Pickles in the decorated carrying case, then takes a seat.

I glance down at the watch adorning my wrist, inhaling a deep breath.

Tick, tick, tick.

For most of my life, the ticking of a clock or the countdown on a scoreboard symbolized anxiety. A race to the finish. Beating the odds.

Survival of the fittest.

Now, it's a welcome sound. Every second that passes is a second spent alive and blessed, celebrating a future I never anticipated—never thought I deserved.

Every second is another blissful second with her.

I let out that breath and straighten my stance.

It's time.

A few more heartbeats pass, and she steps out, arm-in-arm with my father, stealing away the rest of my breath. She's a vision in white, glowing and radiant beneath the sunny sky. Indie doesn't even notice the sailboat behind me because she's only focused on me. Her hair falls over both shoulders in butterscotch waves, her eyes twinkling, cheeks wet with tears.

I fall in love all over again.

My father walks her right to me, and I force my gaze away from my bride to settle upon him. He doesn't speak. He just nods his head through his own tears, then pulls me in for a bone-crushing hug. I hug him back, my emotions high, and mutter, "Thanks, Dad."

He gives my back a slap, stepping away with another terse nod, and places a kiss to Indie's temple before taking a seat.

And then... it's just us.

The officiant says his opening words, but I hear nothing. All I hear is the ocean behind me, the beating of my heart with hers, and the little sound she makes when a new wave of tears claim her. I lift my thumb, dusting away the moisture. "Don't cry, honey."

Indie inhales a shuddering breath, reaching for my hands. "They're happy tears," she says quietly. "The happiest."

The ceremony continues on. We exchange our vows, and when the officiant proclaims our official union, I swoop her back and steal a cinema-worthy kiss as our guests clap and celebrate. Lifting her to her feet, I savor the kiss for another moment, sweeping our tongues together, then pull back, forehead to forehead. "I love you, Indigo Reed."

She laughs through a cry of joy. "I love you, husband."

When the applause subsides, Daisy's high-pitched voice calls out, her little finger pointing behind us. "Mom, look! Did you see it?"

Indie pivots to the left, craning her neck to see beyond the trellis. Her voice hitches with wonder. "Dax..." she breathes out.

I kiss her nose. "Are you ready to finally take that boat ride?"

Our friends and family watch as Indie hikes up her dress and skips through the sand, our hands interlocked, our laughter contagious. We run down the dock, waving over our shoulders, then climb aboard the beautiful sailing vessel, the side painted with her name, "Indigo Blue."

"This is incredible, Dax," she whispers, squeezing my fingers for balance while our captain unmoors us and begins to work the rigging. "I can't believe..."

Emotion seizes her words, and as the boat starts to float along the easy chop of the protected bay, I pull her to me. "I know it's not the same. I know I'm not your father, but..." Pressing a kiss to her windswept hair, I finish, "I hope it's still everything you ever imagined."

Tears track down her pink cheeks as she nods fervently. "He's here," she says with conviction. "He's here with me… I know he is. He always has been, whispering in my ear to keep moving forward. To live the life I've always dreamed of."

I cradle her face between my hands, caressing away her tearstains. "And 'so we be beat on,'" I reply.

Her eyes shimmer with magic beneath the sun-kissed Maui sky.

Green. They look green today.

As the salty sea breeze kisses our skin, a wave laps at the boat with gusto, almost causing us to stumble. I squeeze her hands, keeping myself steady. Centered.

Anchored.

We laugh at the near-fall, finding balance within each other, and as our fingers interlace, hearts beating in perfect rhythm, more vows are said before our voices meet the air.

Our eyes lock.

I'll fight every current with you, Indigo Reed.

You better.

Trust me.

I pull her closer, exhaling my promise against her lips as our eyes hold tight. She's my calm. She's my comfort.

She's my peace.

I do.

The End

CHAPTER 38

Acknowledgments

When Jennifer and I decided to join forces and co-write a book, neither of us had any idea what to expect. I think we envisioned meme-filled chat threads where plot magically came to life, chapters that blinked into existence, and a meeting of the minds that was historic.

And it was. Kind of.

It was also rife with "now-that-we've-written-6000-words,-I-don't-think-this-is-working" moments. "Let's just change fucking everything" convos. "We are never, ever going to finish this" days.

Through it all, though, there were moments that taught us, days that grew us, and people that held us together through the inevitable entropy of … well, Entropy.

One of those moments was learning from those who had gone before exactly how to work in a co-write environment. Much gratitude, in particular, goes to the inimitable Josi Beck for shoring us up and giving us a few private words of advice. Without you, we'd no doubt still be scratching our heads and wondering how to do the thing.

There were days when the advice of our inestimable beta readers, Vanessa Harradine Sheets, Caelan Fine, Jennifer Rose, and others helped pinpoint areas that needed work and showed us how to grow. Days when people like models Nicole Vaughn and Rhylan Streloff challenged us, made us laugh, and gave us a sense of future. Days when the talents of individuals like Jake Hartmann created the brilliant cover we celebrate today.

And then there were the people--or really, the person--that held us together. Our alpha gal, the only one we allowed to read over our shoulders from point A to point Z and question everything. Our Caesar of all early readers, the thumb that decided yea or nay on a plot point or a tricky bit of wording... our Chelley.

Everyone should have a Chelley.

I don't know what we'd have done without Chelley St. Clair. I'm sure you've seen her name and presence on The Thorns Remain by now, as she moved immediately into that magnificent co-write as soon as she finished alpha-reading Entropy. (I mean, whut-whut??) She gave of herself and her time so devotedly through this entire process, committing herself to seeing us produce this unique and beautiful story. Her insight and editorial eye are incredible, but even more—she's a friend neither Jen nor I cannot imagine ever being without. Hail, Caesar.

Thank you, everyone, who assisted with this amazing, career-changing book. The one that earned us a USA Today Bestselling Author designation. The one that we poured so much of ourselves into. There is simply no flipping way we could've done it without you, and we know that. We love you. We see you. We appreciate you.

About the Authors

Jennifer Hartmann

Jennifer Hartmann resides in northern Illinois with her devoted husband, Jake, and three children, Willow, Liam, and Violet. When she is not writing angsty love stories, she is likely thinking about writing them. She enjoys sunsets (because mornings are hard), bike riding, traveling anywhere out of Illinois, binging Buffy the Vampire Slayer reruns, and that time of day when coffee gets replaced by wine. Jennifer is a wedding photographer with her husband and a self-love enthusiast. She is excellent at making puns and finding inappropriate humor in mundane situations. She loves tacos. She also really, really wants to pet your dog. Xoxo.

E.R. Whyte

E(lle) R(ae) Whyte lives in south central Virginia with her youngest son. She's a textbook Capricorn with a tendency to overthink things and word vomit when she gets nervous. She loves good poetry, tacos, dirty jokes, and simple things like couch cuddles. An avid photographer, Elle can often be found wandering little-traveled highways or busy city streets in search of the perfect shot. E.R. writes contemporary reverse harem under her pseudonym Evie Rae.

Also By Jennifer Hartmann

Feel free to join my reader's group!

Queen of Harts: Jennifer Hartmann's Reader Group

Follow me on social media:

Instagram: @author.jenniferhartmann

Facebook: @jenhartmannauthor

Twitter: @authorjhartmann

TikTok: @jenniferhartmannauthor

www.jenniferhartmannauthor.com

STILL BEATING

#1 Amazon Bestseller in three categories!

When Cora leaves her sister's birthday party, she doesn't expect to wake up in shackles in a madman's basement.

To make matters worse, her arch nemesis and ultimate thorn in her side, Dean, shares the space in his own set of chains. The two people who always thought they'd end up killing each other must now work together if they want to survive.

LOTUS

To the rest of the world, he was the little boy who went missing on the Fourth of July.

To Sydney, he was everything.

Twenty-two years later, he's back.

This is Oliver Lynch's story...

This is their story.

THE WRONG HEART

When my husband died, he left my broken heart behind.

He left another heart behind, too—his. I know it's wrong. I shouldn't be contacting the recipient of my husband's heart. I don't even expect him to reply...

But there's a desperate, twisted part of me that hopes he will.

No names.

No personal details.

Just a conversation.

The only thing I have left of my husband is inside him.

THE DUET SERIES —ARIA & CODA

When the lead singer of his rock band starts falling for a pretty waitress, Noah will do whatever it takes to make sure she doesn't get in the way of their dreams. But it would be easier if that waitress didn't accidentally spill her darkest secrets to him one night, triggering a profound connection neither of them saw coming.

CLAWS AND FEATHERS

Small town cop, Cooper, is intrigued by the mysterious new girl who walks into his father's bar, but the last thing he expects is for her to go missing that same night.

Finding Abby is just the beginning. The only way to truly save her is to unravel her secrets—a task that proves to be more challenging than he could ever anticipate.

THE THORNS REMAIN

Co-authored with Chelley St Clair

Revenge was the goal, and she was my way in.

I wasn't supposed to fall for her.

Now... there's no way out.

June First — Coming Soon

Jennifer has an angsty, new standalone in the works, hopefully releasing Spring of 2022!

At the center of my tragedy, there is a love story.

At the center of my love story,

There is June.

Also By E.R. Whyte

FEEL FREE TO JOIN my reader's group!

The Epilogue: E.R. Whyte's Reader Group
Follow me on social media:
Instagram: @authorerwhyte
Facebook: @elleraewhyte
Twitter: @authorerwhyte
TikTok: @erwhyte
♡

SAY YOU LOVE ME and SAY YOU'LL BE MINE

A sexy debut story of forbidden love and looming danger, these books are my first book babies and first loves. I love the stories and want to perfect them, and made the decision to tweak a few things recently. They are currently undergoing extensive edits and being combined to cancel that awful cliffhanger. :) Stay tuned for big changes!

They kissed five years ago, igniting a spark. Now that spark might lead to their destruction.

High school teacher Shiloh Brookings is struggling to pay her brother's medical bills on a teacher's salary. With students only a few years younger than she is, things are difficult enough, but when Gunner Ford enrolls in class things become complicated.

Her brother's best friend, a grown-up Gunner is a temptation she doesn't need. But their long ago, toe-curling kiss makes him hard to ignore.

Gunner is an unapologetic romantic who makes no secret of his feelings for Shiloh. They're both adults and he has no intention of walking away, even if their romance is considered taboo.

As Gunner and Shiloh navigate their way around each other, a deadly stalker hunts in their community. With an unsuspecting Shiloh under his eye, his obsession knows no bounds. He will have her, and he will do anything and destroy anyone who gets in his way.

IN LIES WE TRUST

Emery "Cotton" Bishop has things she wants to forget. Secrets that need to stay buried.

After a trouble-filled stint in the military, Cotton is returning to her small Virginia hometown to heal and move on.

Nothing's ever that easy, though.

It was a favor for a friend that brought Brodie Gallagher to Jessup Falls, Virginia. It's a murder-for-hire contract that keeps him there.

A hitman for the Irish mafia, Brodie wasn't expecting instant sparks upon meeting Cotton. He really wasn't anticipating the order from his boss telling him to kill her. Why would anyone want to kill this woman with shadows in her eyes?

When a second assassin is dispatched to do the job Brodie is struggling with, he does the only thing he can think of...

...he kidnaps her to make Cotton disappear.

REMEMBER ME

Bernadette has it all. A hot fiancé who coaches baseball at a local college, a gorgeous farmhouse she's busy fixing up, and a new career doing what she loves. The only problem? She can't remember any of it.

After an accident results in amnesia, she's released all too soon into a world that makes little sense, haunted by a nagging conviction that something is not as it seems.

With only her intuition and the accounts of strangers to be her guide, she must piece together the puzzle that defines her existence, and decide whether or not to trust the stranger by her side.

Will she get a second chance at love, or will her accident cost more than just her memory?

And as EVIE RAE... Exciting Reverse Harem

BAD NEIGHBORS

After a scandal implodes my family and life, switching to a new university is my only avenue to providing for myself and my younger sister.

When a data entry error assigns me to an all-male quad dormitory with three far-too-attractive men, I'm willing to make it work. We all have our own rooms, and I can just avoid the common areas.

My new roommates aren't as willing, though. They don't want me disrupting their male utopia, and are going to do whatever it takes to make me leave. They leave the toilet seat up, eat my food, drink my last Dr. Peppy, and do their best to make my life hell—all to get me to leave.

Until one day... they stop. Instead of trying to push me out, they make my head spin when they ramp up the charm.

Something tells me not to trust this complete reversal, that they have ulterior motives. That they may just break my heart.

They can break my heart. But they can't push me out. Not with my sister depending on me...not with our future at stake.

BEASTLY BULLIES

She's the one-time princess of a fallen kingdom. They'll be the villains in her new story.

Once upon a time, I had everything. Status. Wealth. Access.

Now, I'm the fallen. The daughter of a disgraced Wall Street king who's serving time.

After my father's conviction and my mother's suicide, I was shipped off to what I hoped would be a fresh start with my uncle. My new home in Cold Spring is far from the city, far from my prestigious former academy, and far from anyone who knew me when I was the Princess of Chauncey Park.

New family, new school, new me.

Unfortunately, it doesn't quite work out that way.

I'm not the anonymous girl I need to be. The princes that rule this rural school know the secrets that haunt my past, know the transgressions that torment me.

They're not content to let me hide in the shadows and finish out my high school career in peace. No, they want me front and center and miserable every day of my sentence in this little podunk town.

Their reason? That's a mystery for me to solve.

Once upon a time, I was a princess. Now, I'm just the whipping girl.

Made in the USA
Monee, IL
26 February 2022

91923292R00154